THE DRAGON PATH

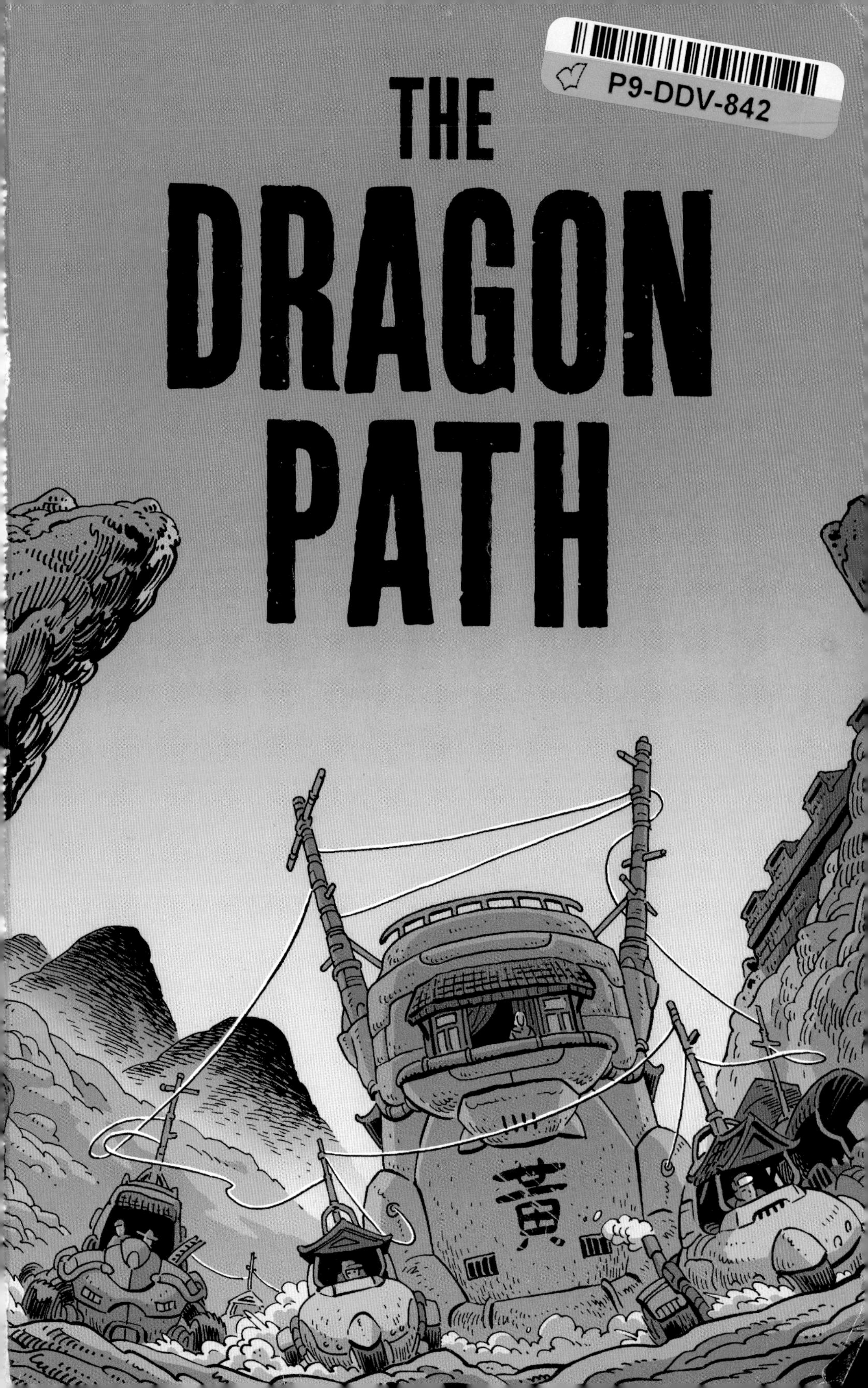
黃

THE DRAGON PATH

ETHAN YOUNG

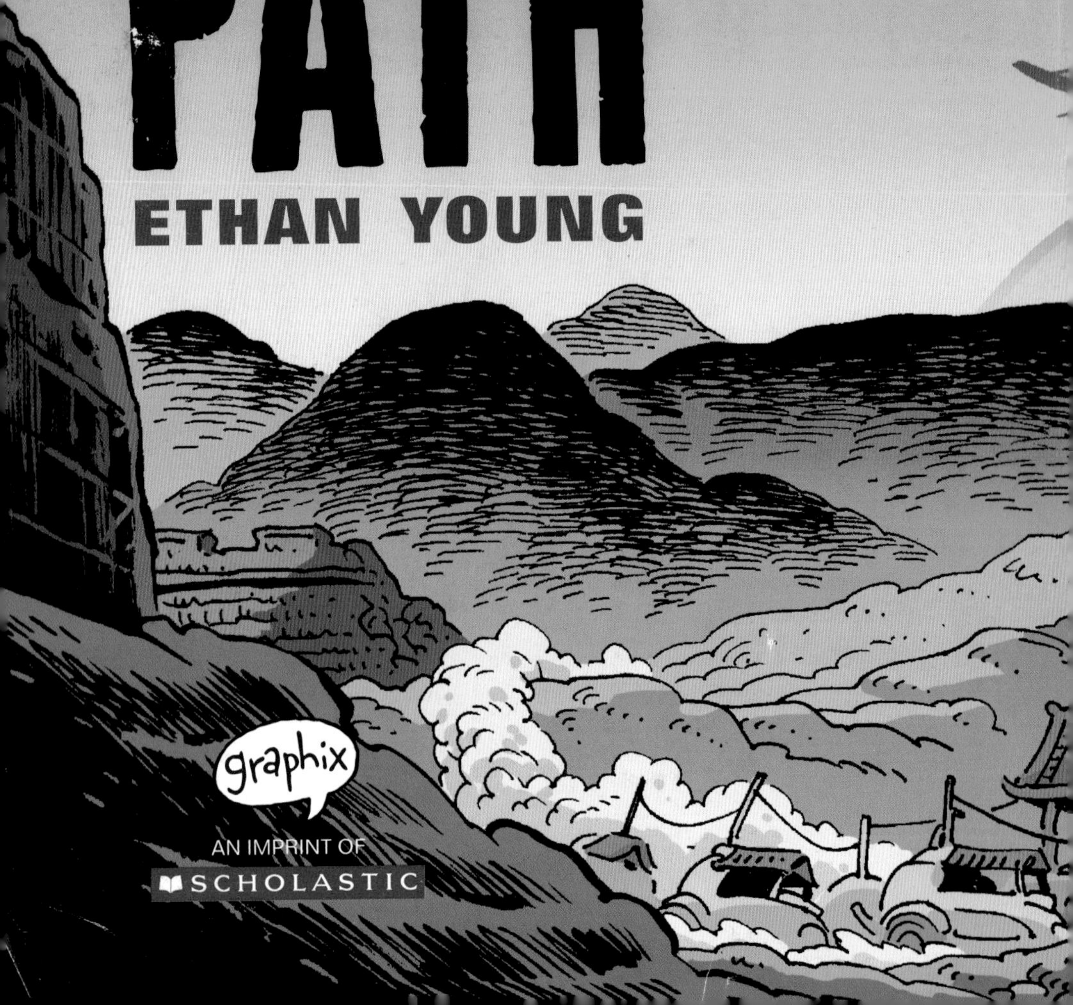

graphix
AN IMPRINT OF
SCHOLASTIC

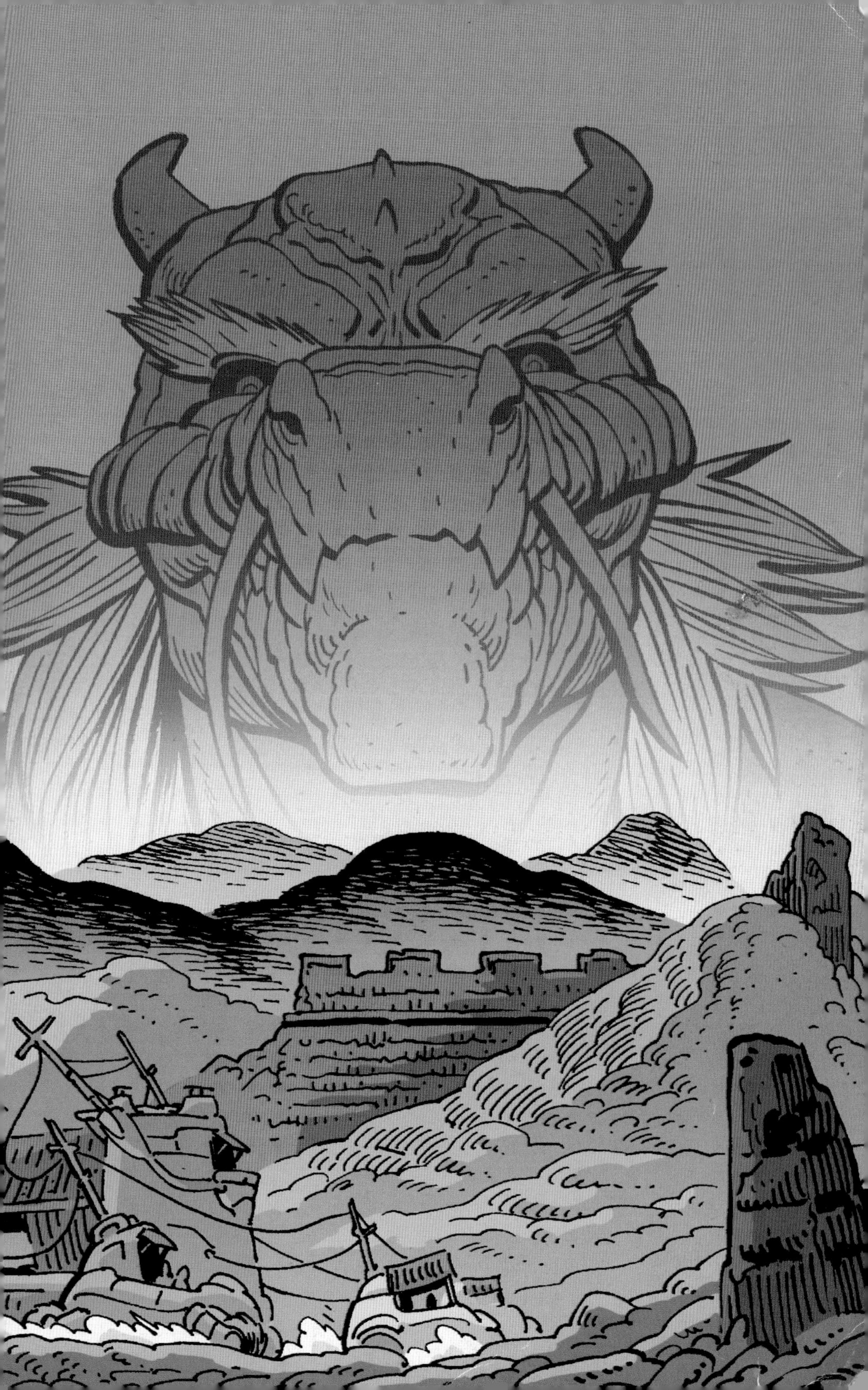

FOR MY SON, ELLIOTT

All rights reserved. Published by Graphix, an imprint of Scholastic Inc.,
Publishers since 1920. SCHOLASTIC, GRAPHIX, and associated logos are
trademarks and/or registered trademarks of Scholastic Inc.

Library of Congress Control Number: 2020943284

ISBN 978-1-338-36330-2 (hardcover)
ISBN 978-1-338-36329-6 (paperback)

10 9 8 7 6 5 4 3 2 1   21 22 23 24 25

Printed in China   62
First edition, May 2021

Color flats by Fernando Argüello
Book design by Steve Ponzo
Creative Director: Phil Falco
Publisher: David Saylor

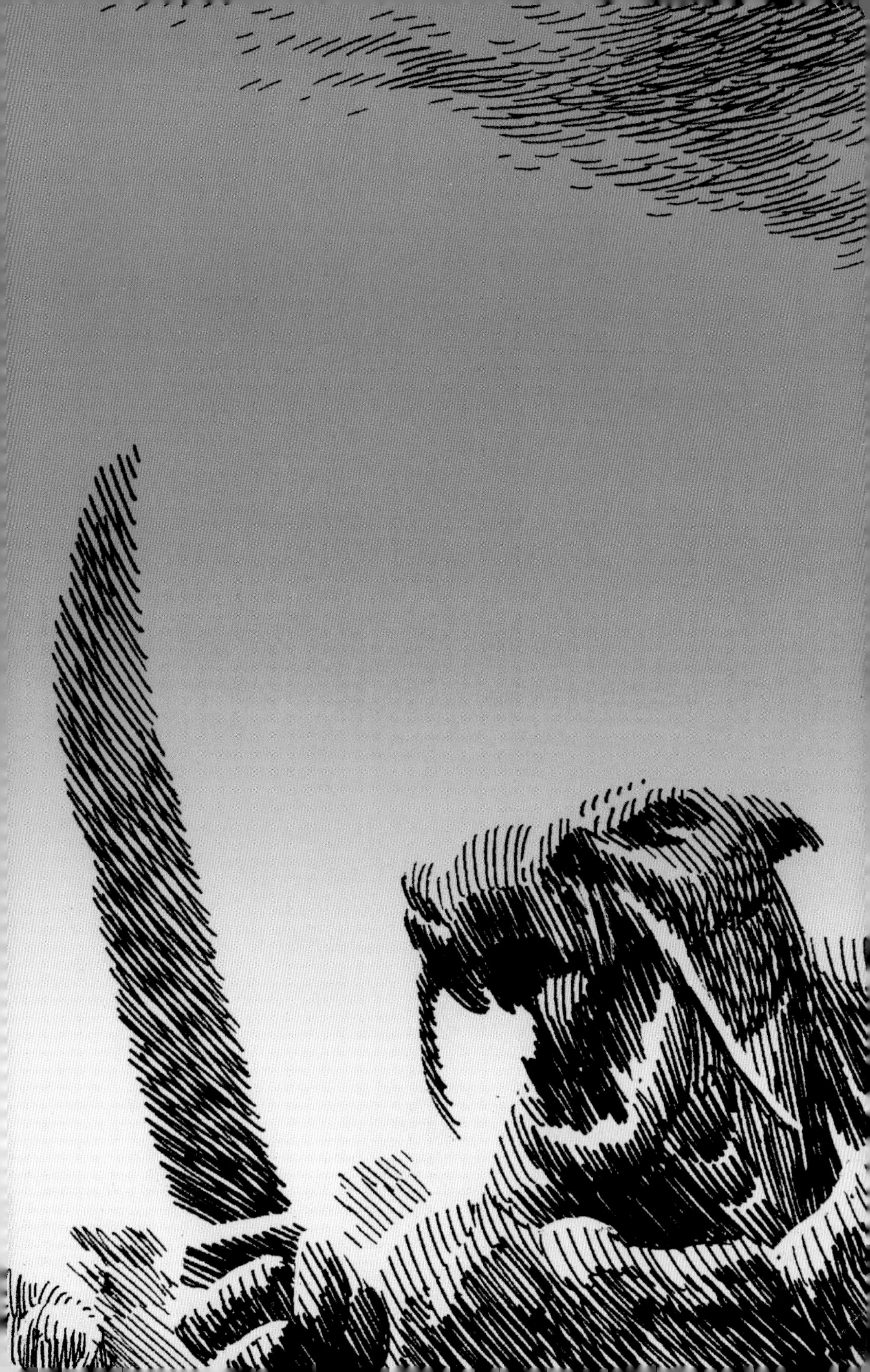

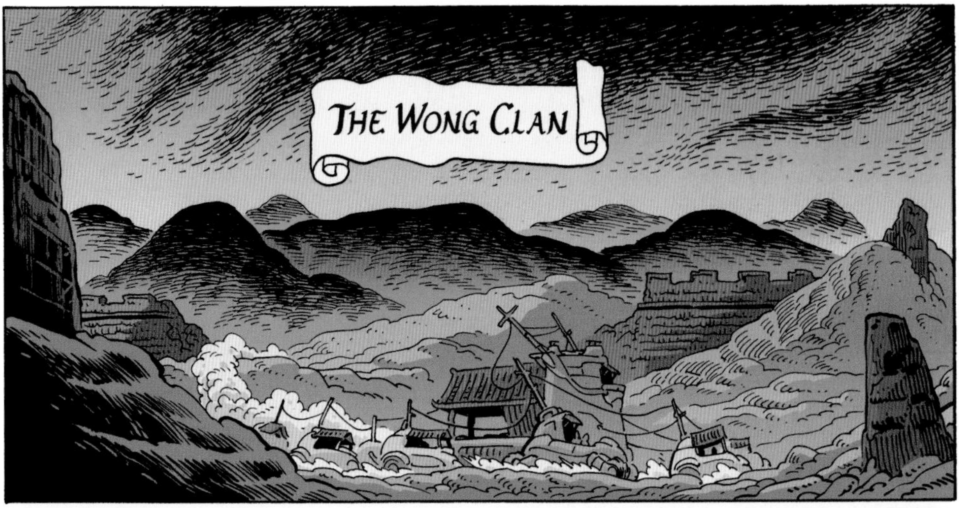
THE WONG CLAN

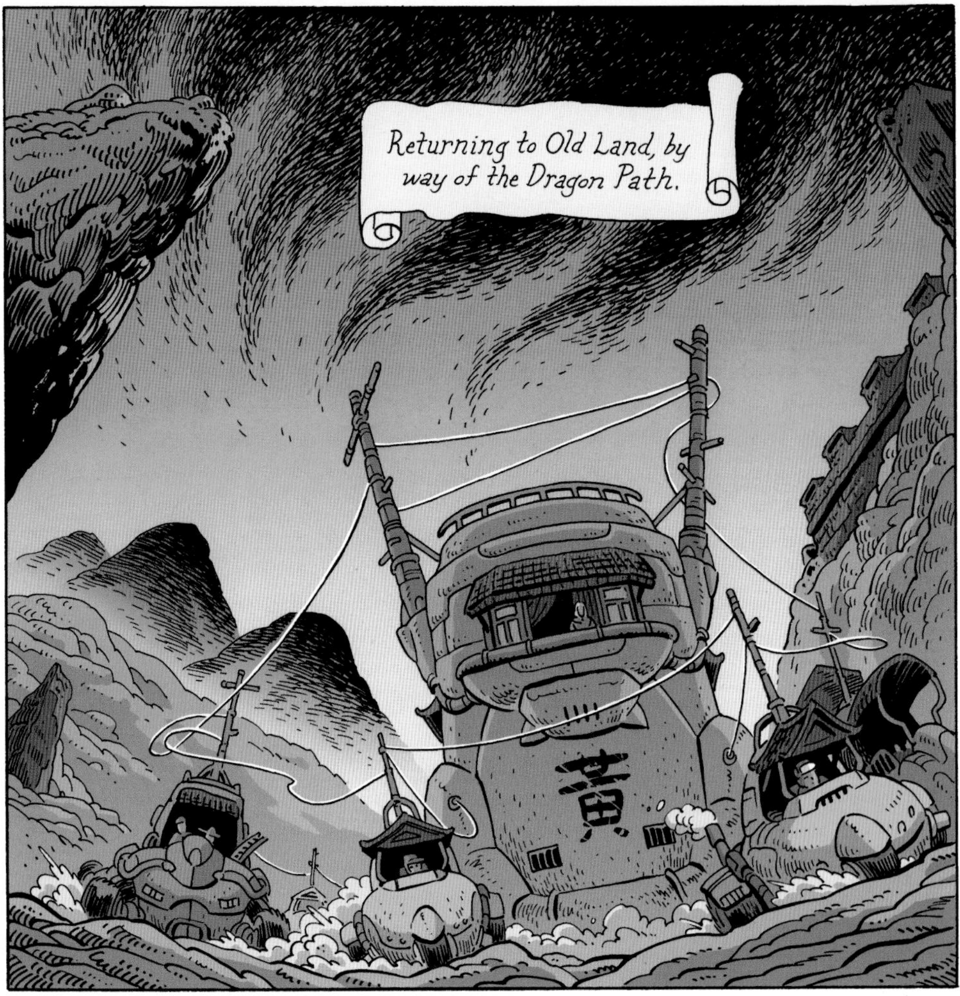
Returning to Old Land, by way of the Dragon Path.
黃

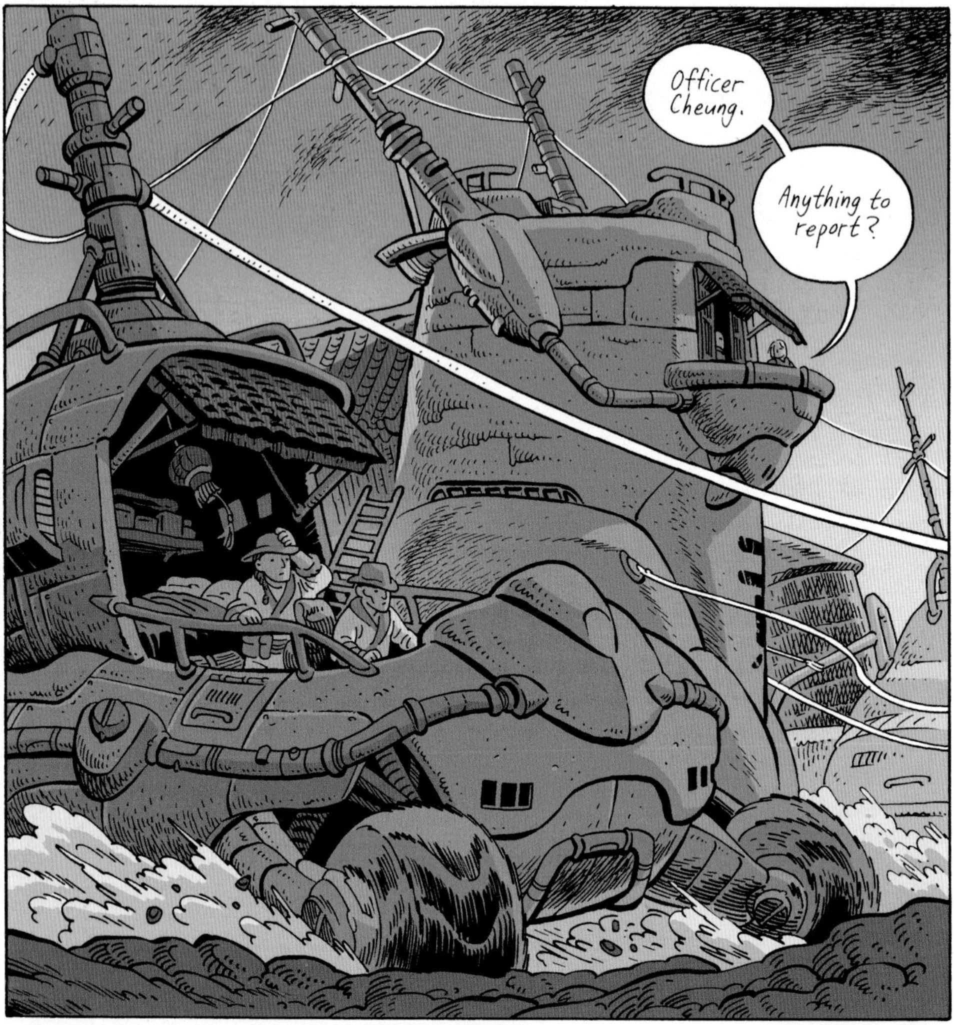
Officer Cheung.
Anything to report?

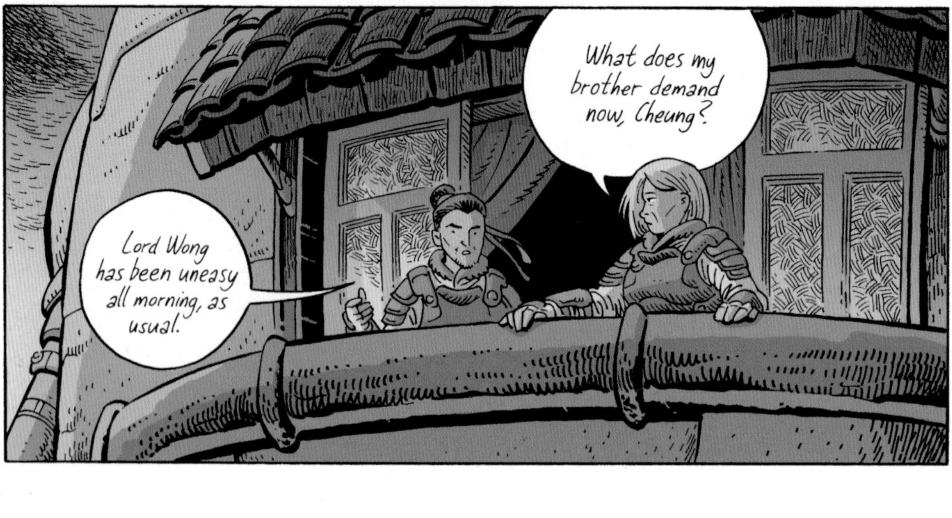
What does my brother demand now, Cheung?
Lord Wong has been uneasy all morning, as usual.

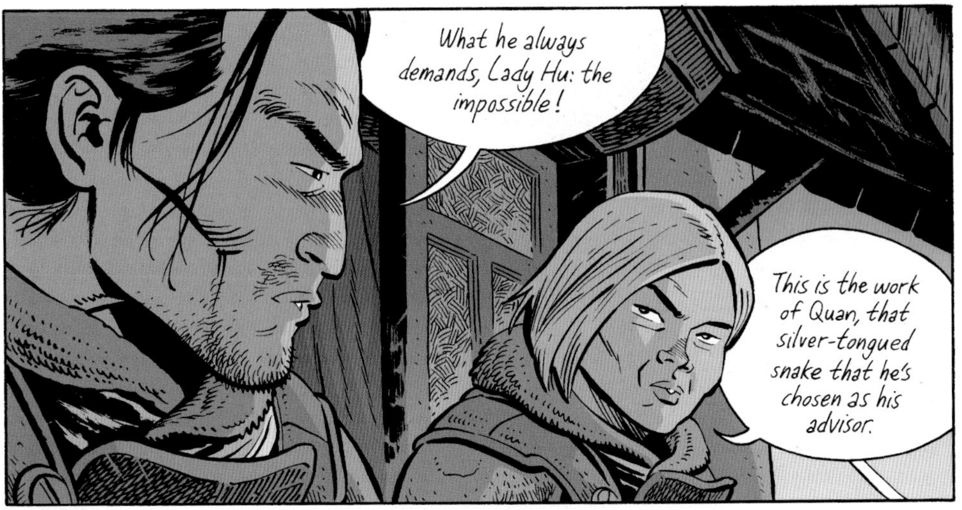
What he always demands, Lady Hu: the impossible!
This is the work of Quan, that silver-tongued snake that he's chosen as his advisor.

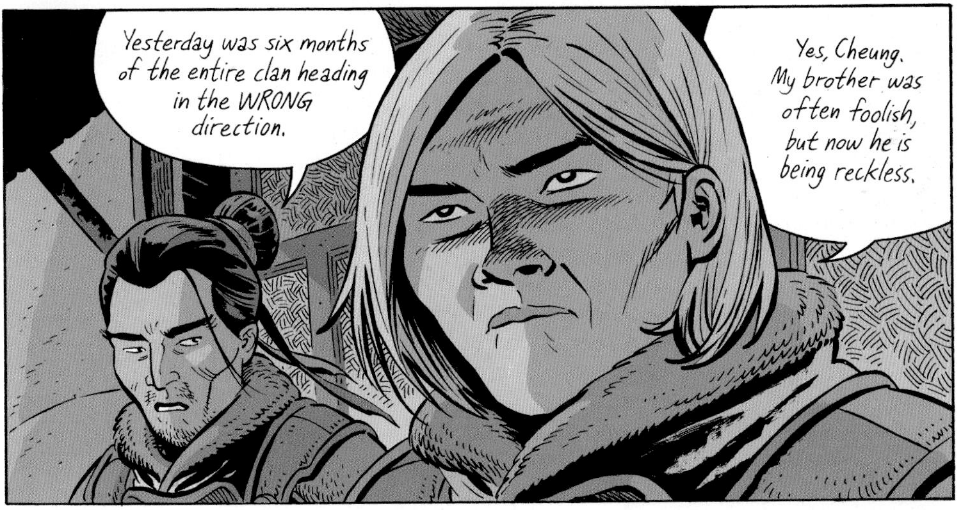
Yesterday was six months of the entire clan heading in the WRONG direction.
Yes, Cheung. My brother was often foolish, but now he is being reckless.

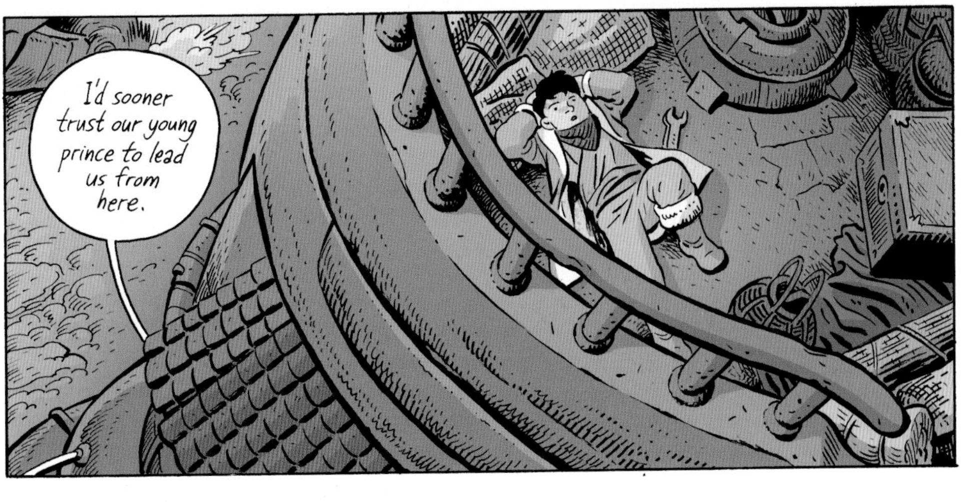
I'd sooner trust our young prince to lead us from here.

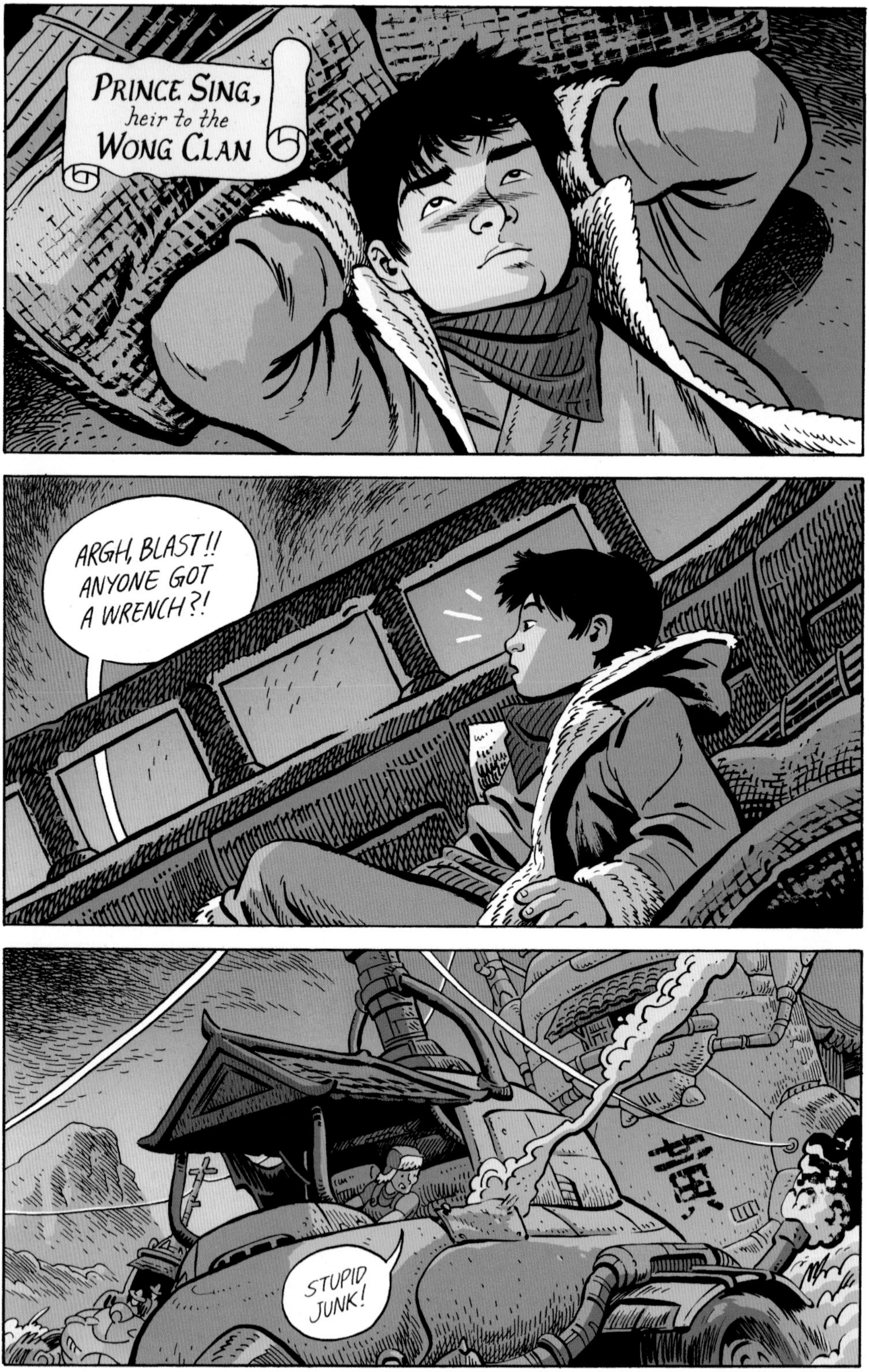
PRINCE SING, heir to the WONG CLAN
ARGH, BLAST!! ANYONE GOT A WRENCH?!
黄
STUPID JUNK!

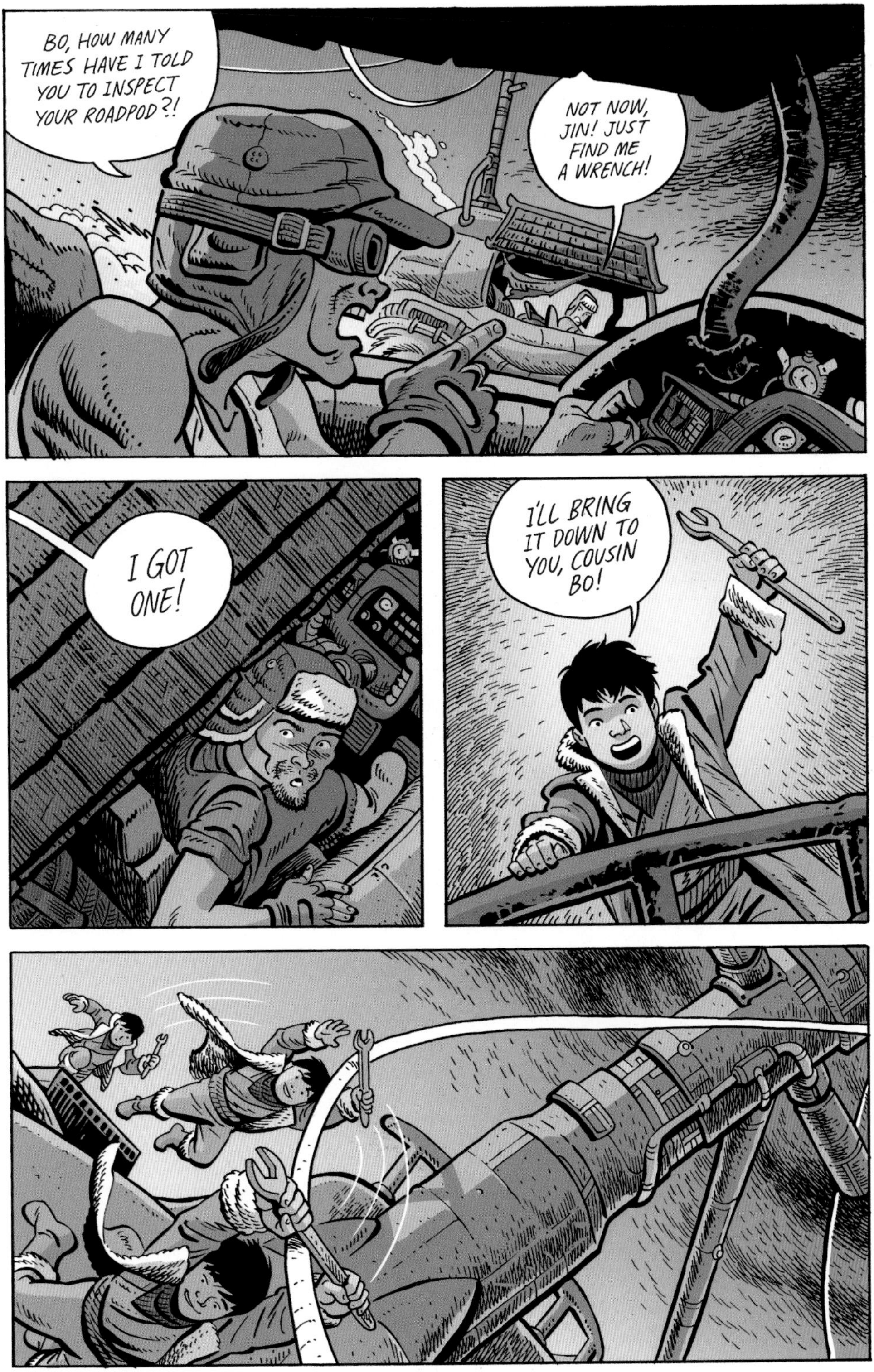
BO, HOW MANY TIMES HAVE I TOLD YOU TO INSPECT YOUR ROADPOD?!
NOT NOW, JIN! JUST FIND ME A WRENCH!
I GOT ONE!
I'LL BRING IT DOWN TO YOU, COUSIN BO!

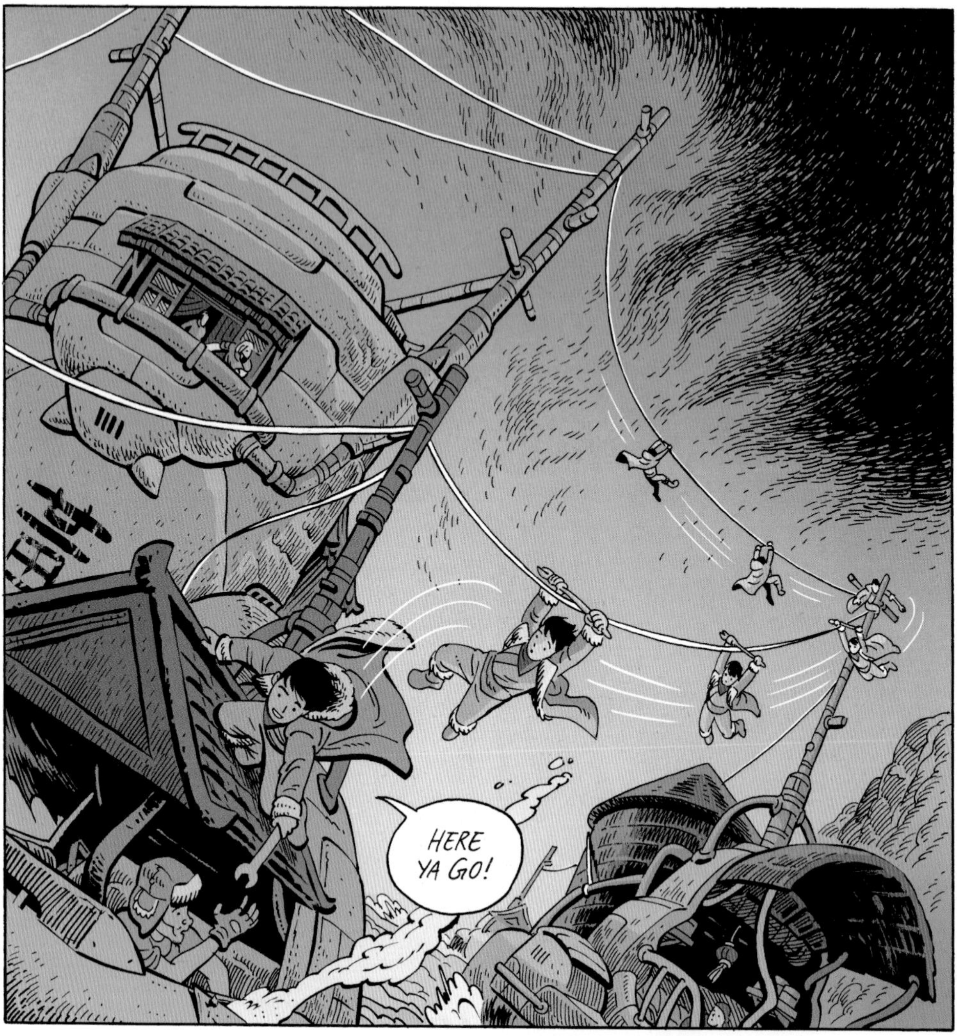
HERE YA GO!

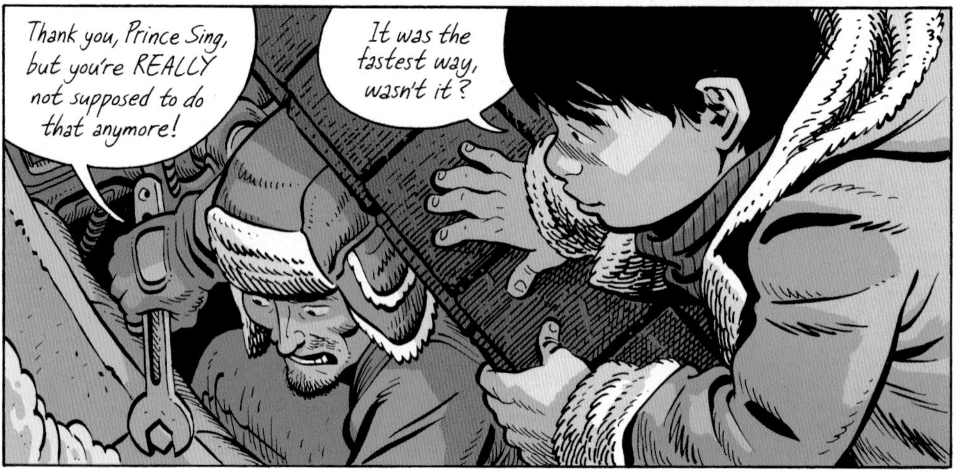
Thank you, Prince Sing, but you're REALLY not supposed to do that anymore!
It was the fastest way, wasn't it?

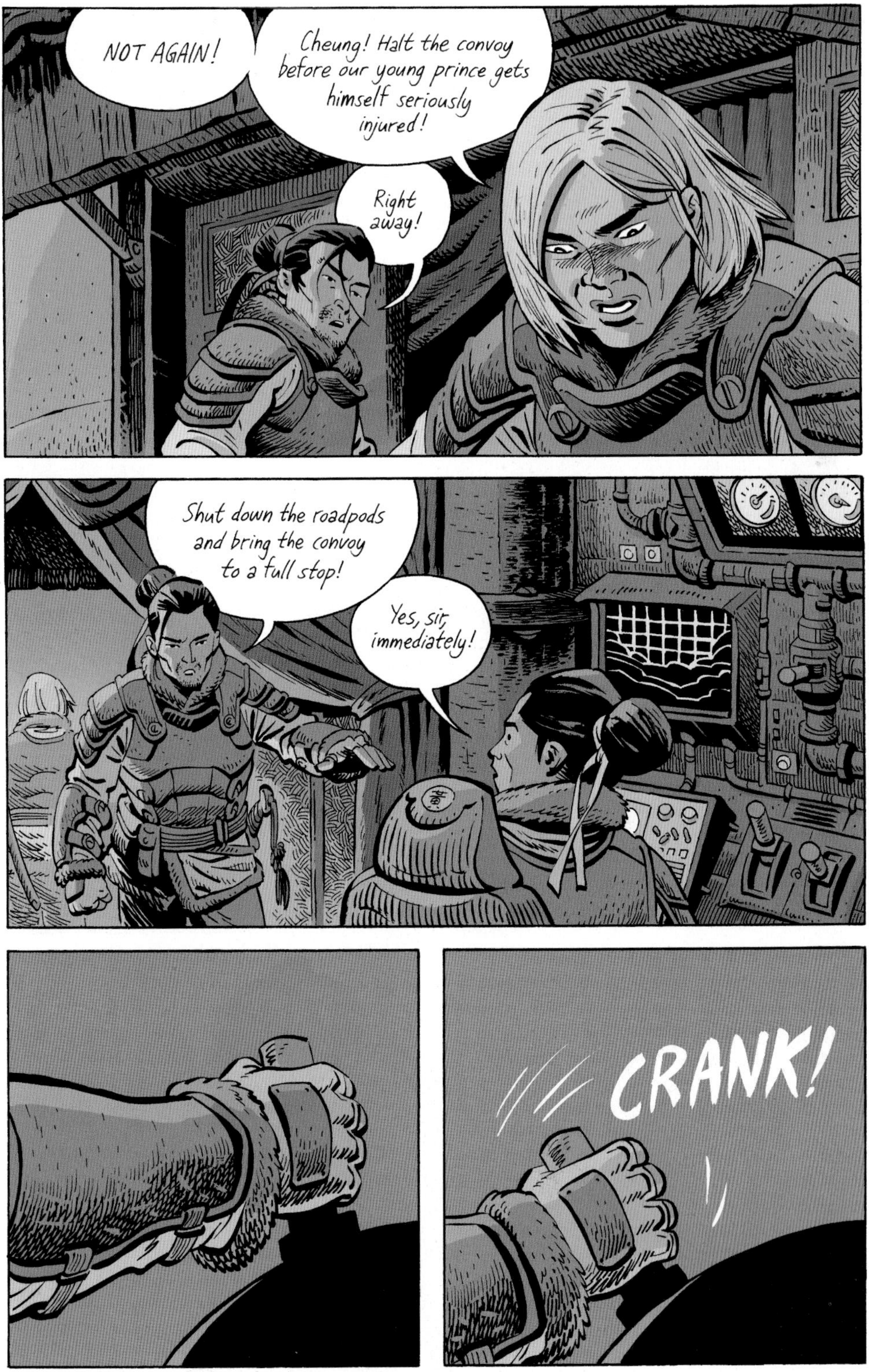
NOT AGAIN!
Cheung! Halt the convoy before our young prince gets himself seriously injured!
Right away!
Shut down the roadpods and bring the convoy to a full stop!
Yes, sir, immediately!
CRANK!

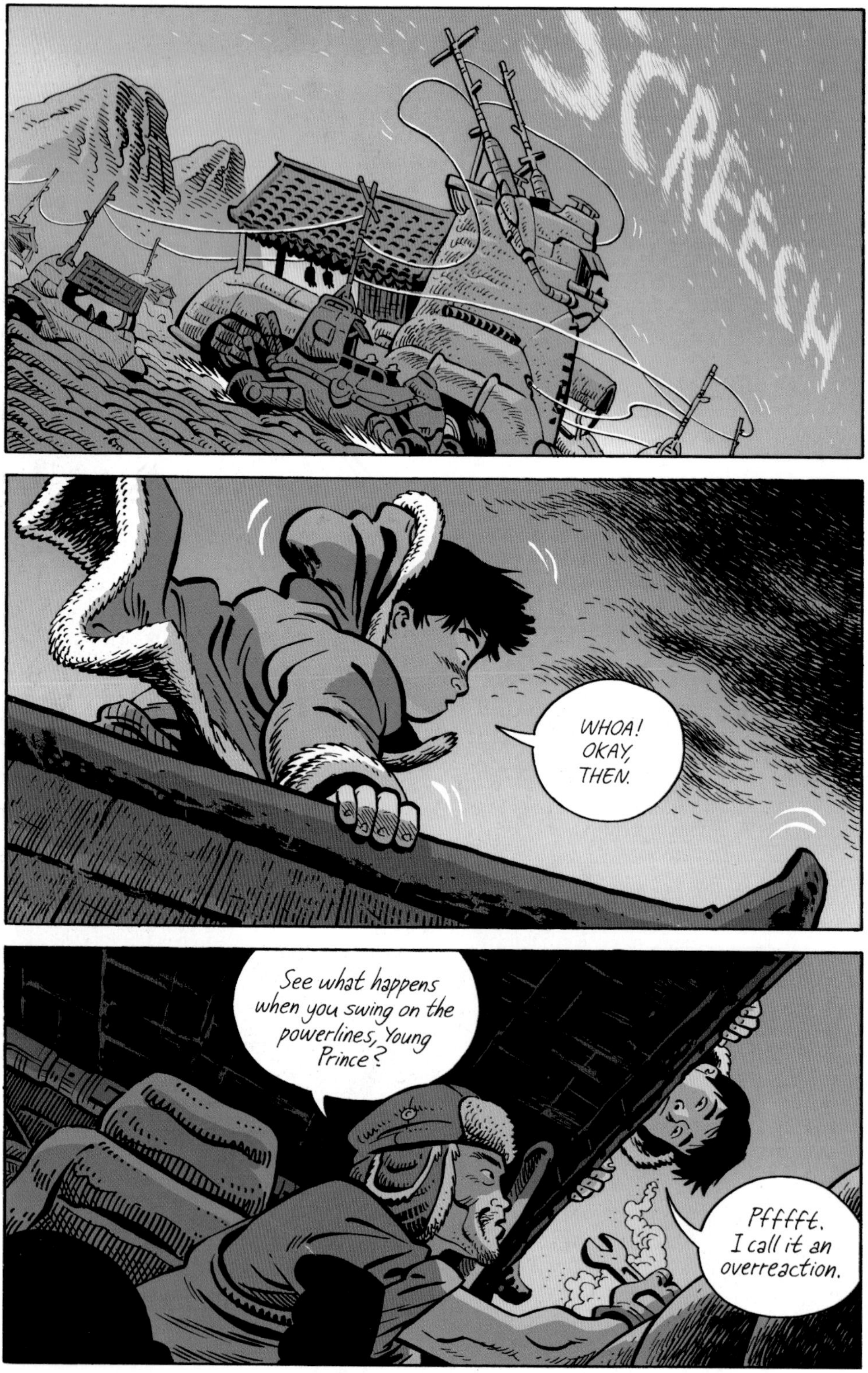
SCREECH
WHOA! OKAY, THEN.
See what happens when you swing on the powerlines, Young Prince?
Pfffft. I call it an overreaction.

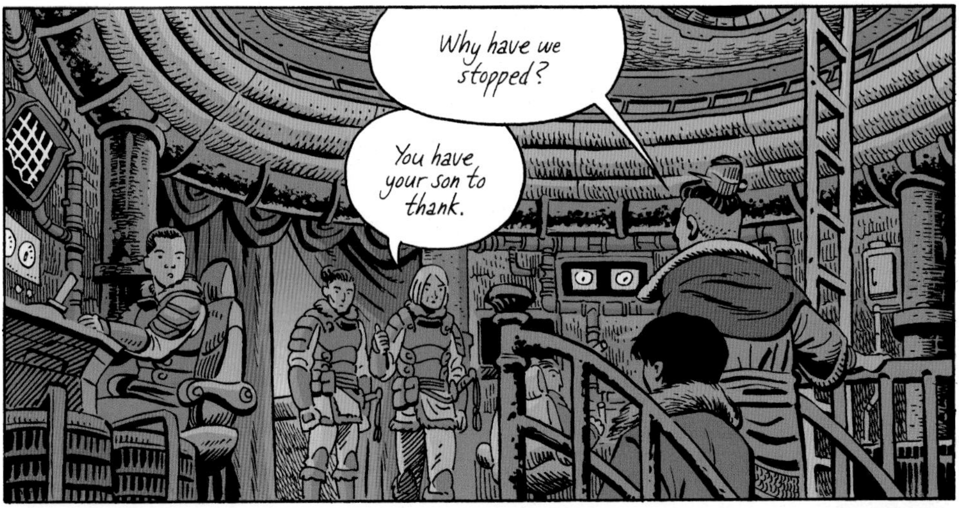
Why have we stopped?
You have your son to thank.

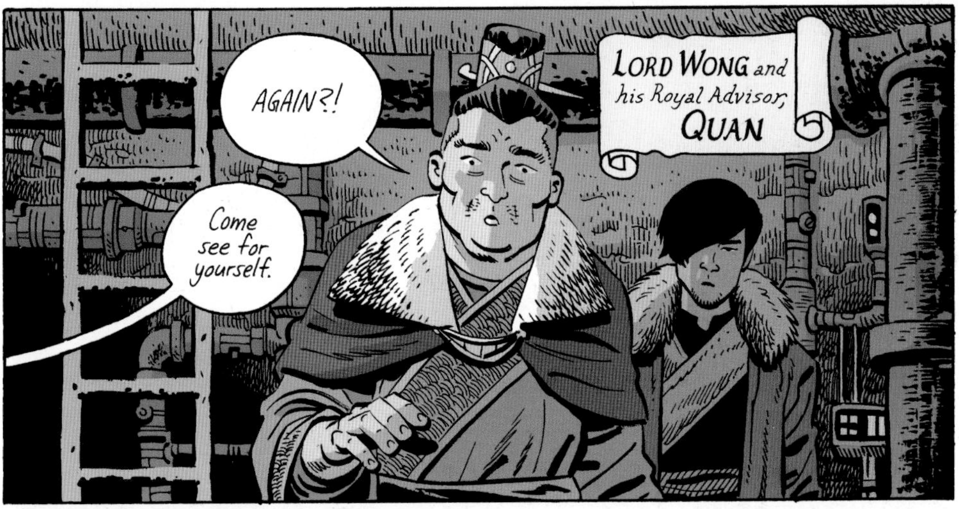
LORD WONG and his Royal Advisor, QUAN
AGAIN?!
Come see for yourself.

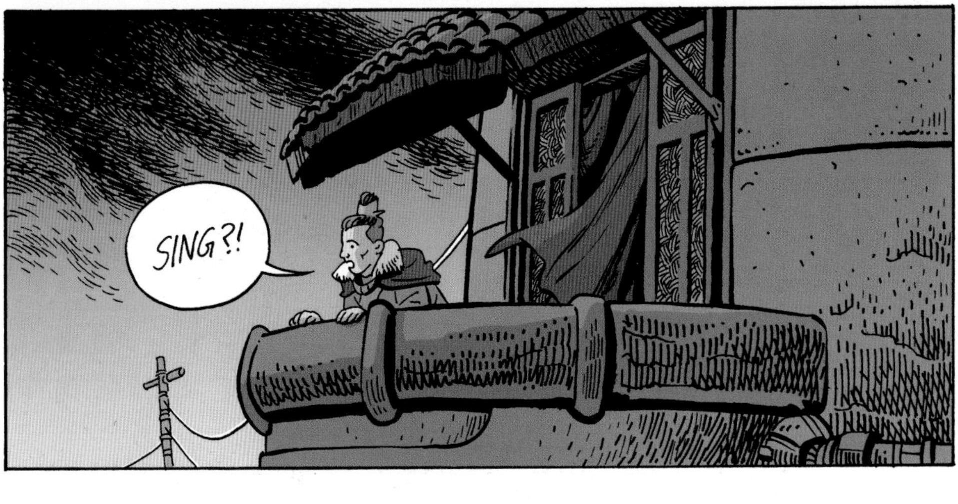
SING?!

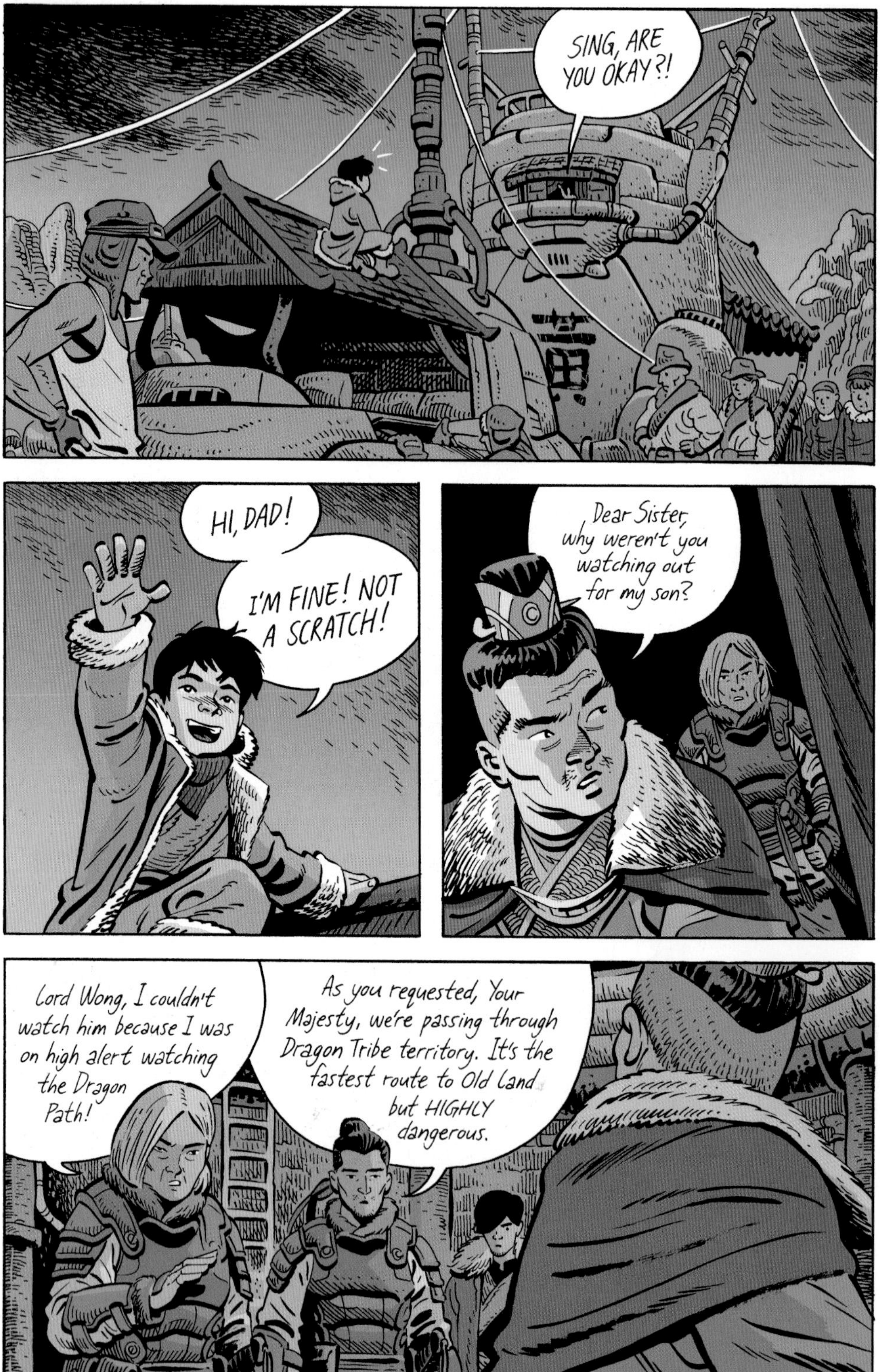
SING, ARE YOU OKAY?!
HI, DAD!
I'M FINE! NOT A SCRATCH!
Dear Sister, why weren't you watching out for my son?
Lord Wong, I couldn't watch him because I was on high alert watching the Dragon Path!
As you requested, Your Majesty, we're passing through Dragon Tribe territory. It's the fastest route to Old Land but HIGHLY dangerous.

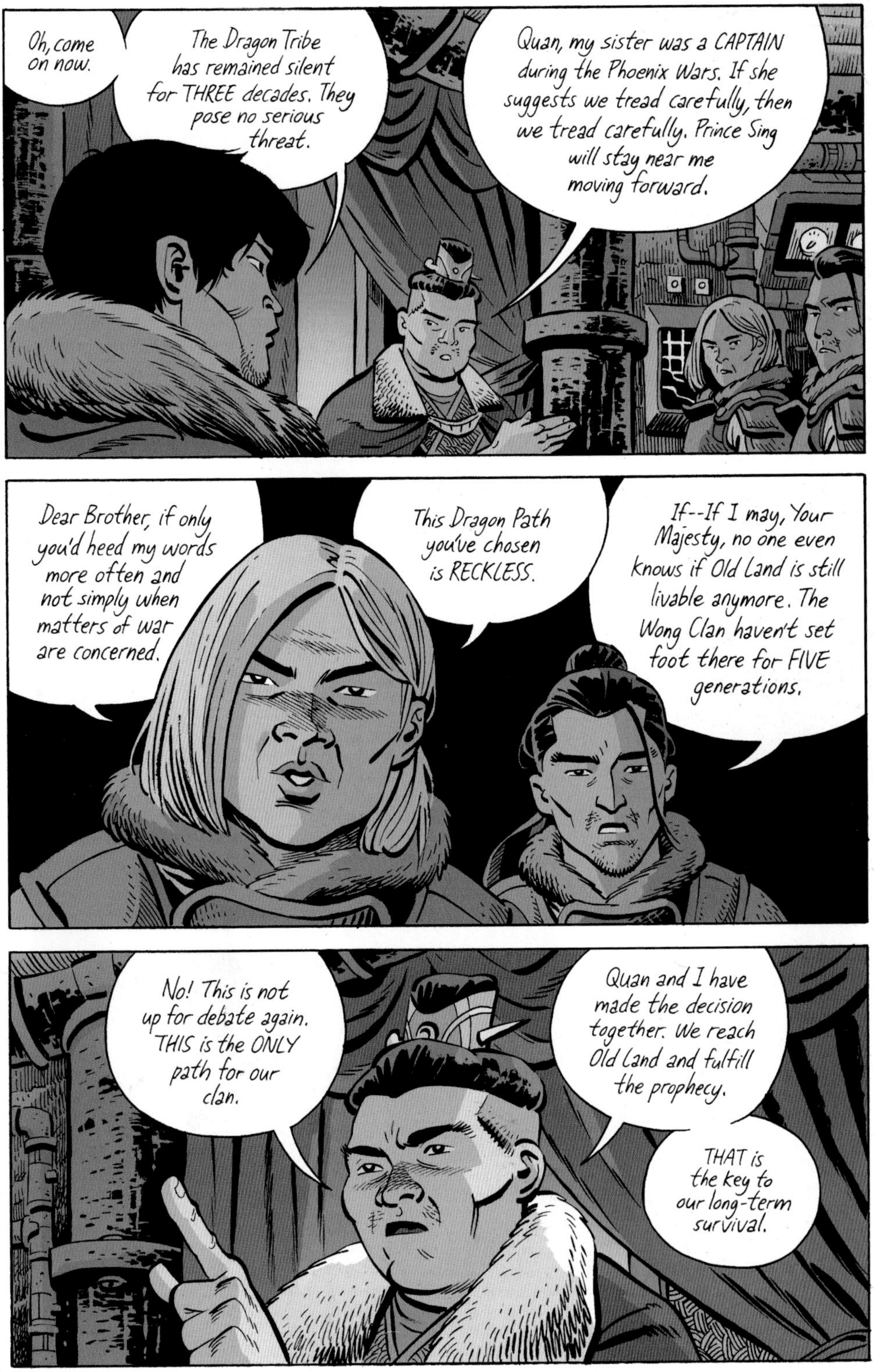
Oh, come on now.
The Dragon Tribe has remained silent for THREE decades. They pose no serious threat.
Quan, my sister was a CAPTAIN during the Phoenix Wars. If she suggests we tread carefully, then we tread carefully. Prince Sing will stay near me moving forward.
Dear Brother, if only you'd heed my words more often and not simply when matters of war are concerned.
This Dragon Path you've chosen is RECKLESS.
If--If I may, Your Majesty, no one even knows if Old Land is still livable anymore. The Wong Clan haven't set foot there for FIVE generations.
No! This is not up for debate again. THIS is the ONLY path for our clan.
Quan and I have made the decision together. We reach Old Land and fulfill the prophecy.
THAT is the key to our long-term survival.

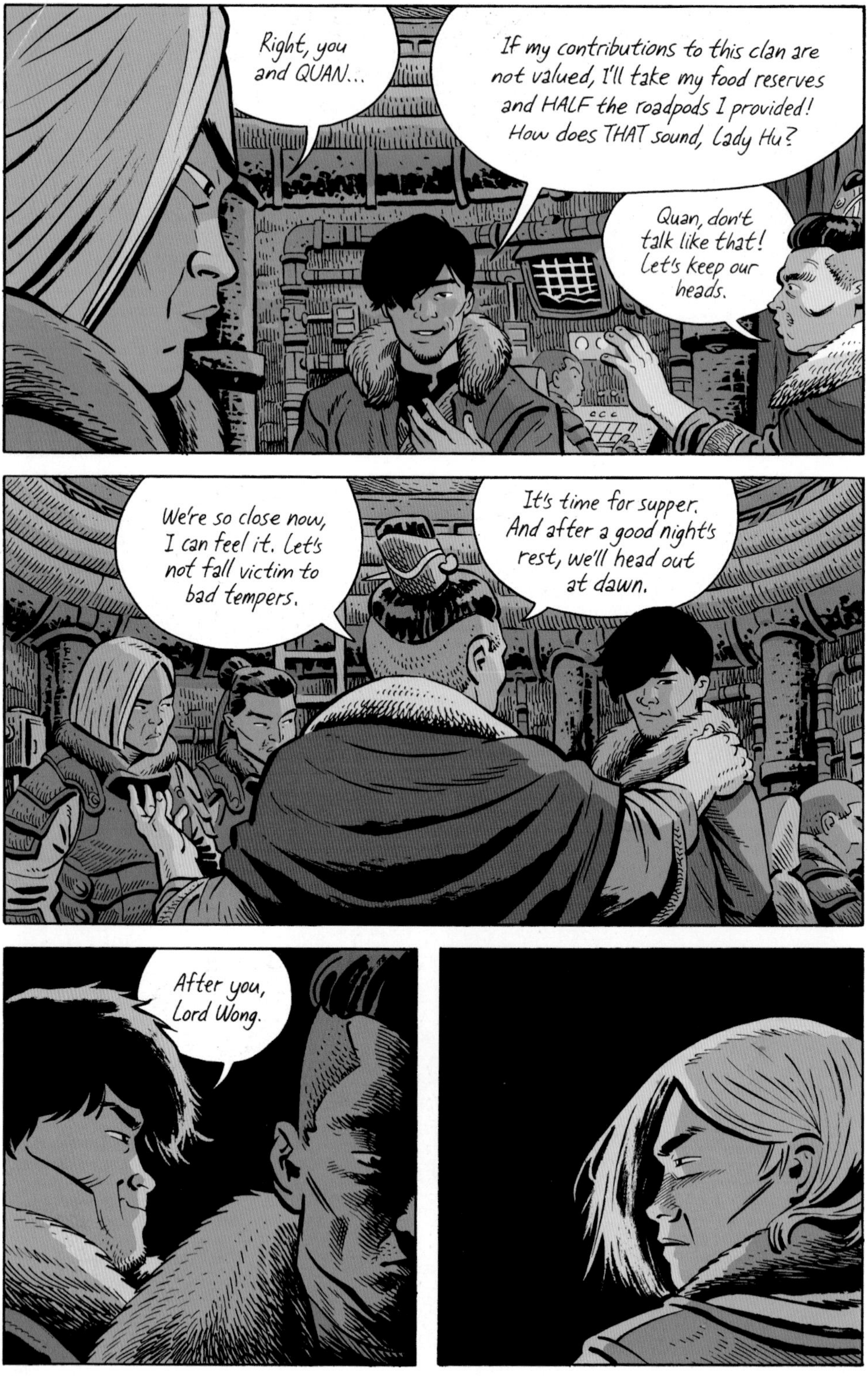
Right, you and QUAN...
If my contributions to this clan are not valued, I'll take my food reserves and HALF the roadpods I provided! How does THAT sound, Lady Hu?
Quan, don't talk like that! Let's keep our heads.
We're so close now, I can feel it. Let's not fall victim to bad tempers.
It's time for supper. And after a good night's rest, we'll head out at dawn.
After you, Lord Wong.

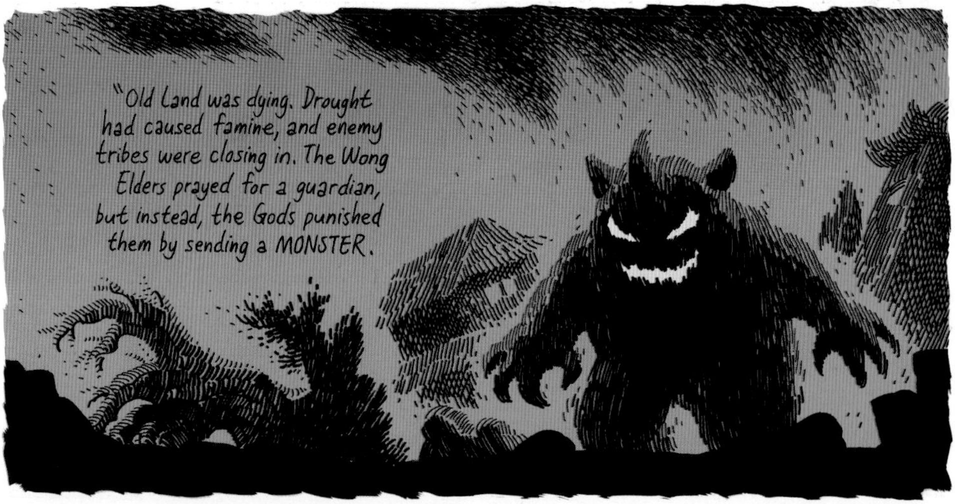
"Old Land was dying. Drought had caused famine, and enemy tribes were closing in. The Wong Elders prayed for a guardian, but instead, the Gods punished them by sending a MONSTER.

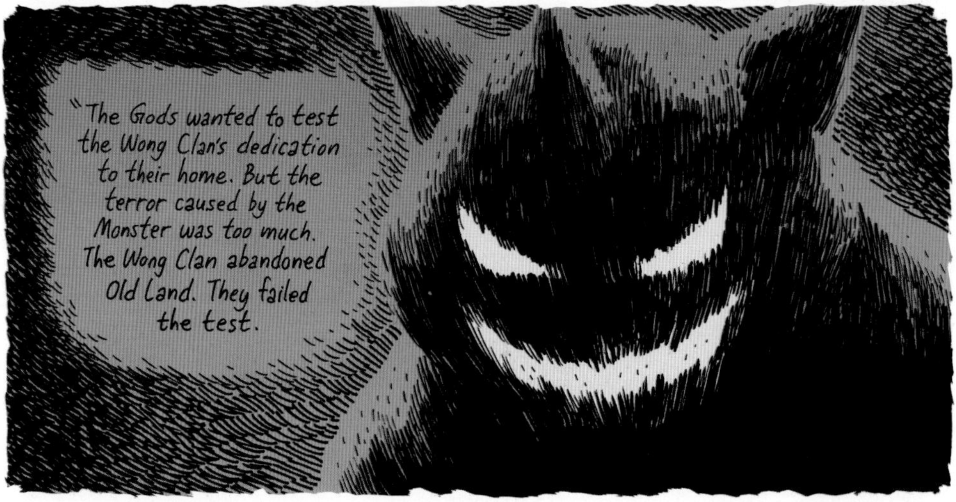
"The Gods wanted to test the Wong Clan's dedication to their home. But the terror caused by the Monster was too much. The Wong Clan abandoned Old Land. They failed the test.

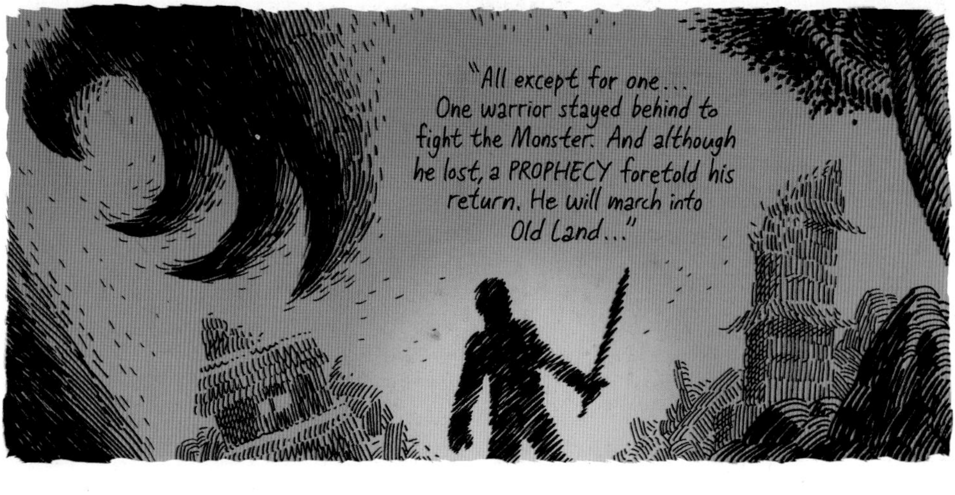
"All except for one... One warrior stayed behind to fight the Monster. And although he lost, a PROPHECY foretold his return. He will march into Old Land..."

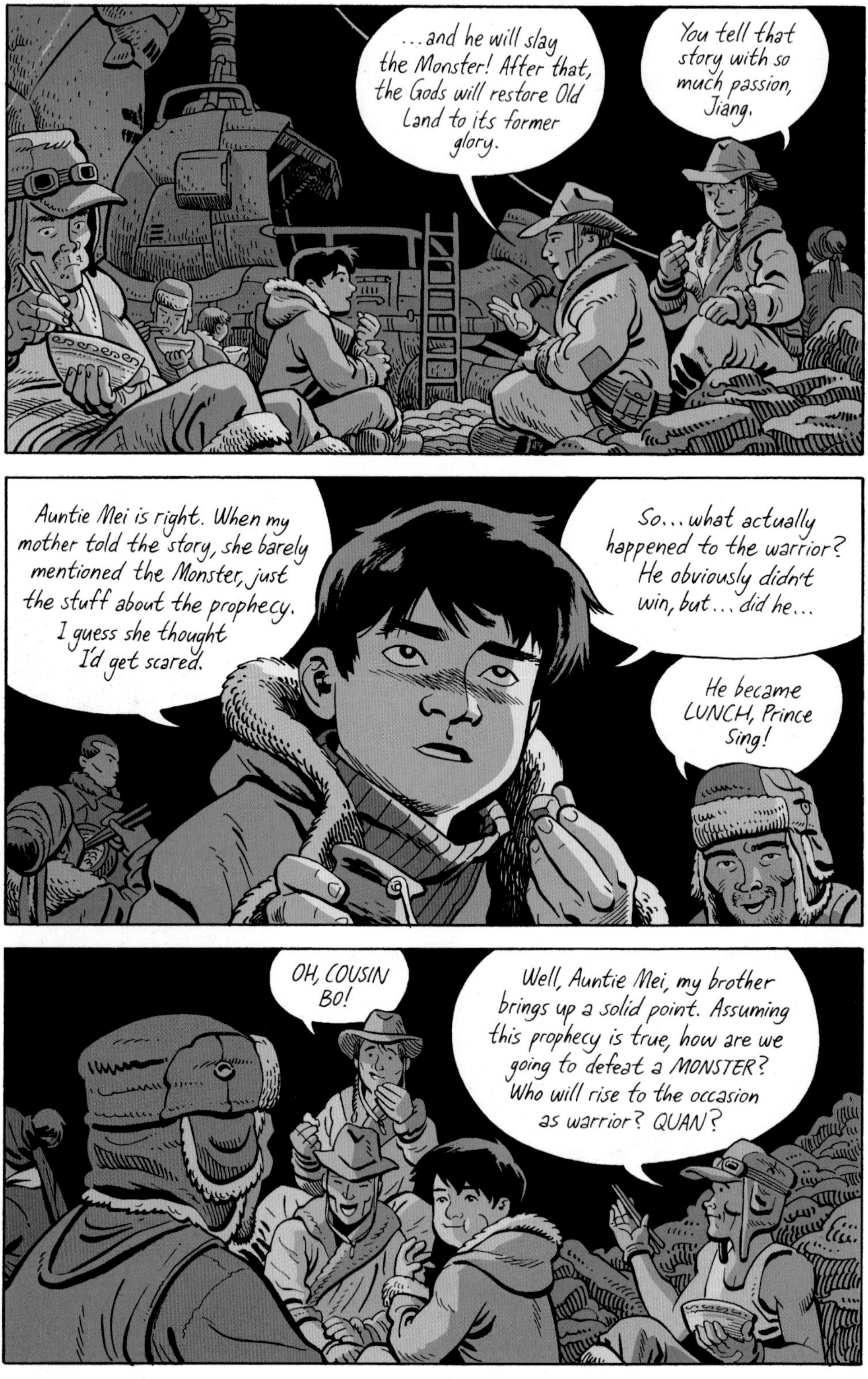
...and he will slay the Monster! After that, the Gods will restore Old Land to its former glory.
You tell that story with so much passion, Jiang.
Auntie Mei is right. When my mother told the story, she barely mentioned the Monster, just the stuff about the prophecy. I guess she thought I'd get scared.
So... what actually happened to the warrior? He obviously didn't win, but... did he...
He became LUNCH, Prince Sing!
OH, COUSIN BO!
Well, Auntie Mei, my brother brings up a solid point. Assuming this prophecy is true, how are we going to defeat a MONSTER? Who will rise to the occasion as warrior? QUAN?

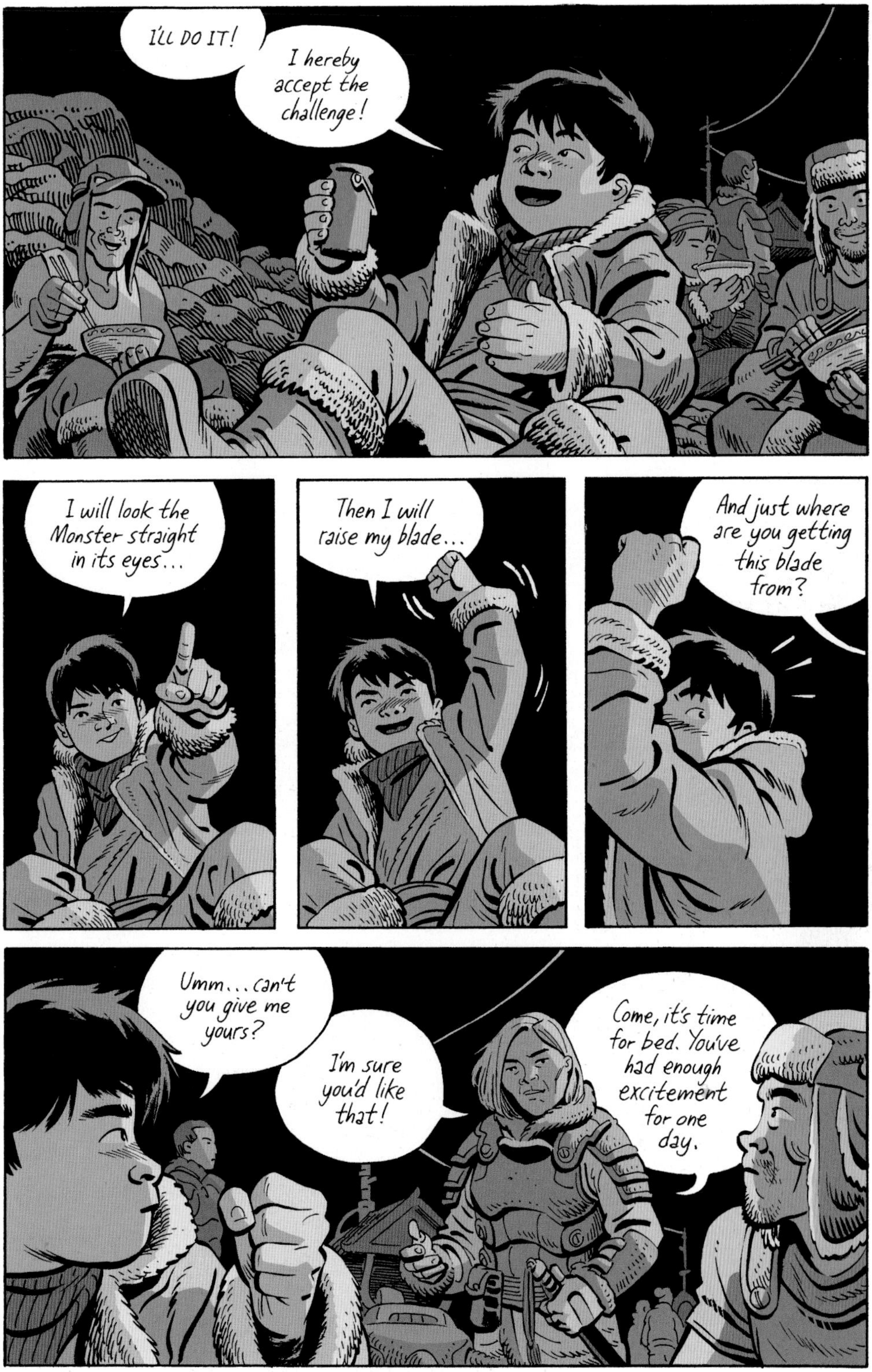
I'LL DO IT!
I hereby accept the challenge!
I will look the Monster straight in its eyes...
Then I will raise my blade...
And just where are you getting this blade from?
Umm... can't you give me yours?
I'm sure you'd like that!
Come, it's time for bed. You've had enough excitement for one day.

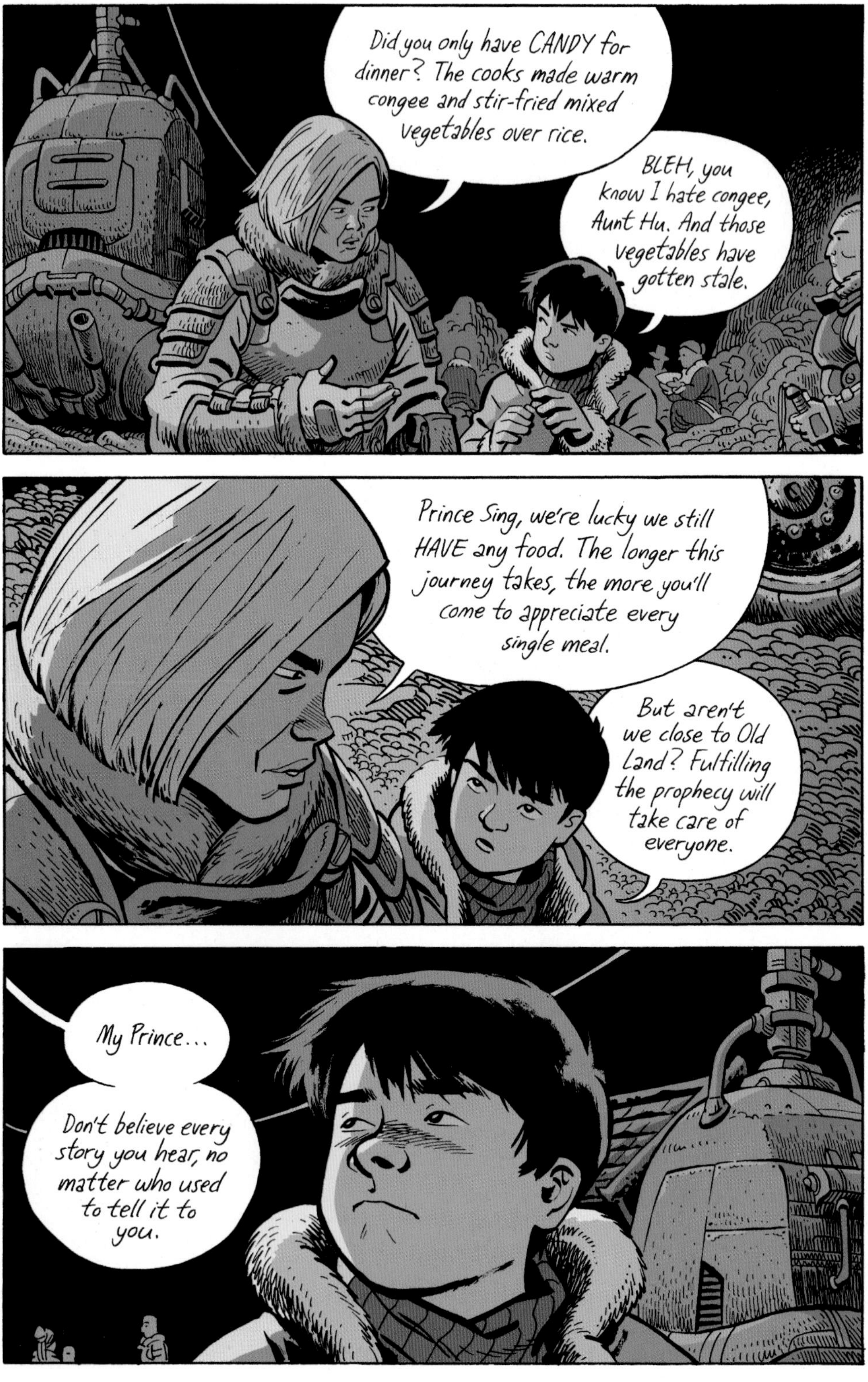
Did you only have CANDY for dinner? The cooks made warm congee and stir-fried mixed vegetables over rice.
BLEH, you know I hate congee, Aunt Hu. And those vegetables have gotten stale.
Prince Sing, we're lucky we still HAVE any food. The longer this journey takes, the more you'll come to appreciate every single meal.
But aren't we close to Old Land? Fulfilling the prophecy will take care of everyone.
My Prince...
Don't believe every story you hear, no matter who used to tell it to you.

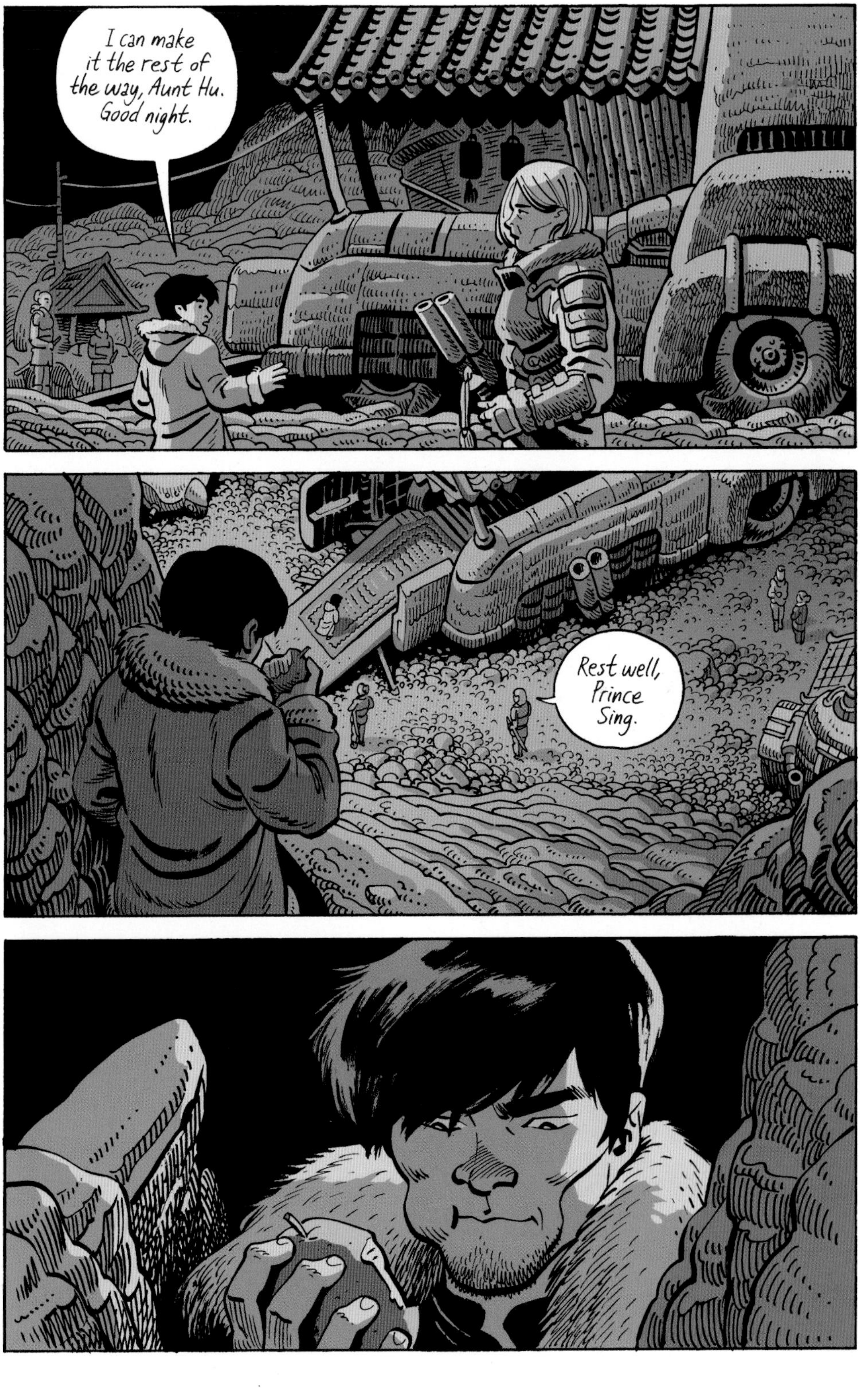
I can make it the rest of the way, Aunt Hu. Good night.
Rest well, Prince Sing.

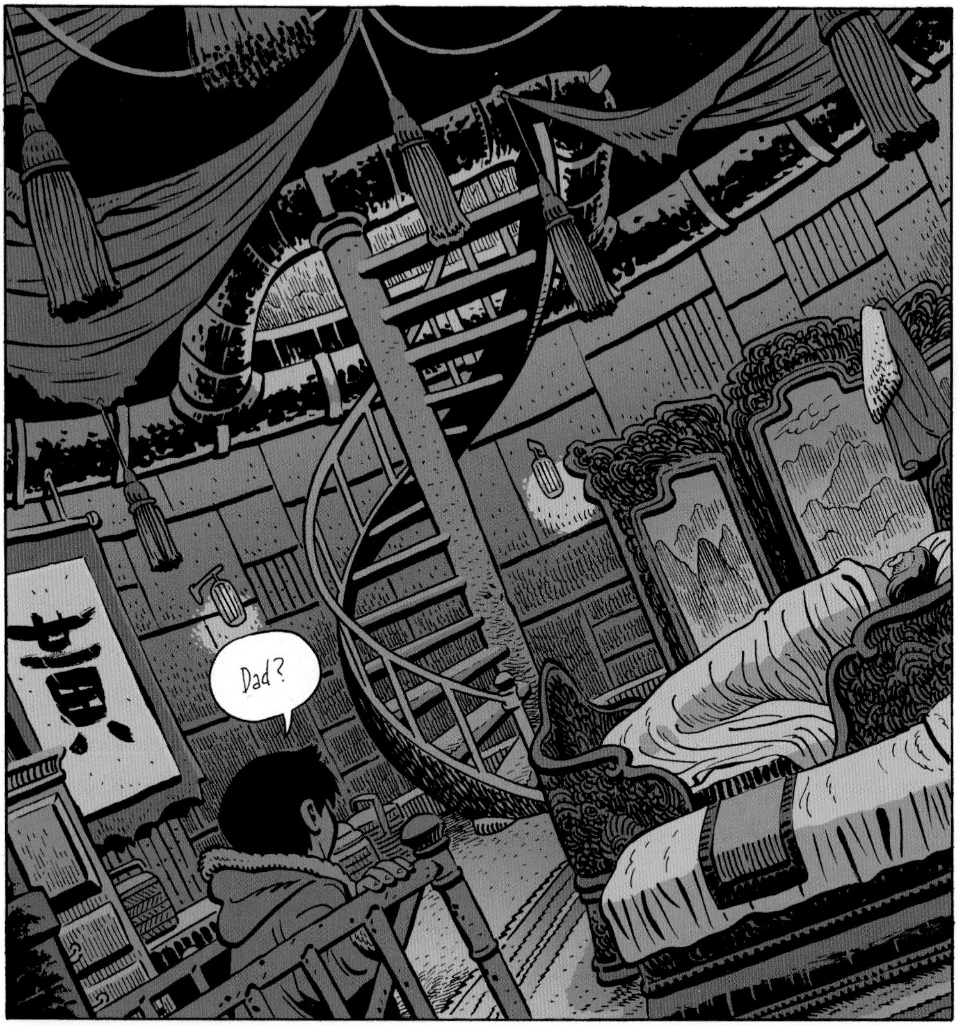
Dad?

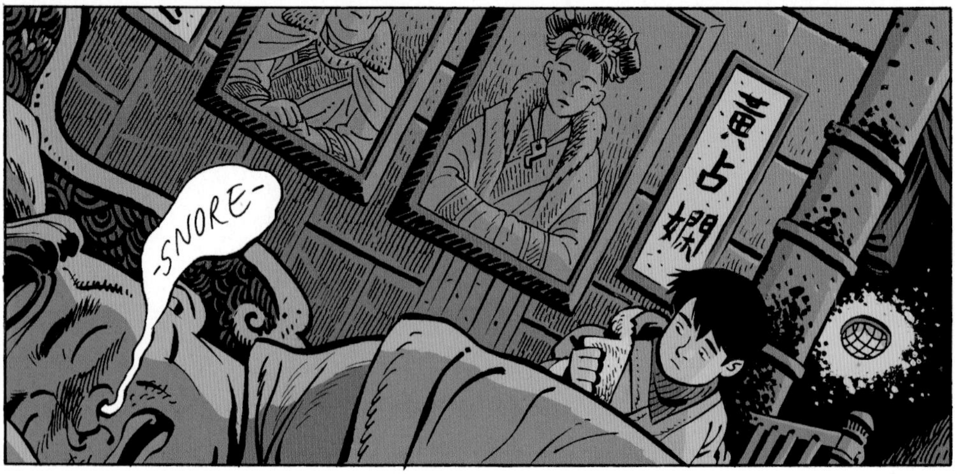
-SNORE-

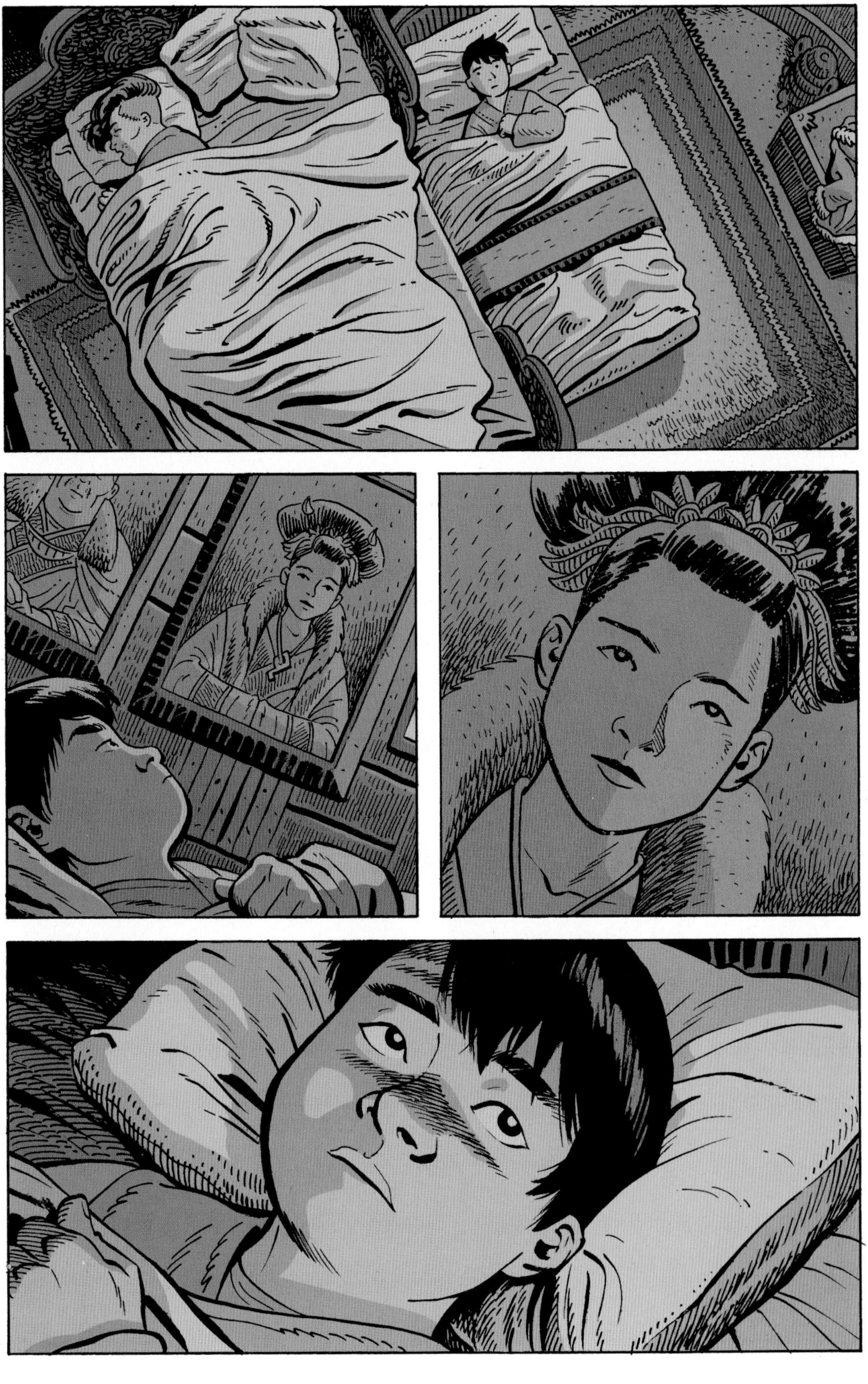

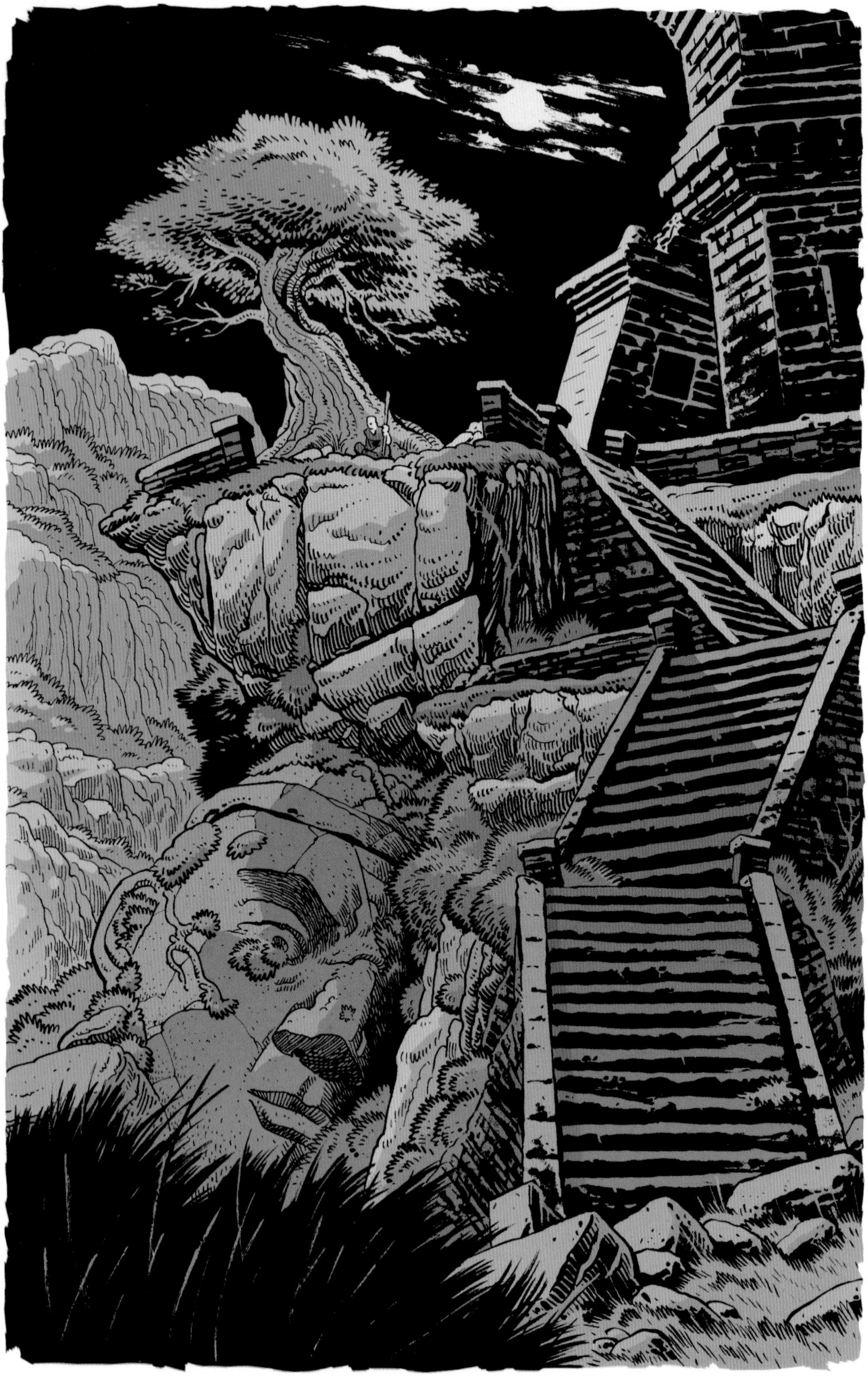

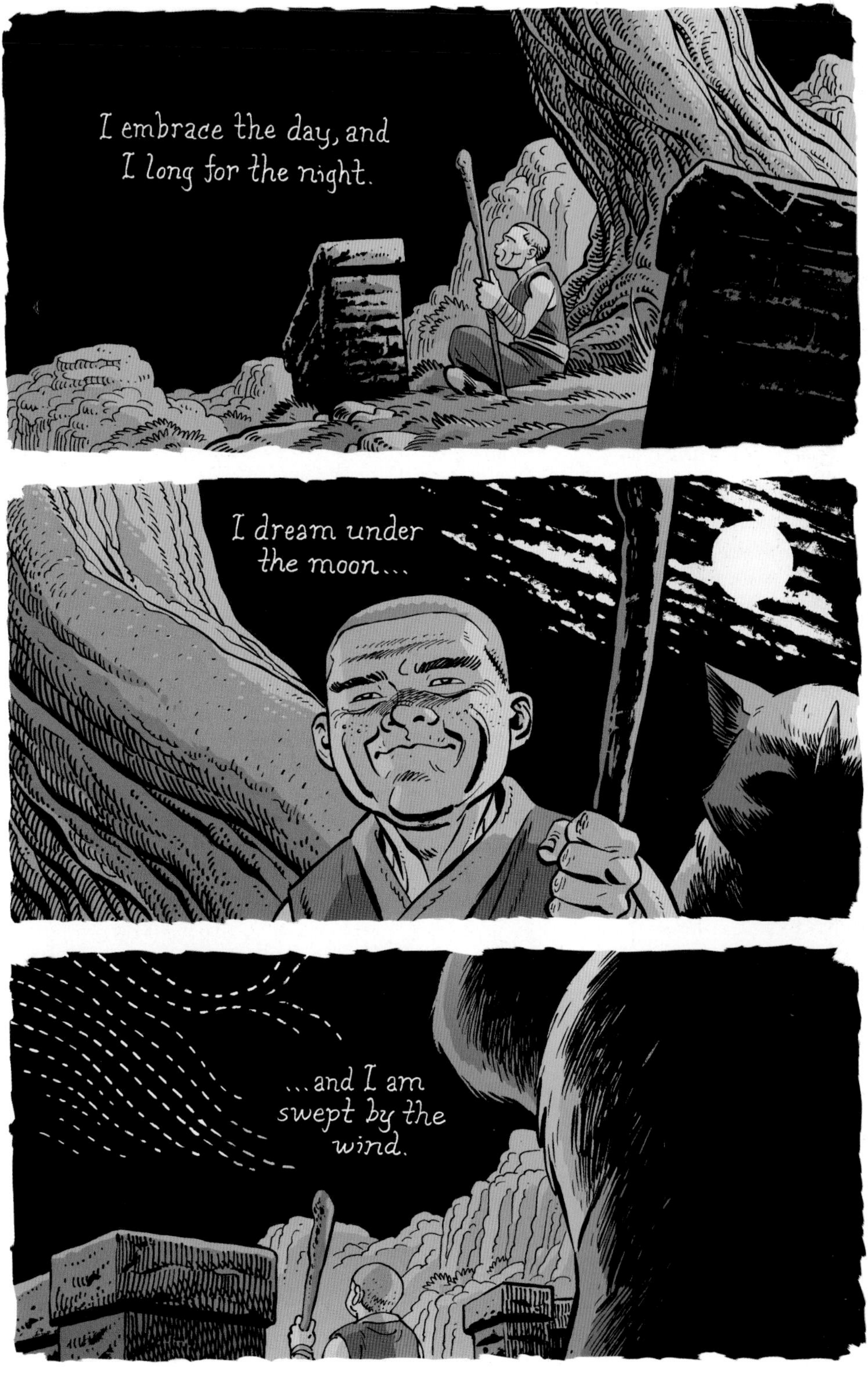
I embrace the day, and I long for the night.
I dream under the moon...
...and I am swept by the wind.

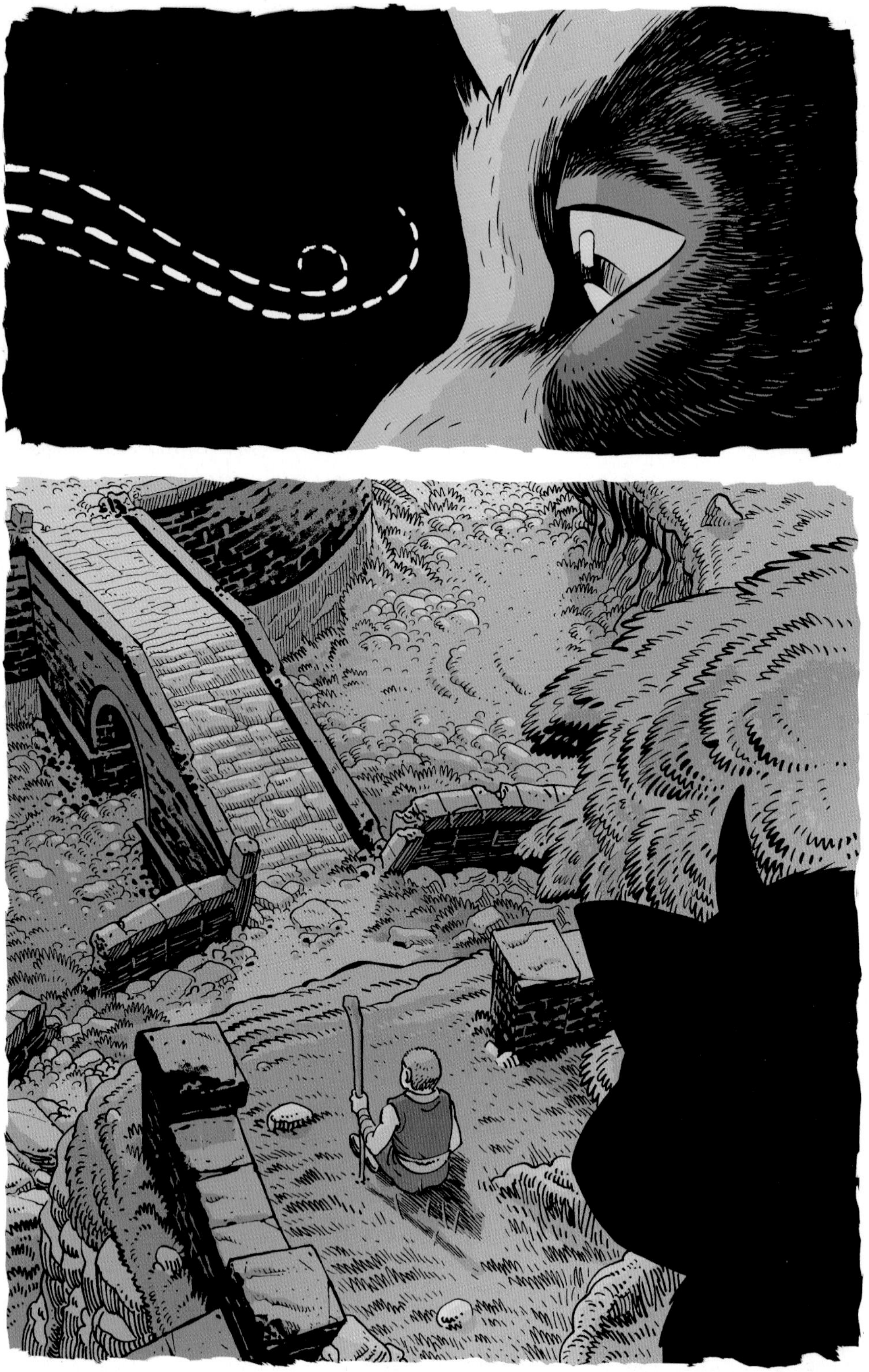

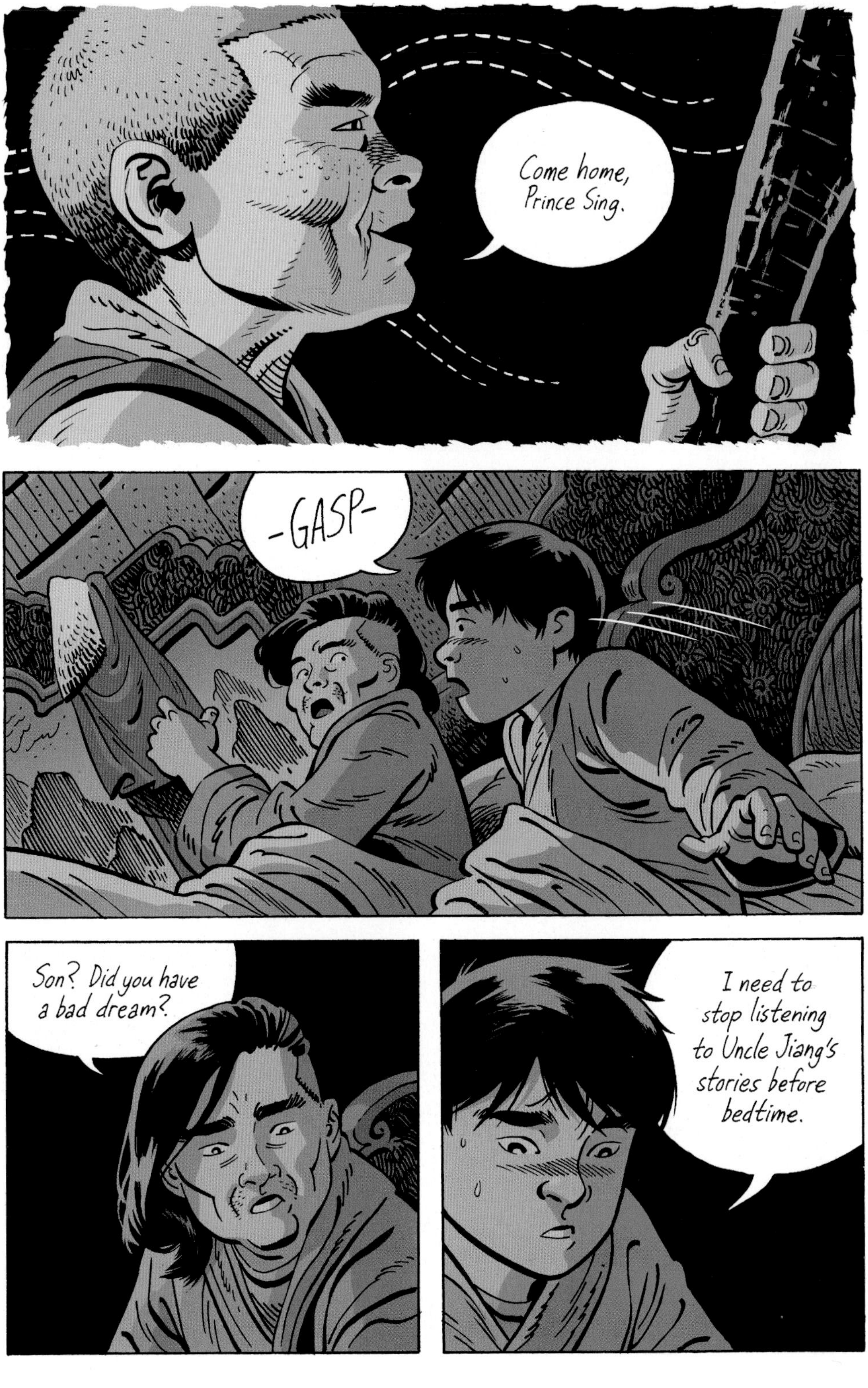
Come home, Prince Sing.
-GASP-
Son? Did you have a bad dream?
I need to stop listening to Uncle Jiang's stories before bedtime.

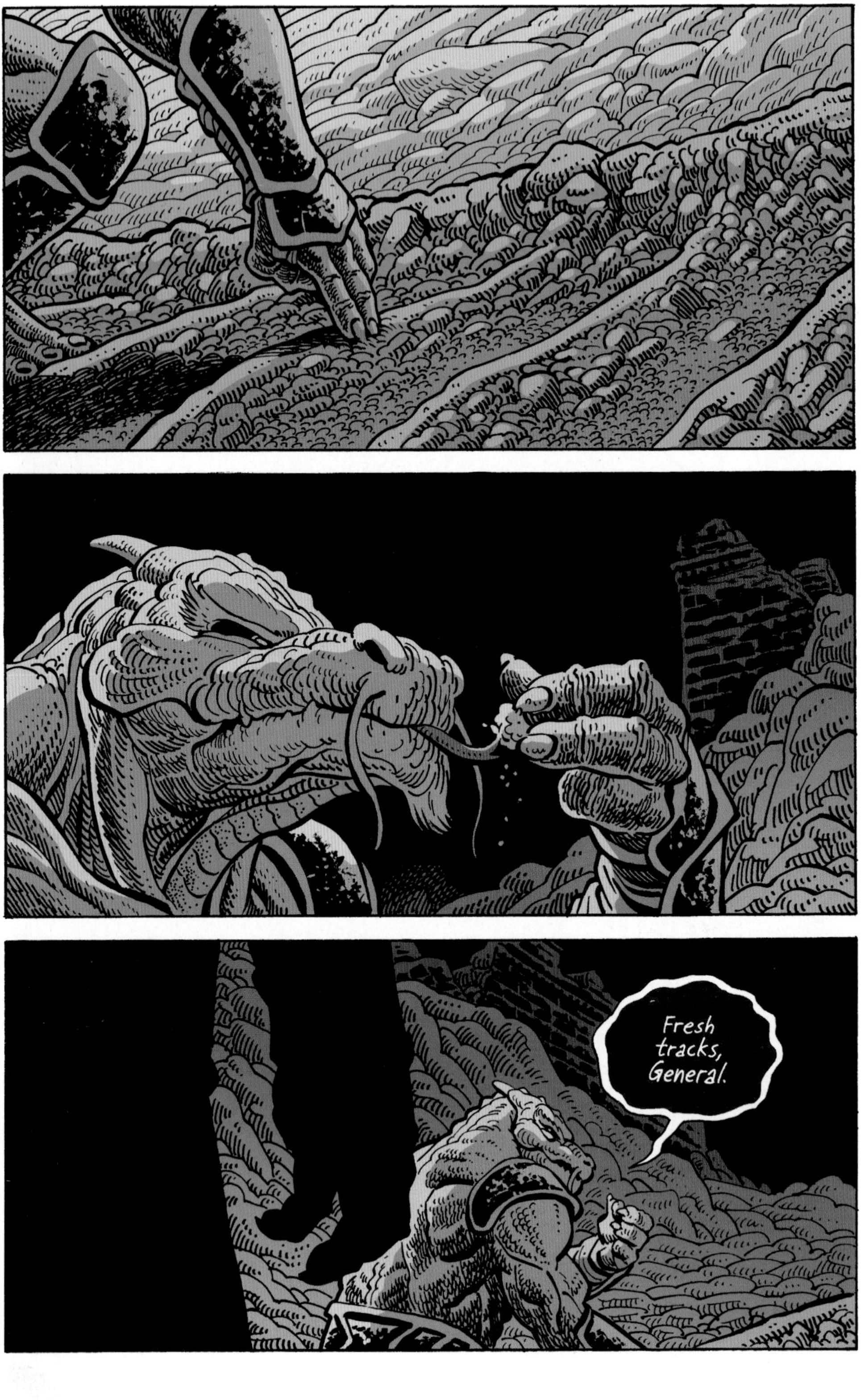
Fresh tracks, General.

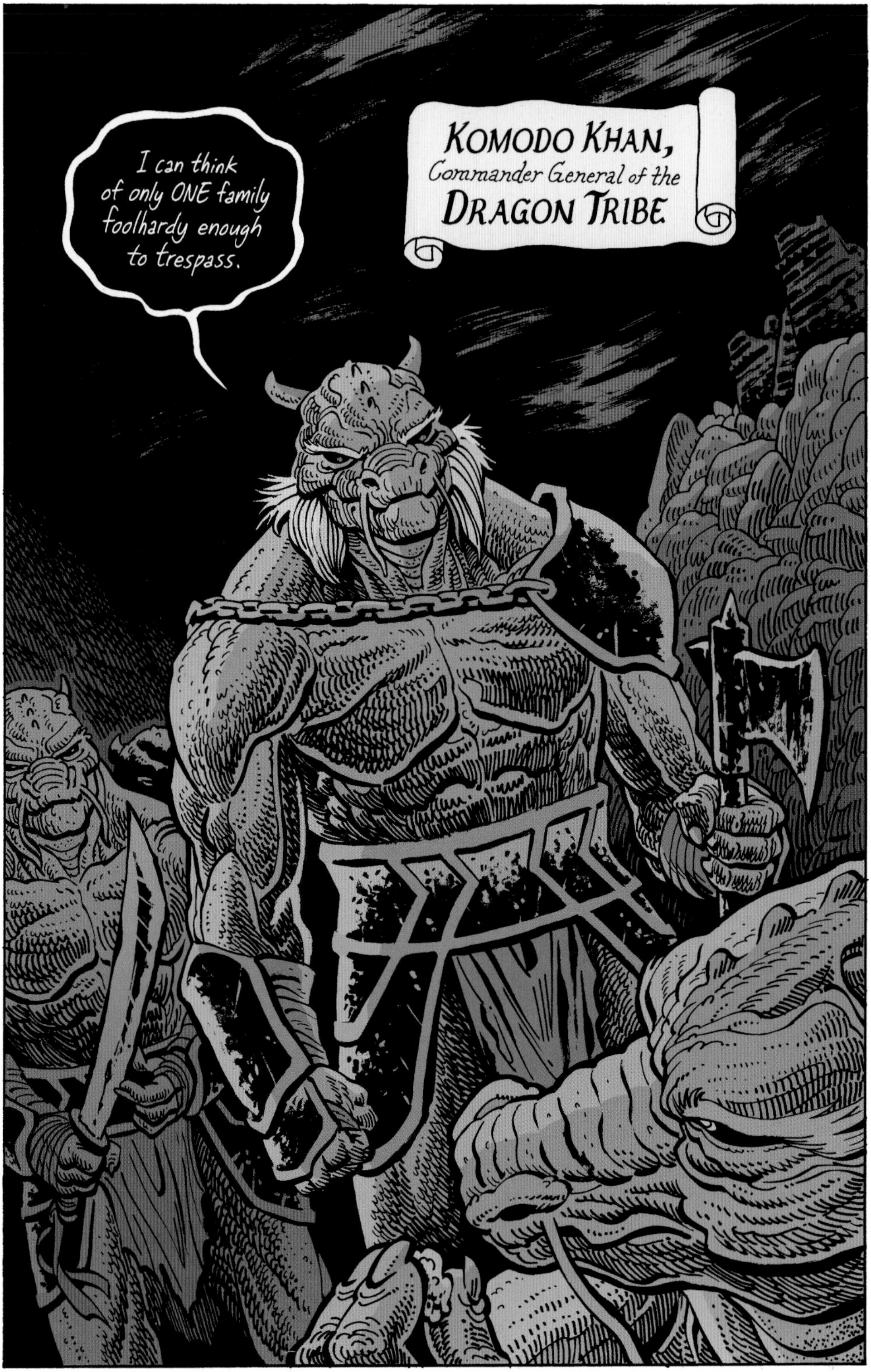
I can think of only ONE family foolhardy enough to trespass.
KOMODO KHAN, Commander General of the DRAGON TRIBE

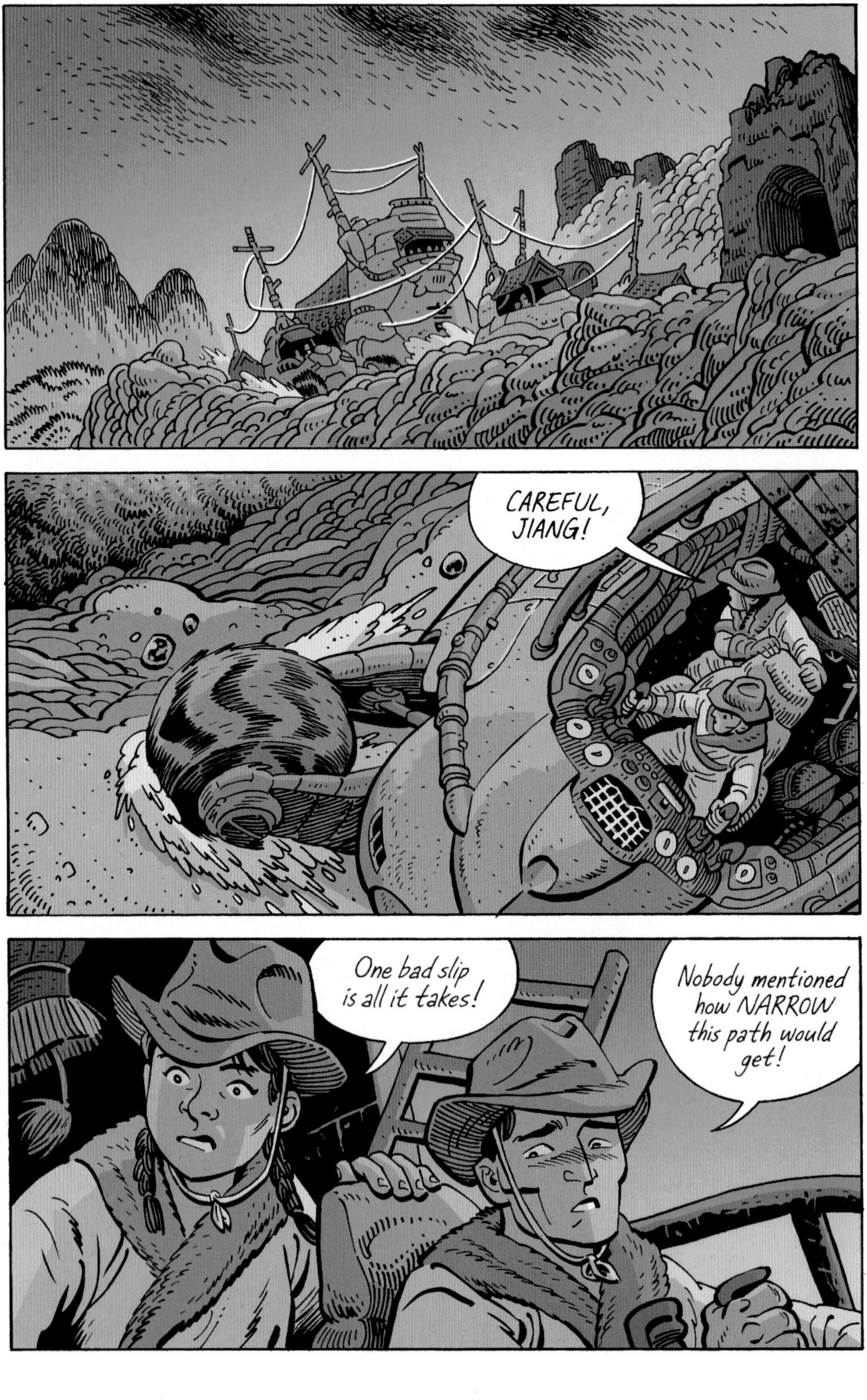
CAREFUL, JIANG!
One bad slip is all it takes!
Nobody mentioned how NARROW this path would get!

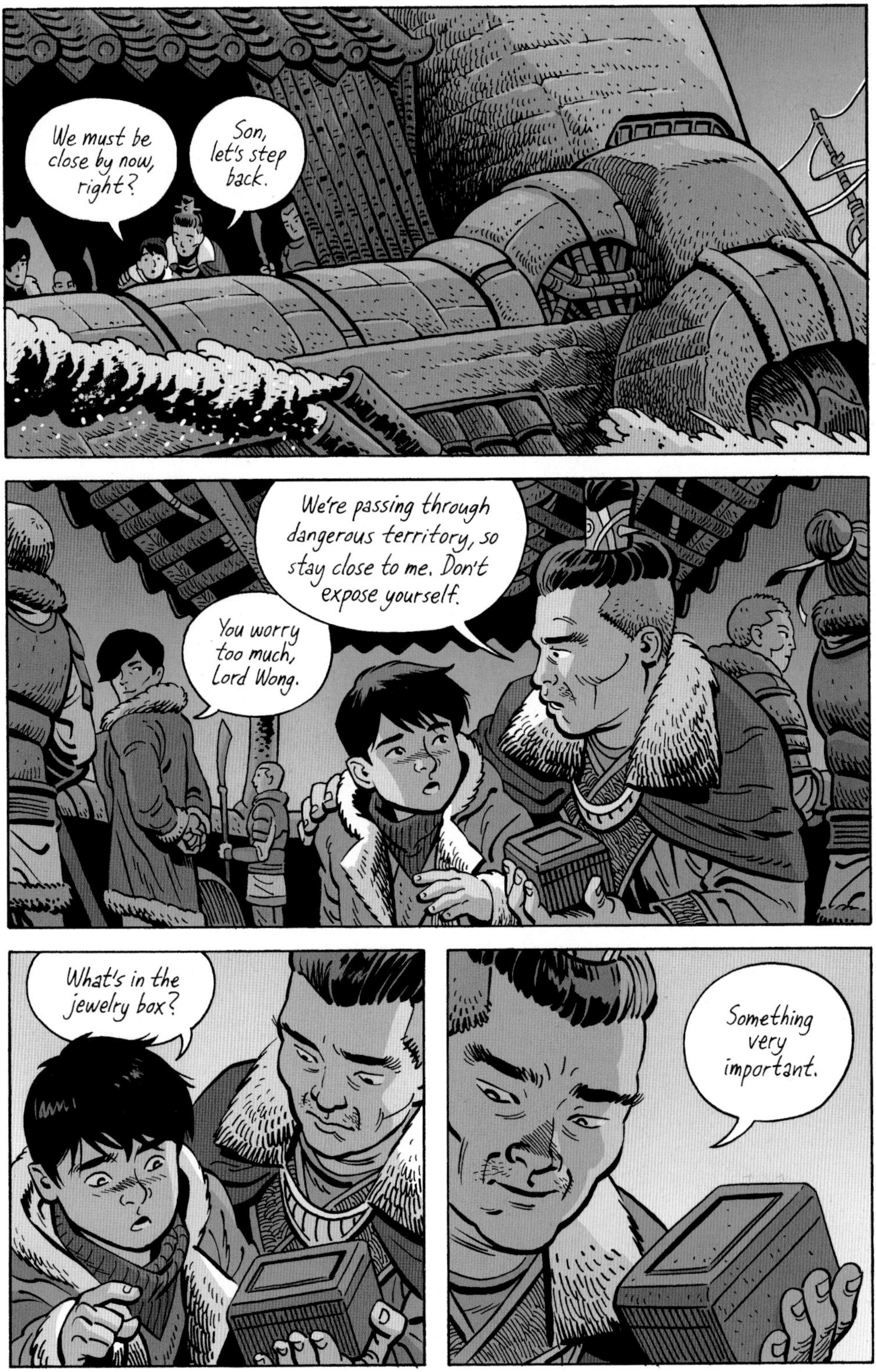
We must be close by now, right?
Son, let's step back.
We're passing through dangerous territory, so stay close to me. Don't expose yourself.
You worry too much, Lord Wong.
What's in the jewelry box?
Something very important.

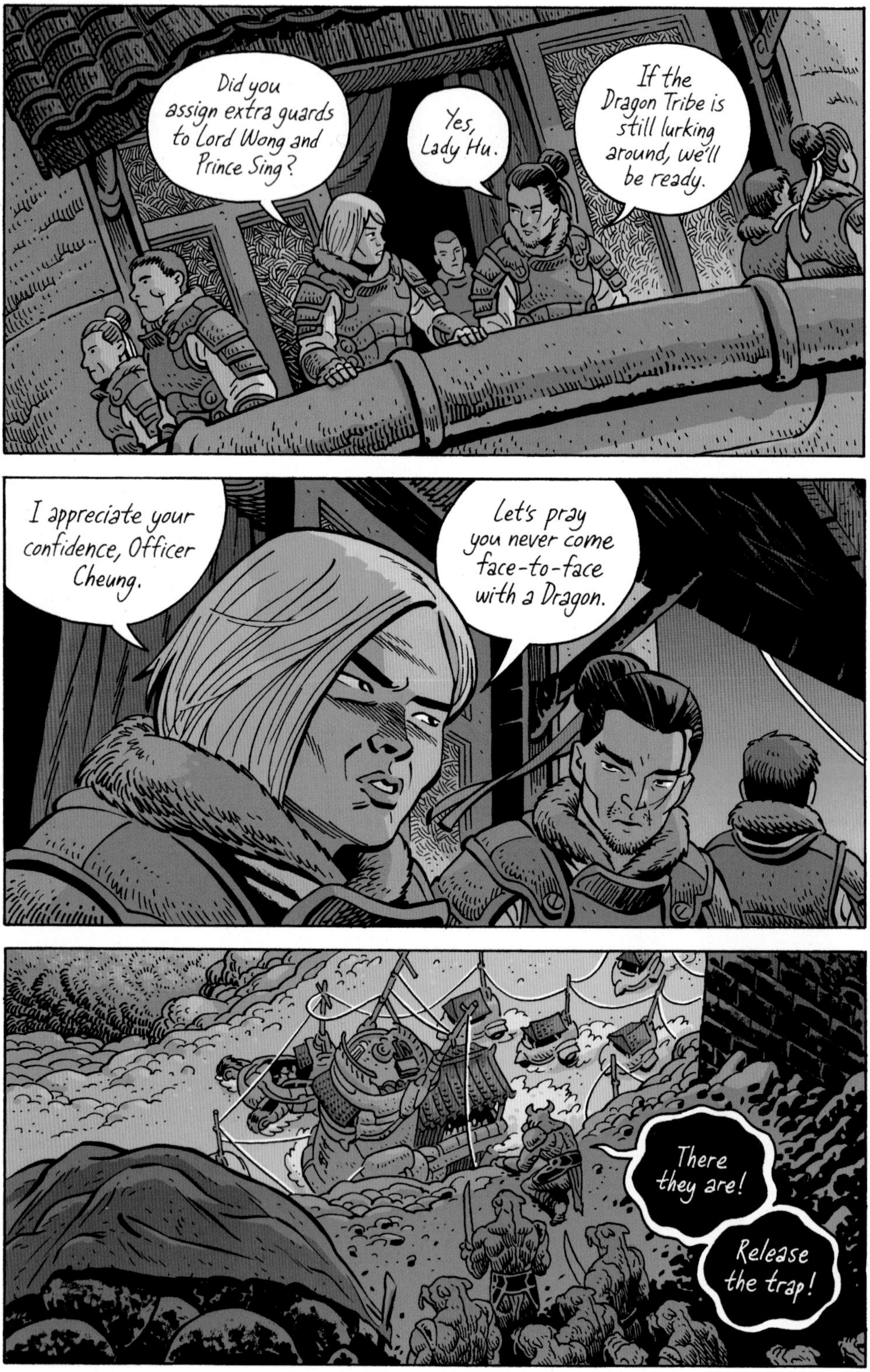
Did you assign extra guards to Lord Wong and Prince Sing?
Yes, Lady Hu.
If the Dragon Tribe is still lurking around, we'll be ready.
I appreciate your confidence, Officer Cheung.
Let's pray you never come face-to-face with a Dragon.
There they are!
Release the trap!

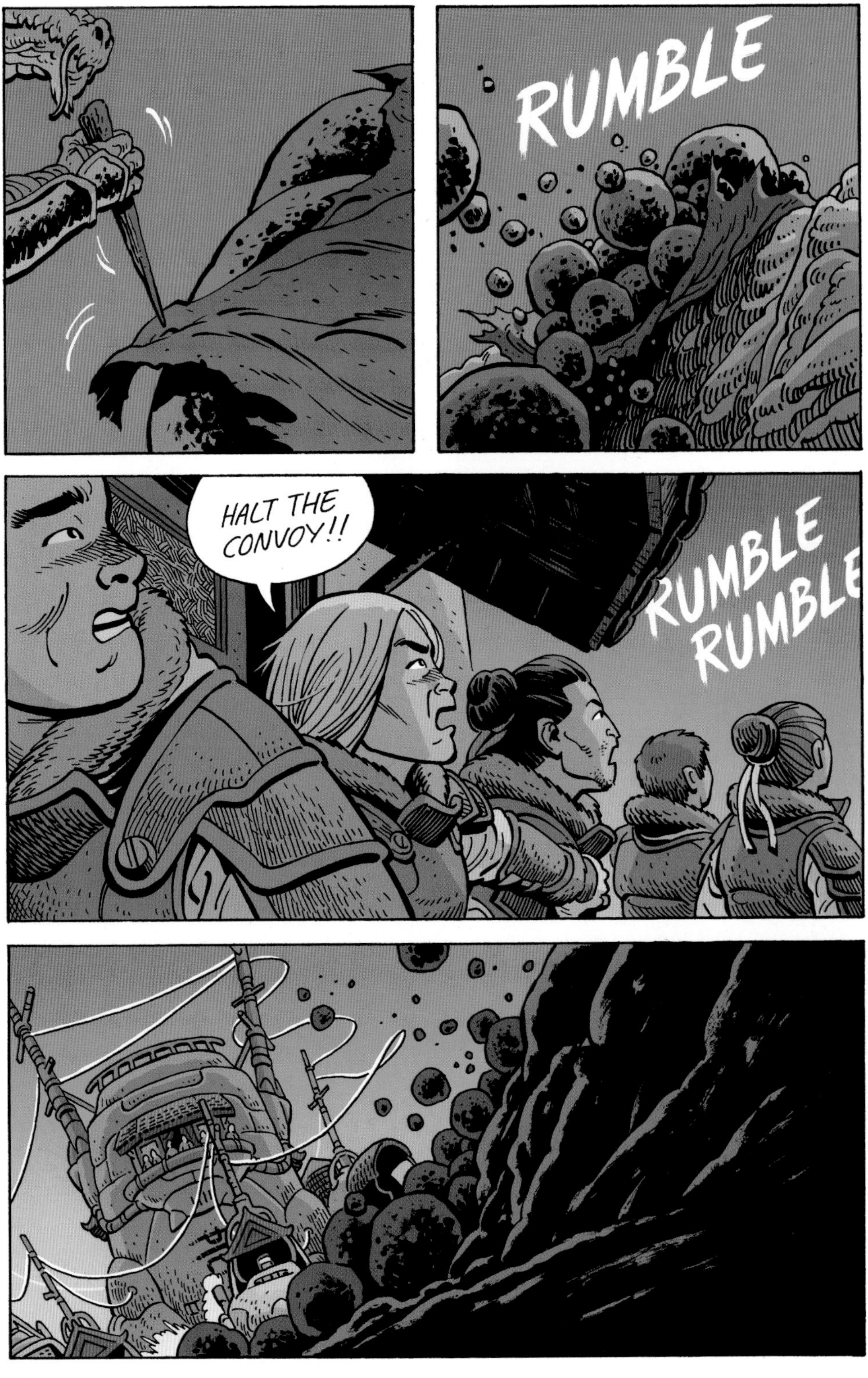

RUMBLE
HALT THE CONVOY!!
RUMBLE RUMBLE

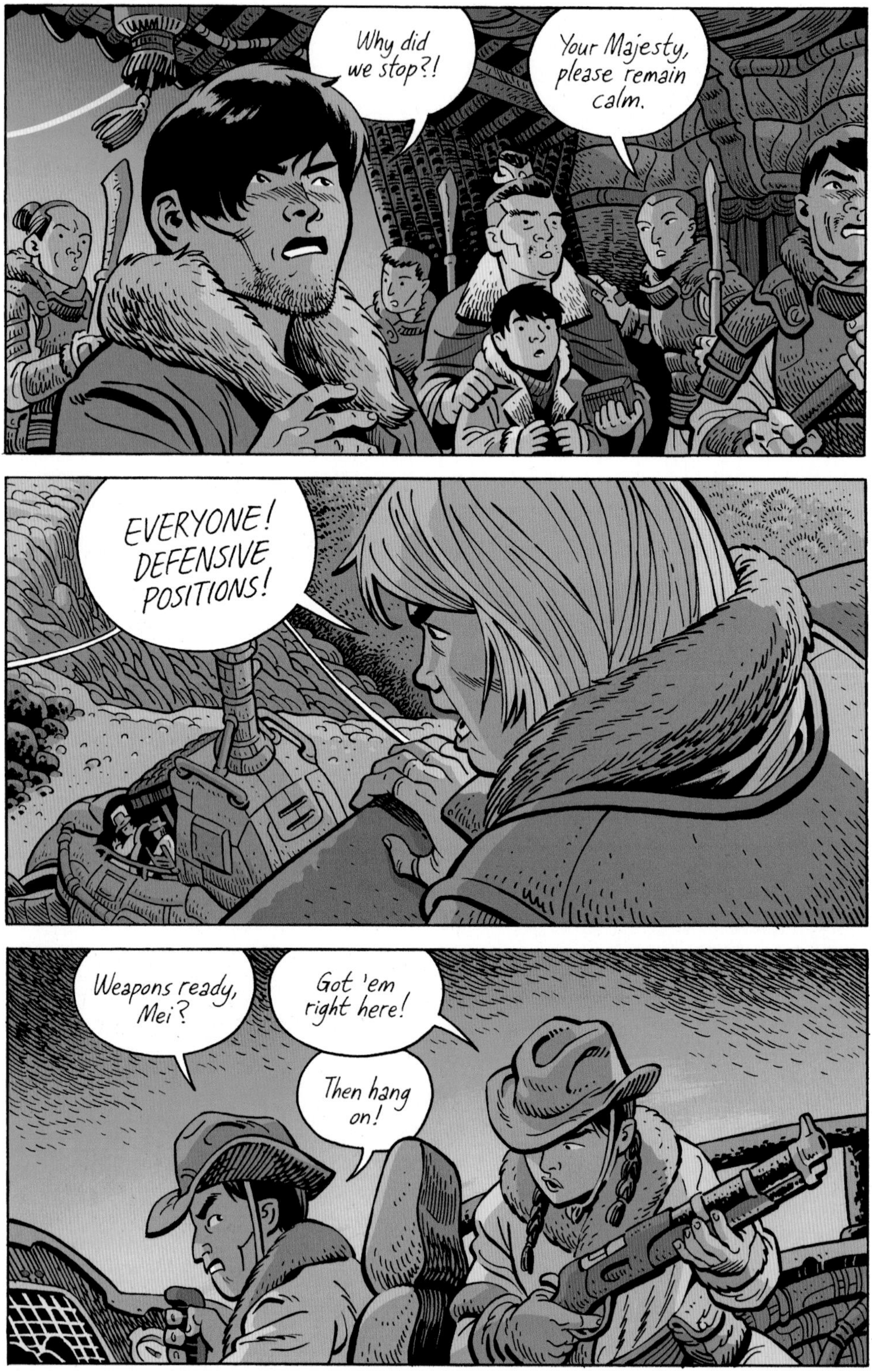
Why did we stop?!
Your Majesty, please remain calm.
EVERYONE! DEFENSIVE POSITIONS!
Weapons ready, Mei?
Got 'em right here!
Then hang on!

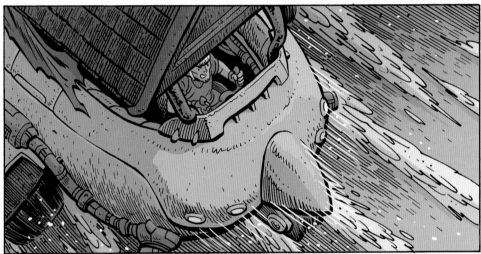

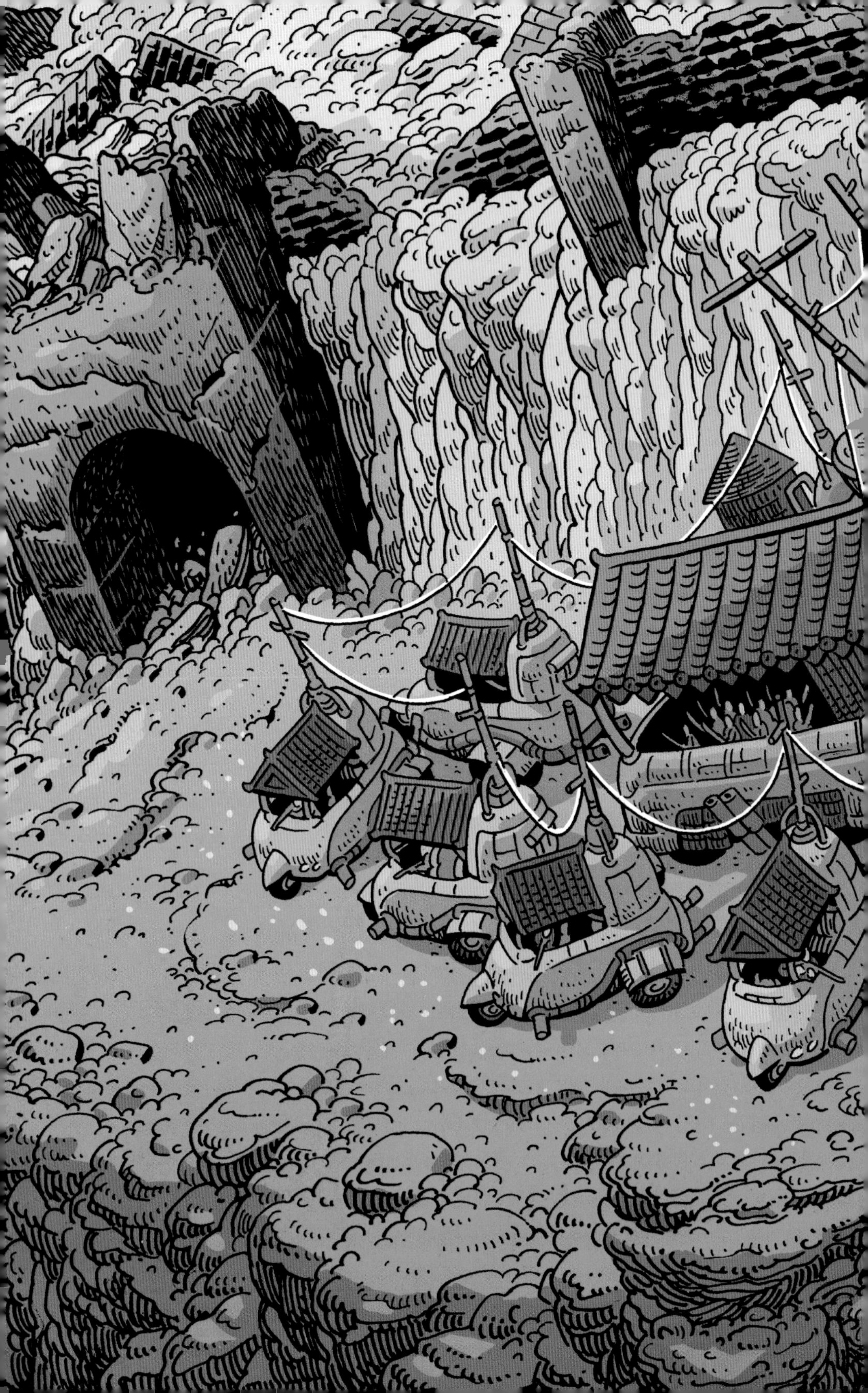

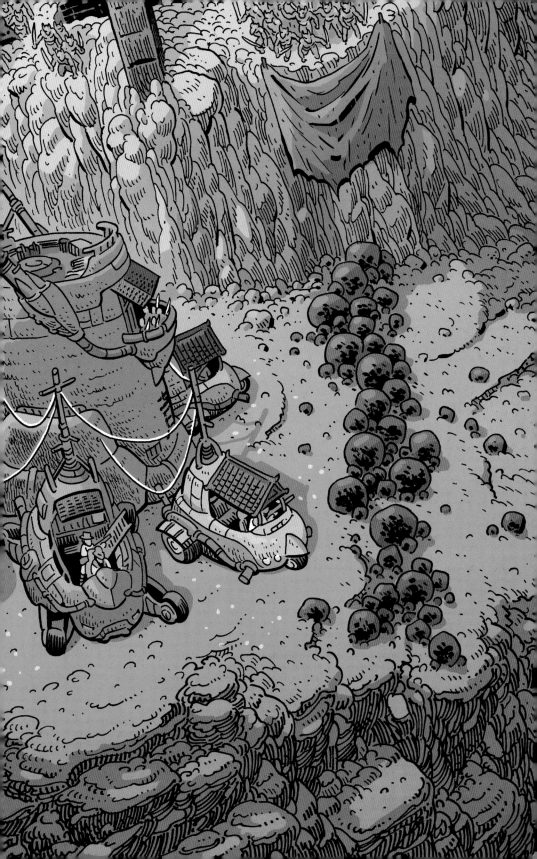

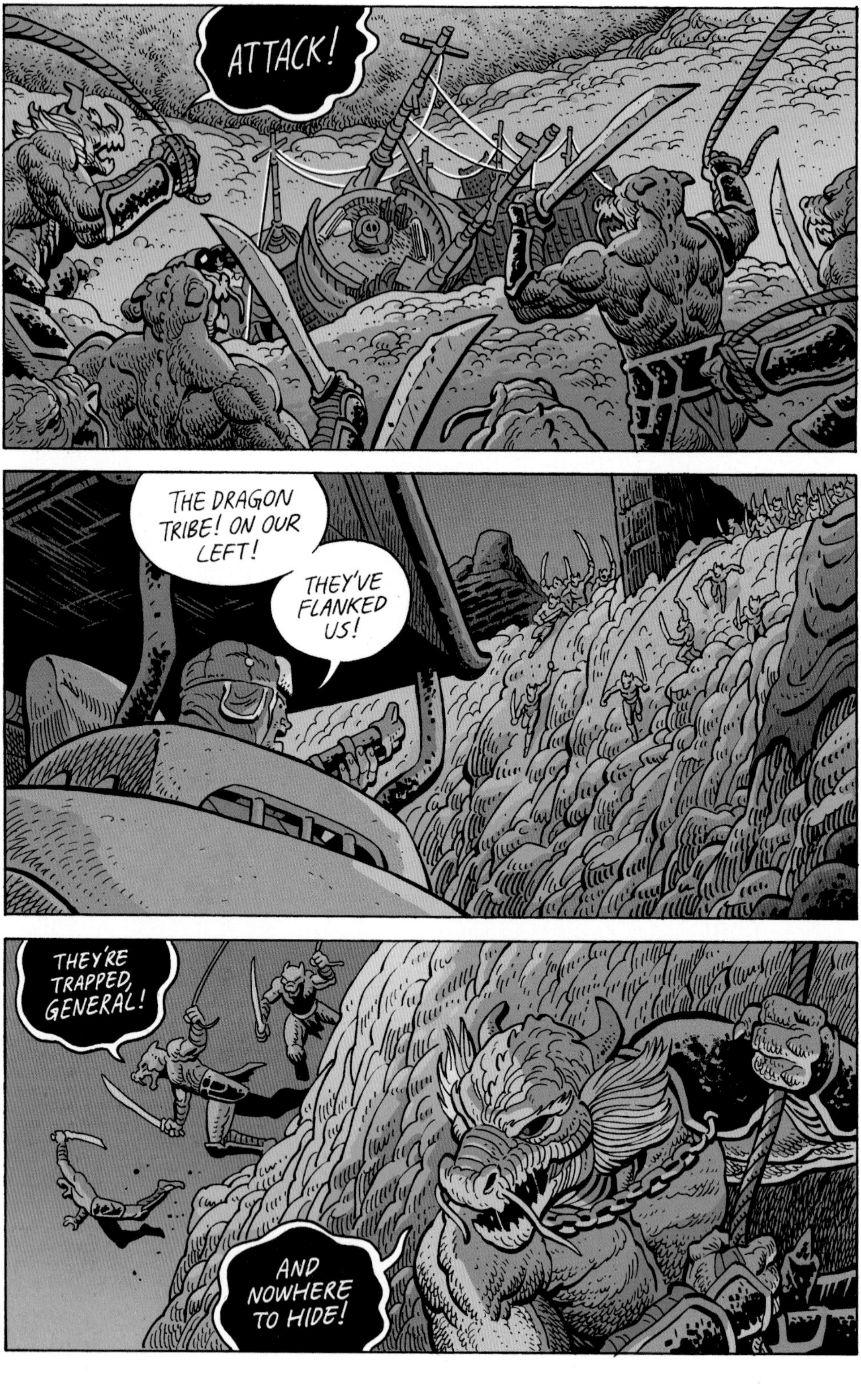
ATTACK!
THE DRAGON TRIBE! ON OUR LEFT!
THEY'VE FLANKED US!
THEY'RE TRAPPED, GENERAL!
AND NOWHERE TO HIDE!

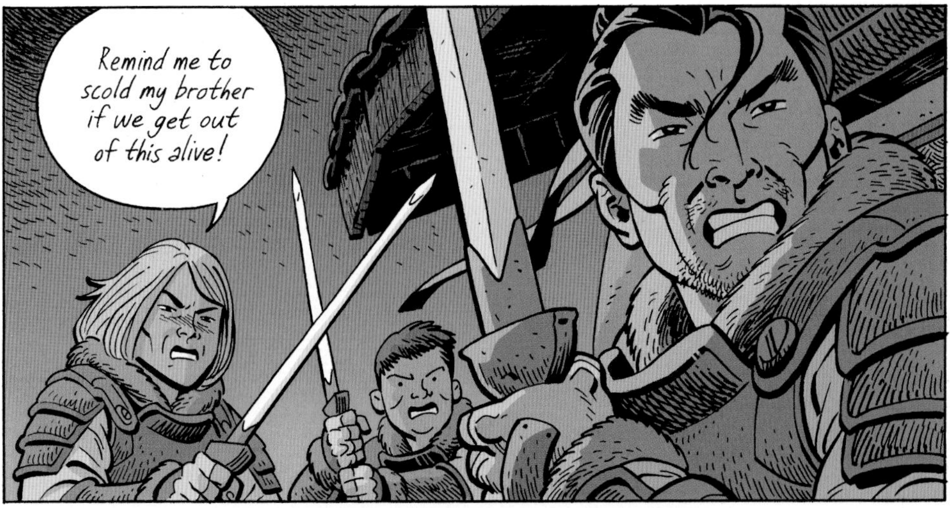
Remind me to scold my brother if we get out of this alive!
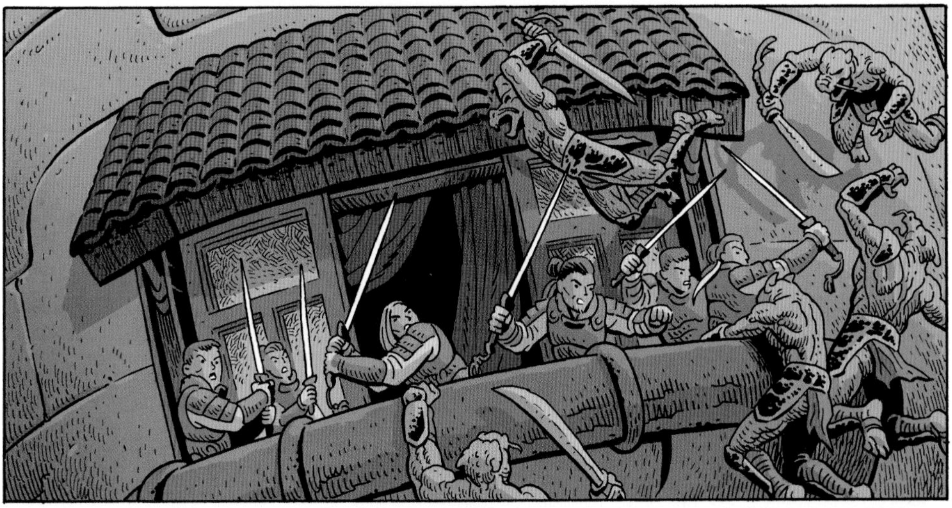
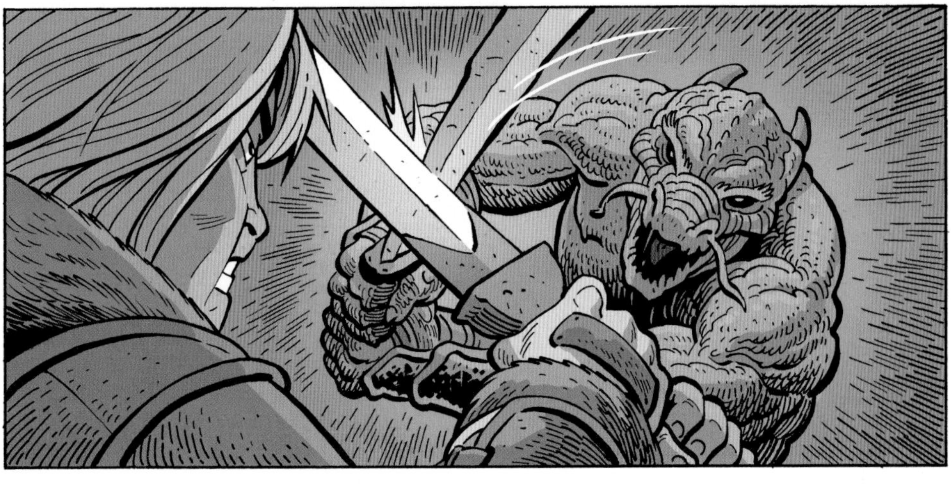

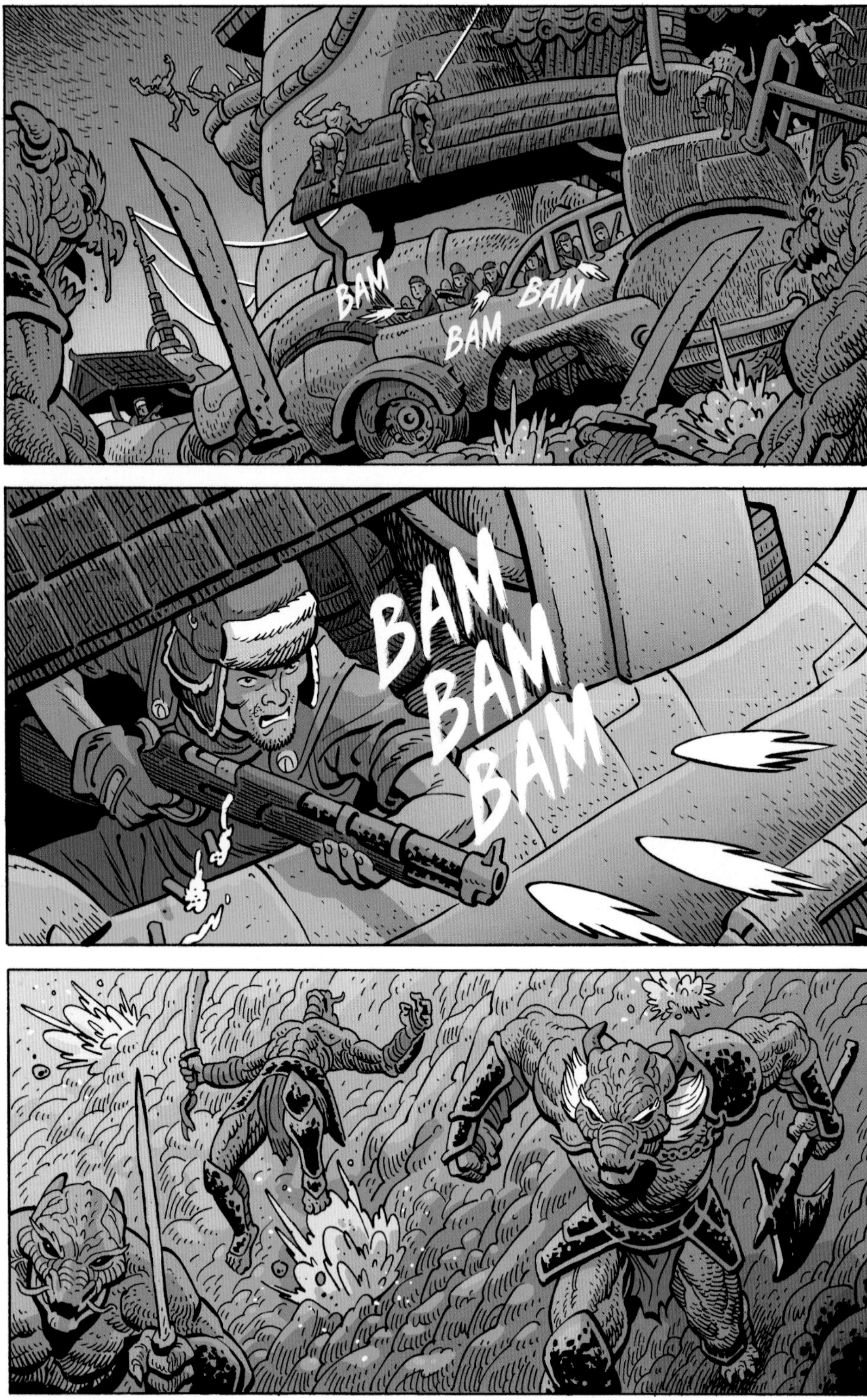
BAM
BAM
BAM
BAM
BAM
BAM
BAM

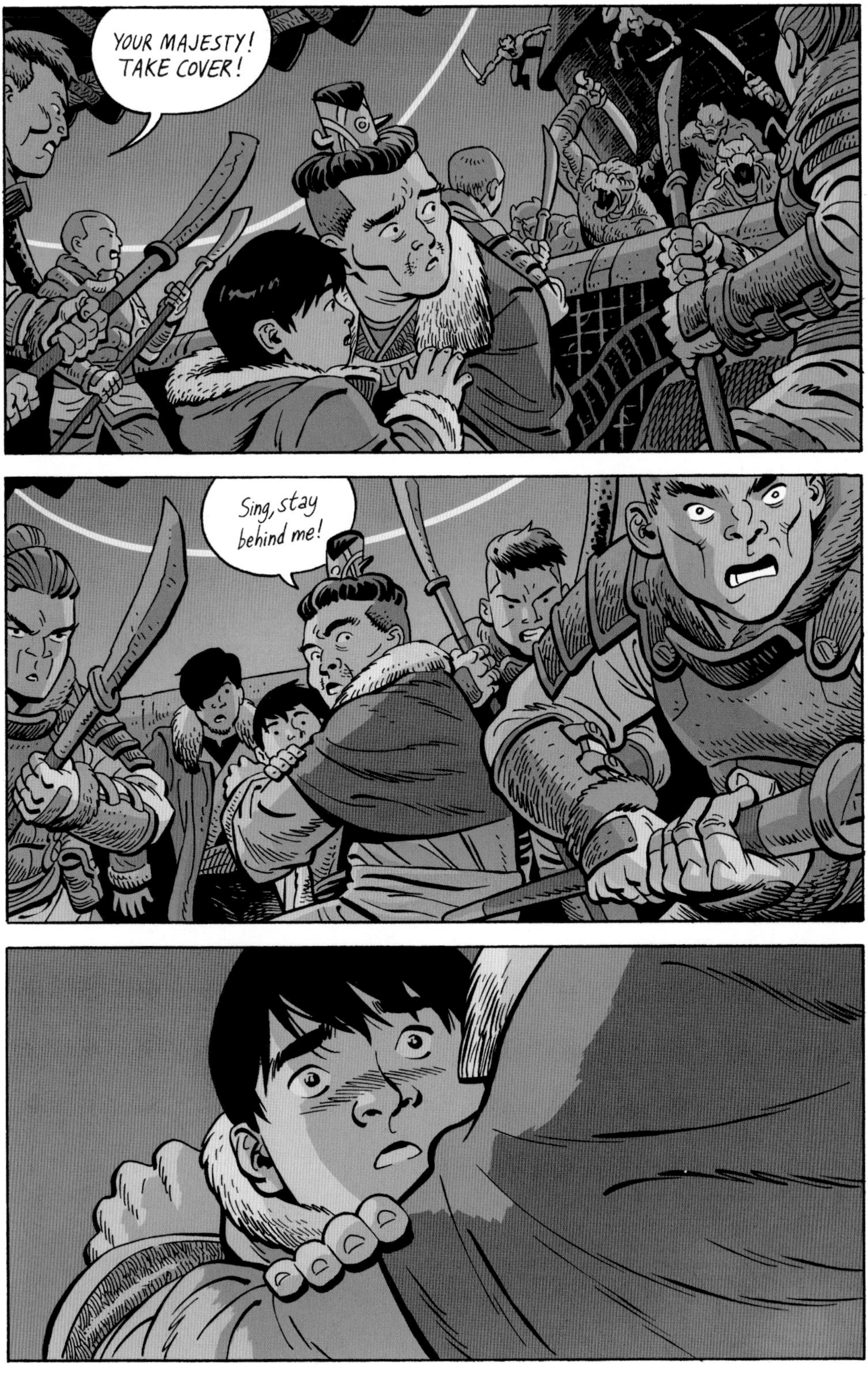
YOUR MAJESTY! TAKE COVER!
Sing, stay behind me!

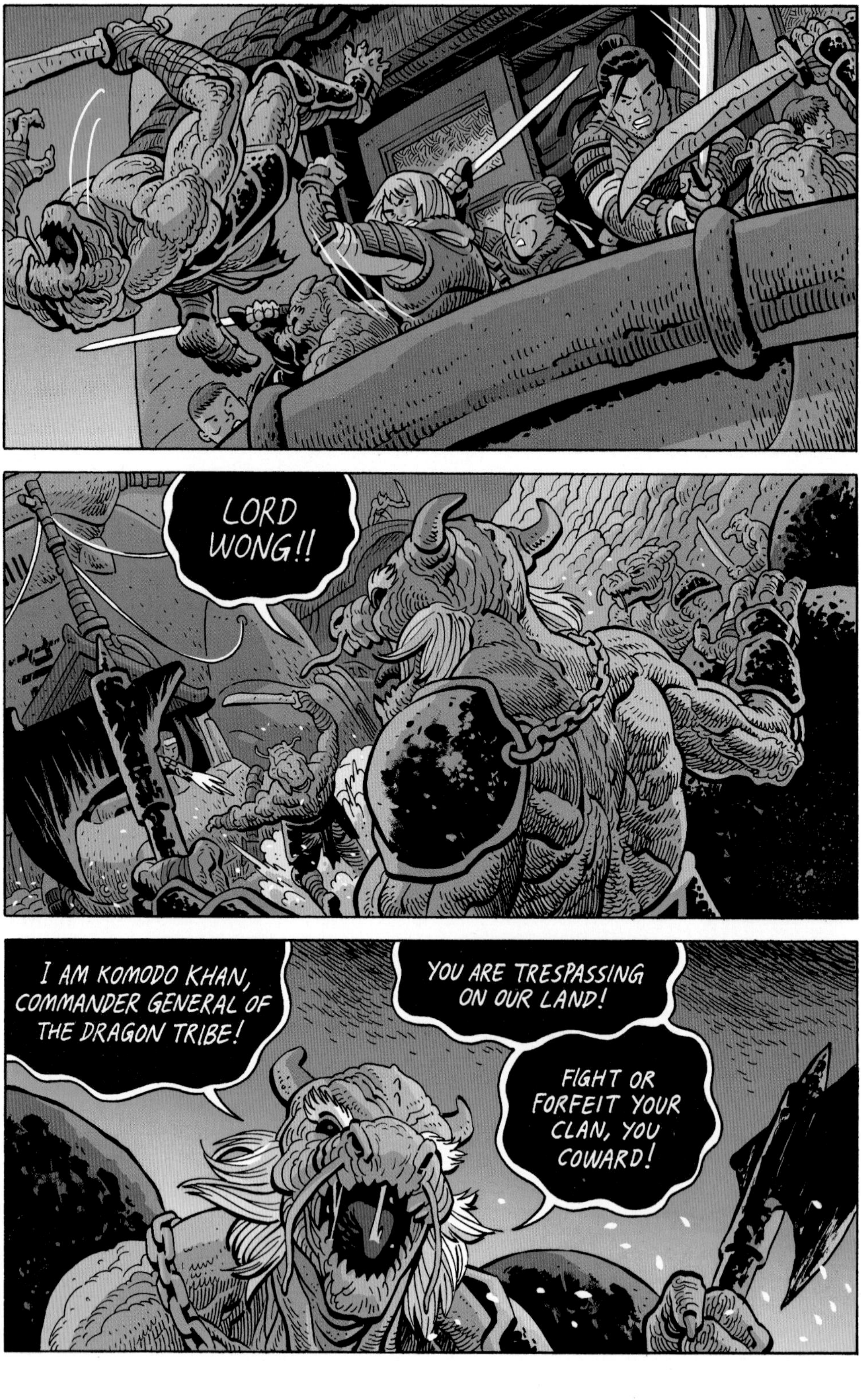
LORD WONG!!
I AM KOMODO KHAN, COMMANDER GENERAL OF THE DRAGON TRIBE!
YOU ARE TRESPASSING ON OUR LAND!
FIGHT OR FORFEIT YOUR CLAN, YOU COWARD!

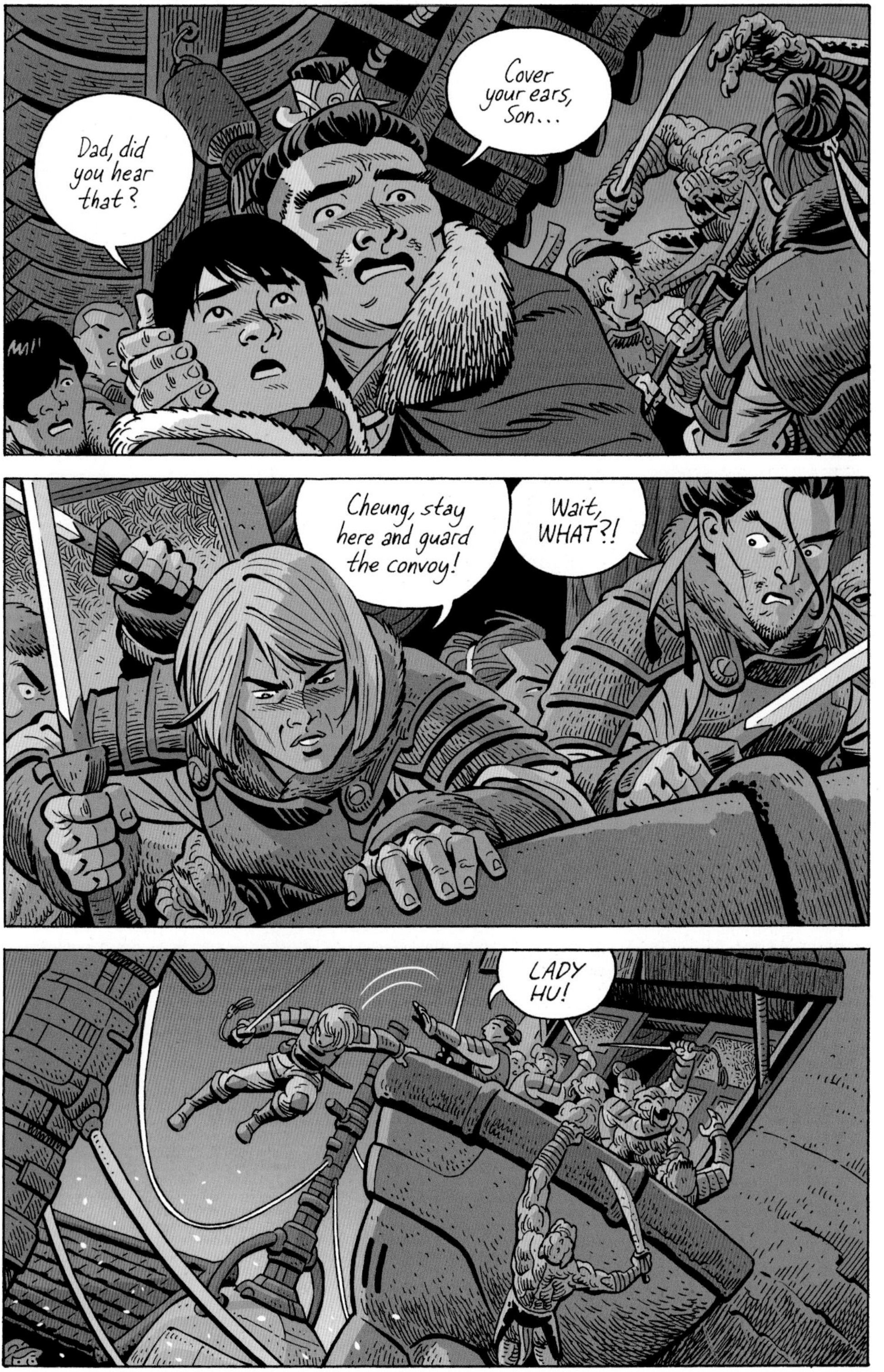
Dad, did you hear that?
Cover your ears, Son...
Cheung, stay here and guard the convoy!
Wait, WHAT?!
LADY HU!

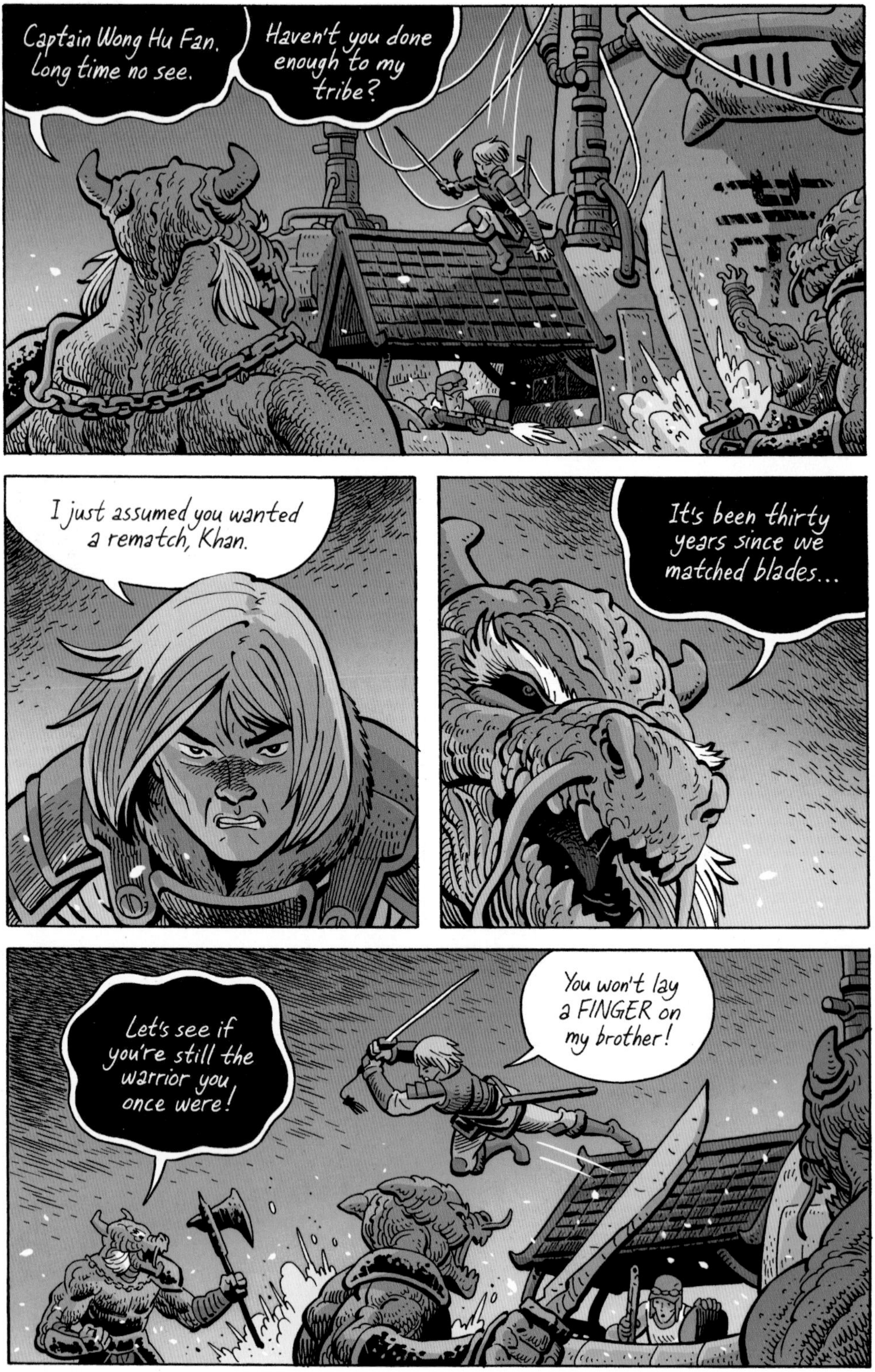

Captain Wong Hu Fan. Long time no see.
Haven't you done enough to my tribe?
I just assumed you wanted a rematch, Khan.
It's been thirty years since we matched blades...
Let's see if you're still the warrior you once were!
You won't lay a FINGER on my brother!

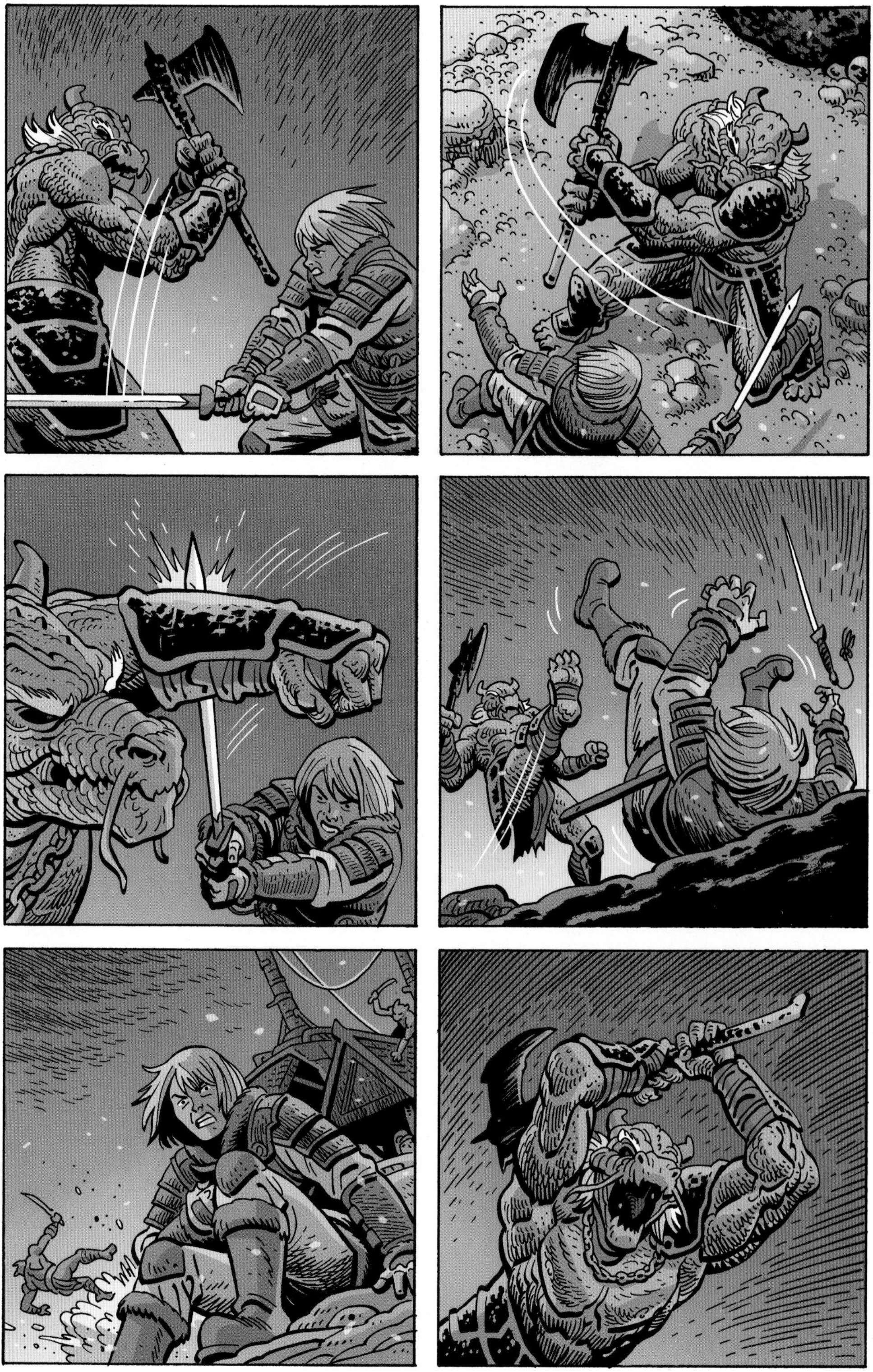

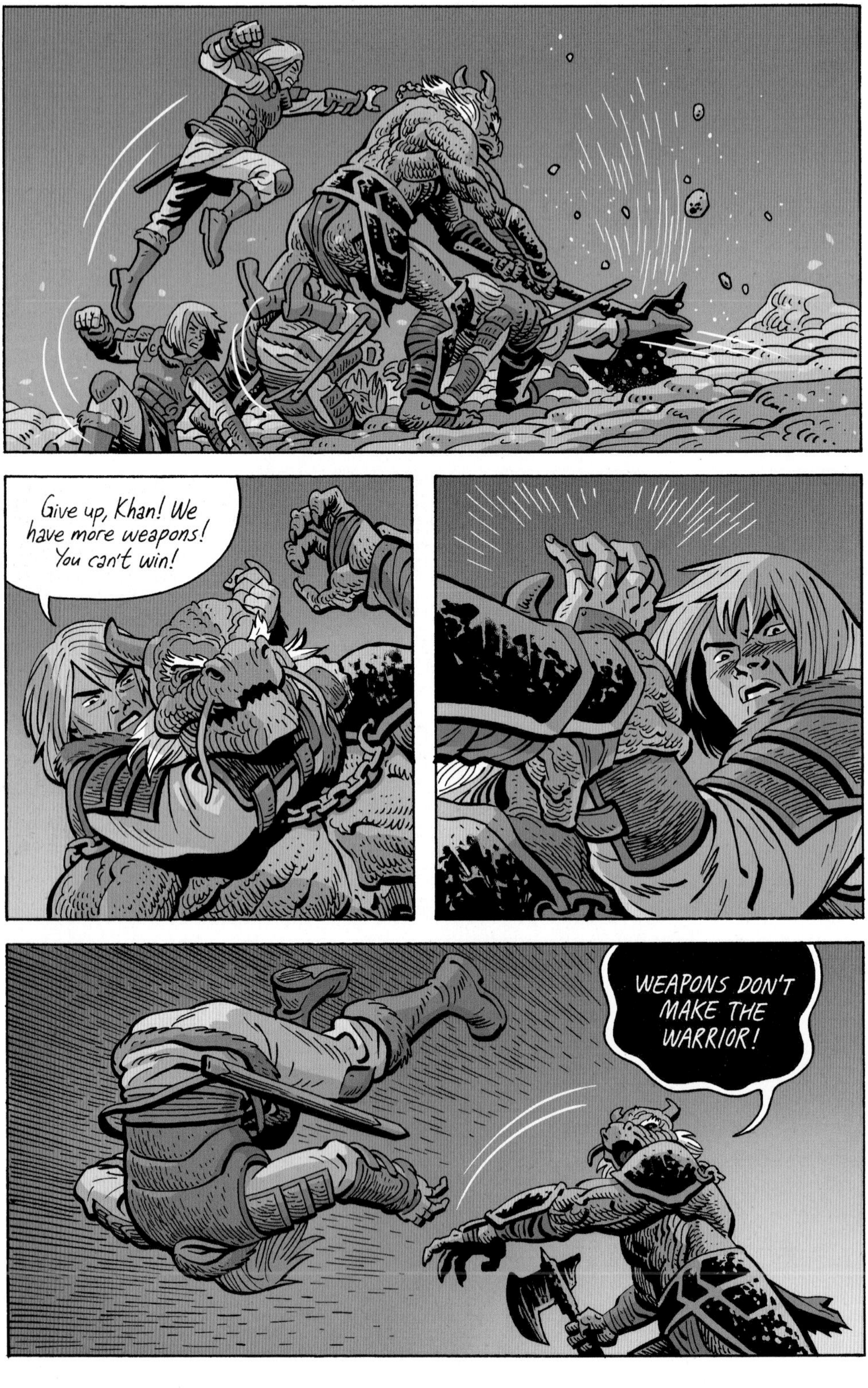
Give up, Khan! We have more weapons! You can't win!
WEAPONS DON'T MAKE THE WARRIOR!

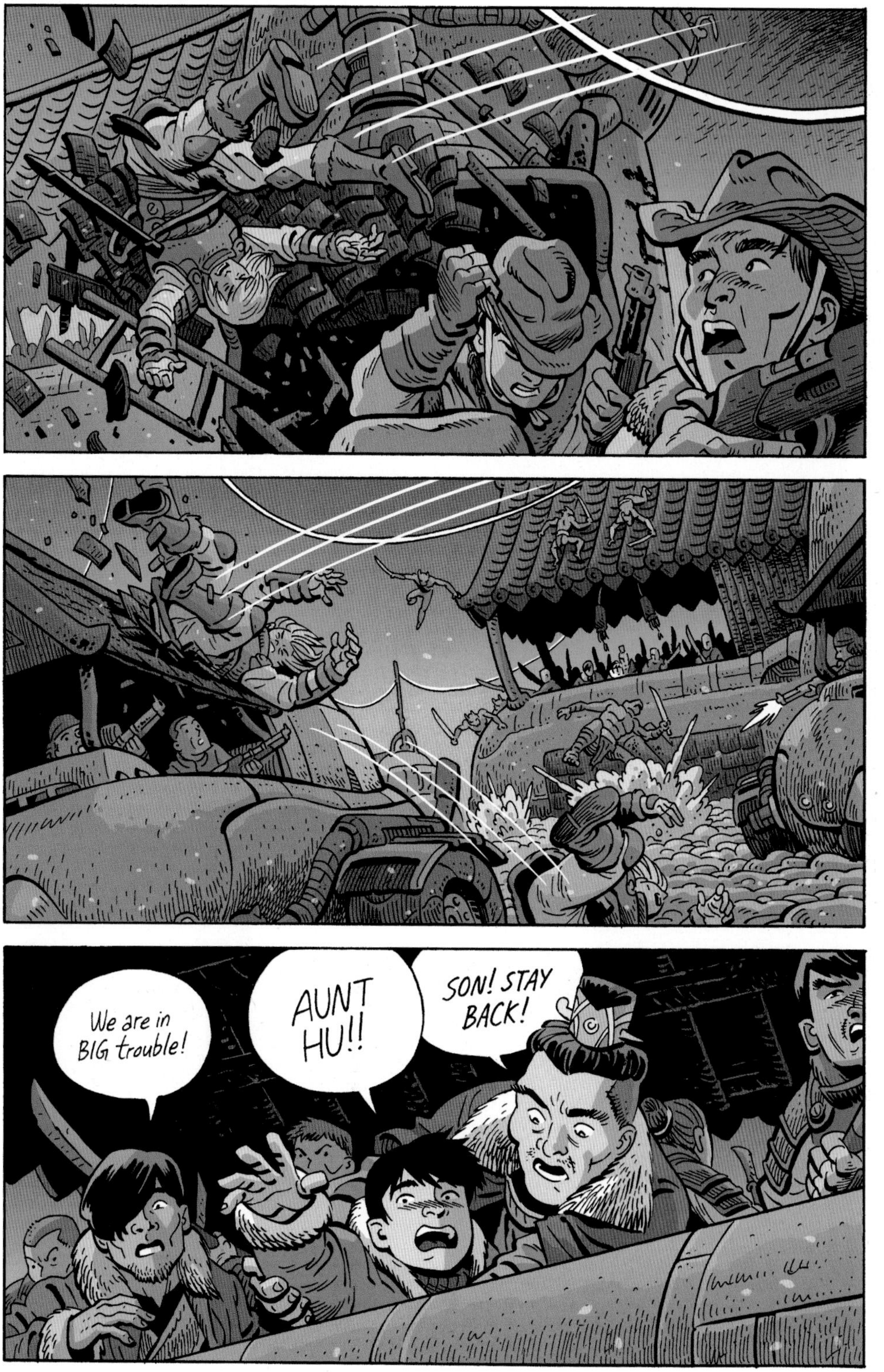
We are in BIG trouble!
AUNT HU!!
SON! STAY BACK!

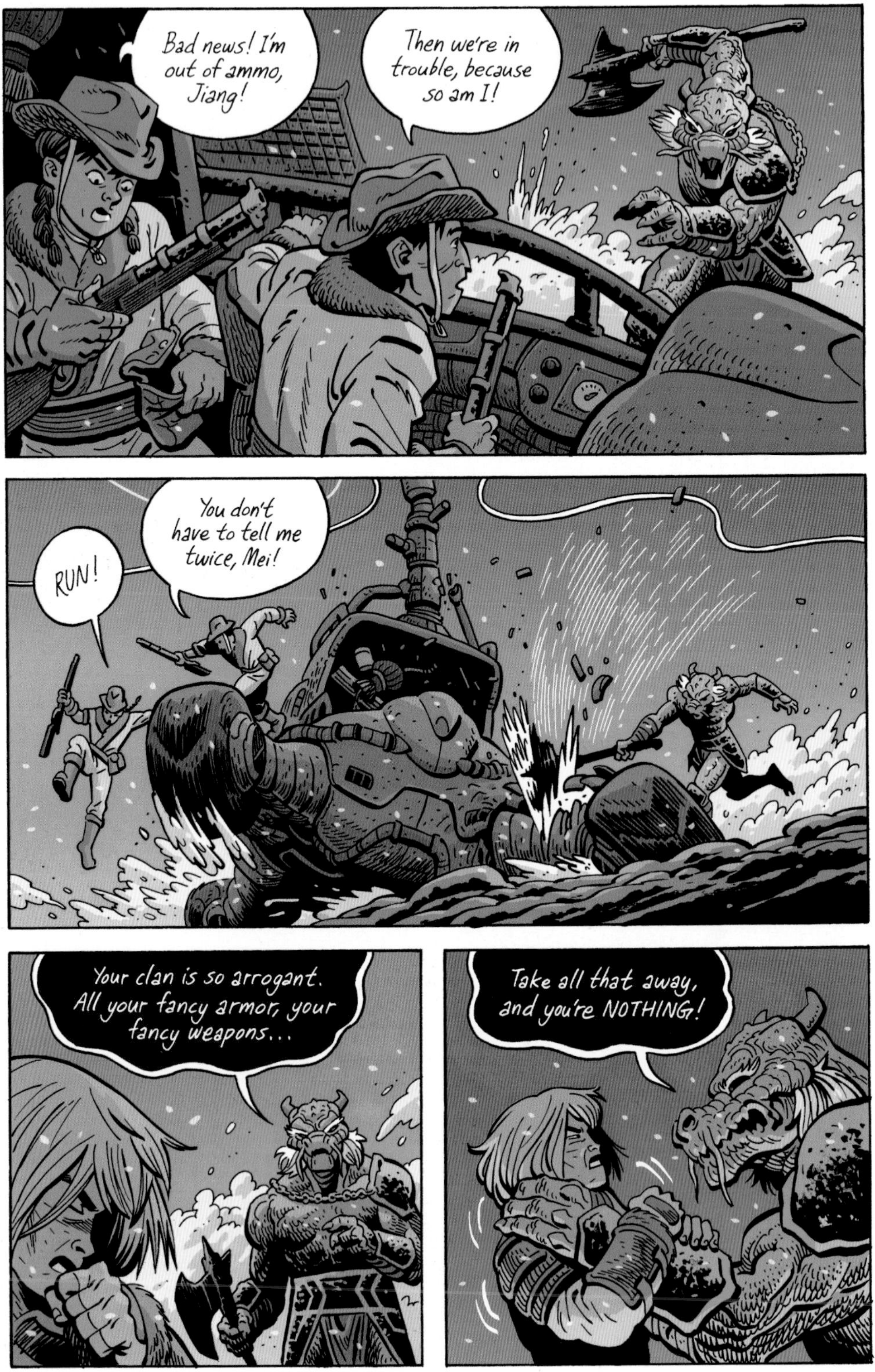
Bad news! I'm out of ammo, Jiang!
Then we're in trouble, because so am I!
RUN!
You don't have to tell me twice, Mei!
Your clan is so arrogant. All your fancy armor, your fancy weapons...
Take all that away, and you're NOTHING!

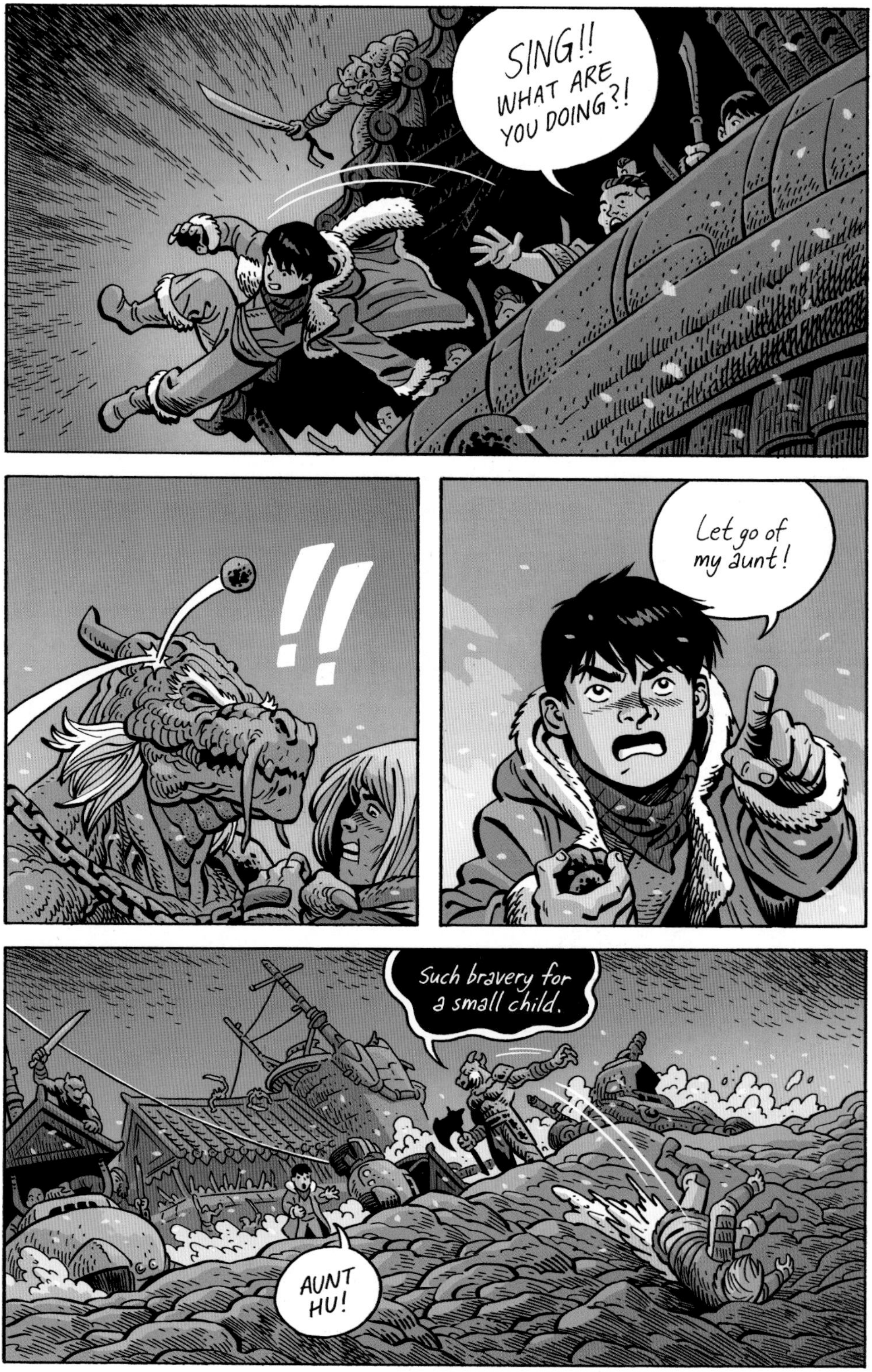
SING!! WHAT ARE YOU DOING?!
!!
Let go of my aunt!
Such bravery for a small child.
AUNT HU!

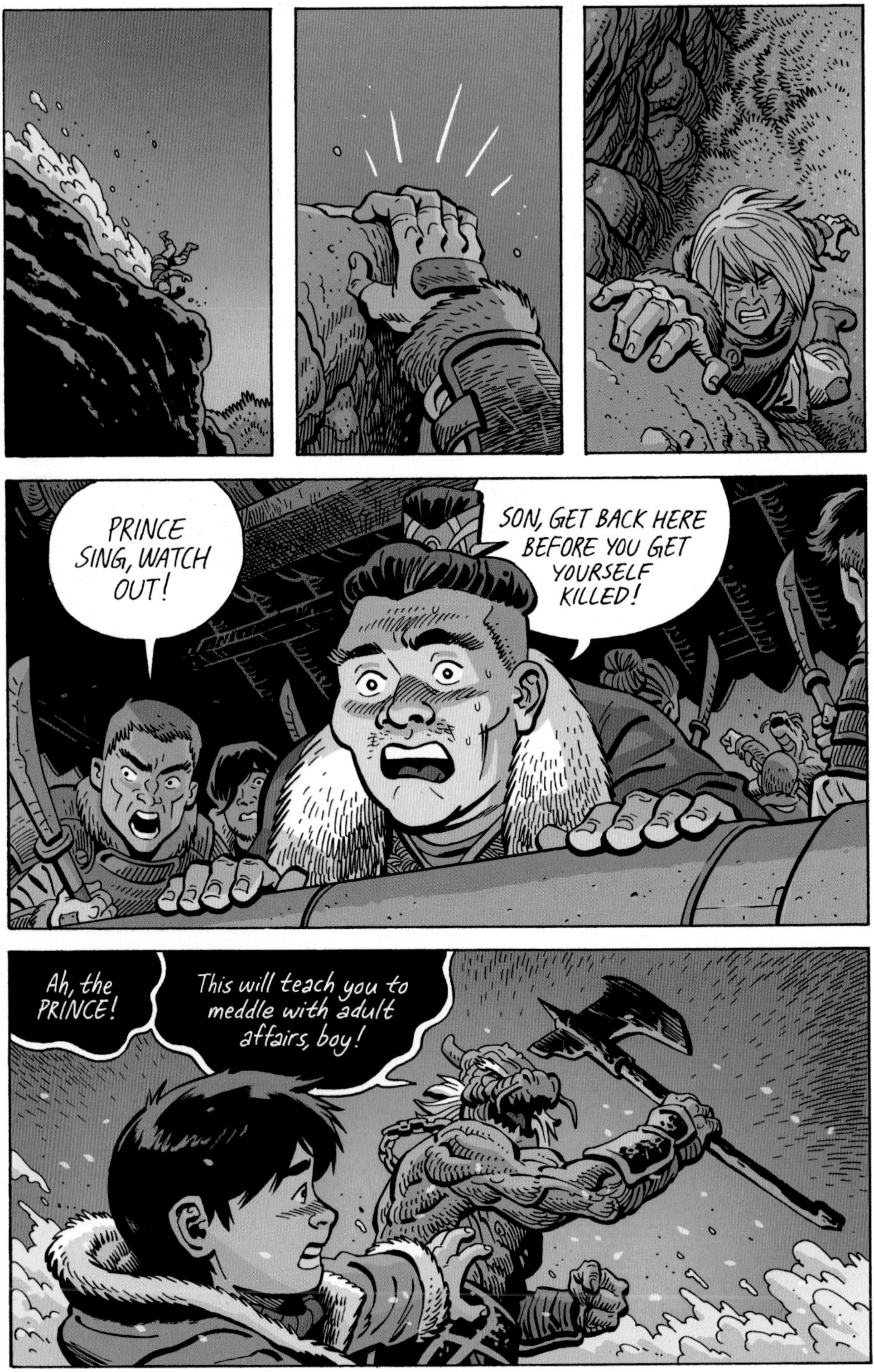
PRINCE SING, WATCH OUT!
SON, GET BACK HERE BEFORE YOU GET YOURSELF KILLED!
Ah, the PRINCE!
This will teach you to meddle with adult affairs, boy!

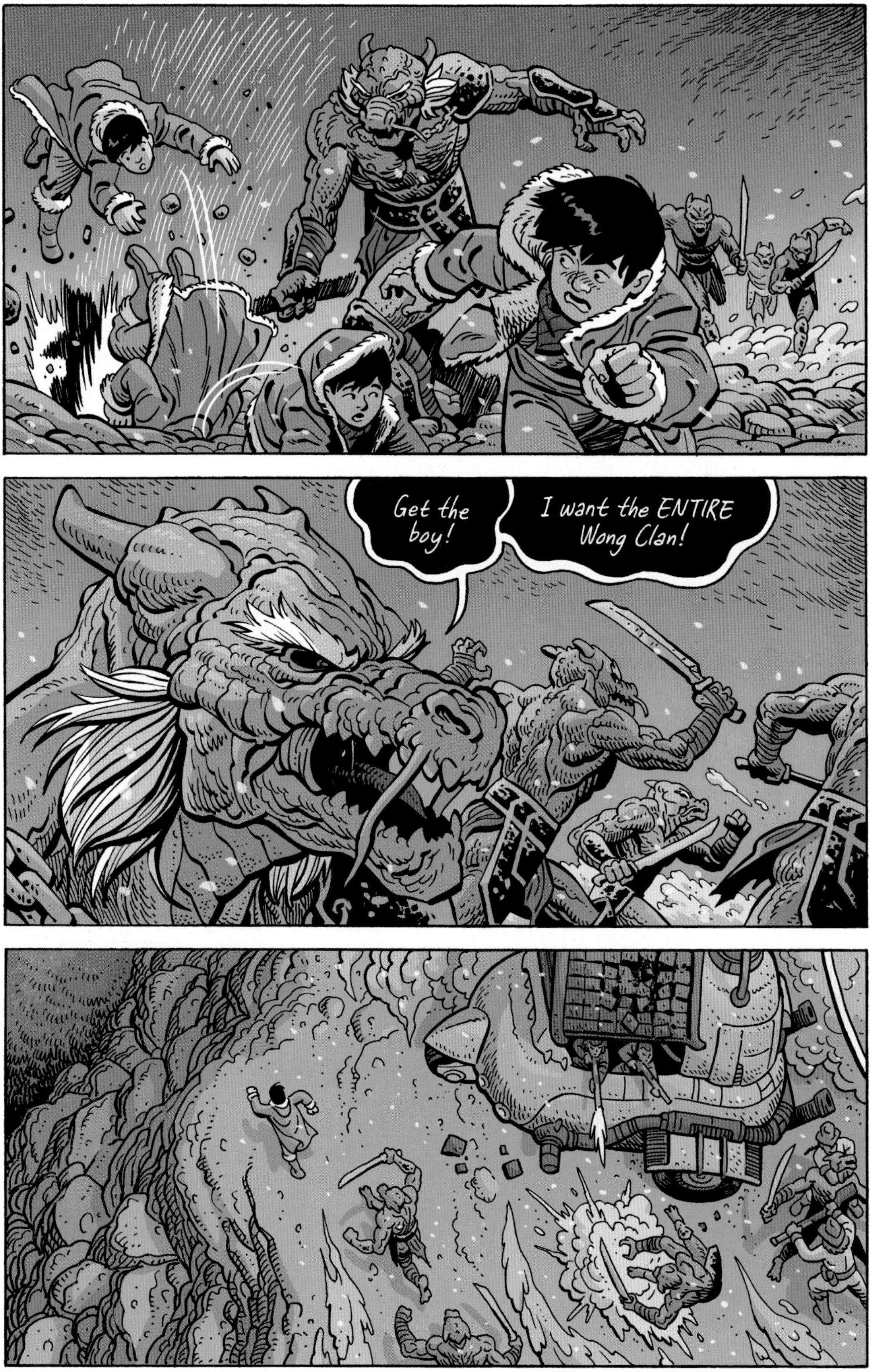
Get the boy!
I want the ENTIRE Wong Clan!

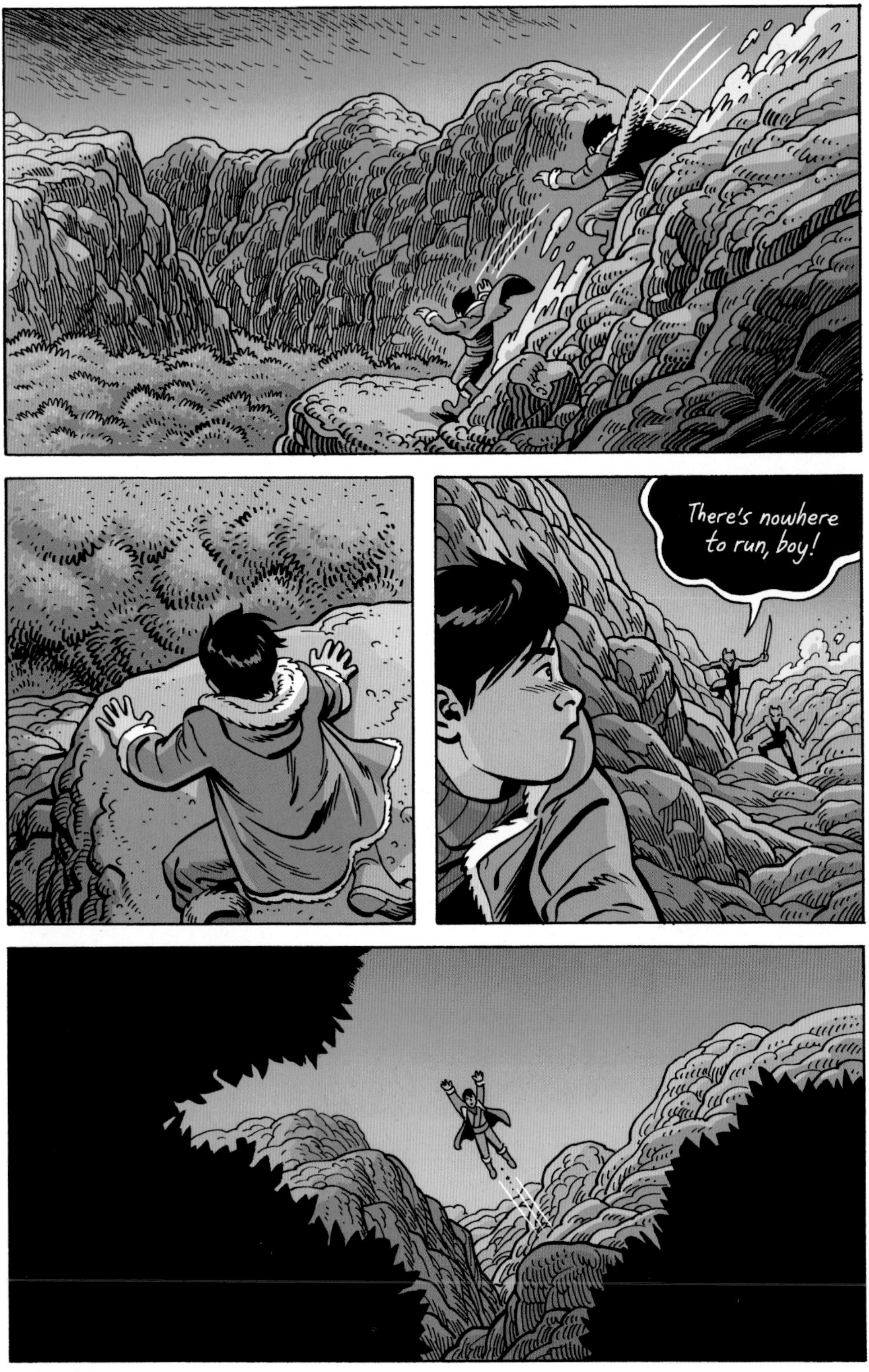
There's nowhere to run, boy!

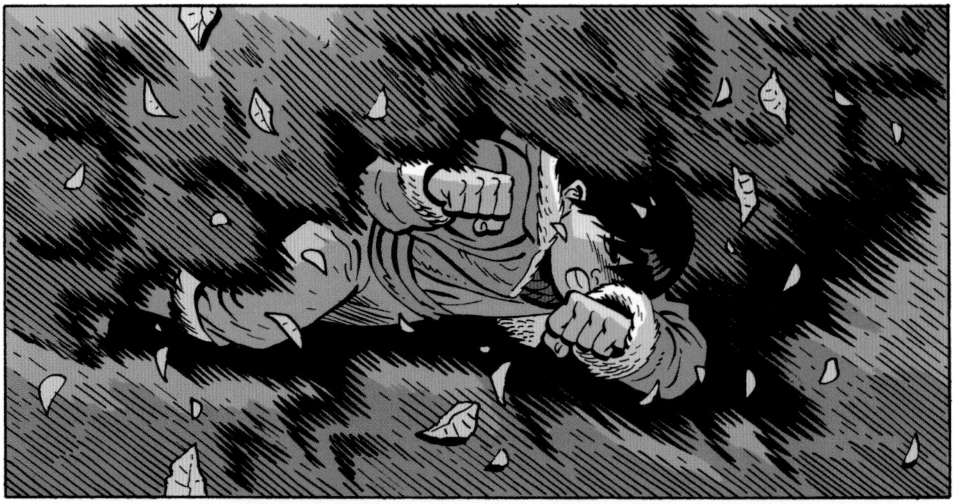

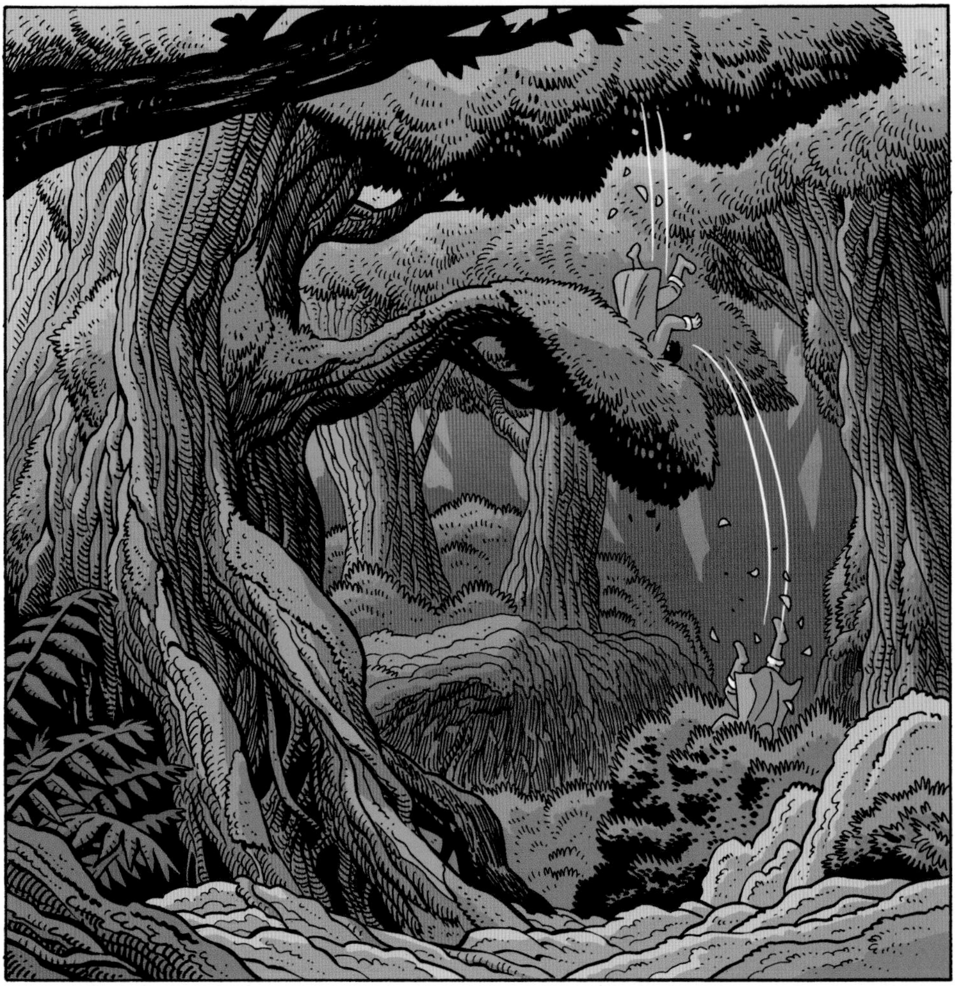

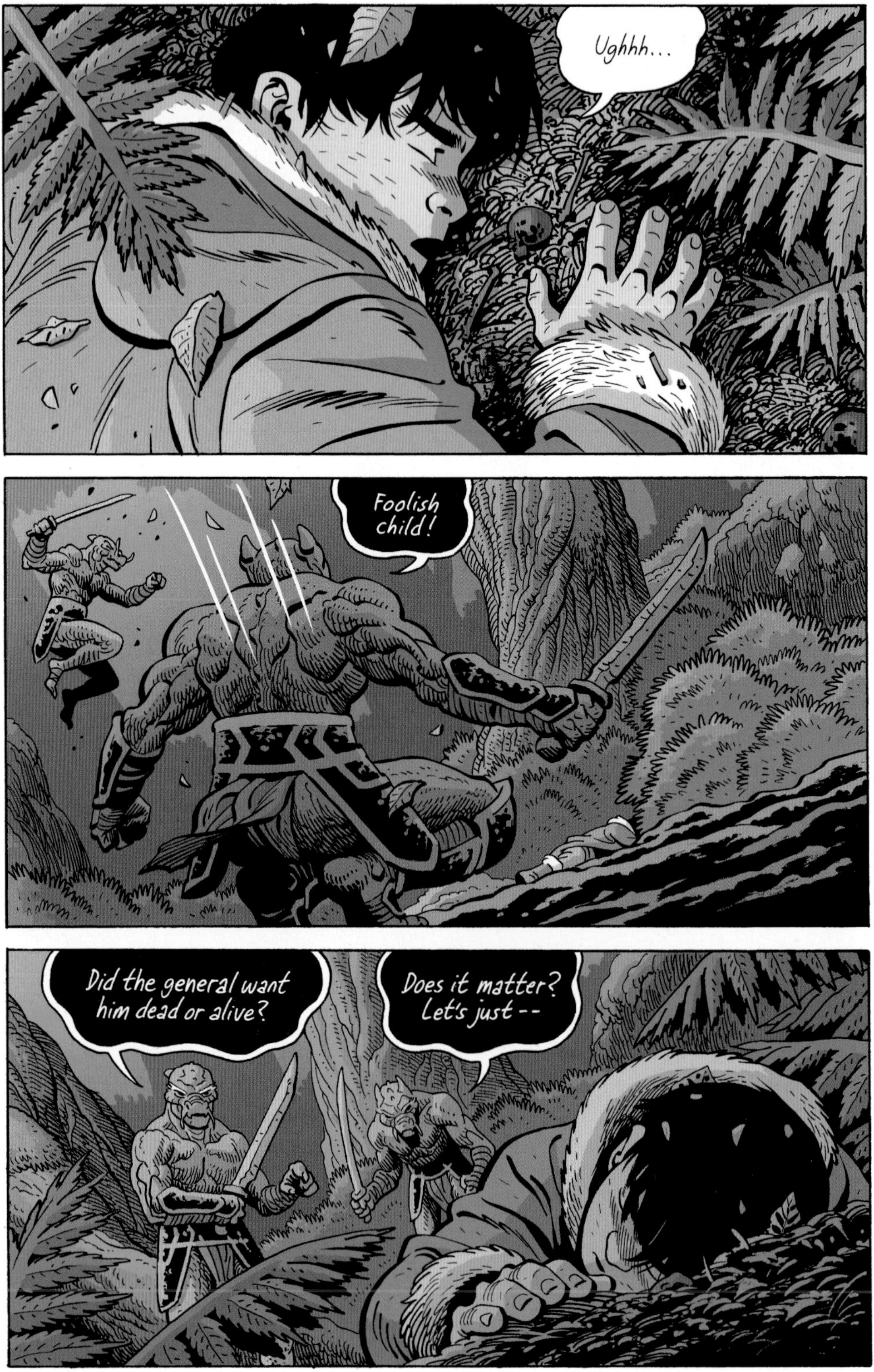
Ughhh...
Foolish child!
Did the general want him dead or alive?
Does it matter? Let's just --

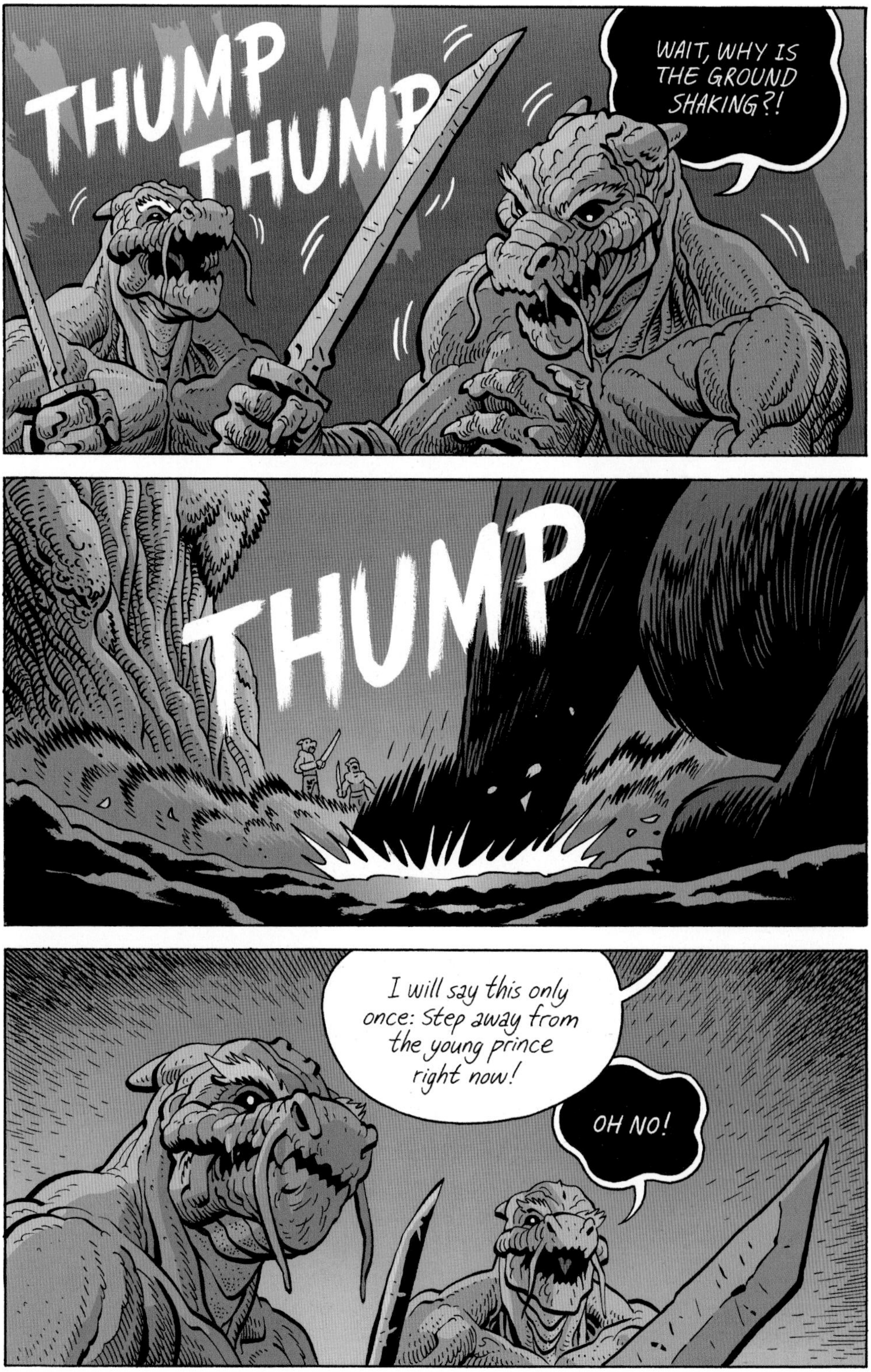
THUMP THUMP
WAIT, WHY IS THE GROUND SHAKING?!
THUMP
I will say this only once: Step away from the young prince right now!
OH NO!

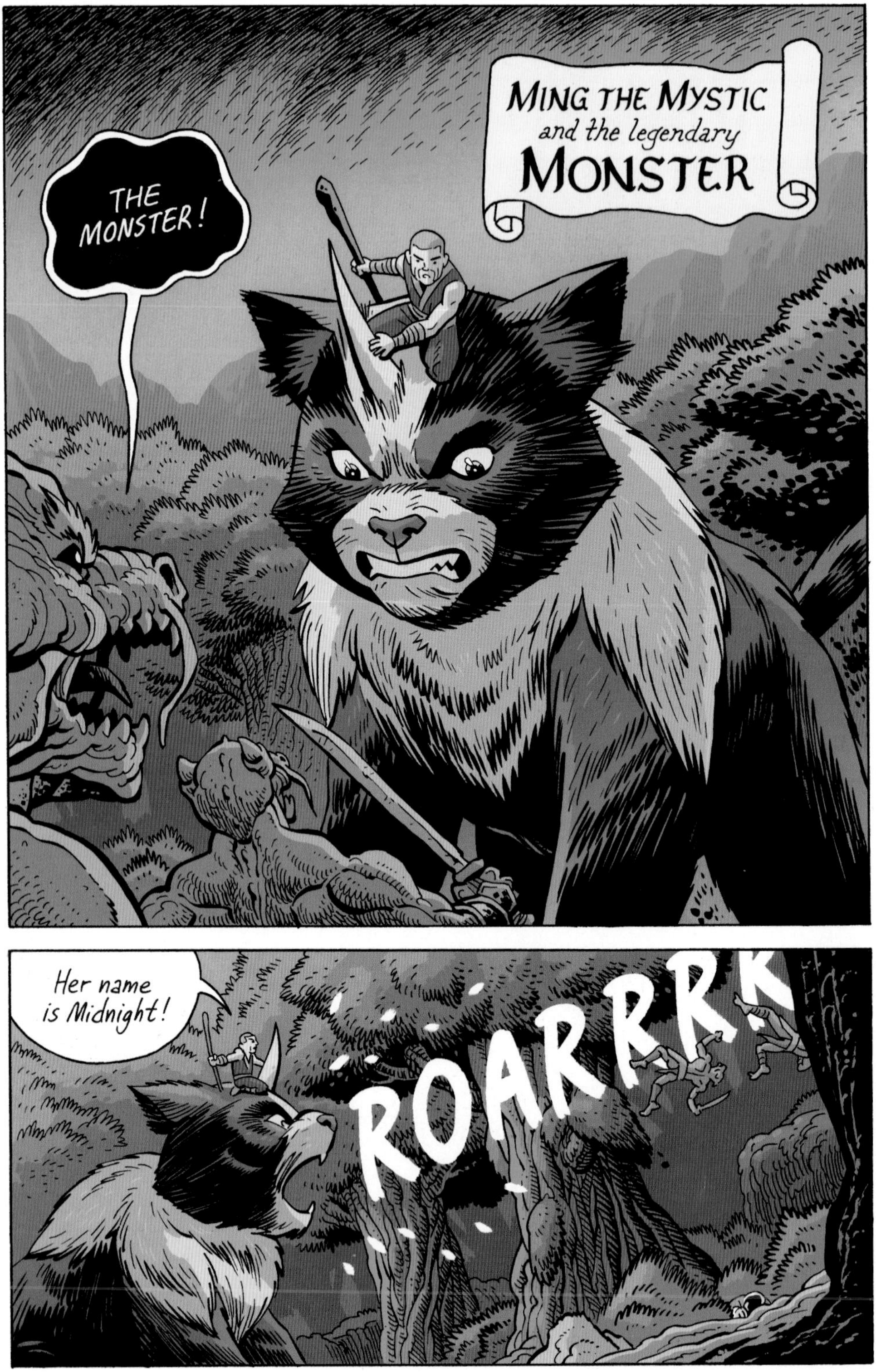
MING THE MYSTIC and the legendary MONSTER
THE MONSTER!
Her name is Midnight!
ROARRRK

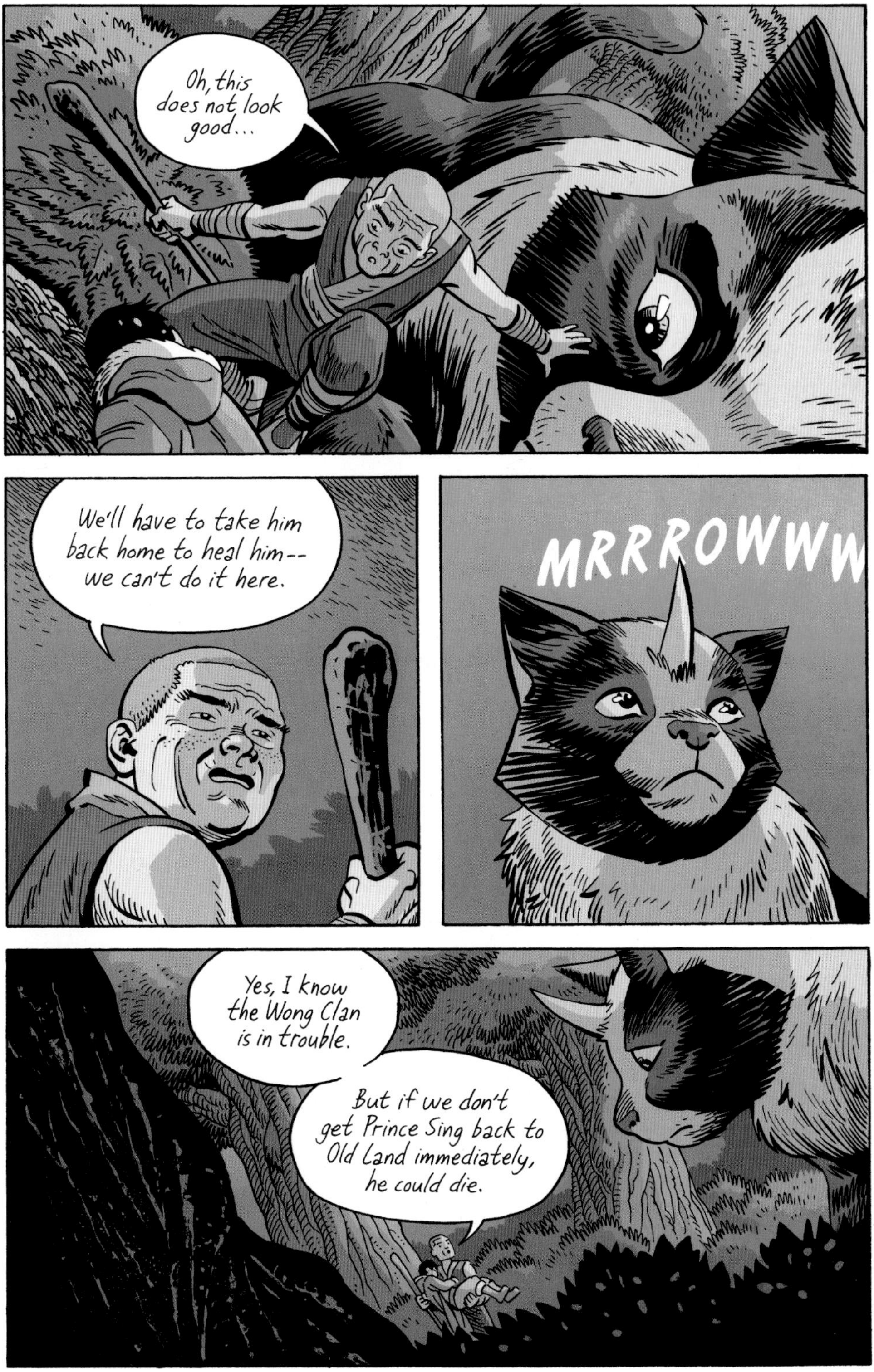
Oh, this does not look good...
We'll have to take him back home to heal him-- we can't do it here.
MRRROWWW
Yes, I know the Wong Clan is in trouble.
But if we don't get Prince Sing back to Old Land immediately, he could die.

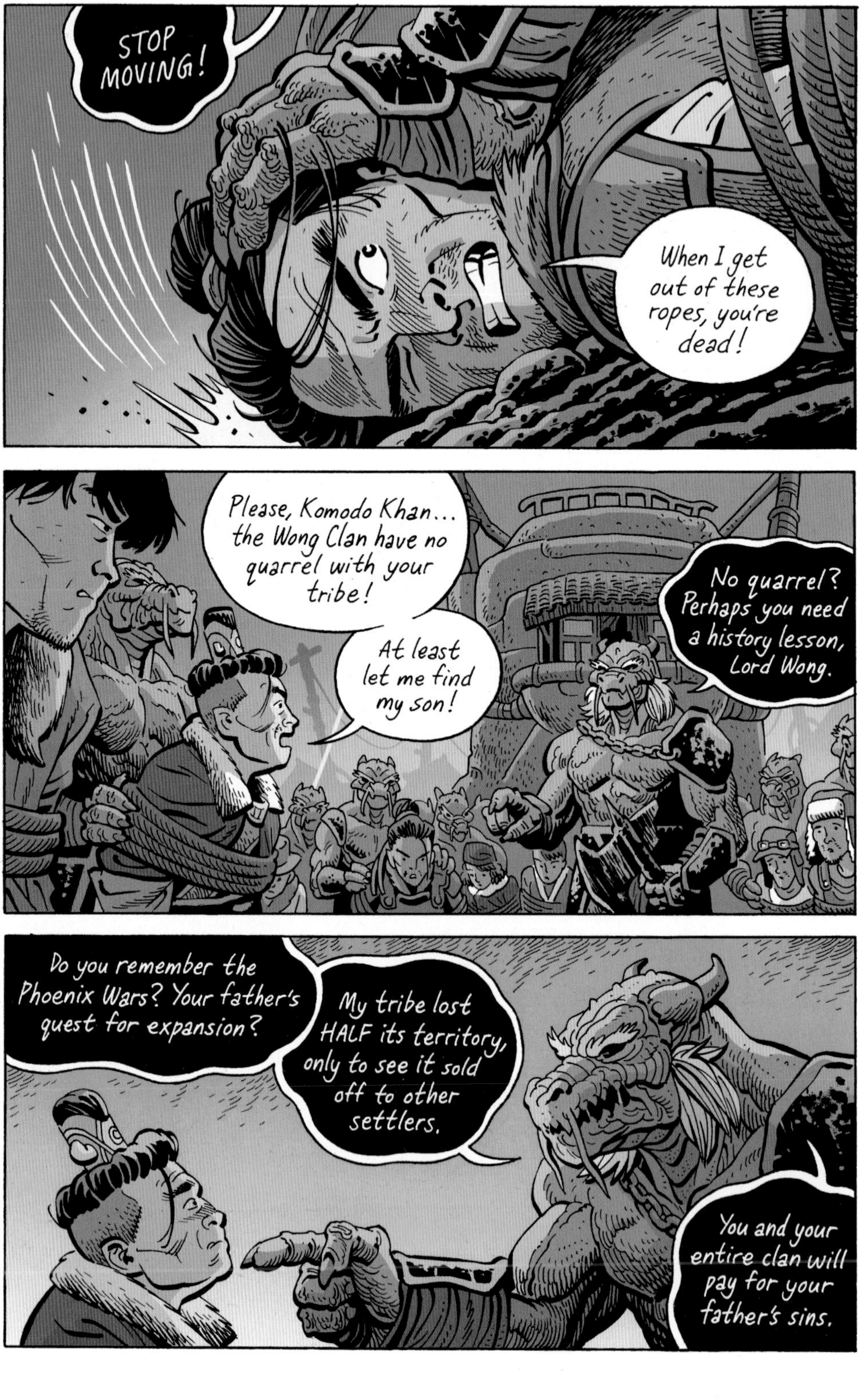
STOP MOVING!
When I get out of these ropes, you're dead!
Please, Komodo Khan... the Wong Clan have no quarrel with your tribe!
At least let me find my son!
No quarrel? Perhaps you need a history lesson, Lord Wong.
Do you remember the Phoenix Wars? Your father's quest for expansion?
My tribe lost HALF its territory, only to see it sold off to other settlers.
You and your entire clan will pay for your father's sins.

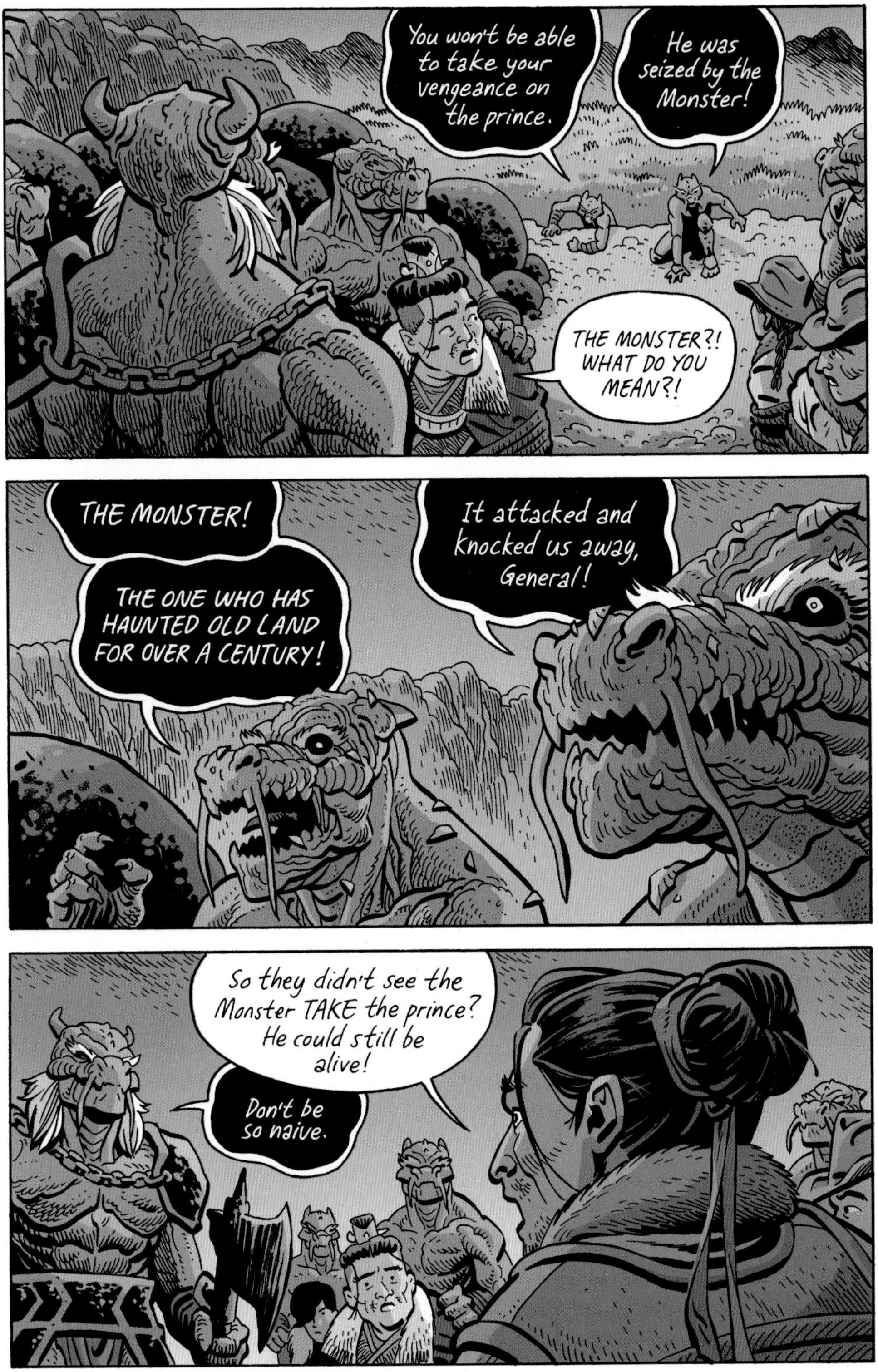

You won't be able to take your vengeance on the prince.
He was seized by the Monster!
THE MONSTER?! WHAT DO YOU MEAN?!
THE MONSTER!
THE ONE WHO HAS HAUNTED OLD LAND FOR OVER A CENTURY!
It attacked and knocked us away, General!
So they didn't see the Monster TAKE the prince? He could still be alive!
Don't be so naive.

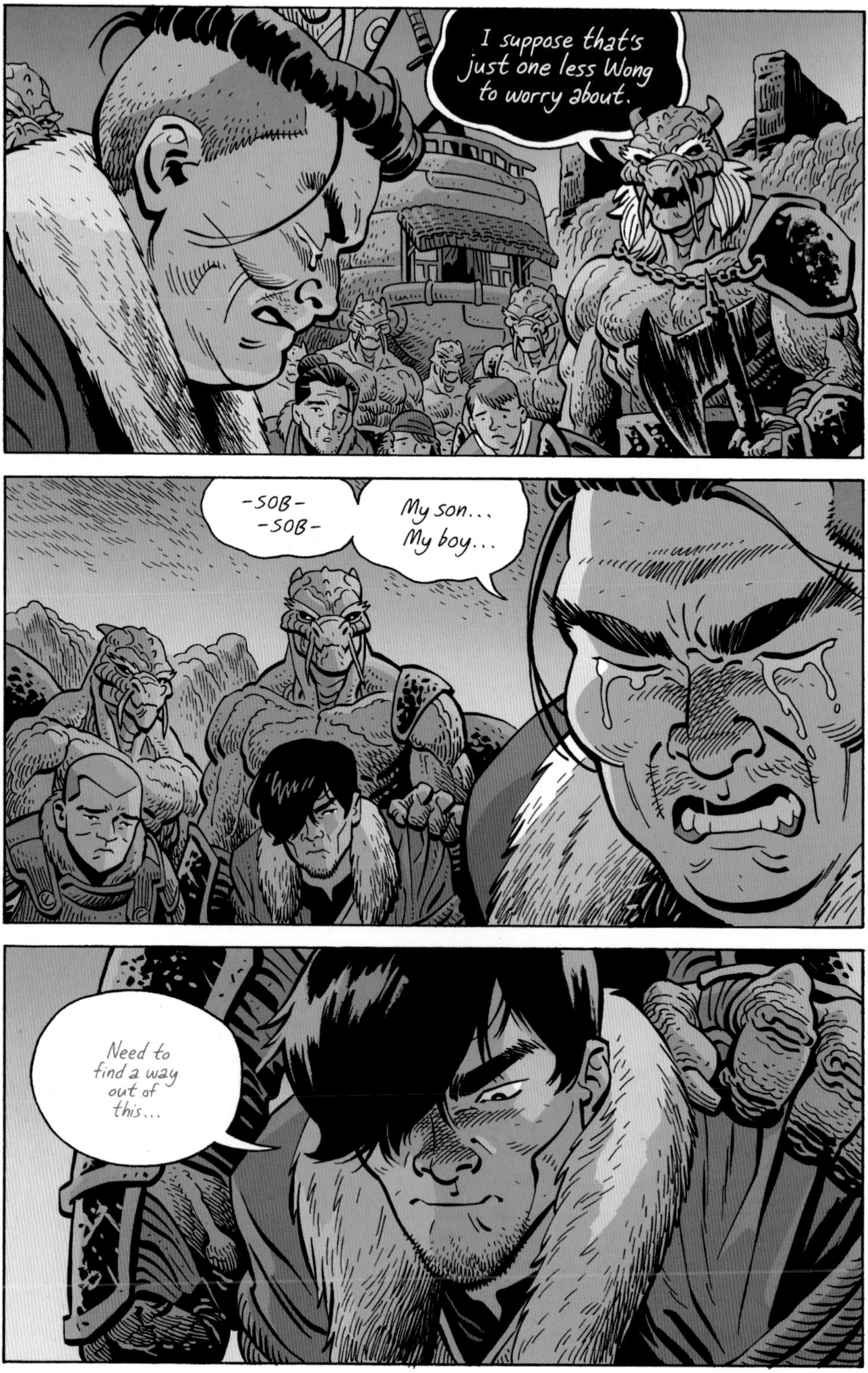
I suppose that's just one less Wong to worry about.
-SOB- -SOB-
My son... My boy...
Need to find a way out of this...

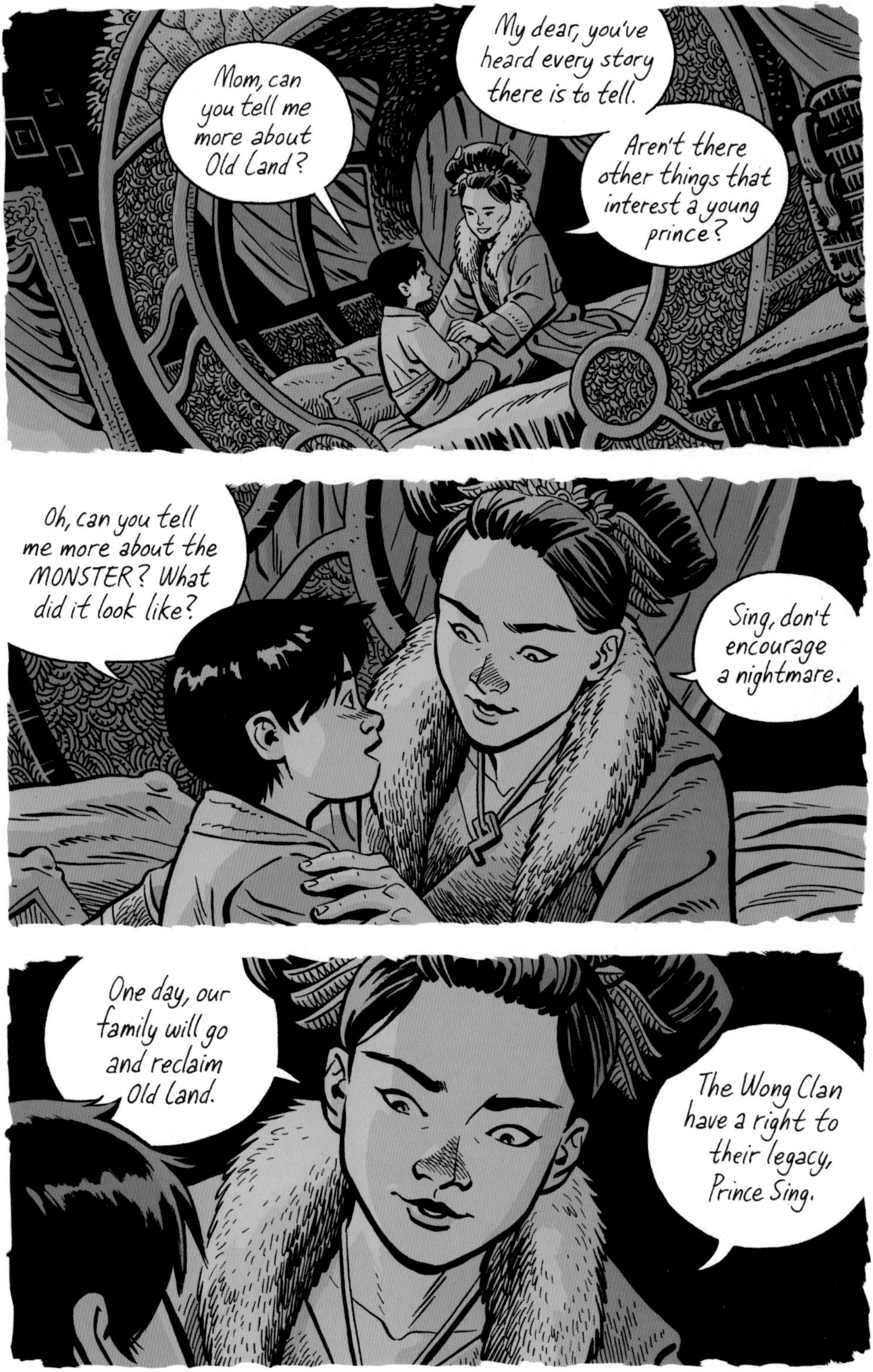
Mom, can you tell me more about Old Land?
My dear, you've heard every story there is to tell.
Aren't there other things that interest a young prince?
Oh, can you tell me more about the MONSTER? What did it look like?
Sing, don't encourage a nightmare.
One day, our family will go and reclaim Old Land.
The Wong Clan have a right to their legacy, Prince Sing.

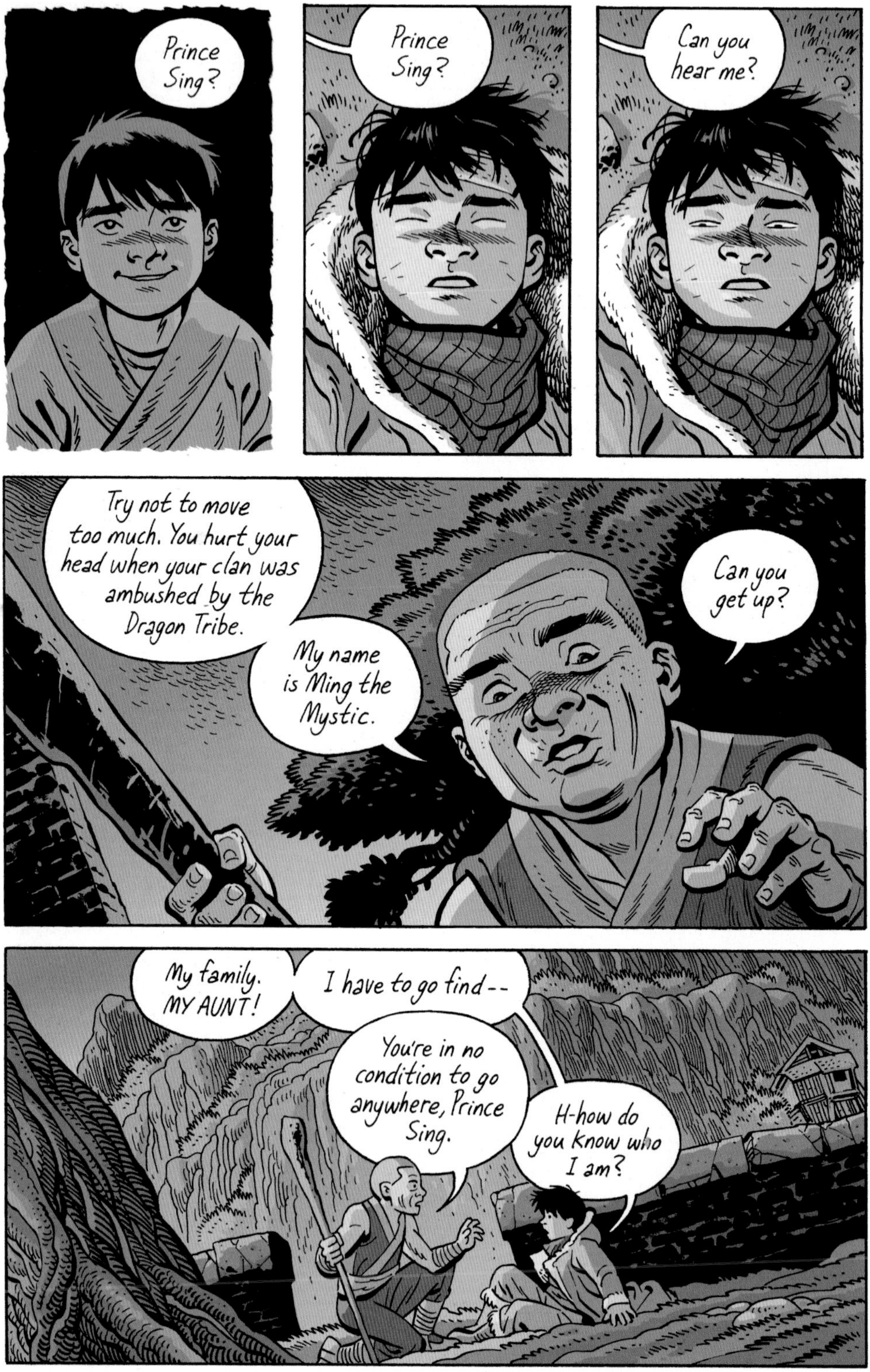
Prince Sing?
Prince Sing?
Can you hear me?
Try not to move too much. You hurt your head when your clan was ambushed by the Dragon Tribe.
My name is Ming the Mystic.
Can you get up?
My family. MY AUNT!
I have to go find--
You're in no condition to go anywhere, Prince Sing.
H-how do you know who I am?

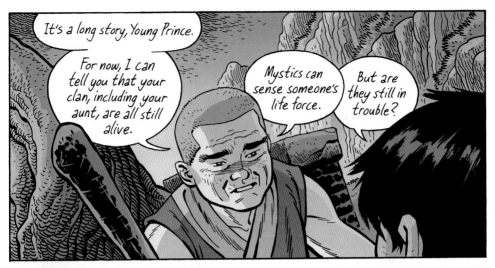

It's a long story, Young Prince.

For now, I can tell you that your clan, including your aunt, are all still alive.

Mystics can sense someone's life force.

But are they still in trouble?

Unfortunately, yes.

The Dragon Tribe captured your clan. I had to bring you back to Old Land to heal your wounds. You were SERIOUSLY injured.

Did...did you say Old Land?

Take a look for yourself, Prince Sing.

Oh, my...

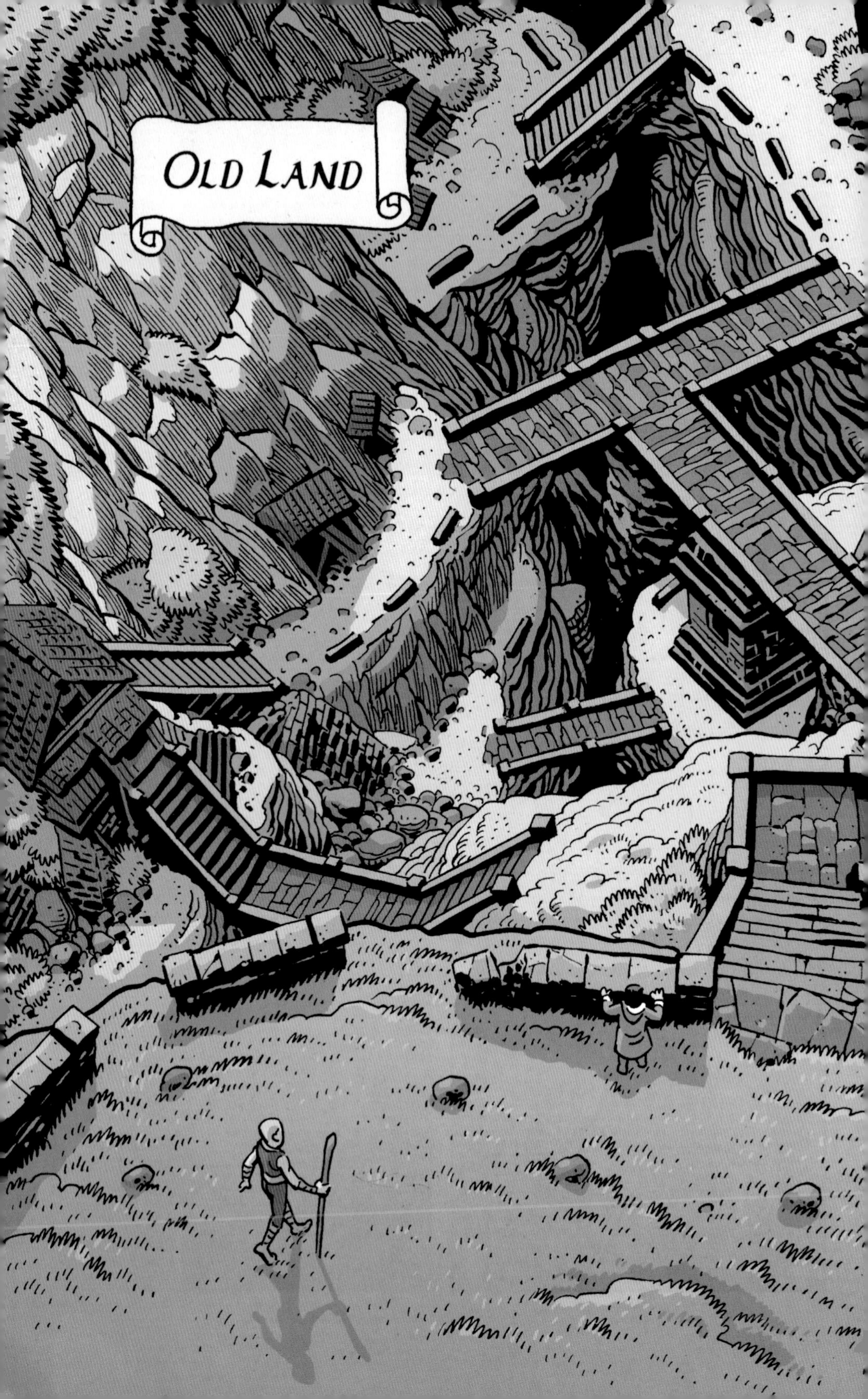
OLD LAND

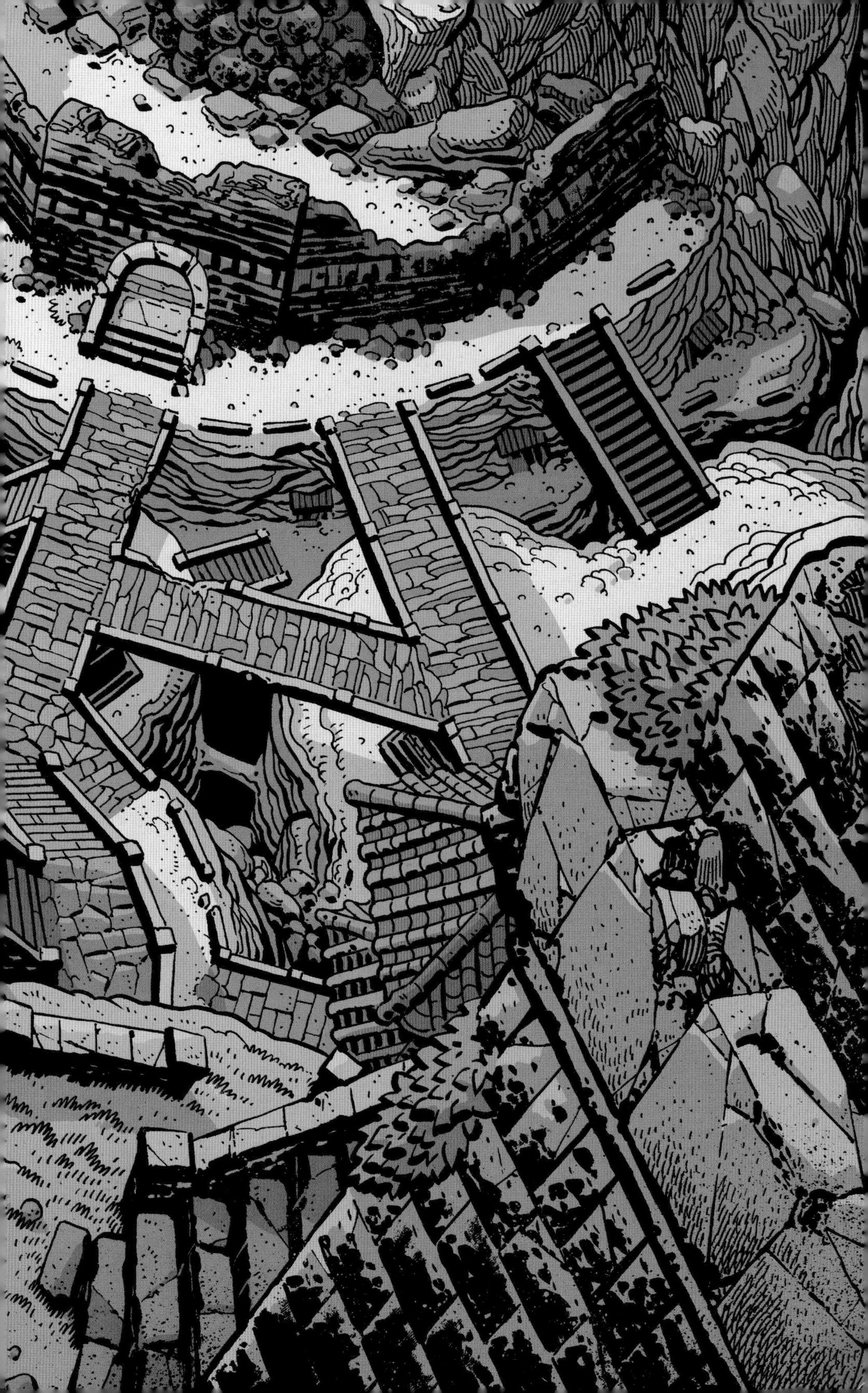

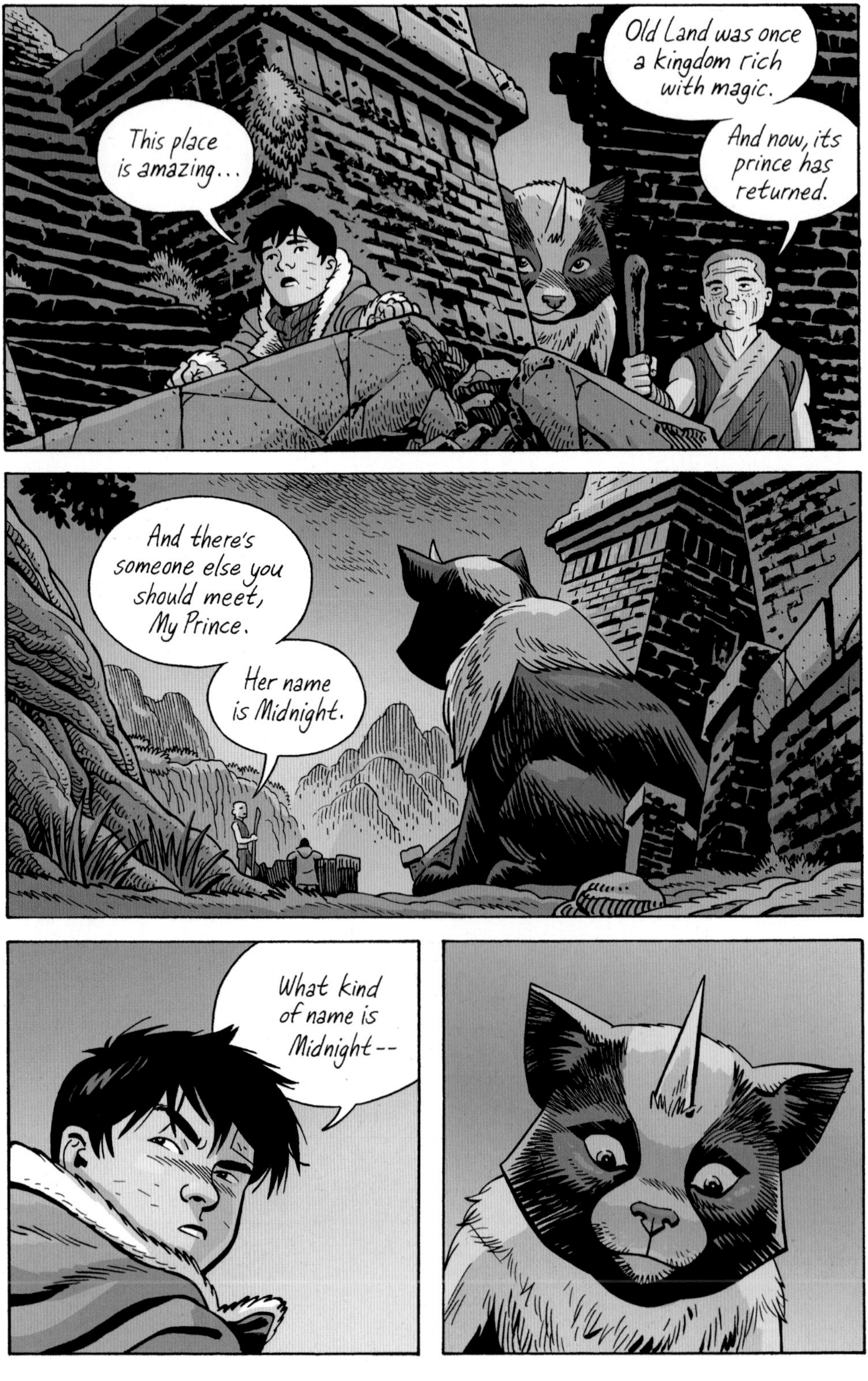
Old Land was once a kingdom rich with magic.
This place is amazing...
And now, its prince has returned.
And there's someone else you should meet, My Prince.
Her name is Midnight.
What kind of name is Midnight--

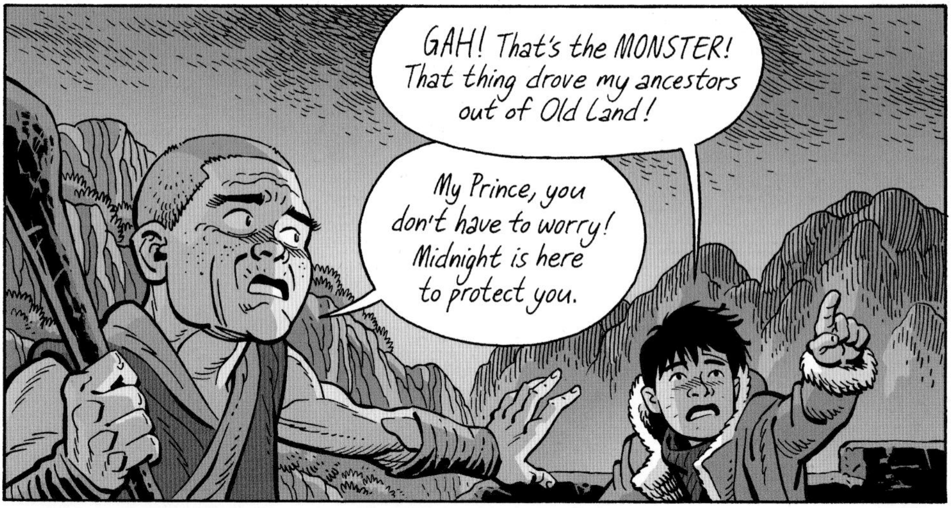
GAH! That's the MONSTER! That thing drove my ancestors out of Old Land!
My Prince, you don't have to worry! Midnight is here to protect you.

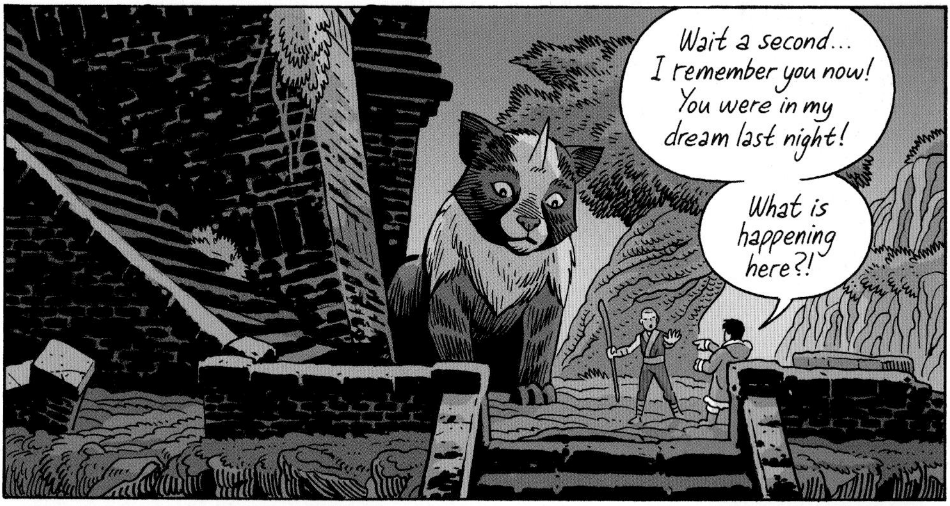
Wait a second... I remember you now! You were in my dream last night!
What is happening here?!

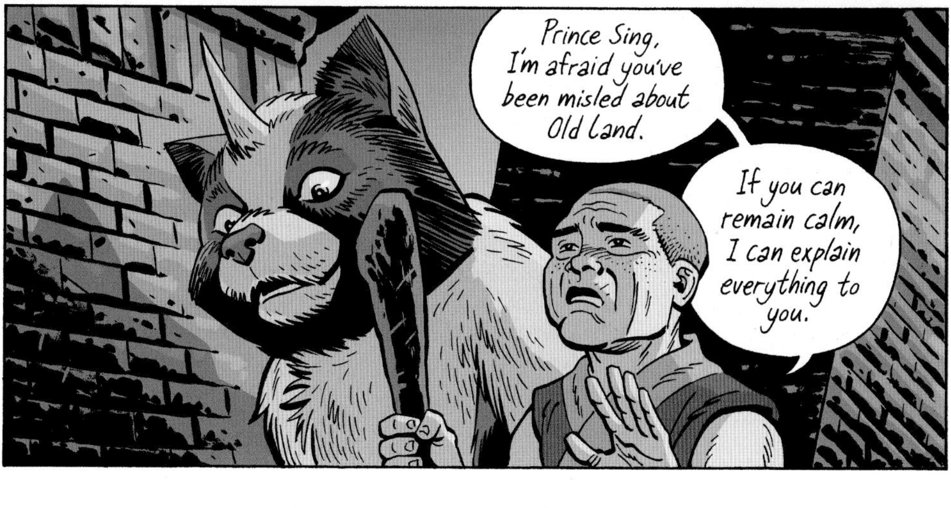
Prince Sing, I'm afraid you've been misled about Old Land.
If you can remain calm, I can explain everything to you.

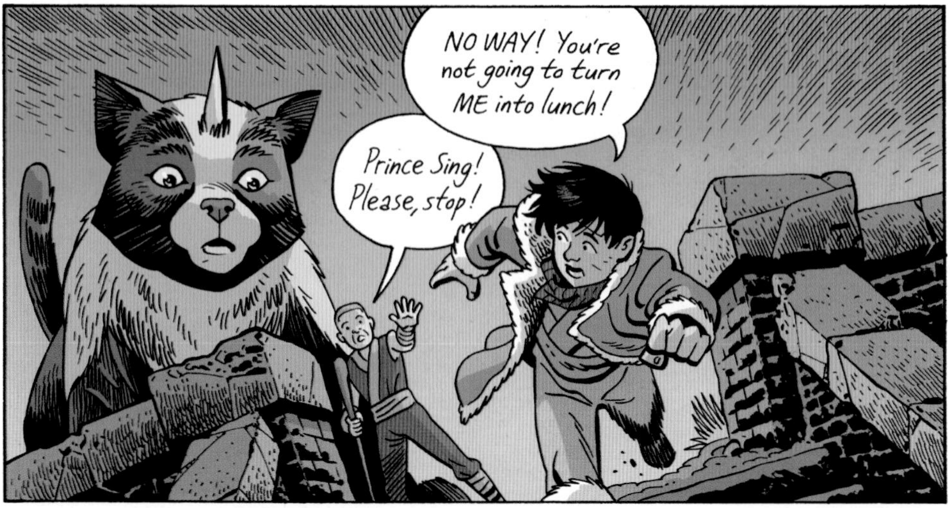
NO WAY! You're not going to turn ME into lunch!
Prince Sing! Please, stop!

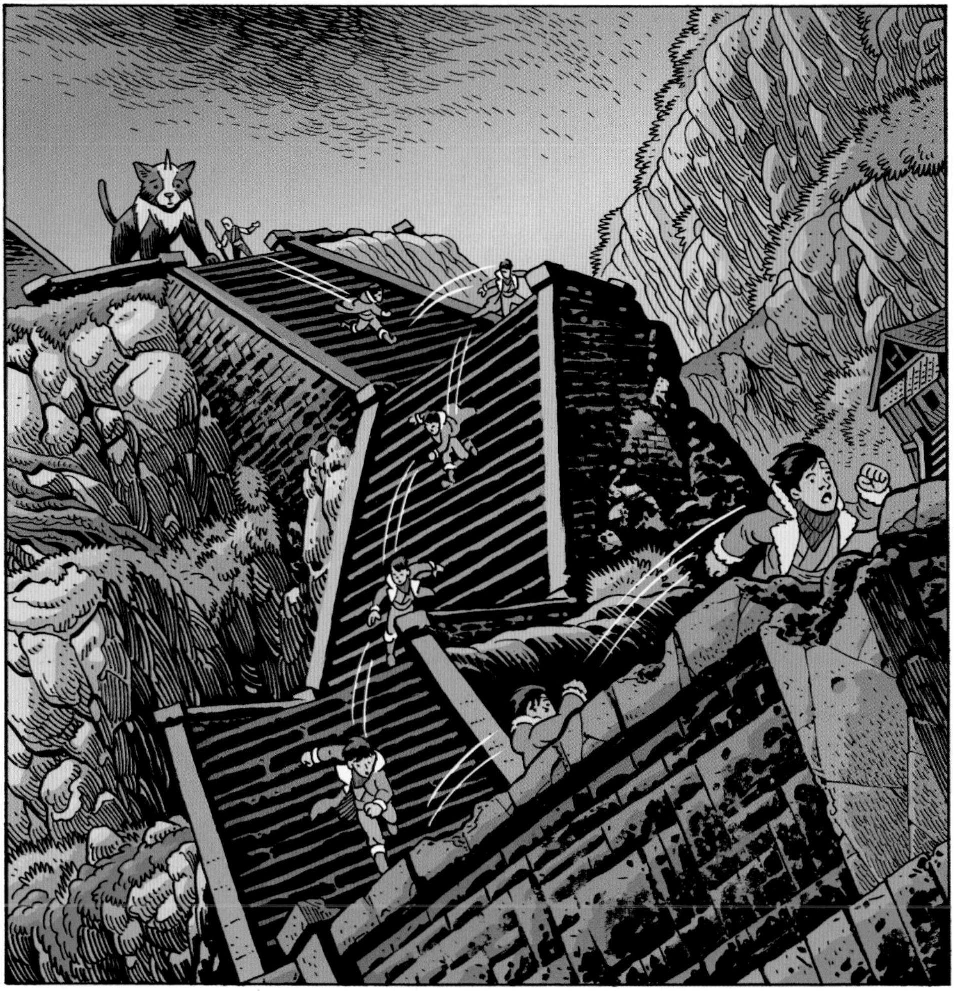

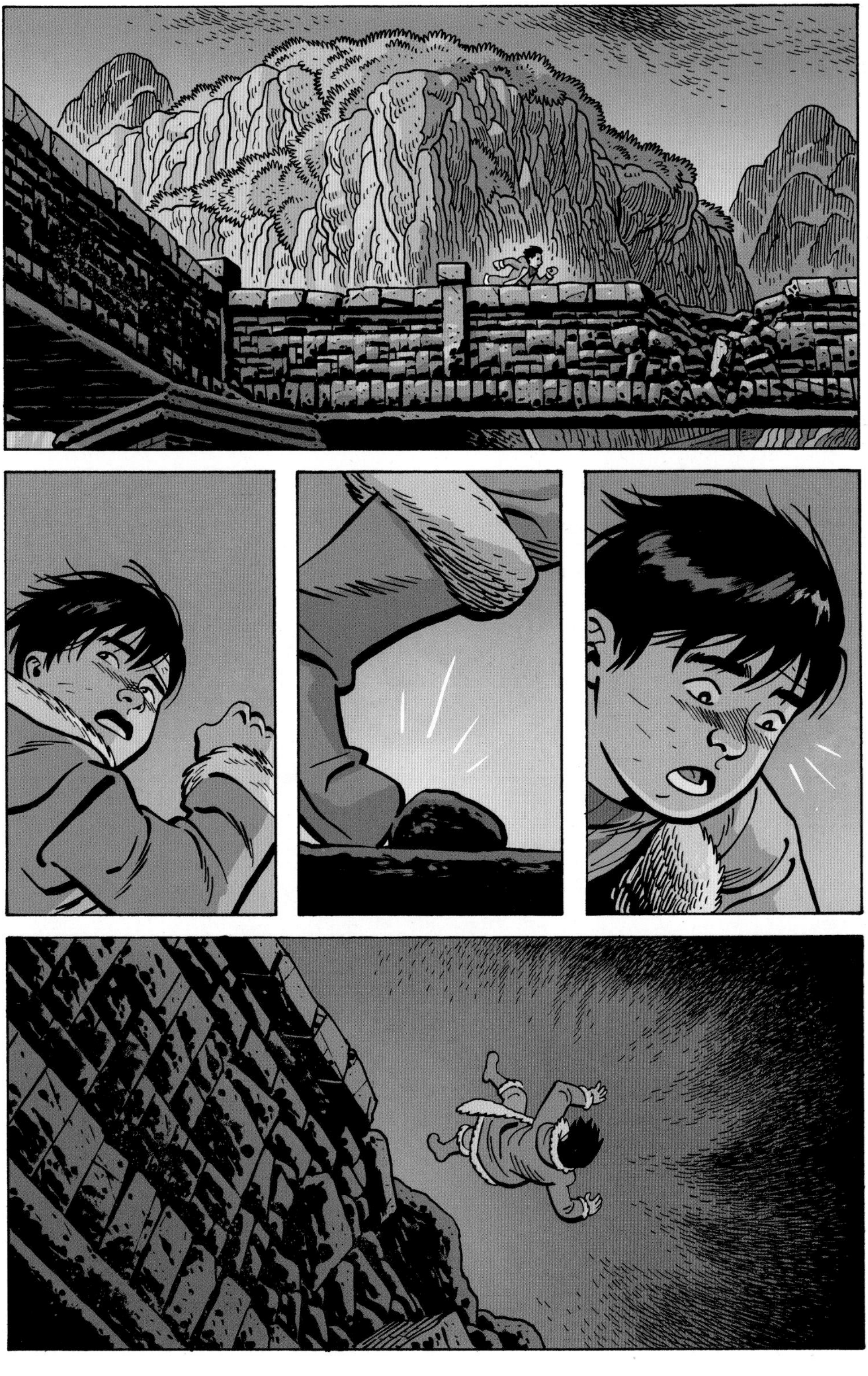

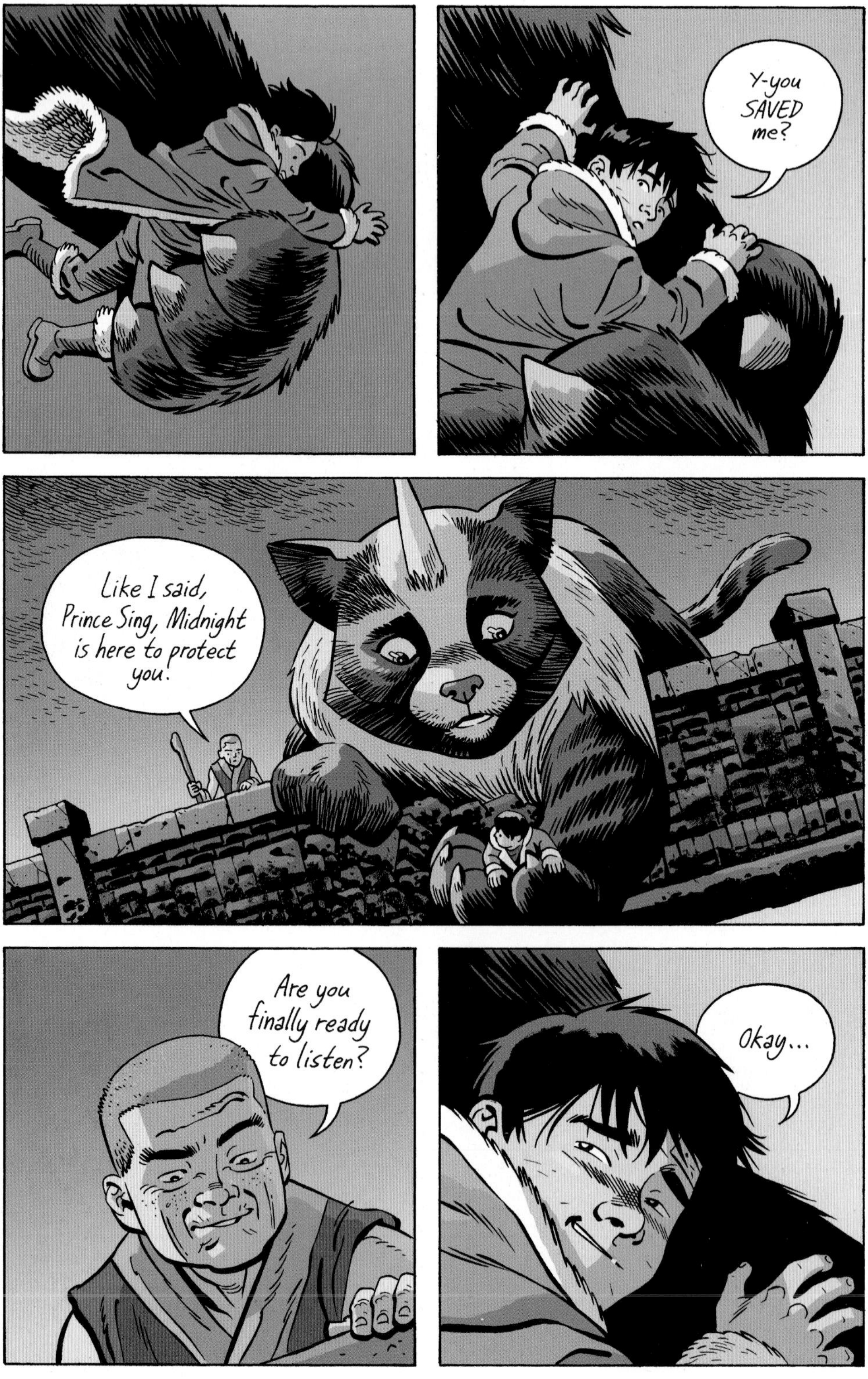
Y-you SAVED me?
Like I said, Prince Sing, Midnight is here to protect you.
Are you finally ready to listen?
Okay...

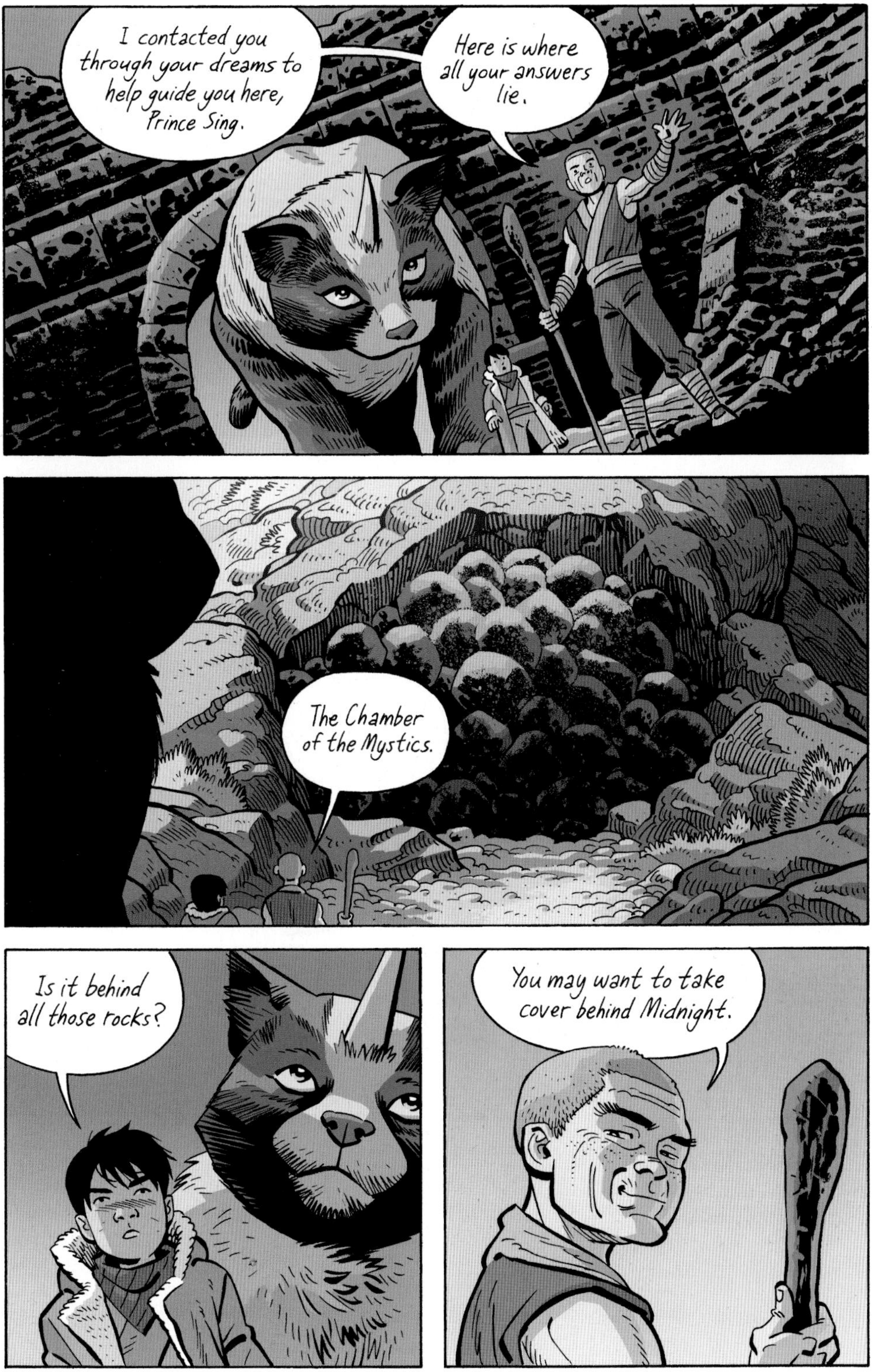
I contacted you through your dreams to help guide you here, Prince Sing.
Here is where all your answers lie.
The Chamber of the Mystics.
Is it behind all those rocks?
You may want to take cover behind Midnight.

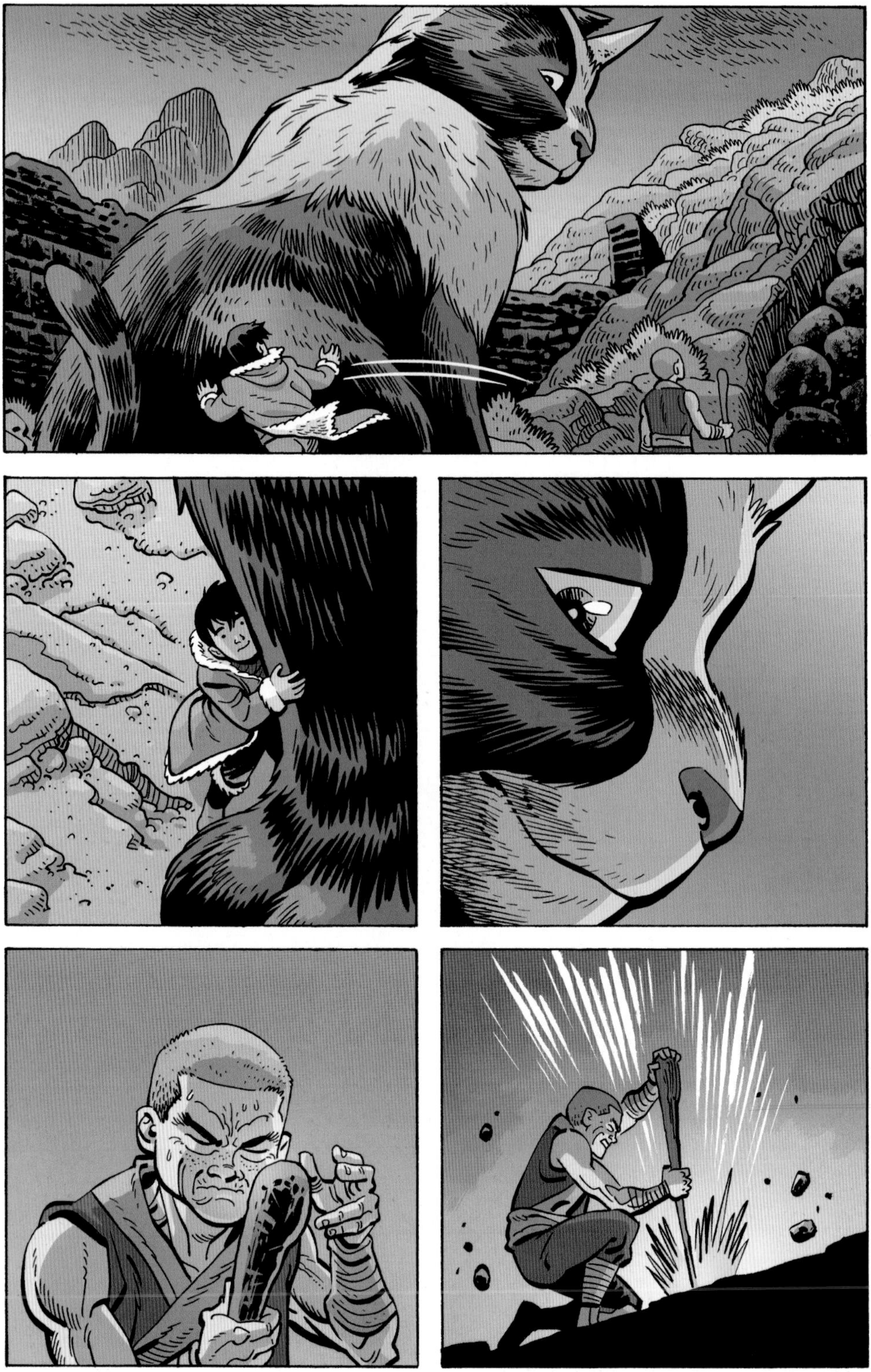

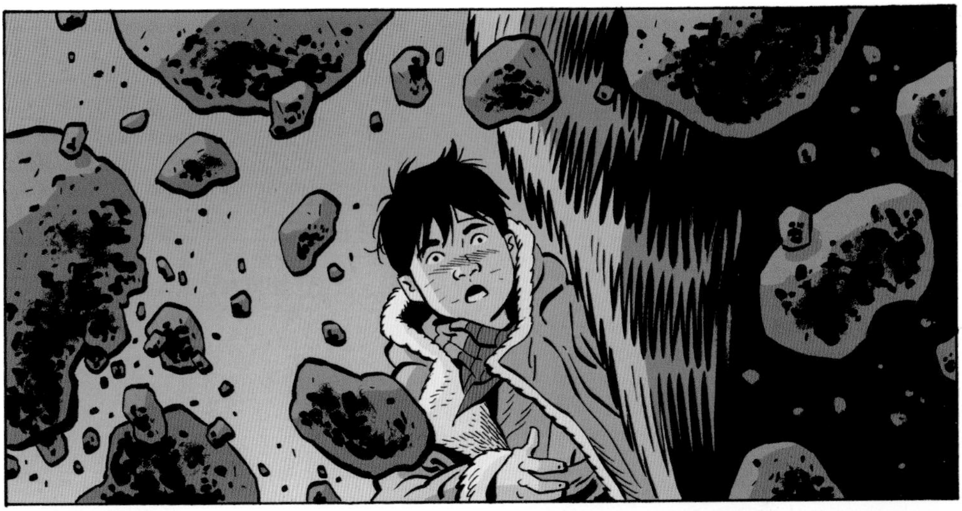

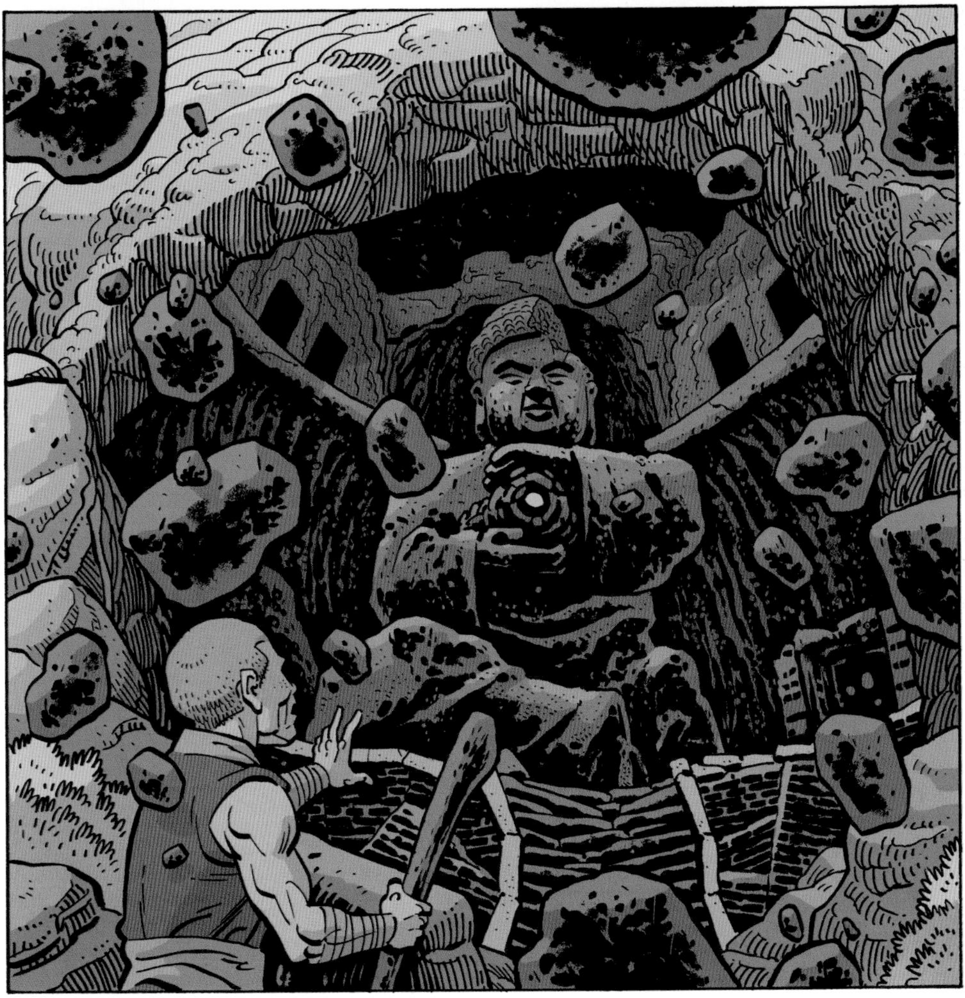

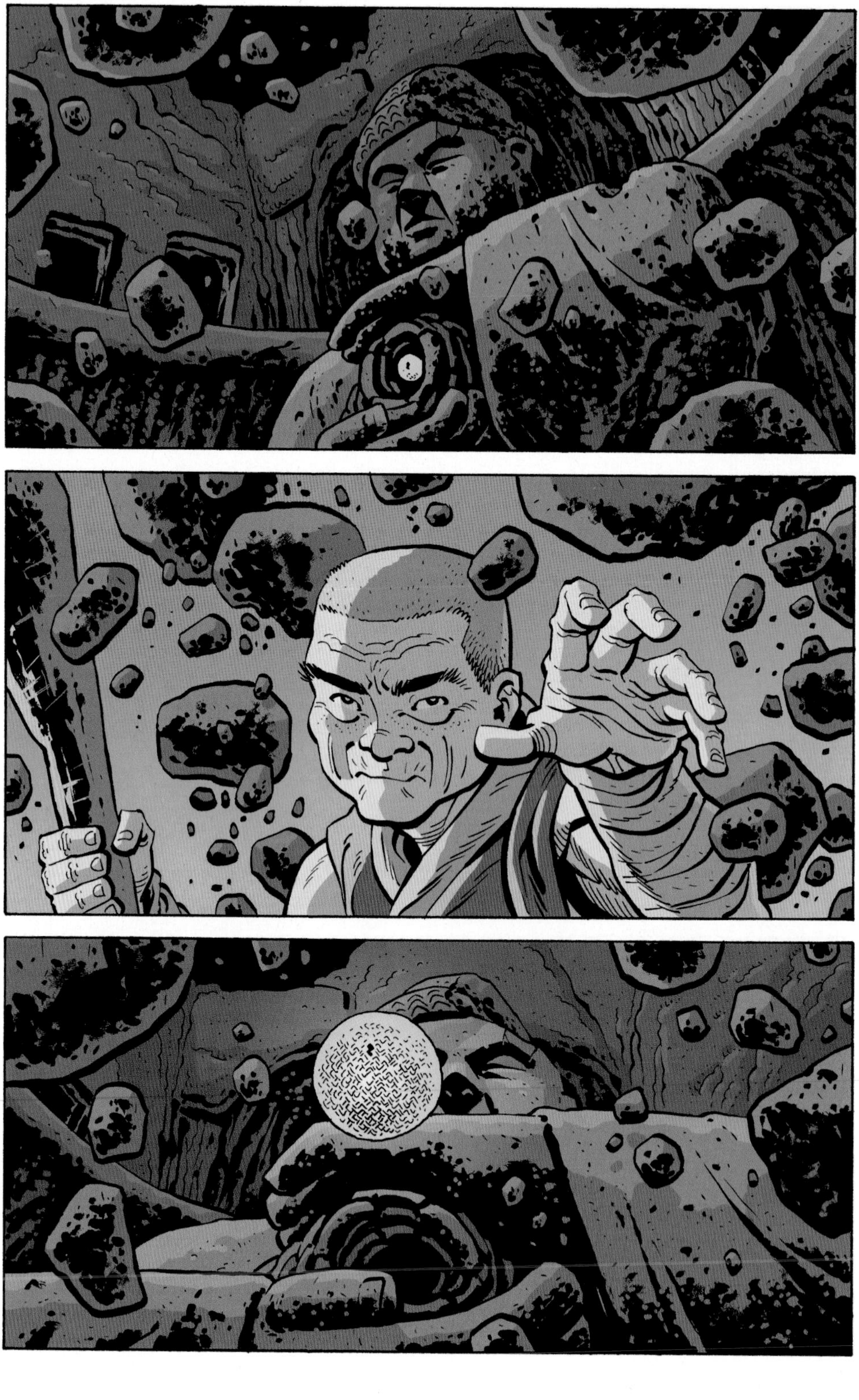

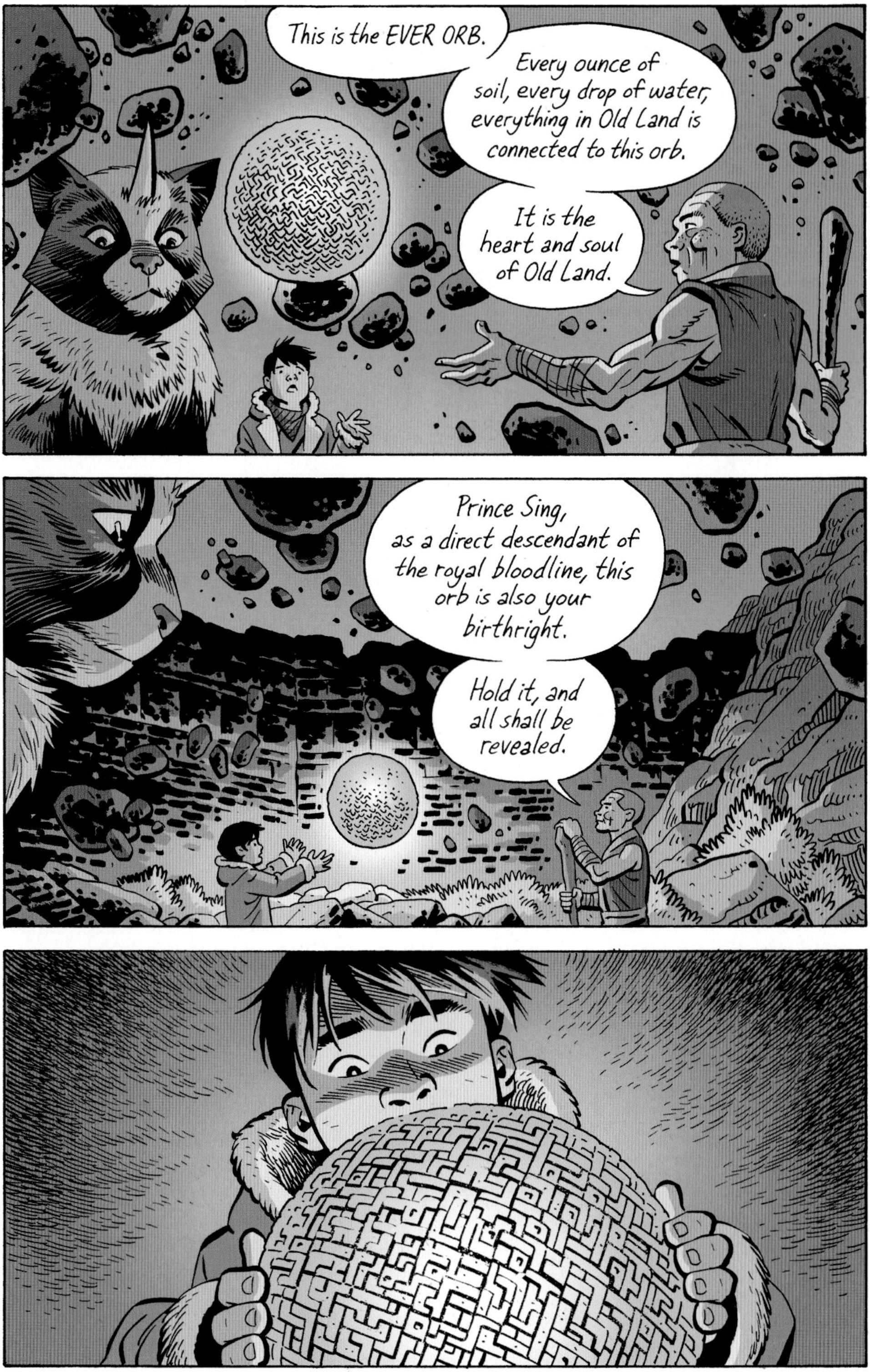
This is the EVER ORB.
Every ounce of soil, every drop of water, everything in Old Land is connected to this orb.
It is the heart and soul of Old Land.
Prince Sing, as a direct descendant of the royal bloodline, this orb is also your birthright.
Hold it, and all shall be revealed.

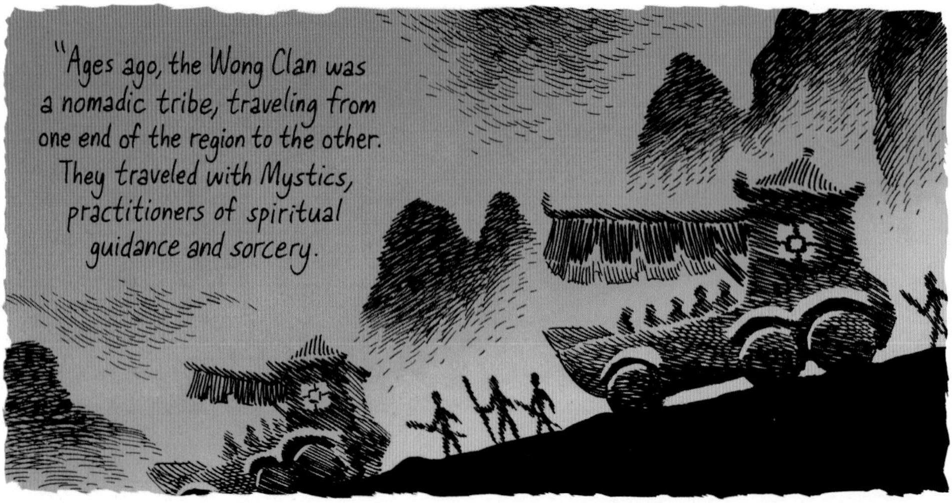
"Ages ago, the Wong Clan was a nomadic tribe, traveling from one end of the region to the other. They traveled with Mystics, practitioners of spiritual guidance and sorcery.

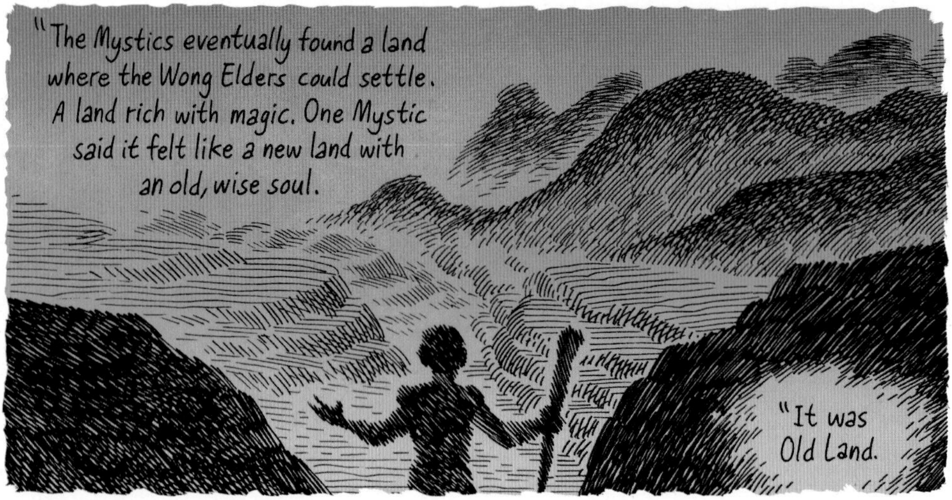
"The Mystics eventually found a land where the Wong Elders could settle. A land rich with magic. One Mystic said it felt like a new land with an old, wise soul.
"It was Old Land.

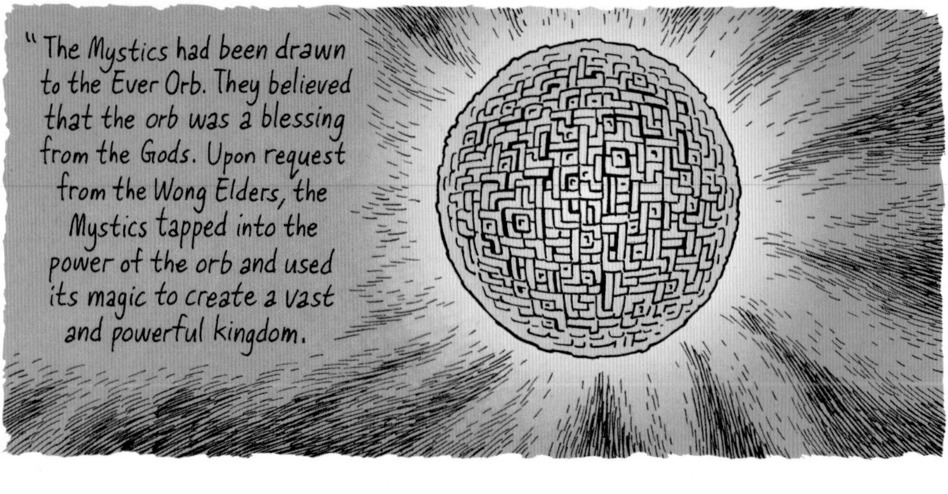
"The Mystics had been drawn to the Ever Orb. They believed that the orb was a blessing from the Gods. Upon request from the Wong Elders, the Mystics tapped into the power of the orb and used its magic to create a vast and powerful kingdom.

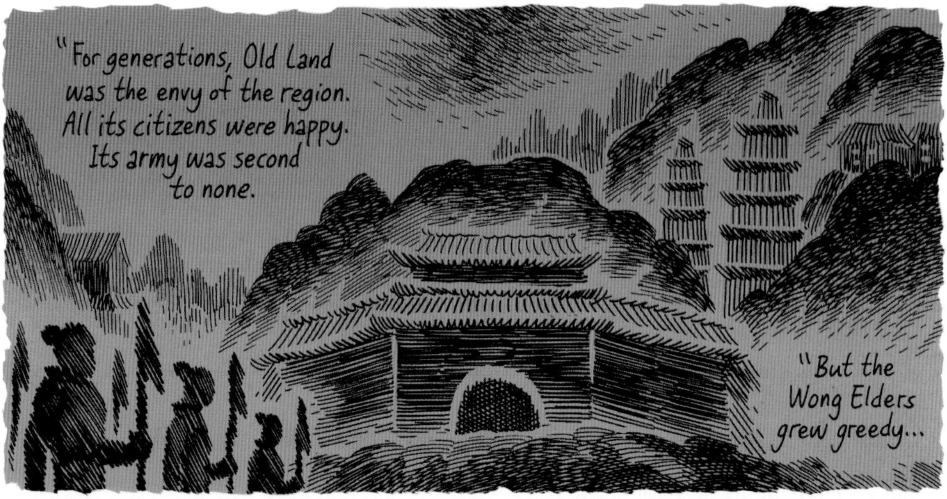
"For generations, Old Land was the envy of the region. All its citizens were happy. Its army was second to none.
"But the Wong Elders grew greedy...

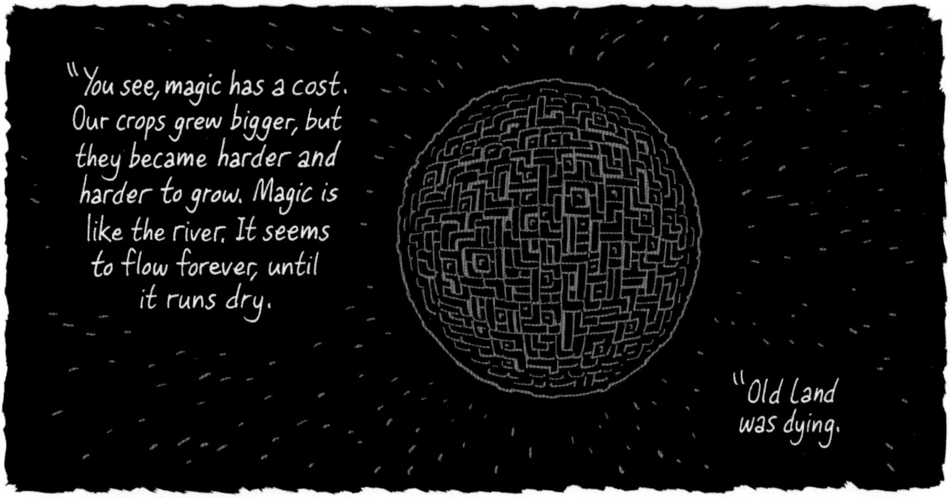
"You see, magic has a cost. Our crops grew bigger, but they became harder and harder to grow. Magic is like the river. It seems to flow forever, until it runs dry.
"Old Land was dying.

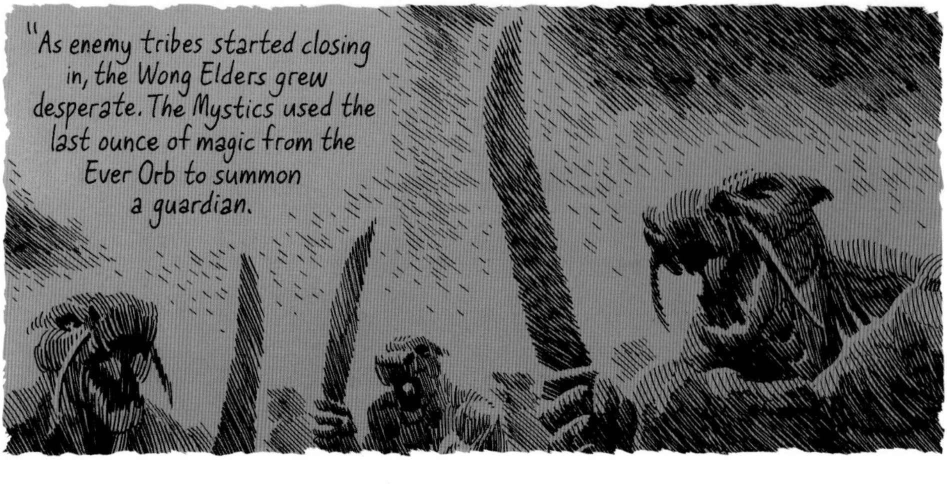
"As enemy tribes started closing in, the Wong Elders grew desperate. The Mystics used the last ounce of magic from the Ever Orb to summon a guardian.

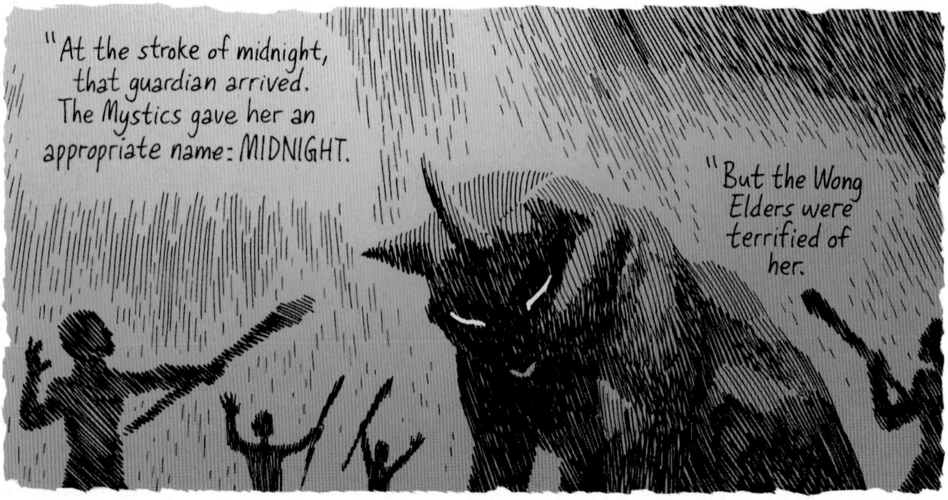
"At the stroke of midnight, that guardian arrived. The Mystics gave her an appropriate name: MIDNIGHT.
"But the Wong Elders were terrified of her.

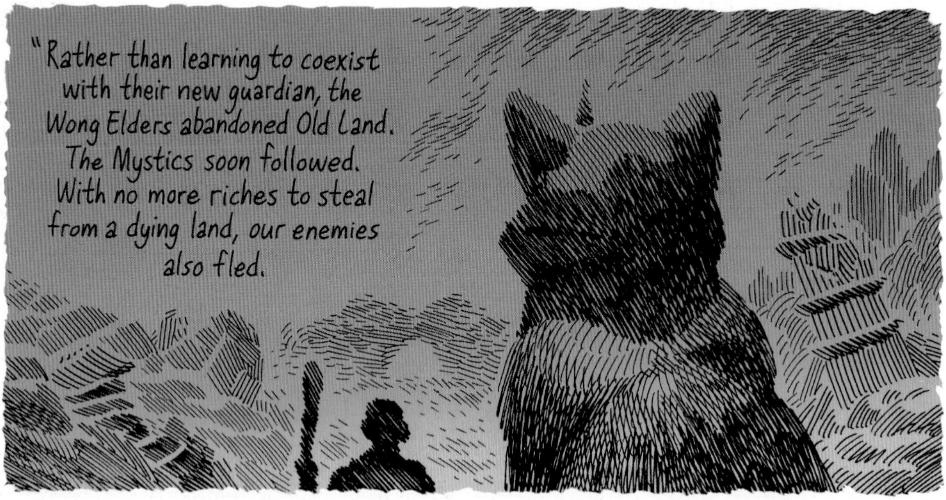
"Rather than learning to coexist with their new guardian, the Wong Elders abandoned Old Land. The Mystics soon followed. With no more riches to steal from a dying land, our enemies also fled.

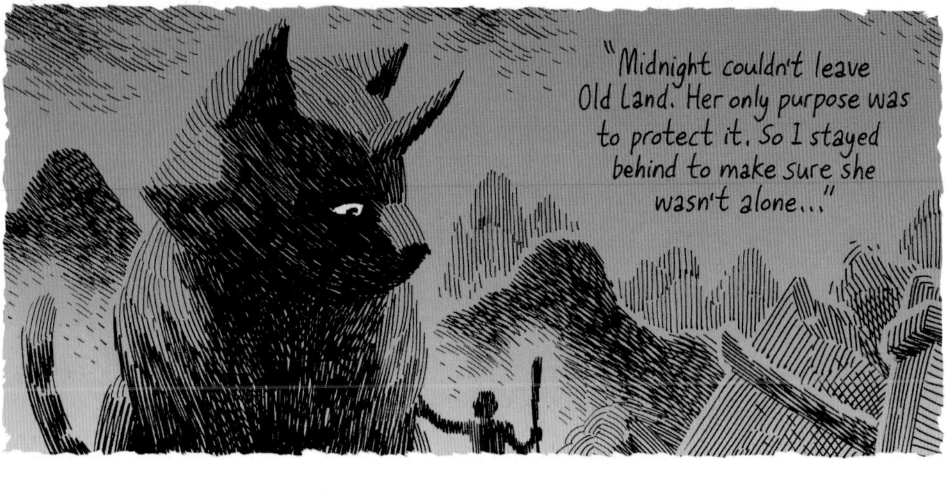
"Midnight couldn't leave Old Land. Her only purpose was to protect it. So I stayed behind to make sure she wasn't alone..."

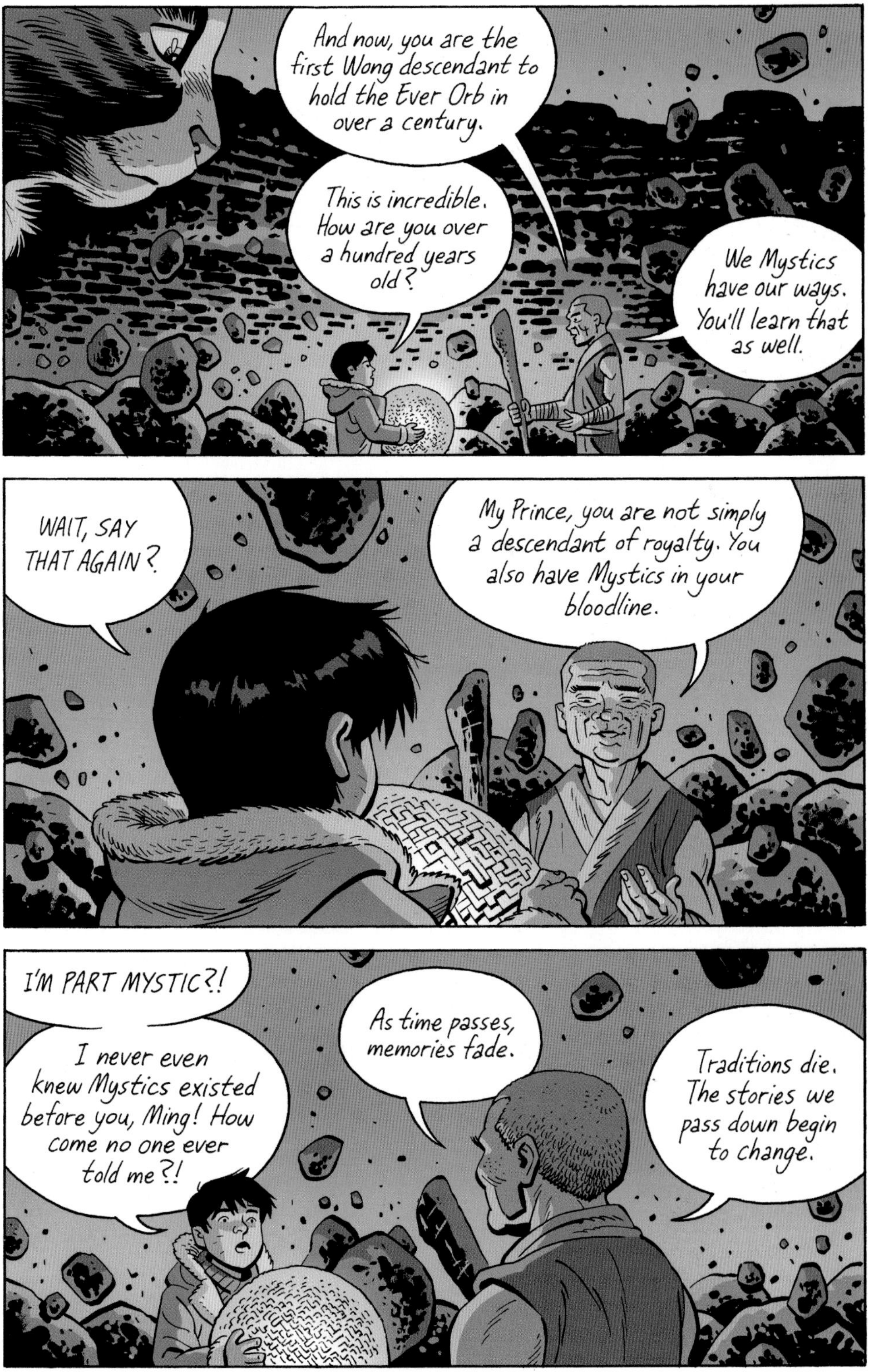
And now, you are the first Wong descendant to hold the Ever Orb in over a century.
This is incredible. How are you over a hundred years old?
We Mystics have our ways. You'll learn that as well.
WAIT, SAY THAT AGAIN?
My Prince, you are not simply a descendant of royalty. You also have Mystics in your bloodline.
I'M PART MYSTIC?!
I never even knew Mystics existed before you, Ming! How come no one ever told me?!
As time passes, memories fade.
Traditions die. The stories we pass down begin to change.

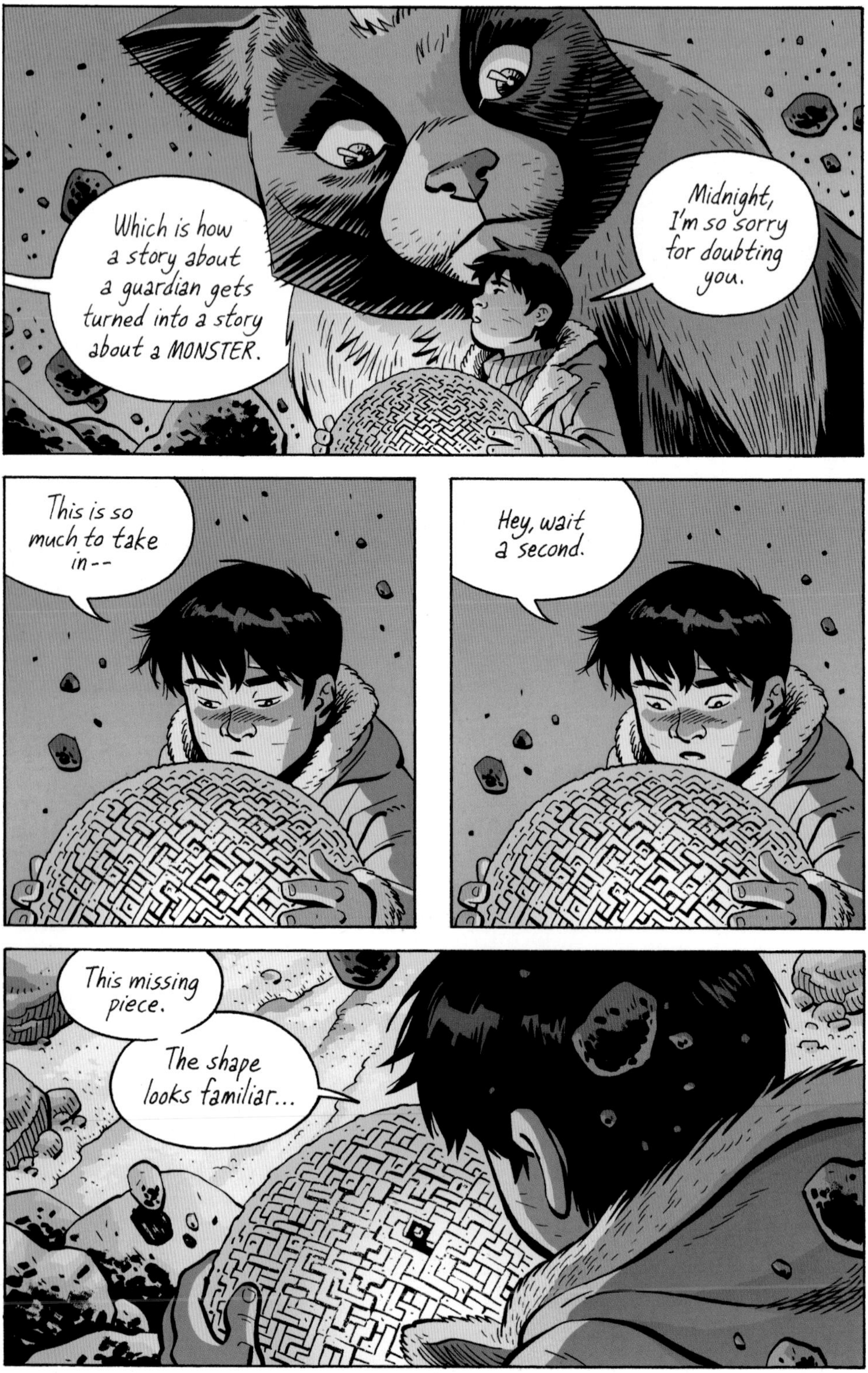
Which is how a story about a guardian gets turned into a story about a MONSTER.
Midnight, I'm so sorry for doubting you.
This is so much to take in--
Hey, wait a second.
This missing piece.
The shape looks familiar...

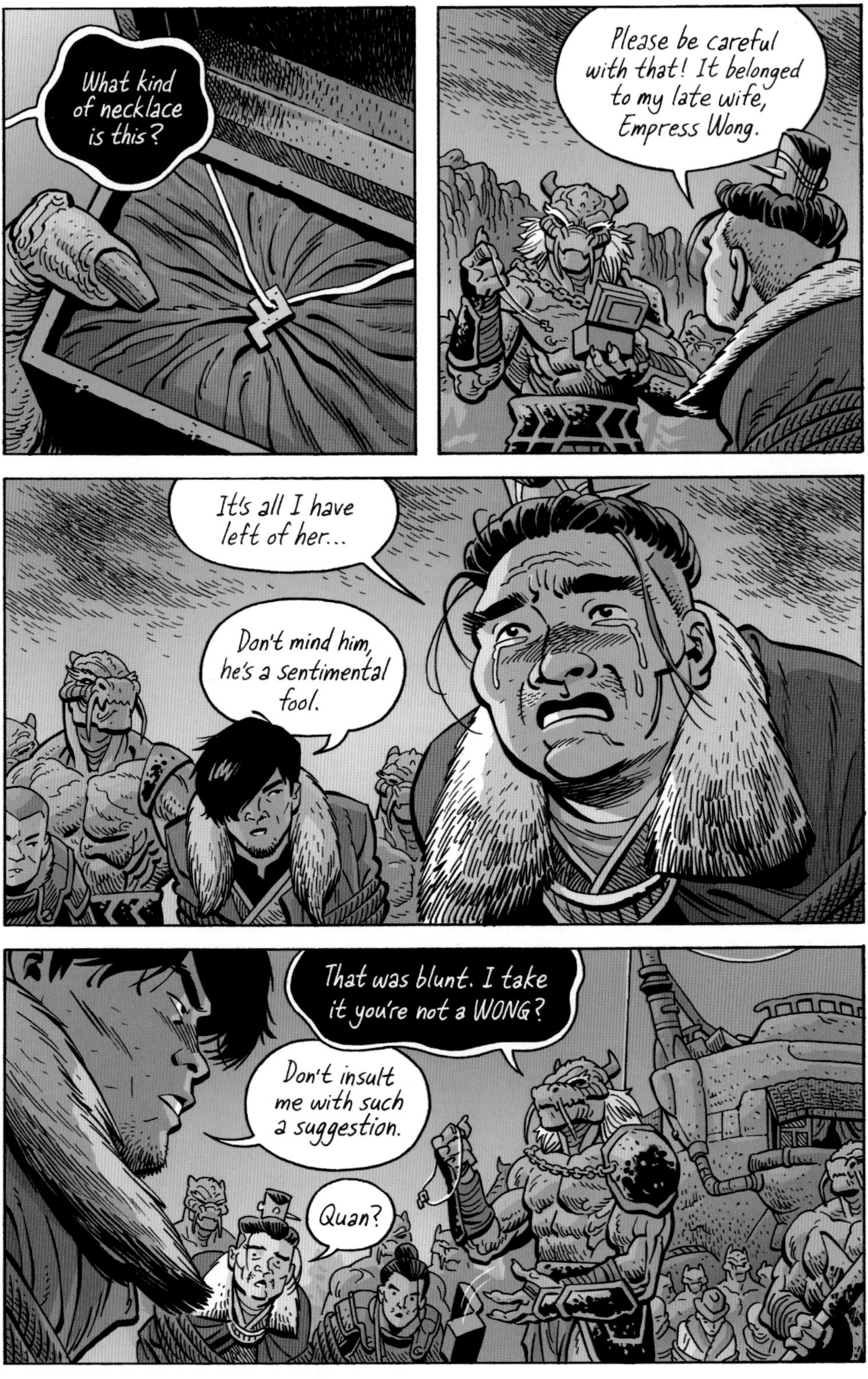
What kind of necklace is this?
Please be careful with that! It belonged to my late wife, Empress Wong.
It's all I have left of her...
Don't mind him, he's a sentimental fool.
That was blunt. I take it you're not a WONG?
Don't insult me with such a suggestion.
Quan?

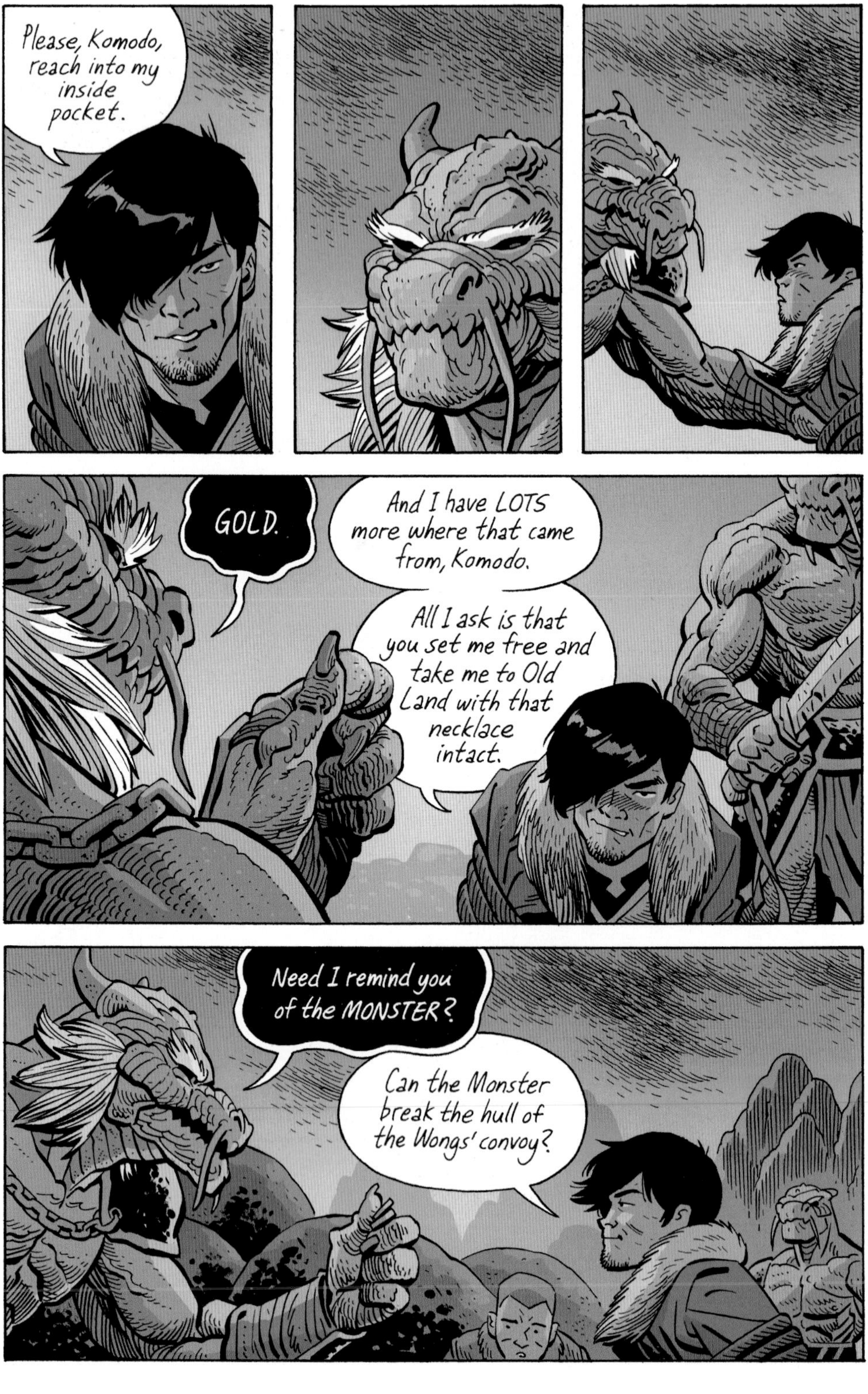
Please, Komodo, reach into my inside pocket.
GOLD.
And I have LOTS more where that came from, Komodo.
All I ask is that you set me free and take me to Old Land with that necklace intact.
Need I remind you of the MONSTER?
Can the Monster break the hull of the Wongs' convoy?

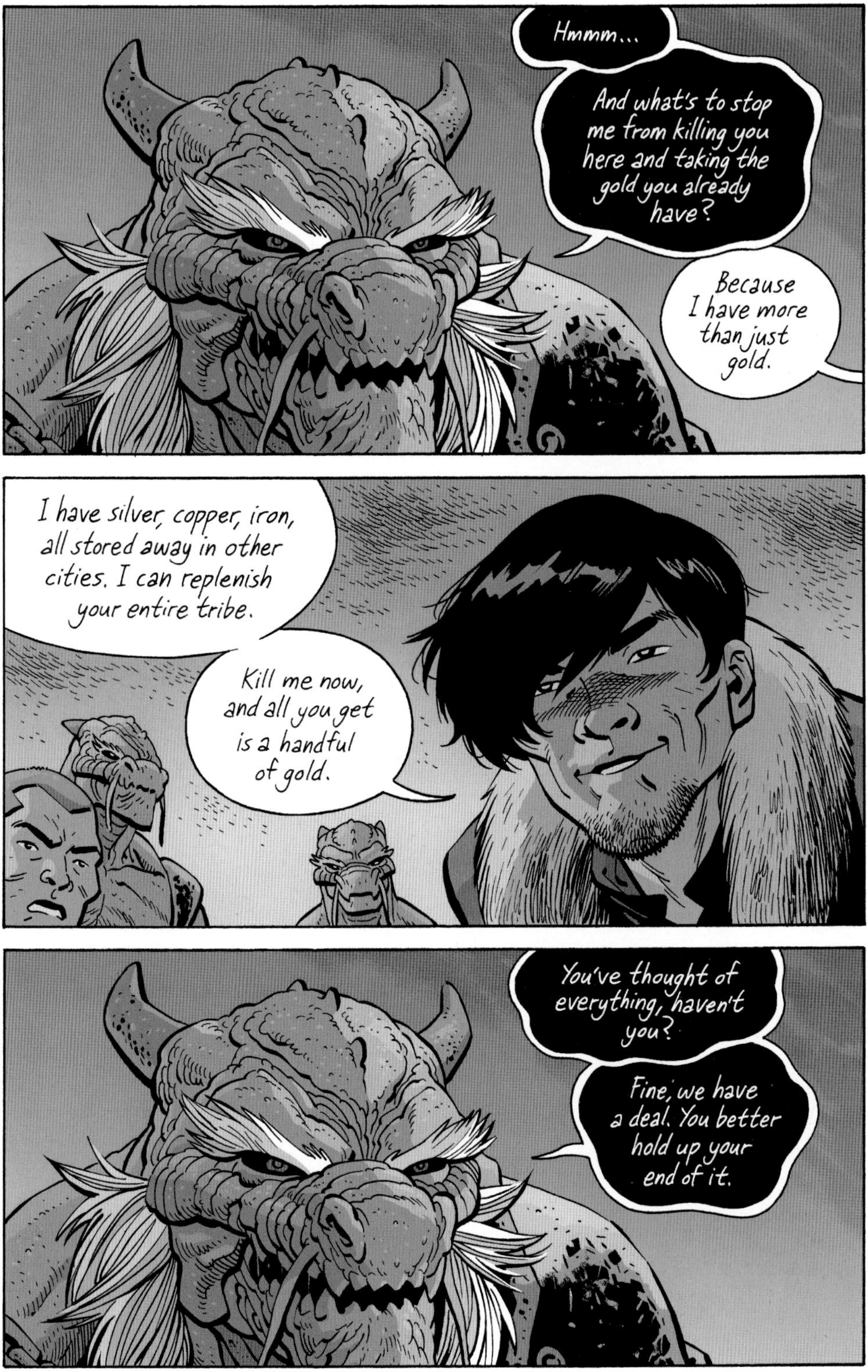

Hmmm...
And what's to stop me from killing you here and taking the gold you already have?
Because I have more than just gold.
I have silver, copper, iron, all stored away in other cities. I can replenish your entire tribe.
Kill me now, and all you get is a handful of gold.
You've thought of everything, haven't you?
Fine, we have a deal. You better hold up your end of it.

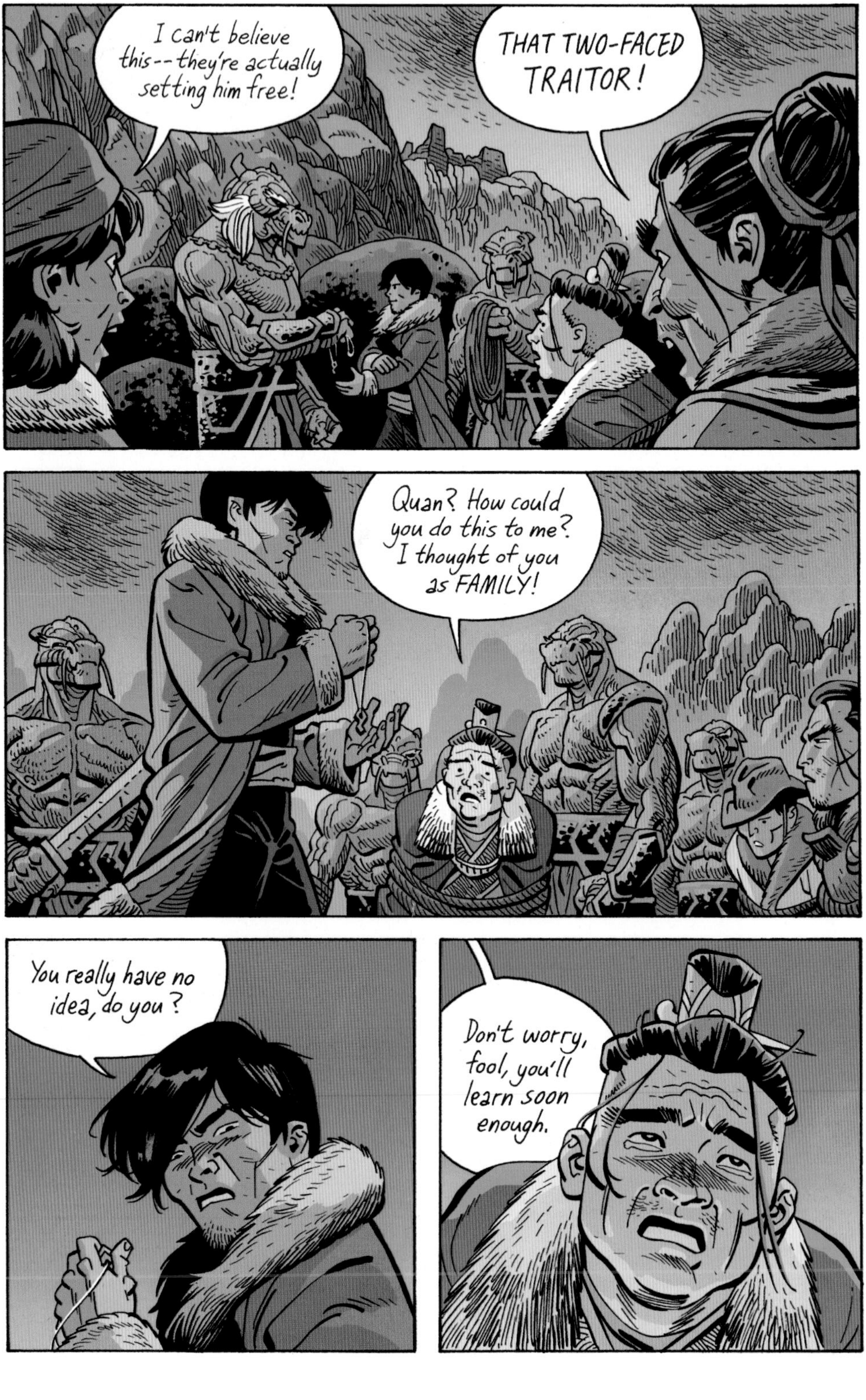
I can't believe this--they're actually setting him free!
THAT TWO-FACED TRAITOR!
Quan? How could you do this to me? I thought of you as FAMILY!
You really have no idea, do you?
Don't worry, fool, you'll learn soon enough.

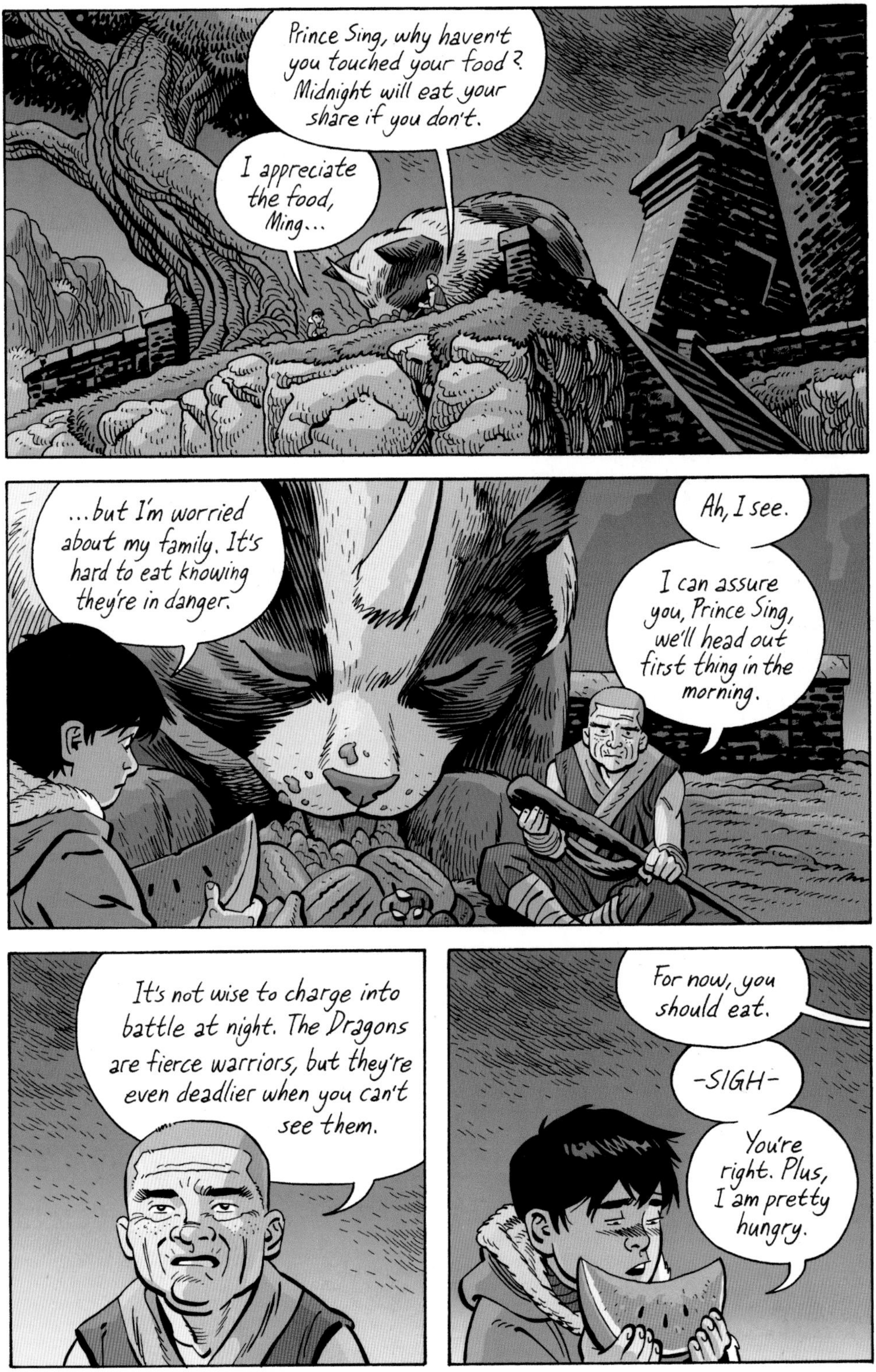
Prince Sing, why haven't you touched your food? Midnight will eat your share if you don't.
I appreciate the food, Ming...
...but I'm worried about my family. It's hard to eat knowing they're in danger.
Ah, I see.
I can assure you, Prince Sing, we'll head out first thing in the morning.
It's not wise to charge into battle at night. The Dragons are fierce warriors, but they're even deadlier when you can't see them.
For now, you should eat.
-SIGH-
You're right. Plus, I am pretty hungry.

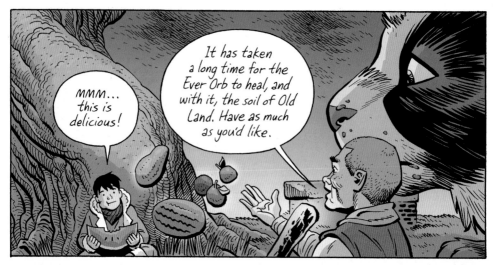

MMM... this is delicious!

It has taken a long time for the Ever Orb to heal, and with it, the soil of Old Land. Have as much as you'd like.

Thank you, Ming. And you can have some of my candy if you're interested.

SNIFF SNIFF

I forgot to warn you, Midnight has quite the sweet tooth.

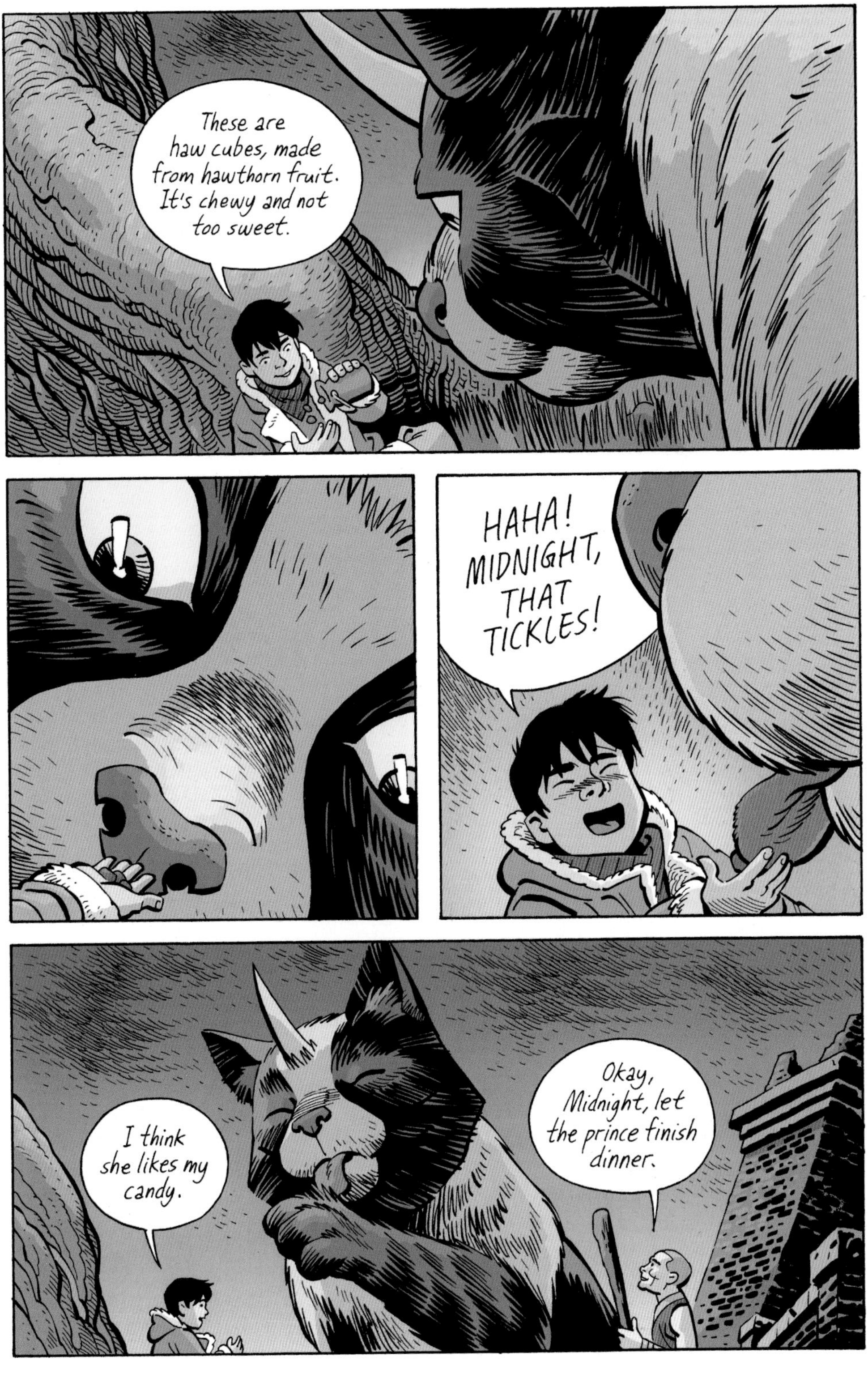
These are haw cubes, made from hawthorn fruit. It's chewy and not too sweet.
HAHA! MIDNIGHT, THAT TICKLES!
I think she likes my candy.
Okay, Midnight, let the prince finish dinner.

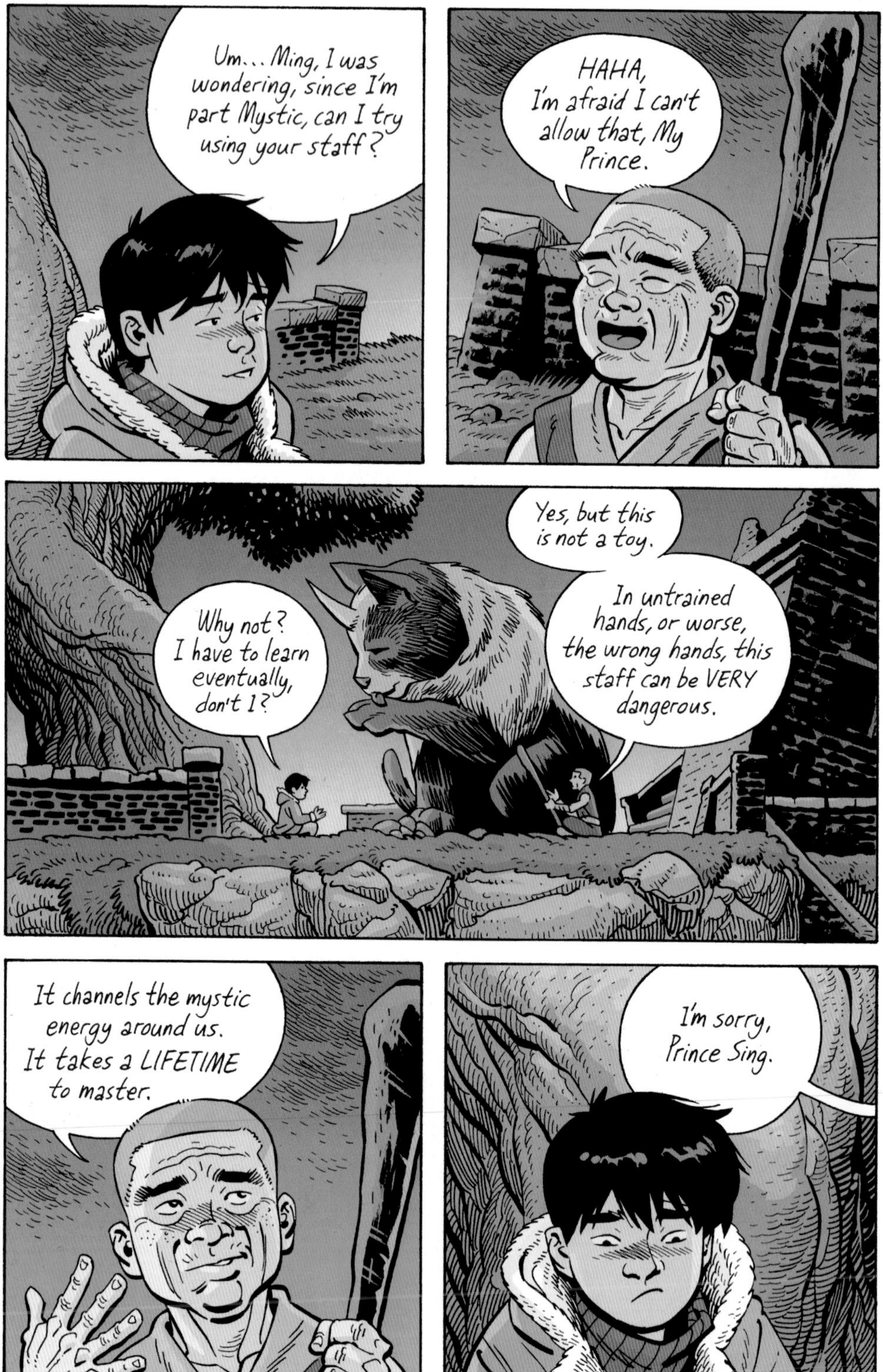
Um... Ming, I was wondering, since I'm part Mystic, can I try using your staff?
HAHA, I'm afraid I can't allow that, My Prince.
Why not? I have to learn eventually, don't I?
Yes, but this is not a toy.
In untrained hands, or worse, the wrong hands, this staff can be VERY dangerous.
It channels the mystic energy around us. It takes a LIFETIME to master.
I'm sorry, Prince Sing.

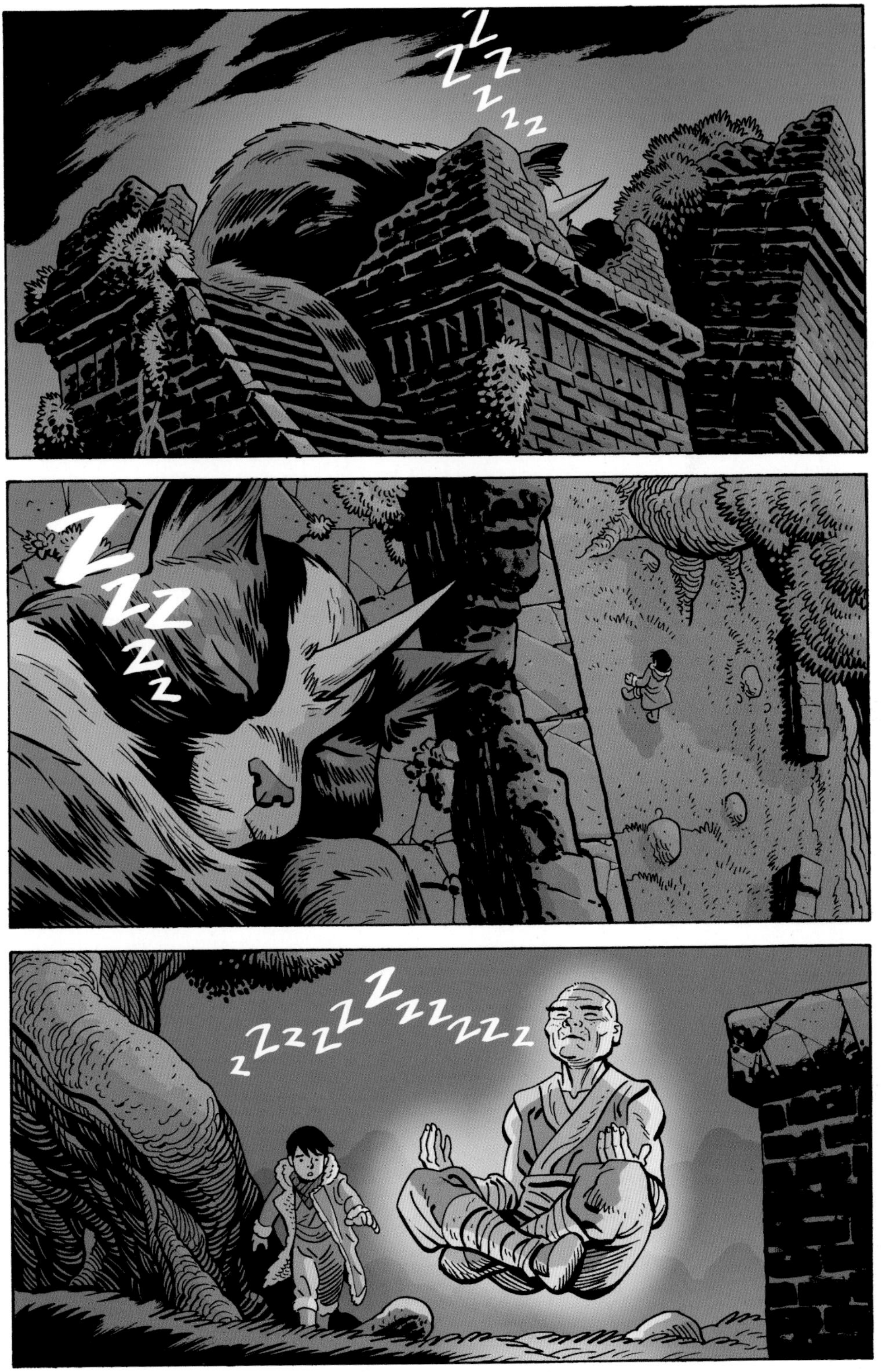
ZZZZZZ
ZZZZZ
ZZZZZZZZZZZ

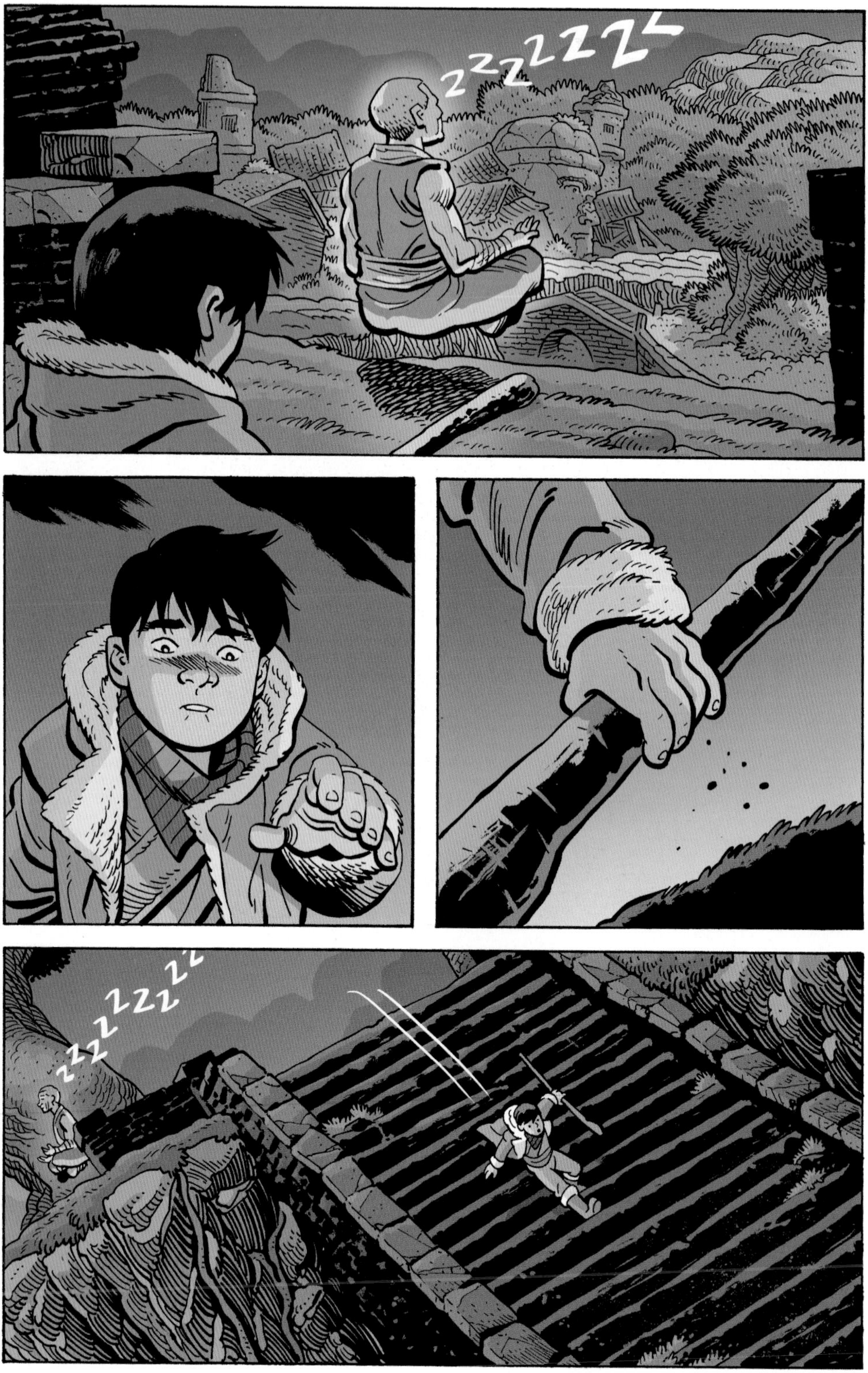

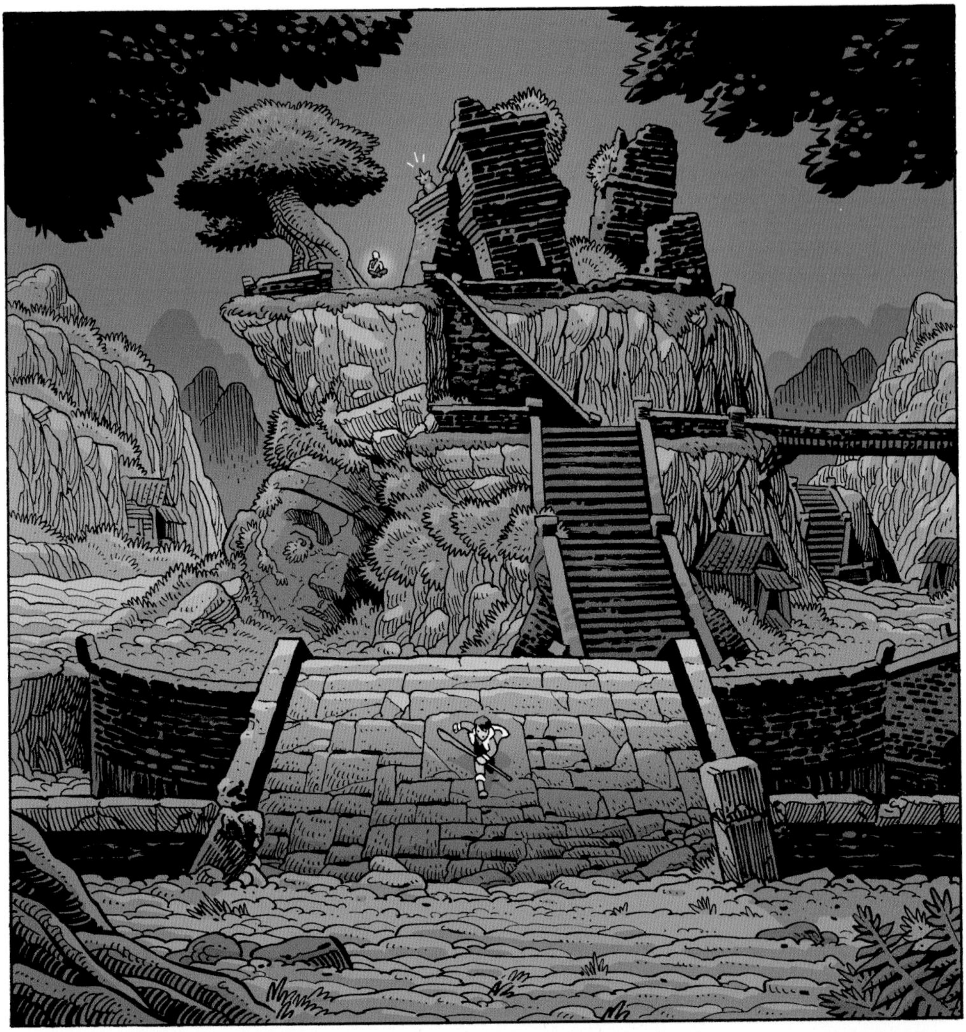

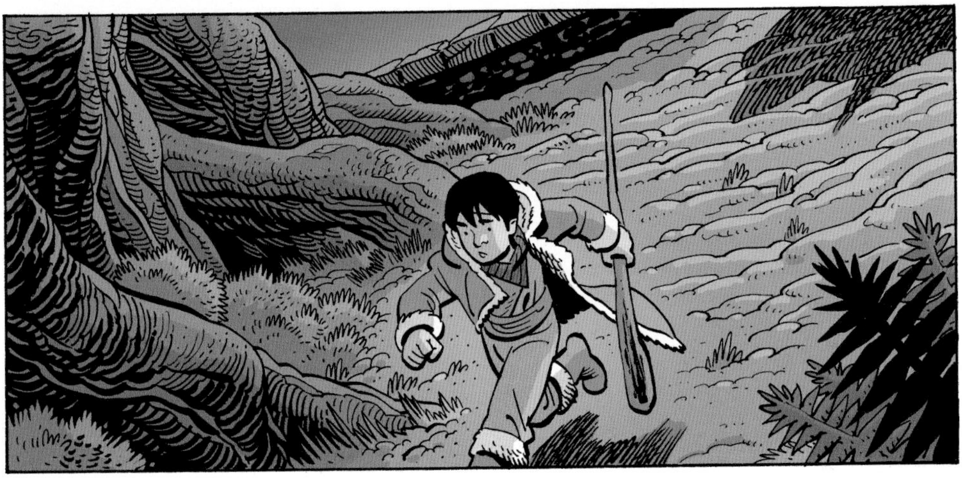

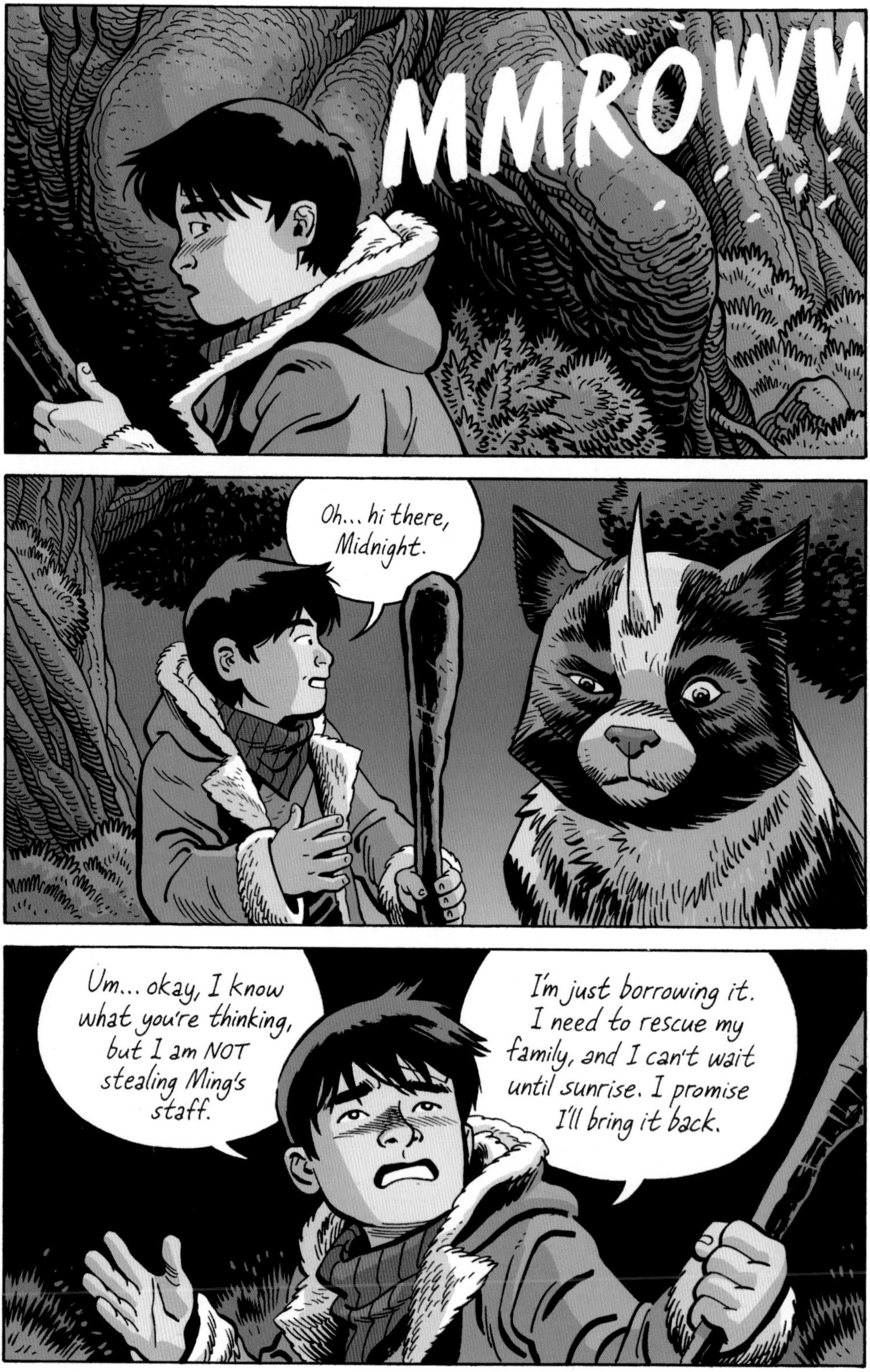
MMROWW
Oh... hi there, Midnight.
Um... okay, I know what you're thinking, but I am NOT stealing Ming's staff.
I'm just borrowing it. I need to rescue my family, and I can't wait until sunrise. I promise I'll bring it back.

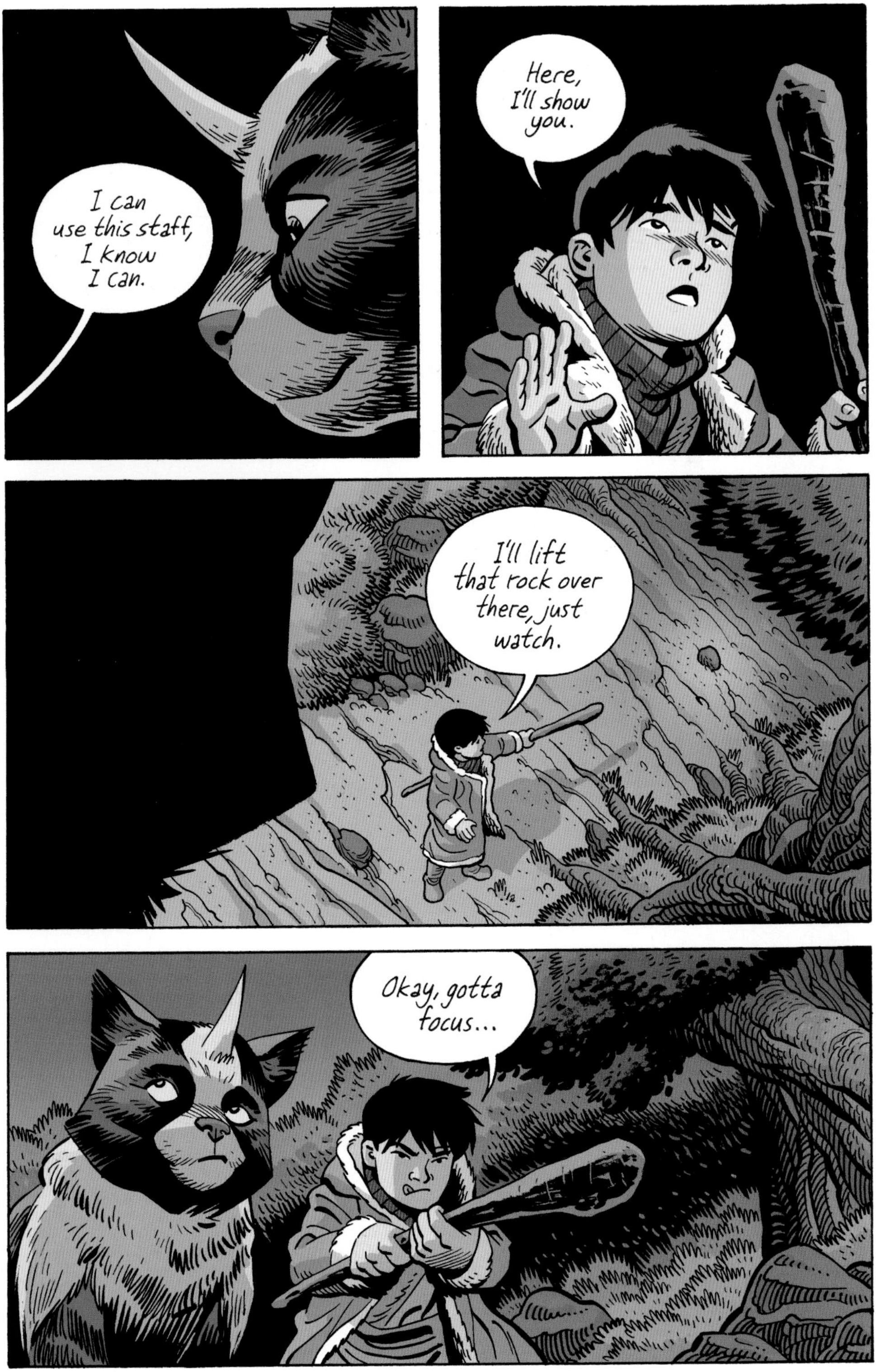
I can use this staff, I know I can.
Here, I'll show you.
I'll lift that rock over there, just watch.
Okay, gotta focus...

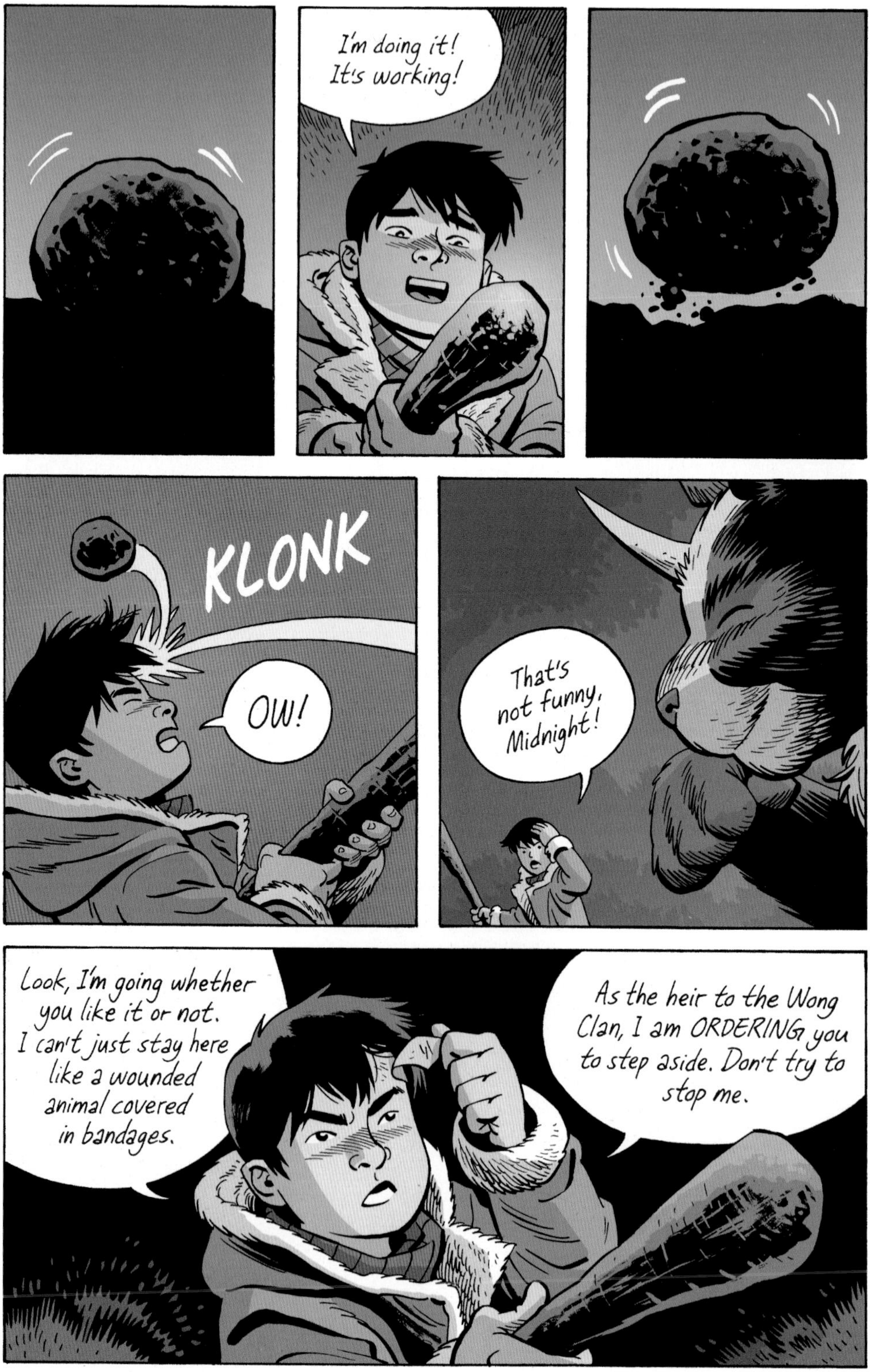
I'm doing it! It's working!
KLONK
OW!
That's not funny, Midnight!
Look, I'm going whether you like it or not. I can't just stay here like a wounded animal covered in bandages.
As the heir to the Wong Clan, I am ORDERING you to step aside. Don't try to stop me.

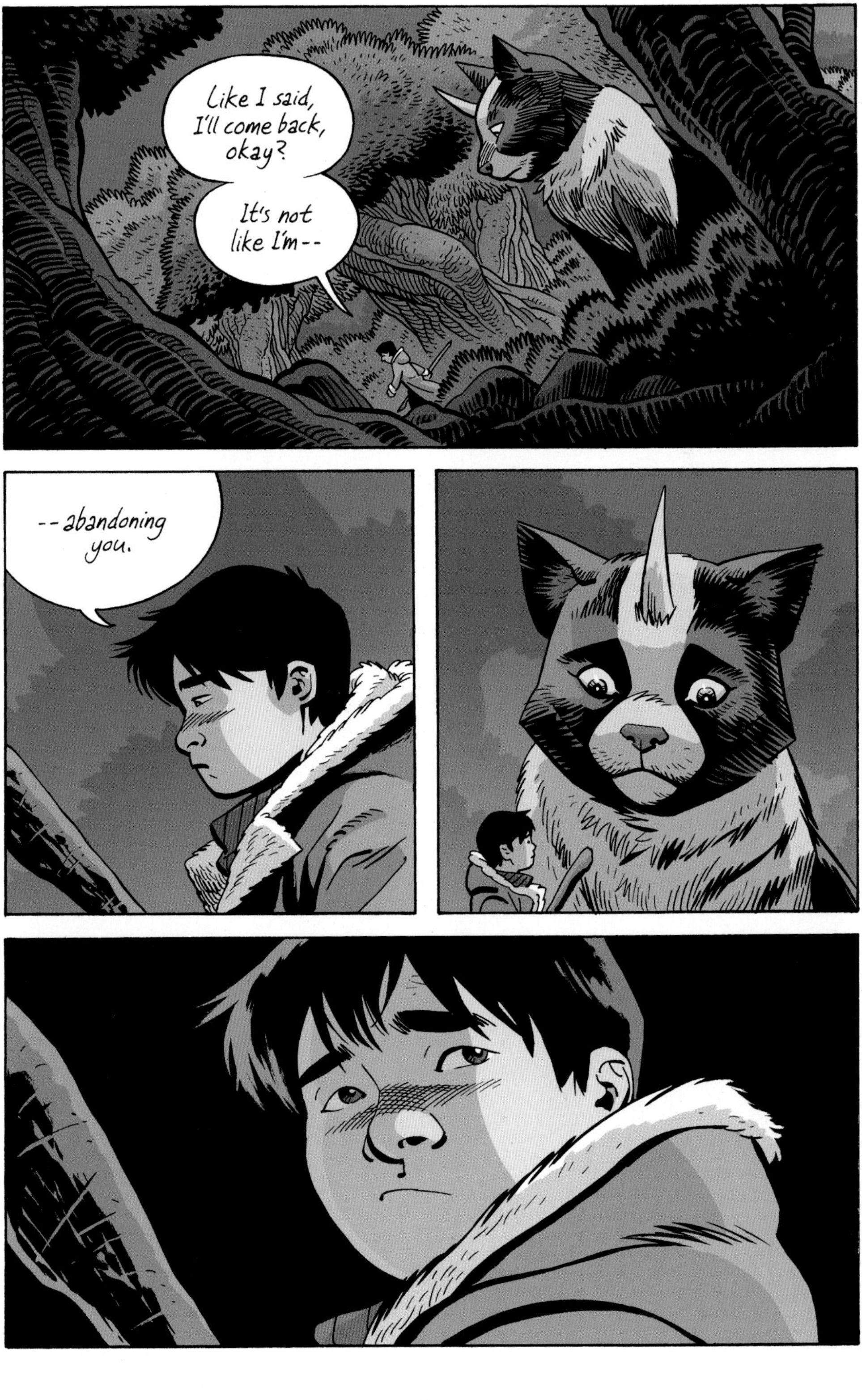
Like I said, I'll come back, okay?
It's not like I'm--
--abandoning you.

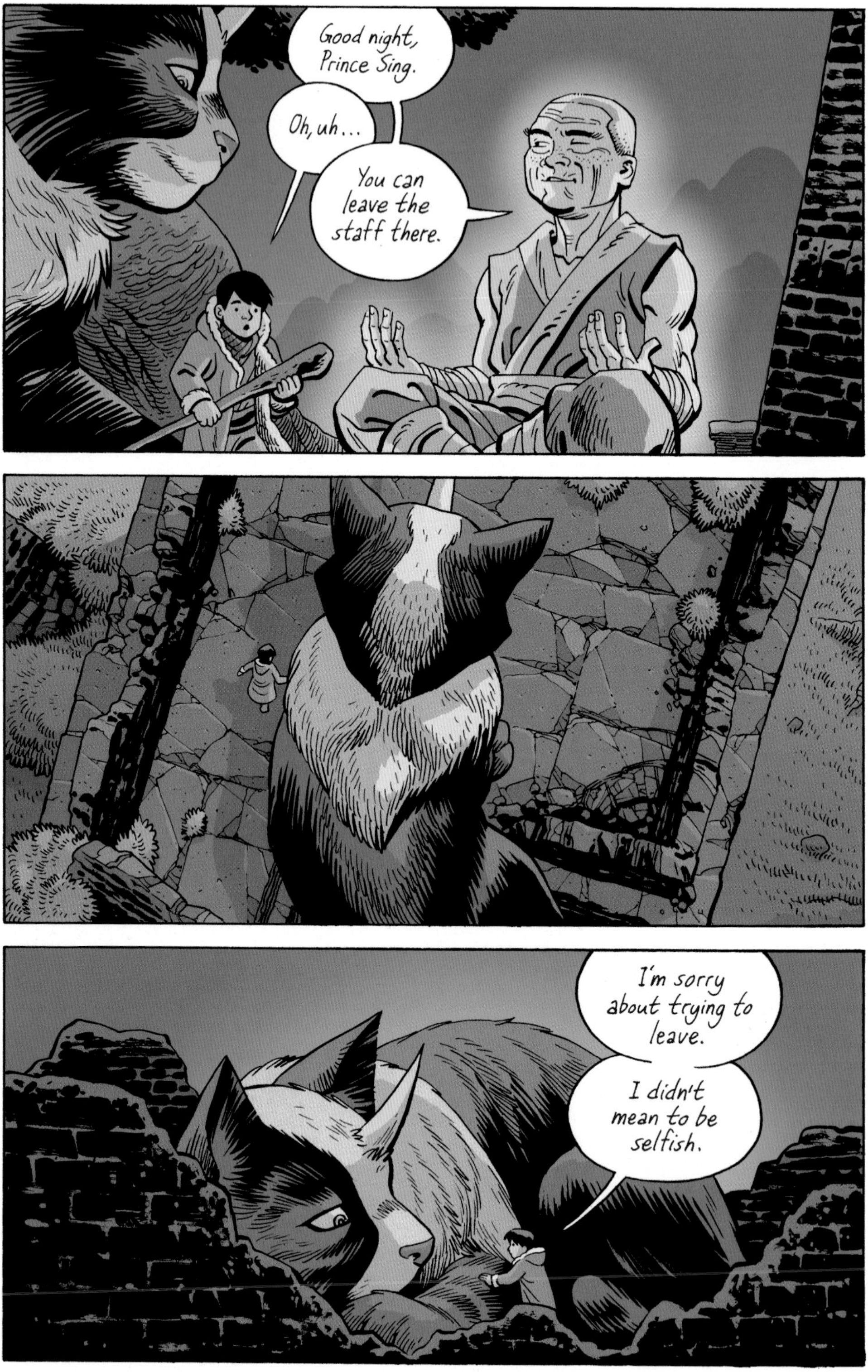
Good night, Prince Sing.
Oh, uh...
You can leave the staff there.
I'm sorry about trying to leave.
I didn't mean to be selfish.

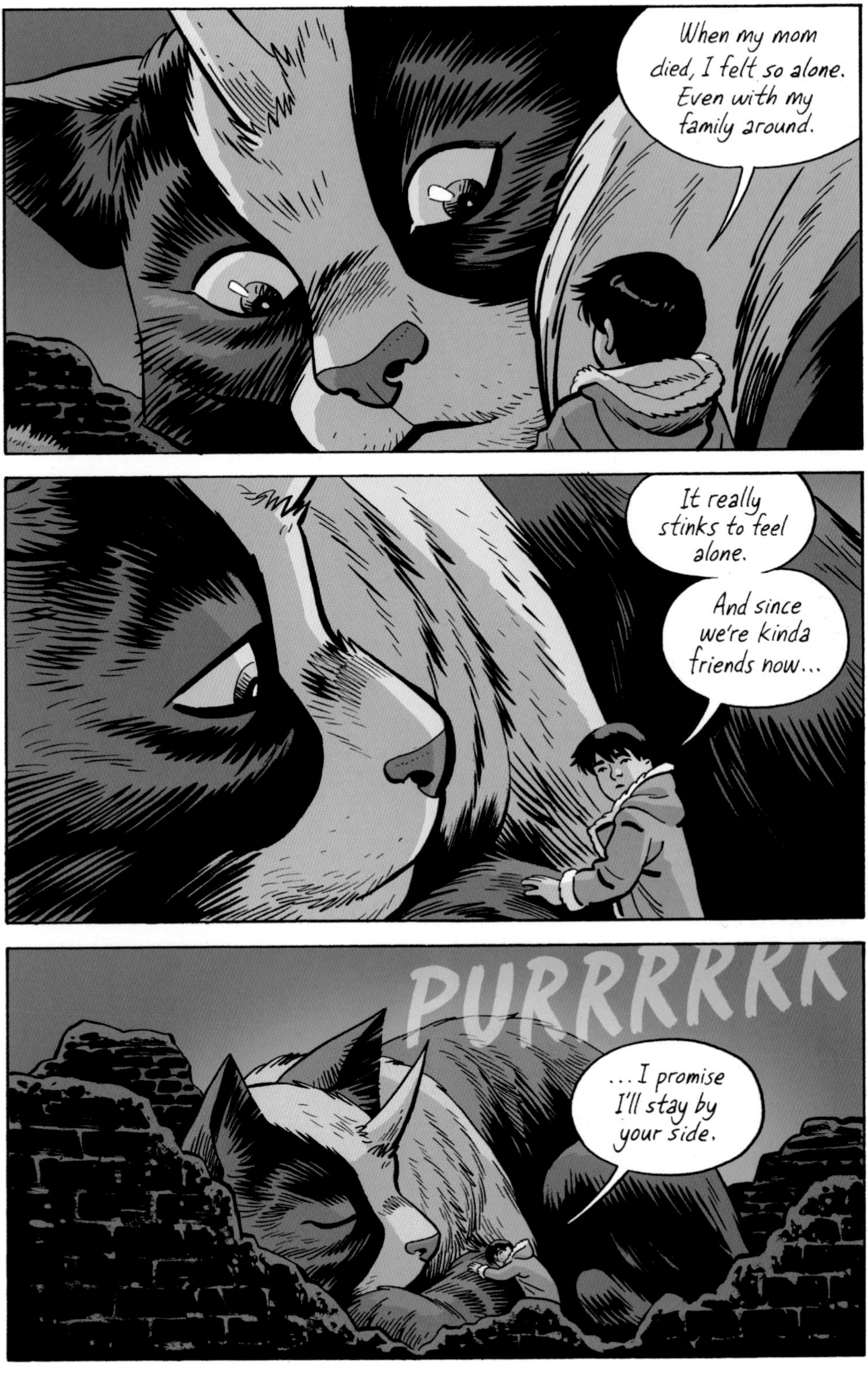
When my mom died, I felt so alone. Even with my family around.
It really stinks to feel alone.
And since we're kinda friends now...
PURRRRRK
...I promise I'll stay by your side.

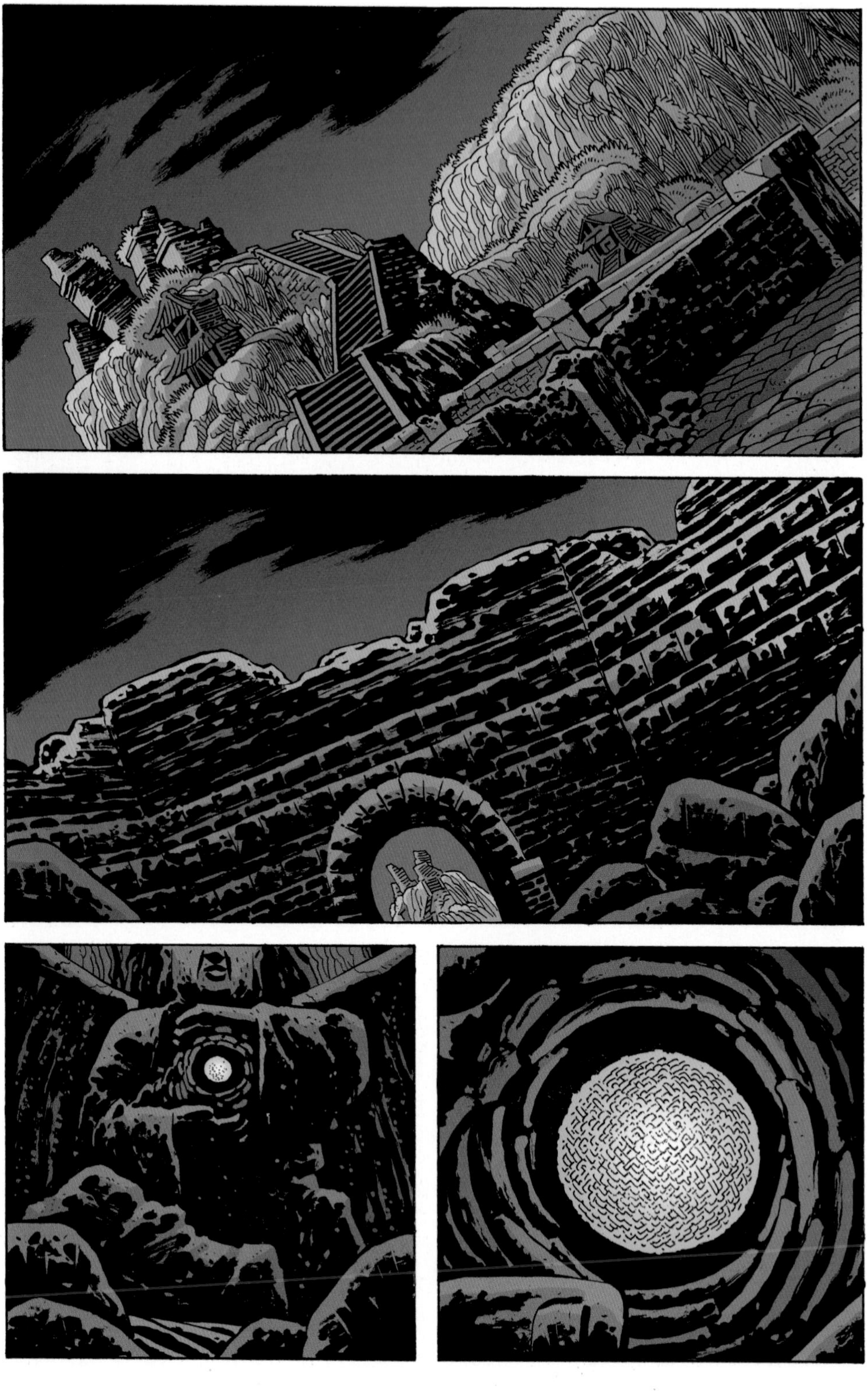

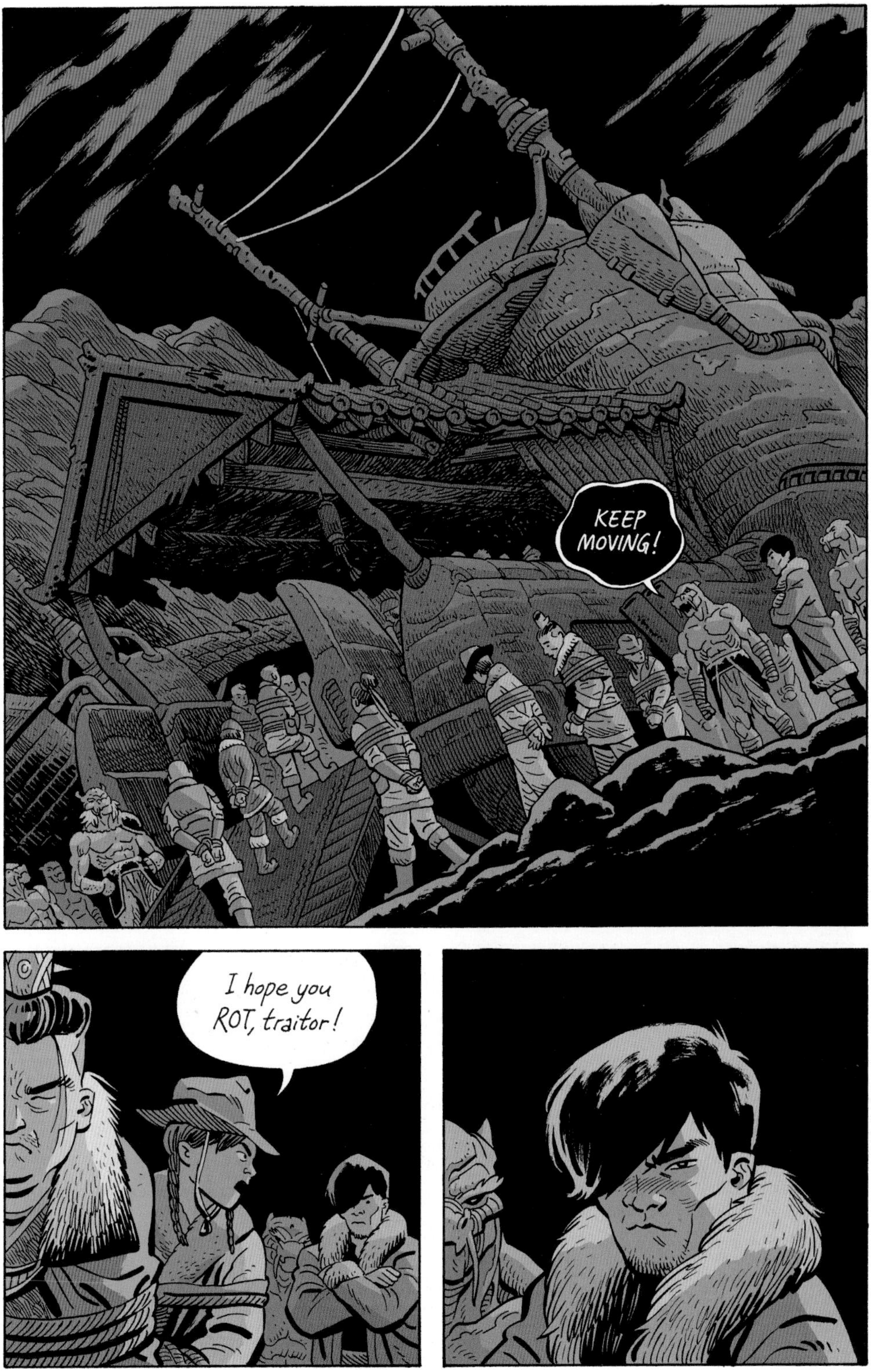
KEEP MOVING!
I hope you ROT, traitor!

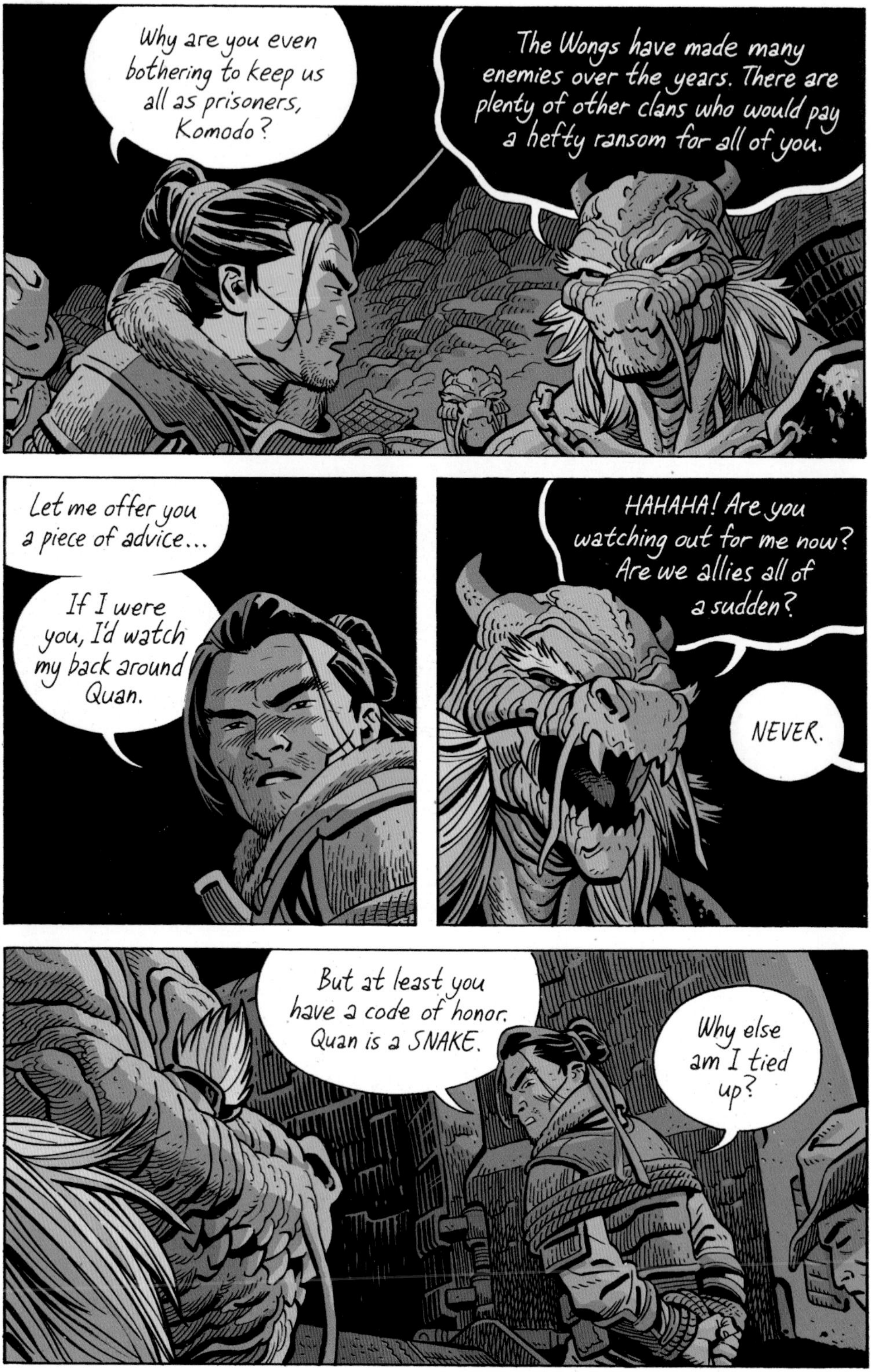
Why are you even bothering to keep us all as prisoners, Komodo?
The Wongs have made many enemies over the years. There are plenty of other clans who would pay a hefty ransom for all of you.
Let me offer you a piece of advice...
If I were you, I'd watch my back around Quan.
HAHAHA! Are you watching out for me now? Are we allies all of a sudden?
NEVER.
But at least you have a code of honor. Quan is a SNAKE.
Why else am I tied up?

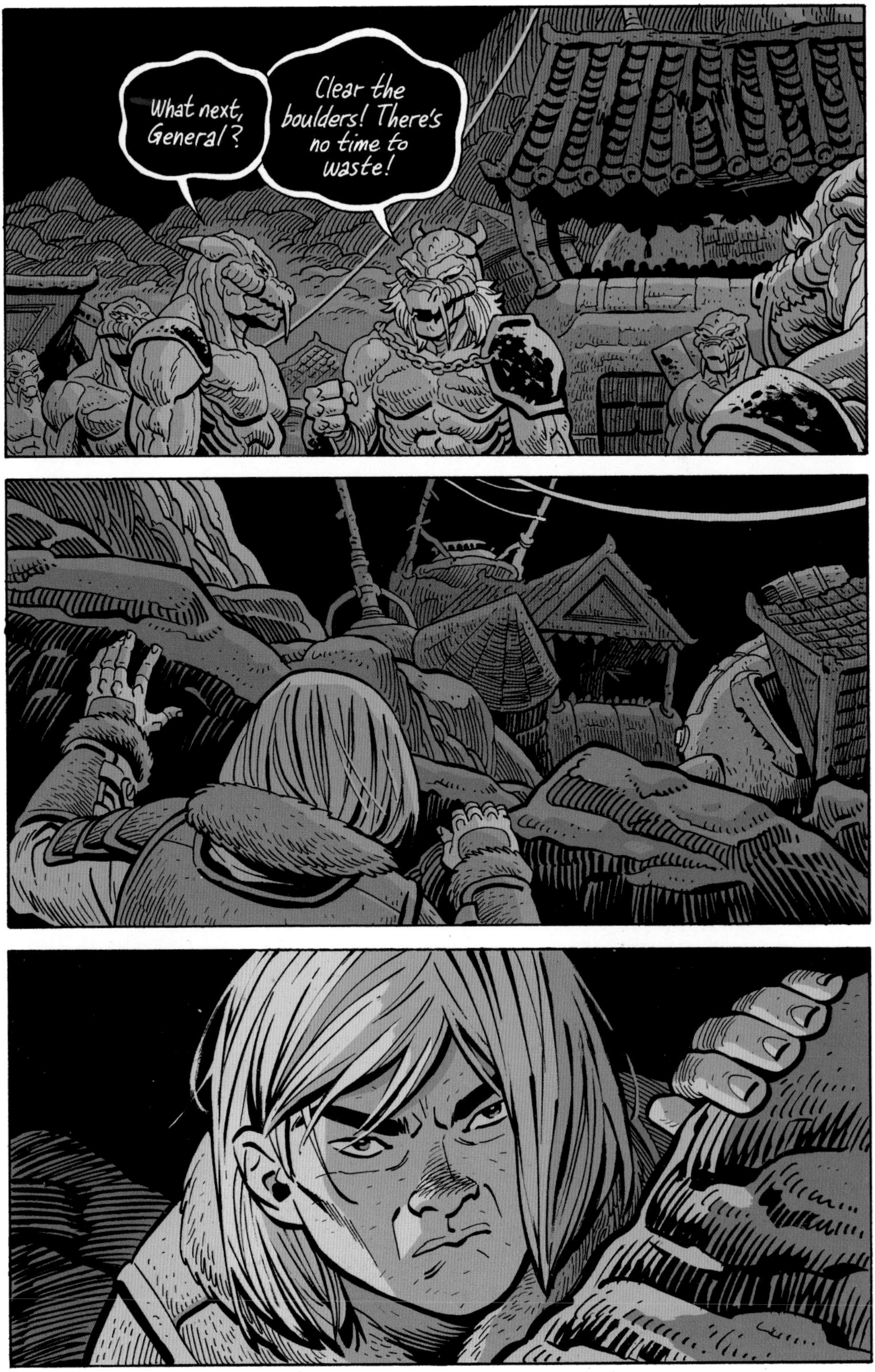
What next, General?
Clear the boulders! There's no time to waste!

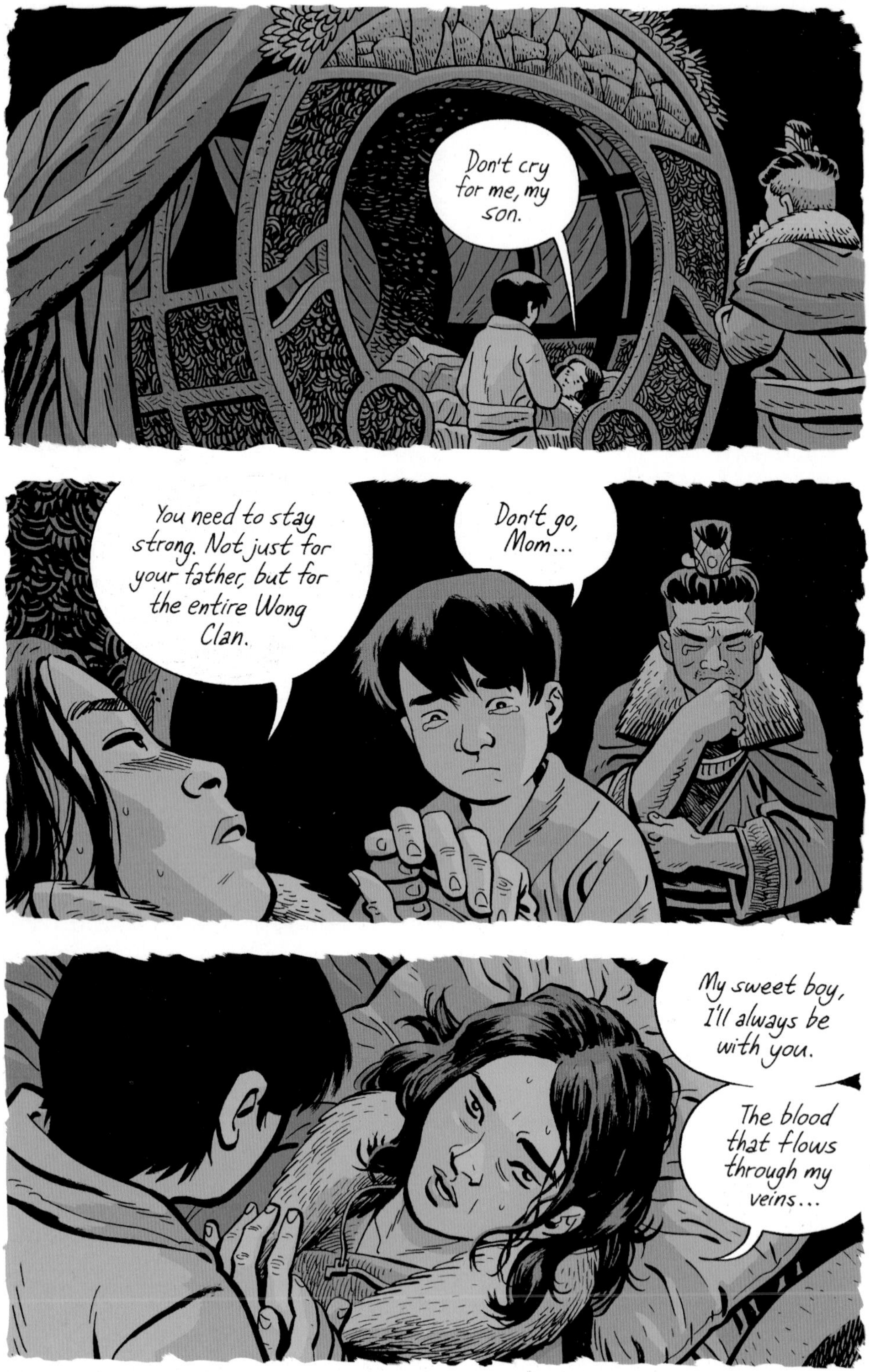
Don't cry for me, my son.
You need to stay strong. Not just for your father, but for the entire Wong Clan.
Don't go, Mom...
My sweet boy, I'll always be with you.
The blood that flows through my veins...

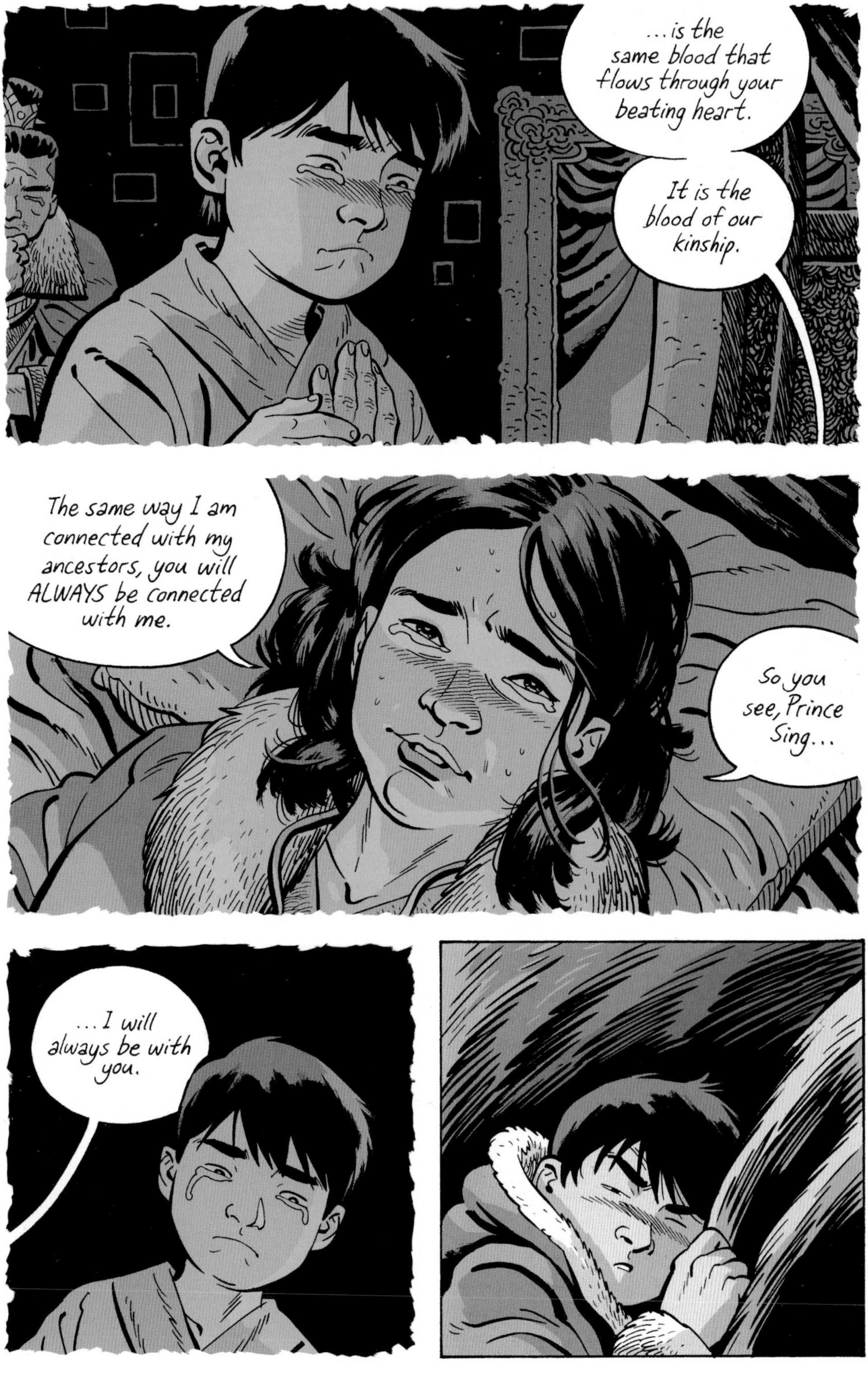
...is the same blood that flows through your beating heart.
It is the blood of our kinship.
The same way I am connected with my ancestors, you will ALWAYS be connected with me.
So you see, Prince Sing...
...I will always be with you.

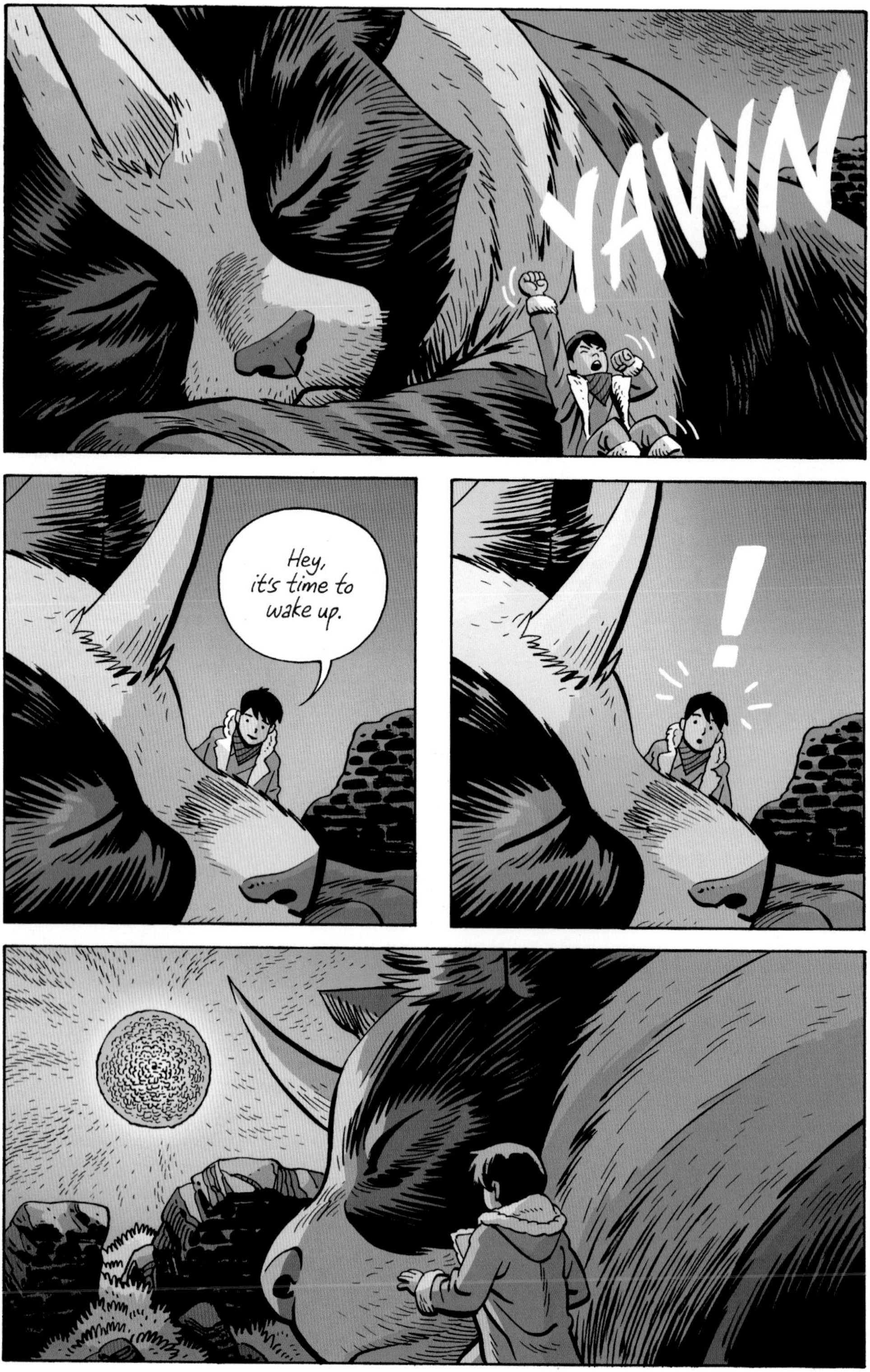
YAWN
Hey, it's time to wake up.
!

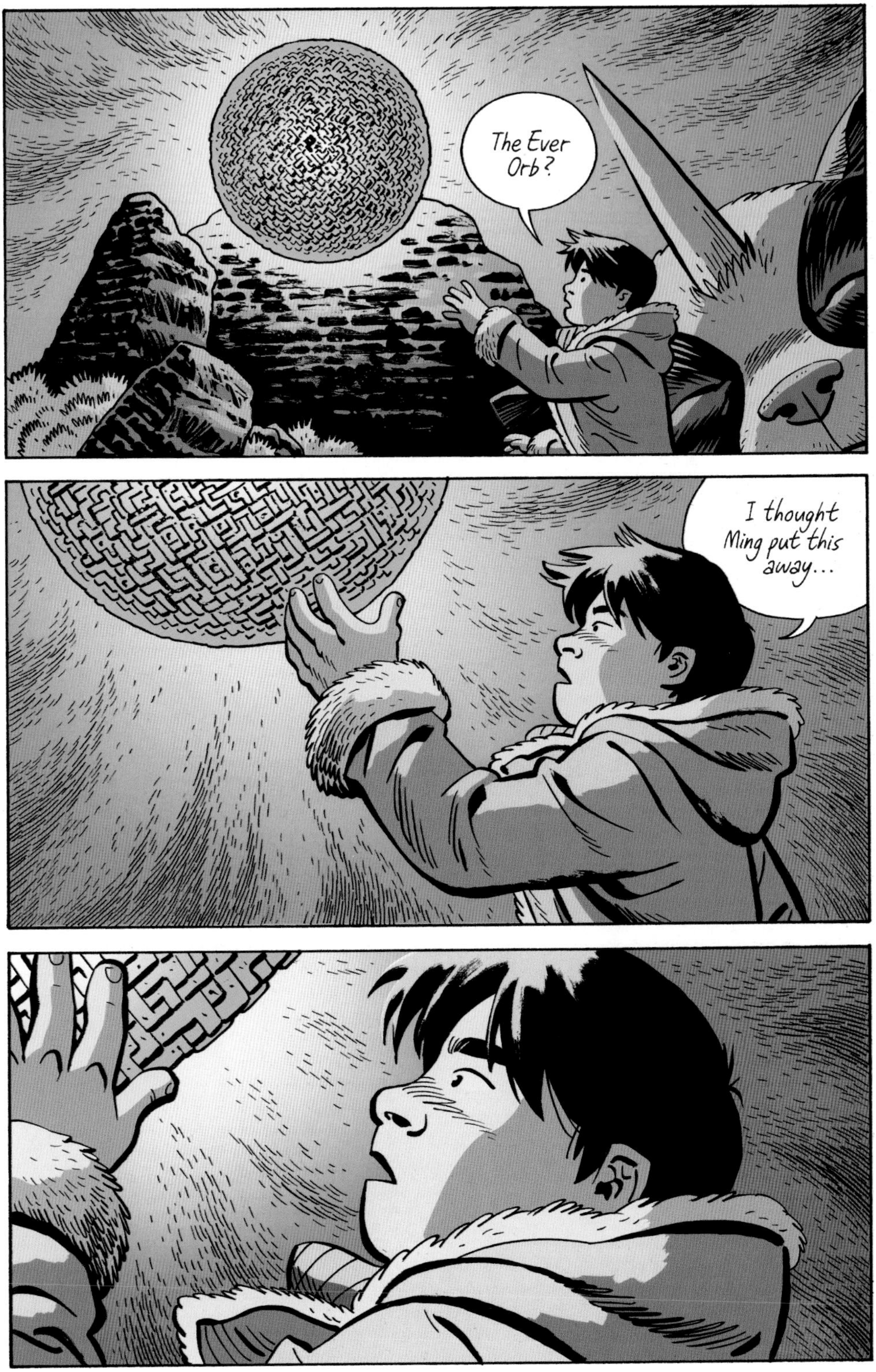
The Ever Orb?
I thought Ming put this away...

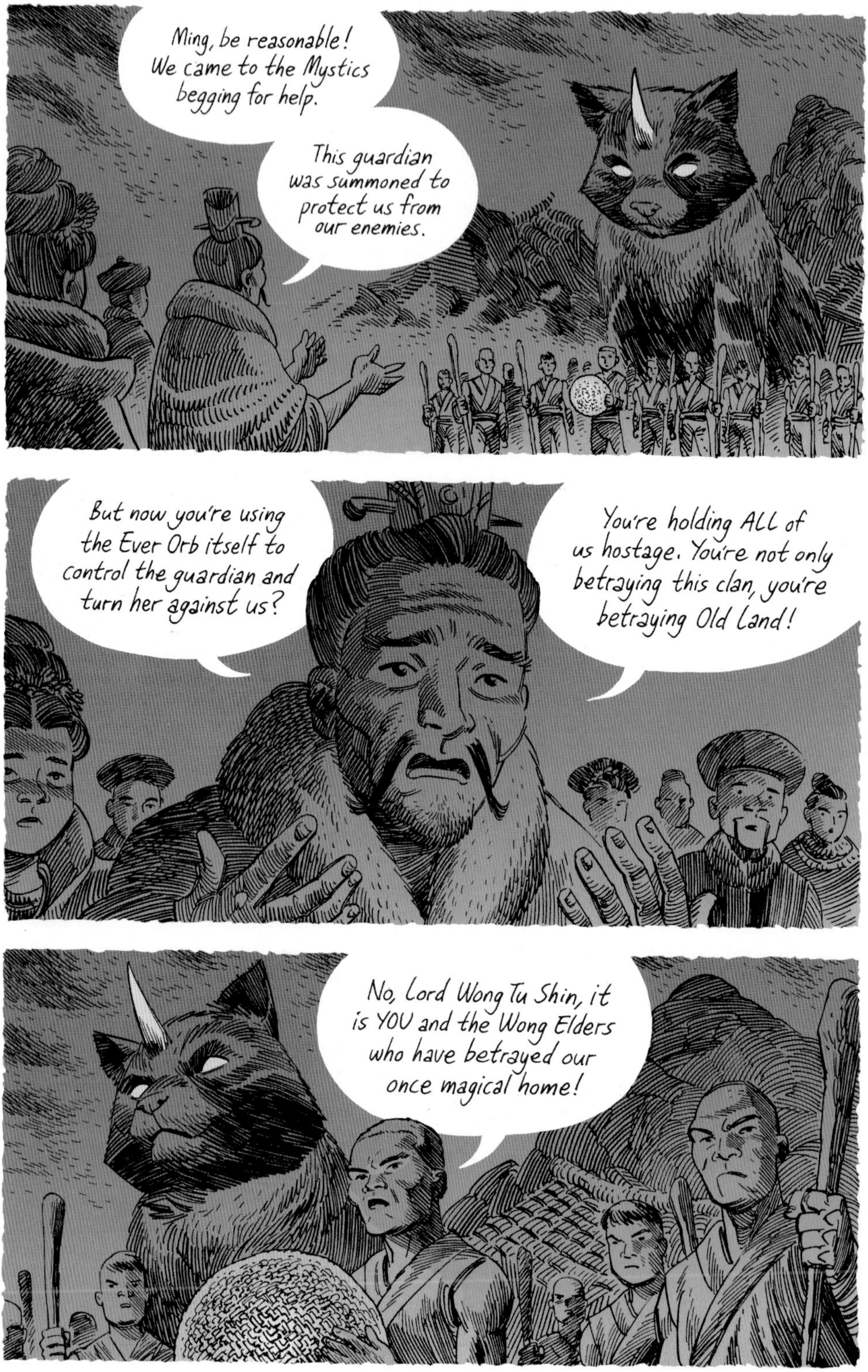
Ming, be reasonable! We came to the Mystics begging for help.
This guardian was summoned to protect us from our enemies.
But now you're using the Ever Orb itself to control the guardian and turn her against us?
You're holding ALL of us hostage. You're not only betraying this clan, you're betraying Old Land!
No, Lord Wong Tu Shin, it is YOU and the Wong Elders who have betrayed our once magical home!

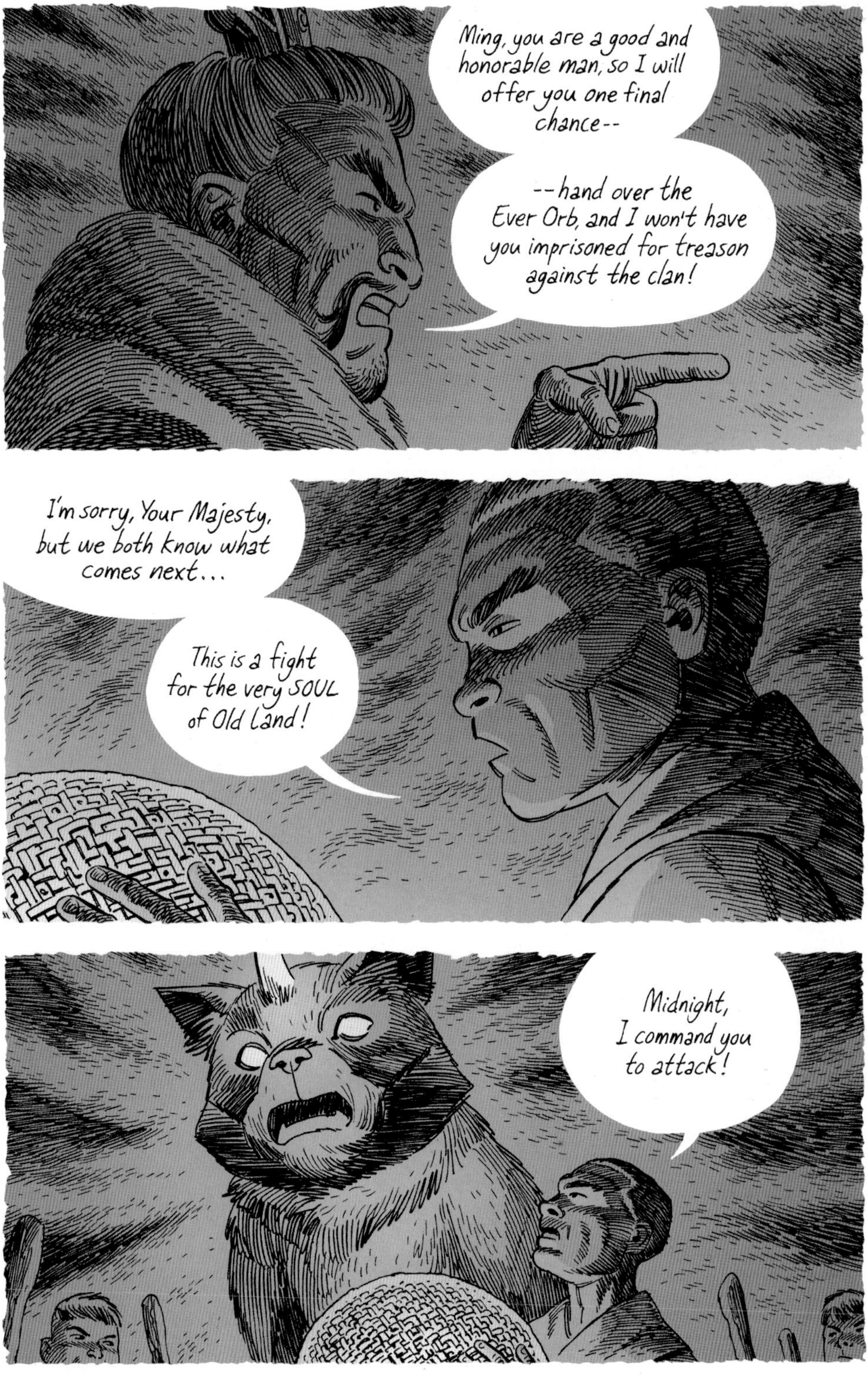
Ming, you are a good and honorable man, so I will offer you one final chance--
--hand over the Ever Orb, and I won't have you imprisoned for treason against the clan!
I'm sorry, Your Majesty, but we both know what comes next...
This is a fight for the very SOUL of Old Land!
Midnight, I command you to attack!

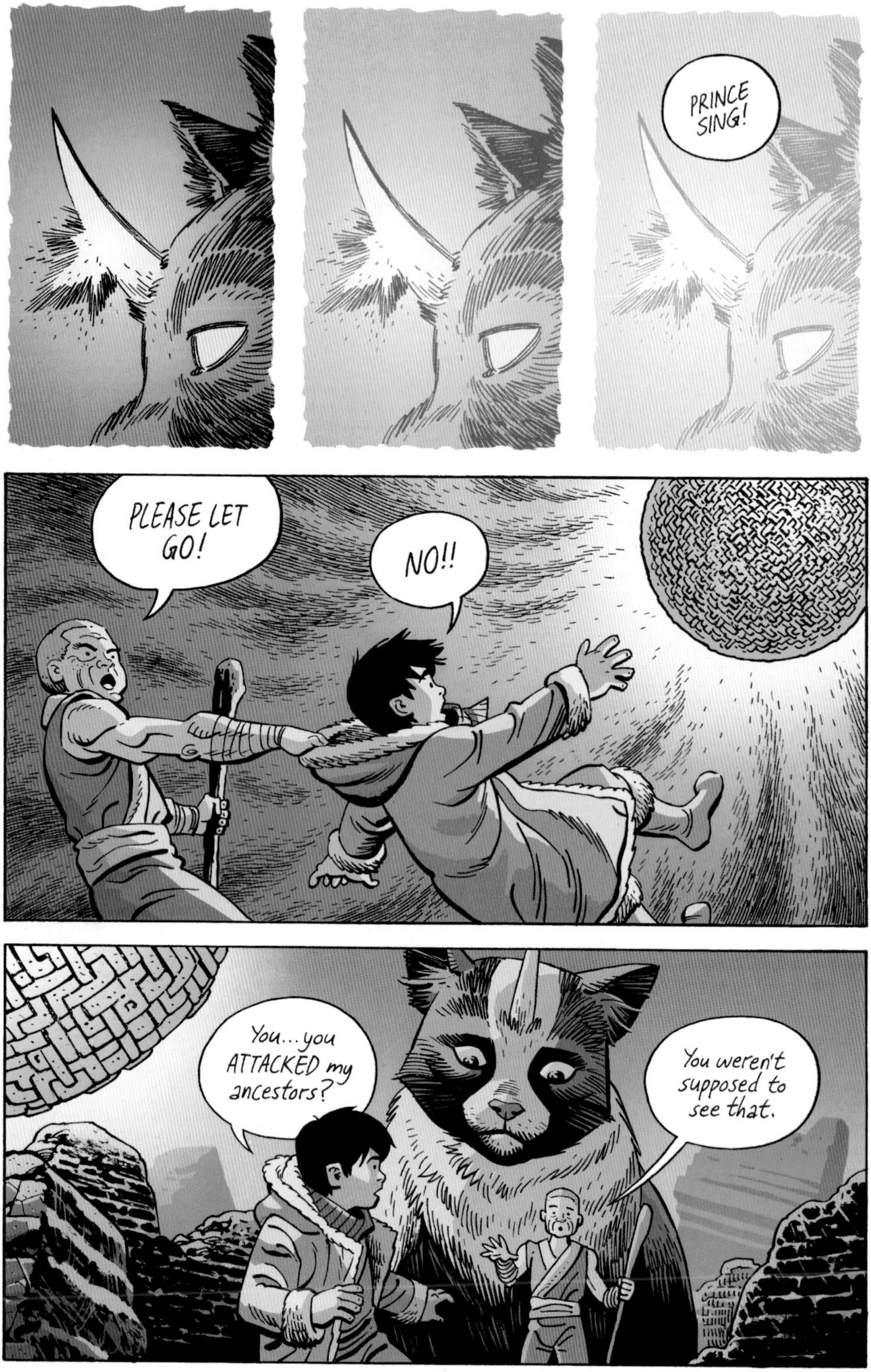
PRINCE SING!
PLEASE LET GO!
NO!!
You...you ATTACKED my ancestors?
You weren't supposed to see that.

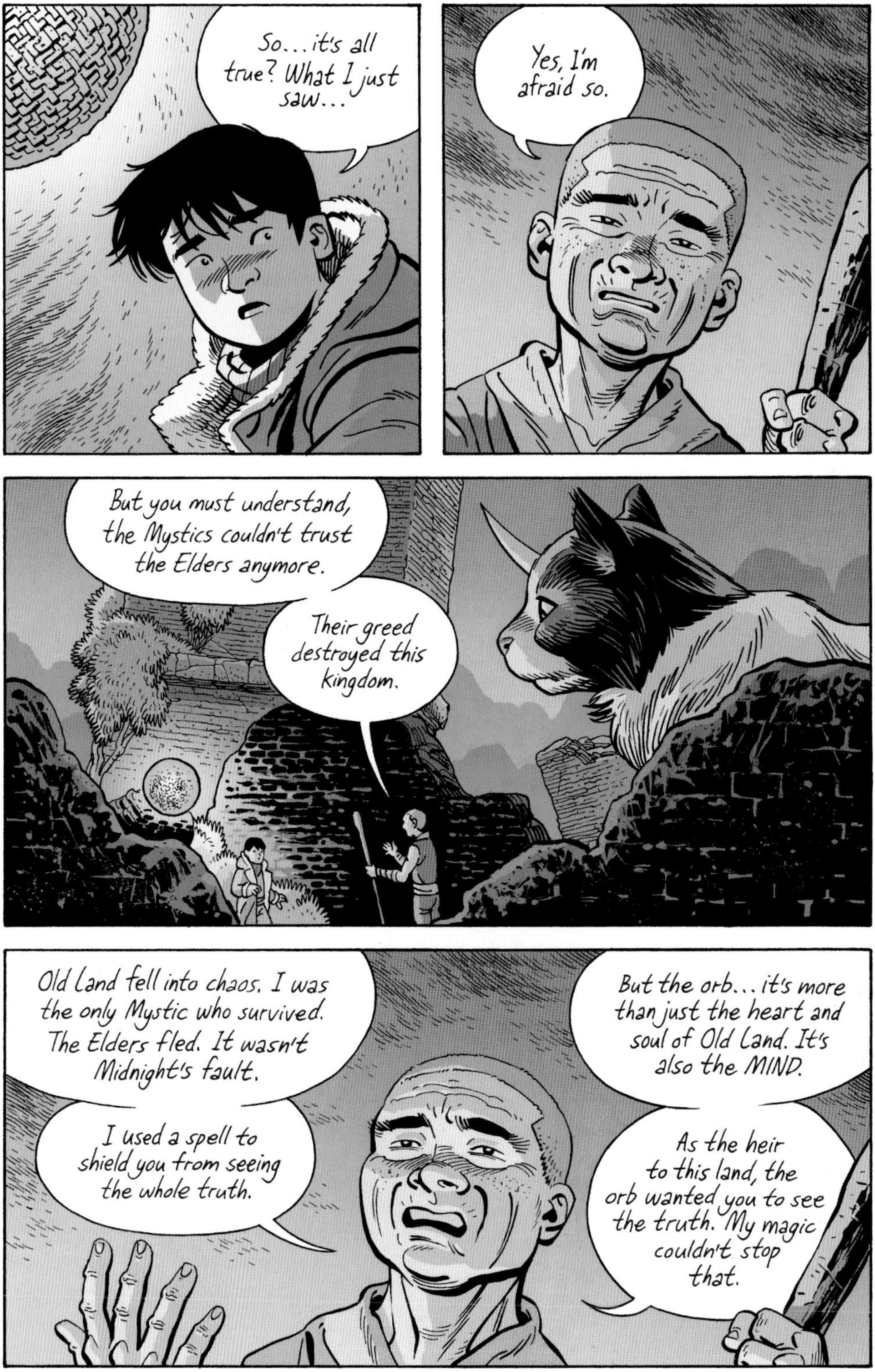
So... it's all true? What I just saw...
Yes, I'm afraid so.
But you must understand, the Mystics couldn't trust the Elders anymore.
Their greed destroyed this kingdom.
Old Land fell into chaos. I was the only Mystic who survived. The Elders fled. It wasn't Midnight's fault.
I used a spell to shield you from seeing the whole truth.
But the orb... it's more than just the heart and soul of Old Land. It's also the MIND.
As the heir to this land, the orb wanted you to see the truth. My magic couldn't stop that.

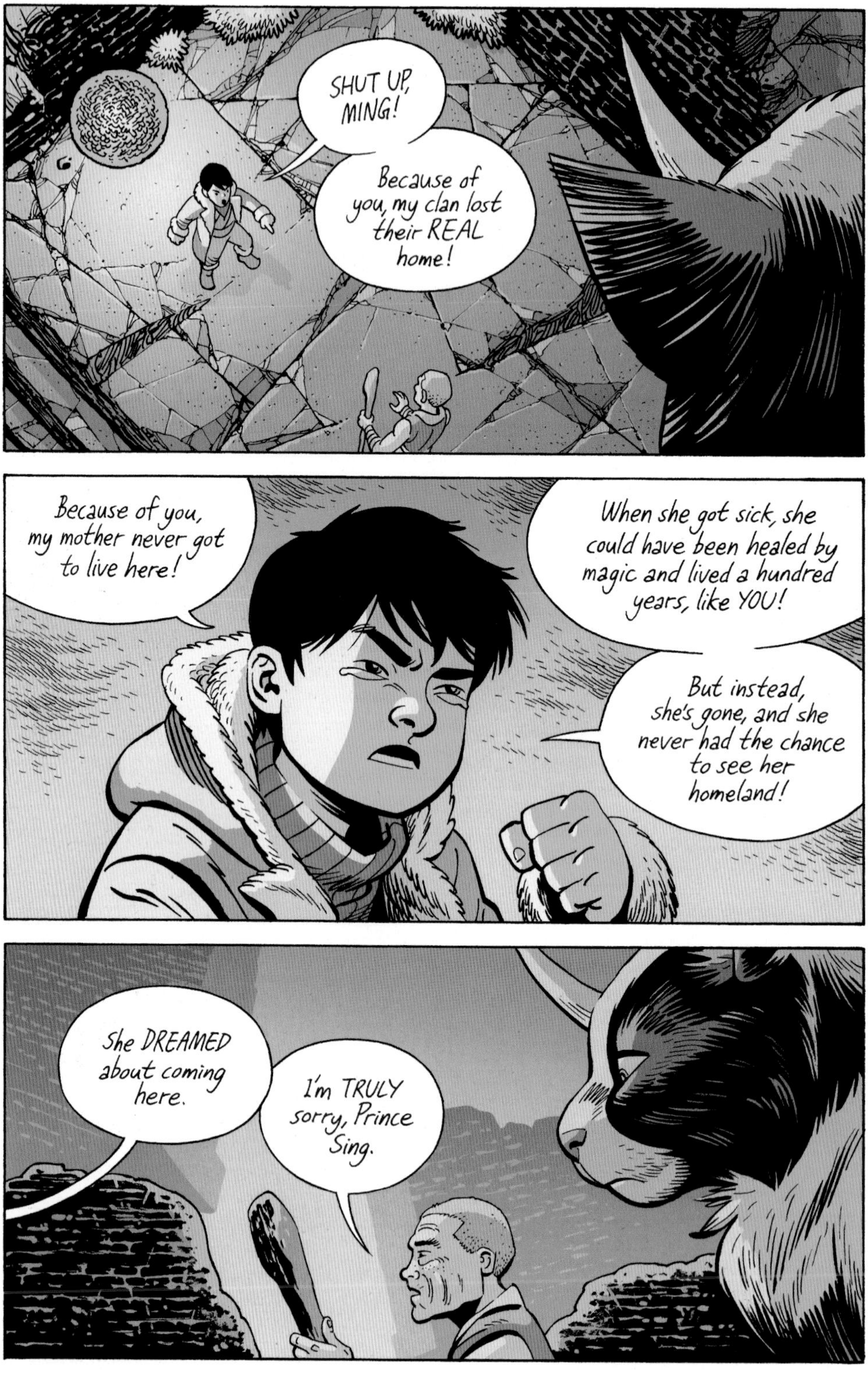
SHUT UP, MING!
Because of you, my clan lost their REAL home!
Because of you, my mother never got to live here!
When she got sick, she could have been healed by magic and lived a hundred years, like YOU!
But instead, she's gone, and she never had the chance to see her homeland!
She DREAMED about coming here.
I'm TRULY sorry, Prince Sing.

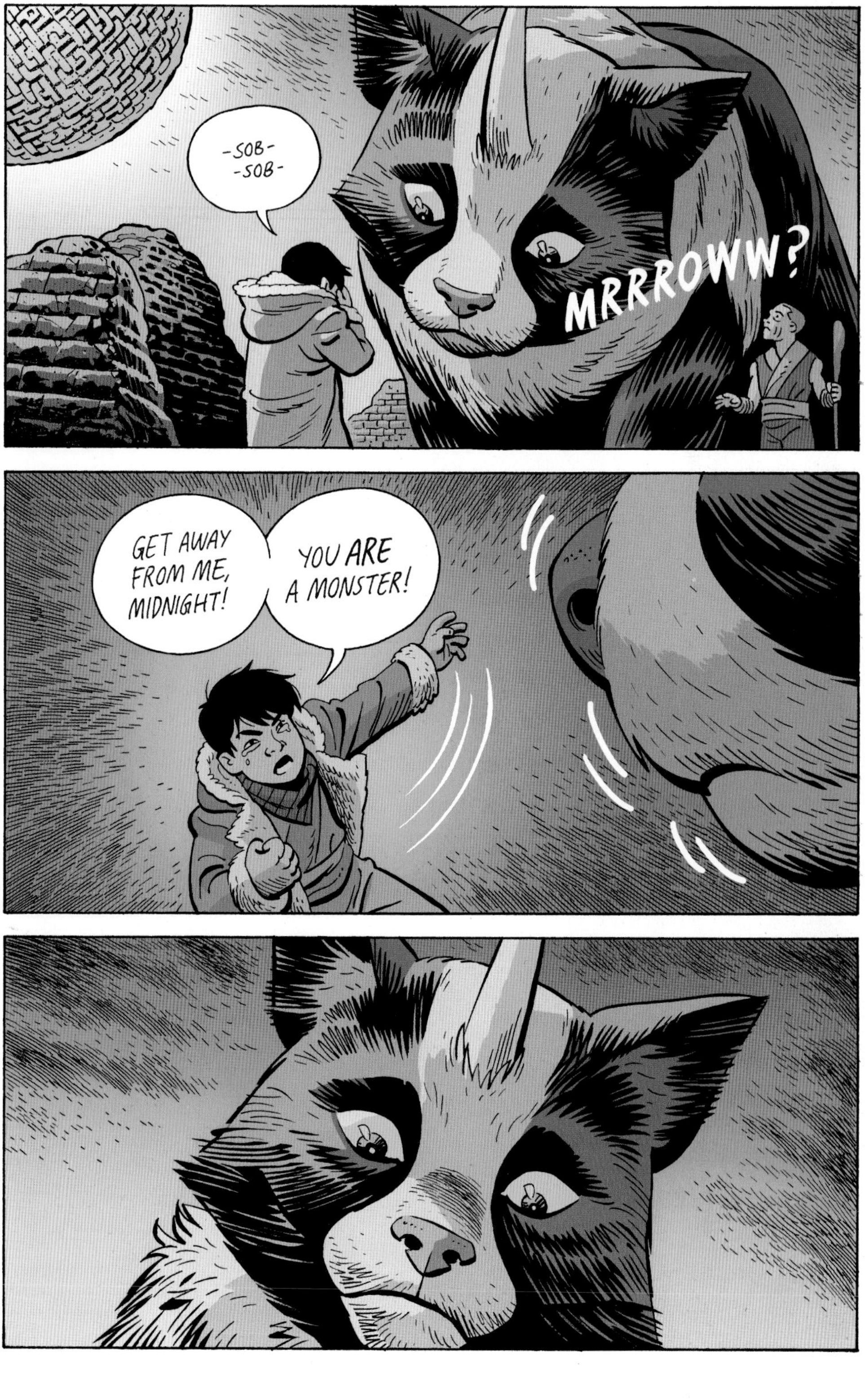
-SOB-
-SOB-
MRRROWW?
GET AWAY FROM ME, MIDNIGHT!
YOU ARE A MONSTER!

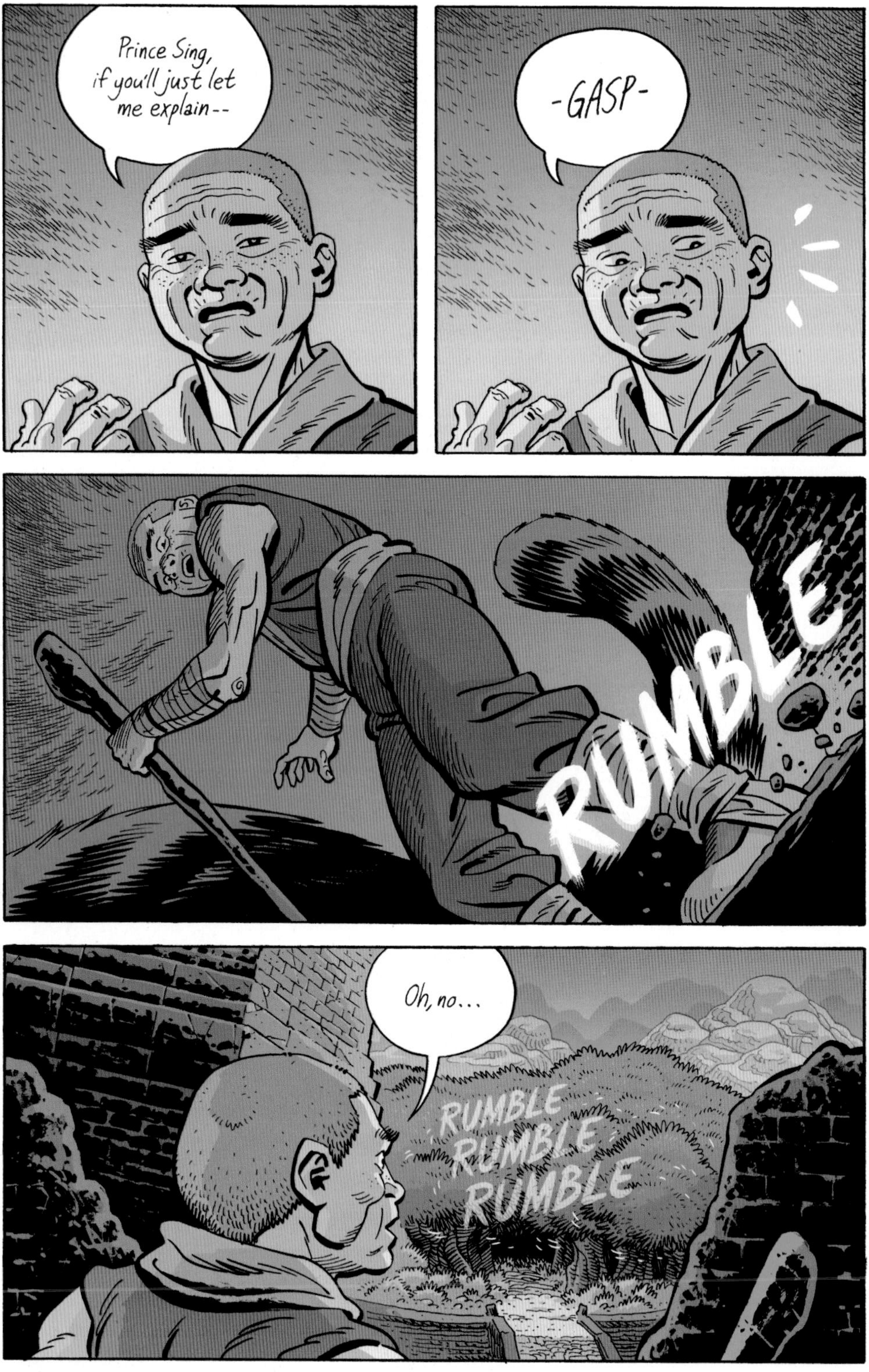
Prince Sing, if you'll just let me explain--
-GASP-
RUMBLE
Oh, no...
RUMBLE RUMBLE RUMBLE

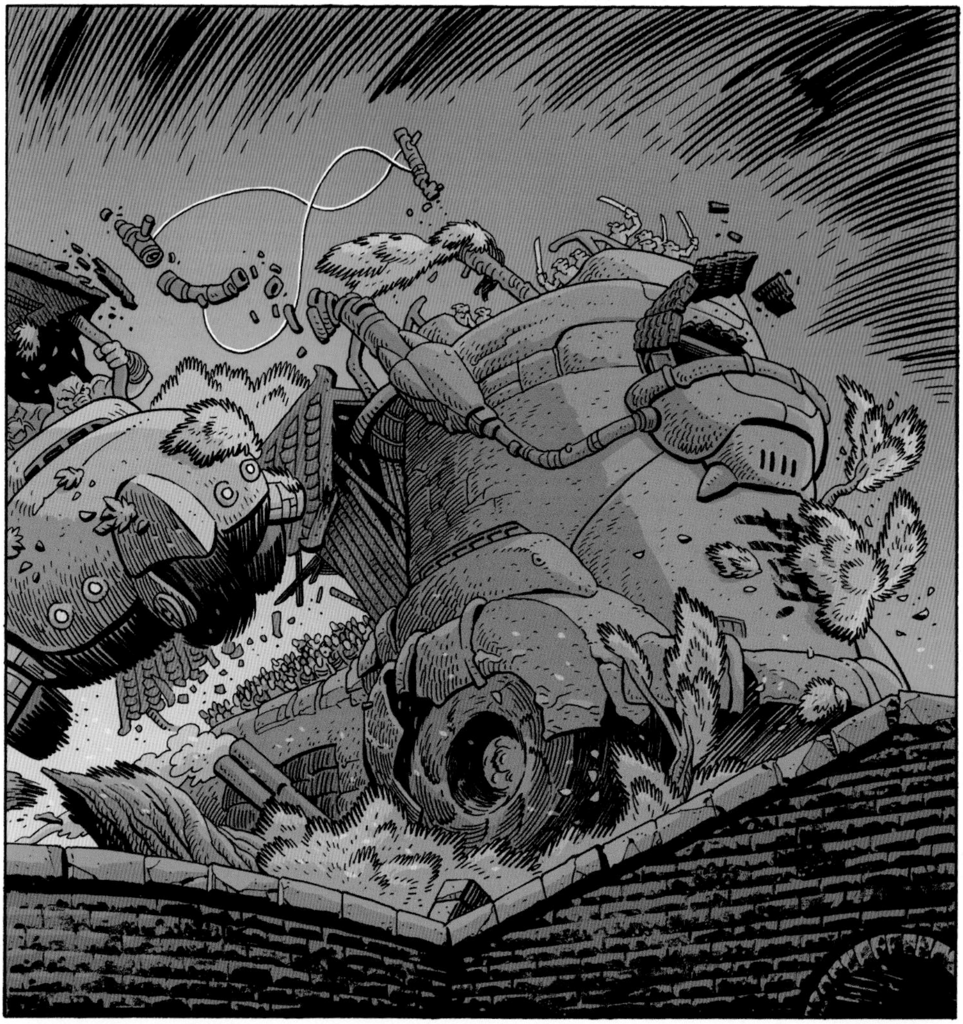

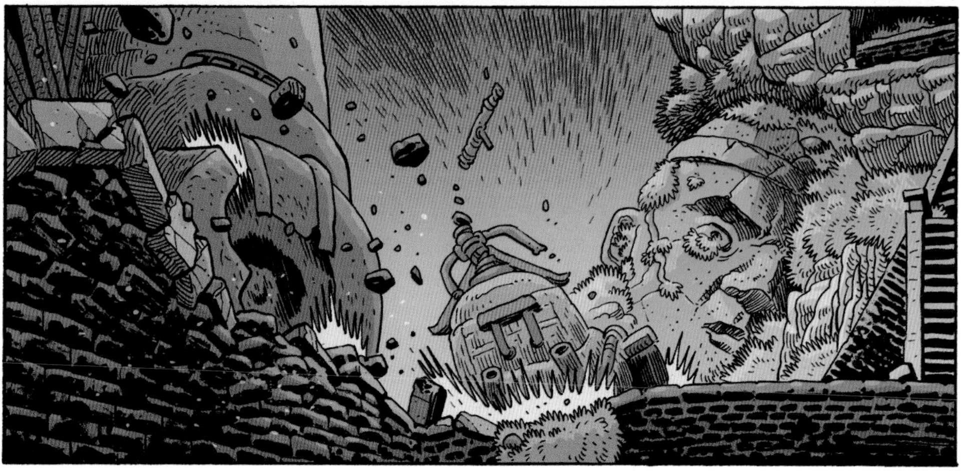

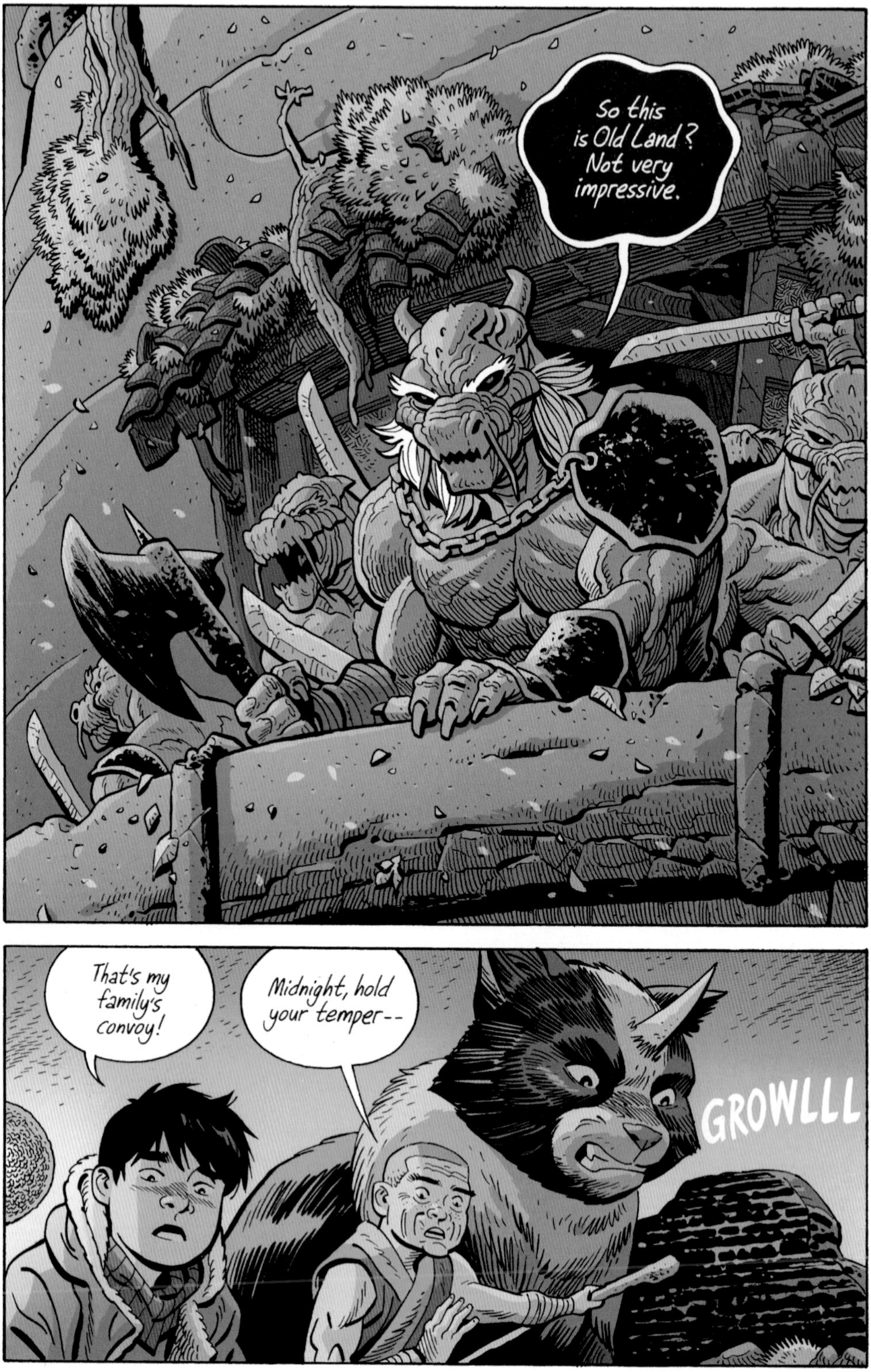

So this is Old Land? Not very impressive.
That's my family's convoy!
Midnight, hold your temper--
GROWLLL

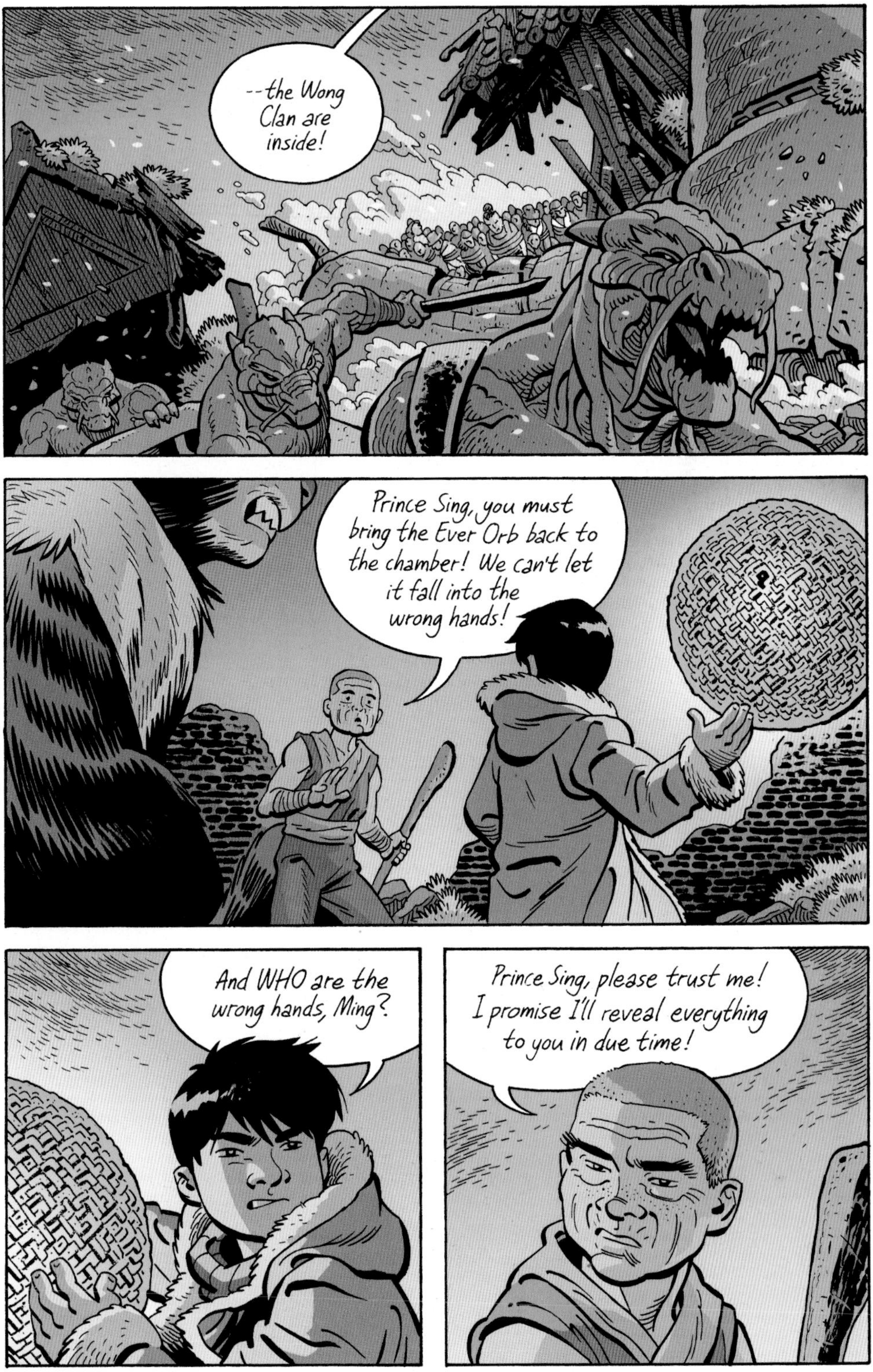
--the Wong Clan are inside!
Prince Sing, you must bring the Ever Orb back to the chamber! We can't let it fall into the wrong hands!
And WHO are the wrong hands, Ming?
Prince Sing, please trust me! I promise I'll reveal everything to you in due time!

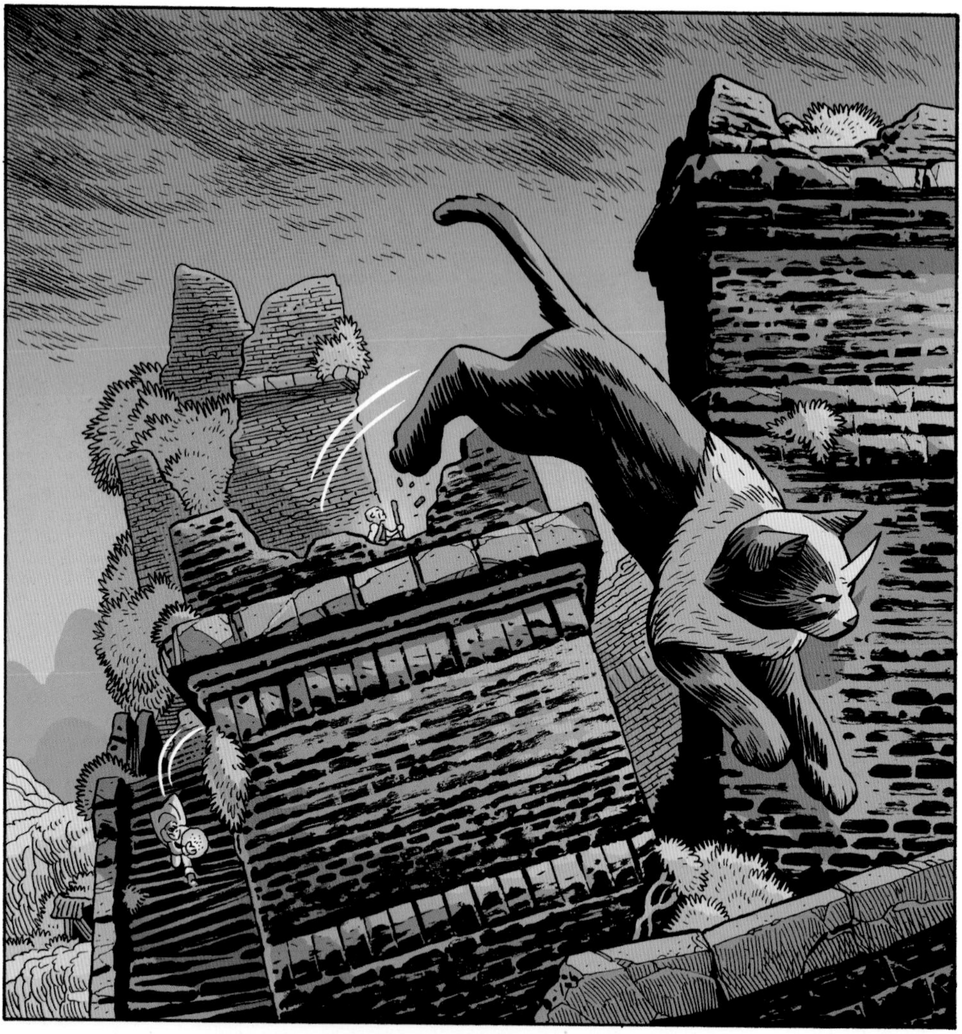

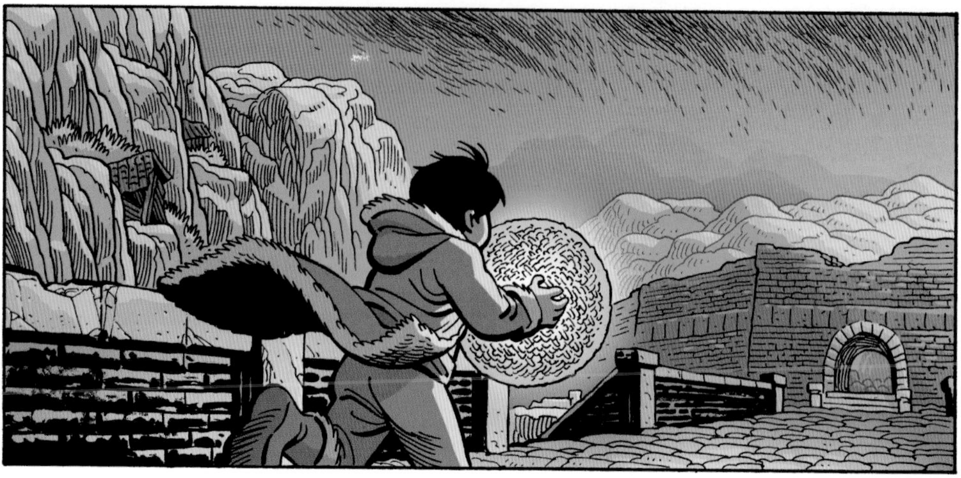

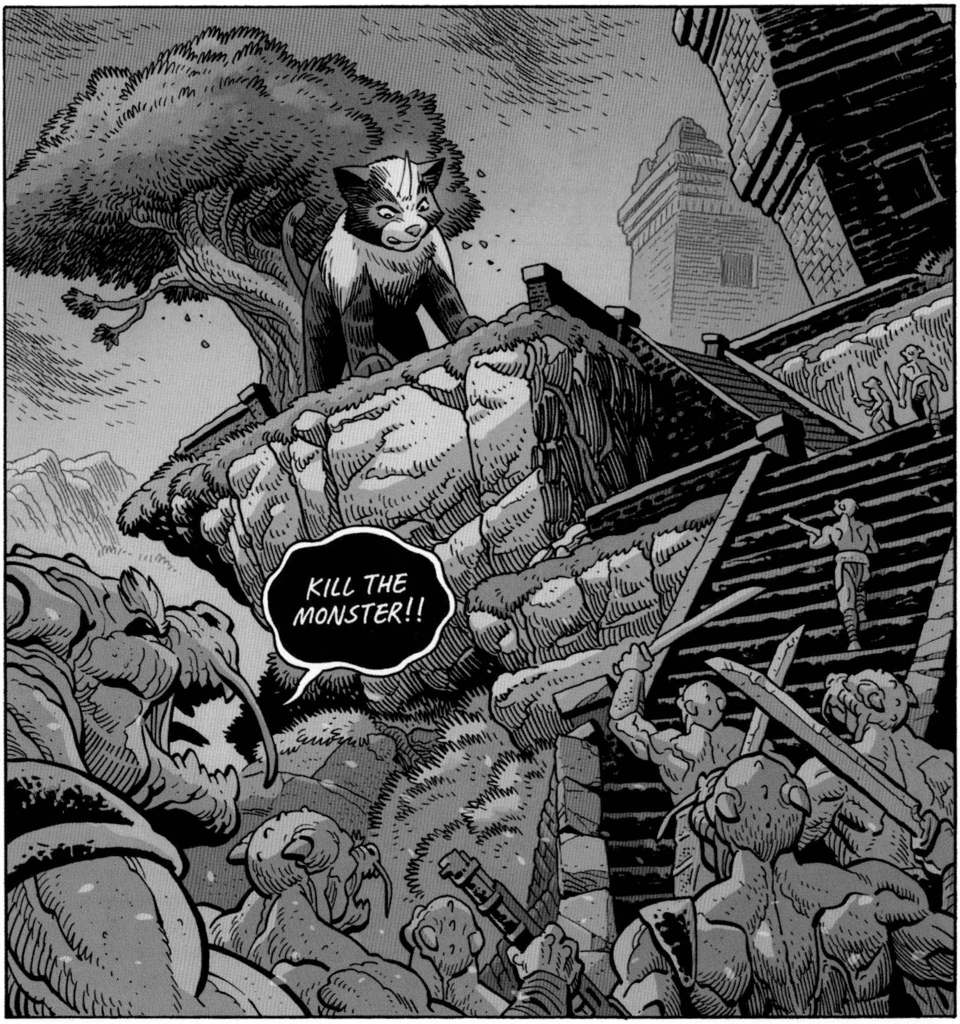
KILL THE MONSTER!!

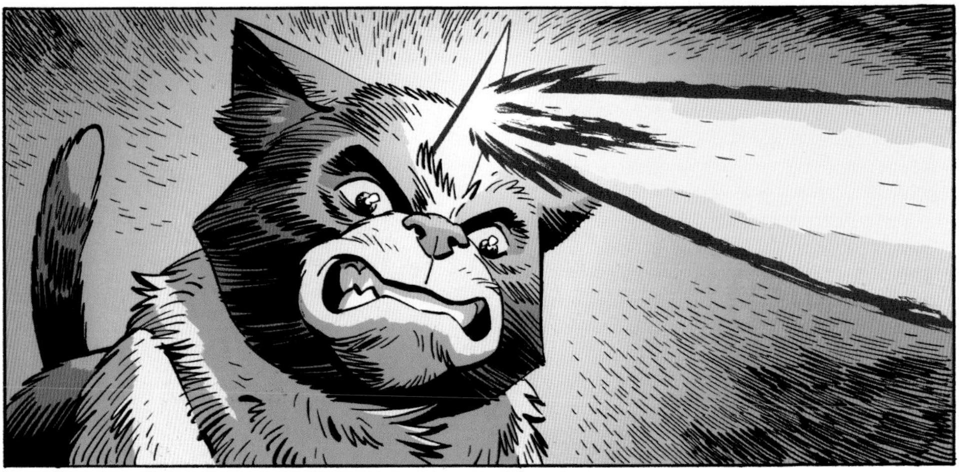

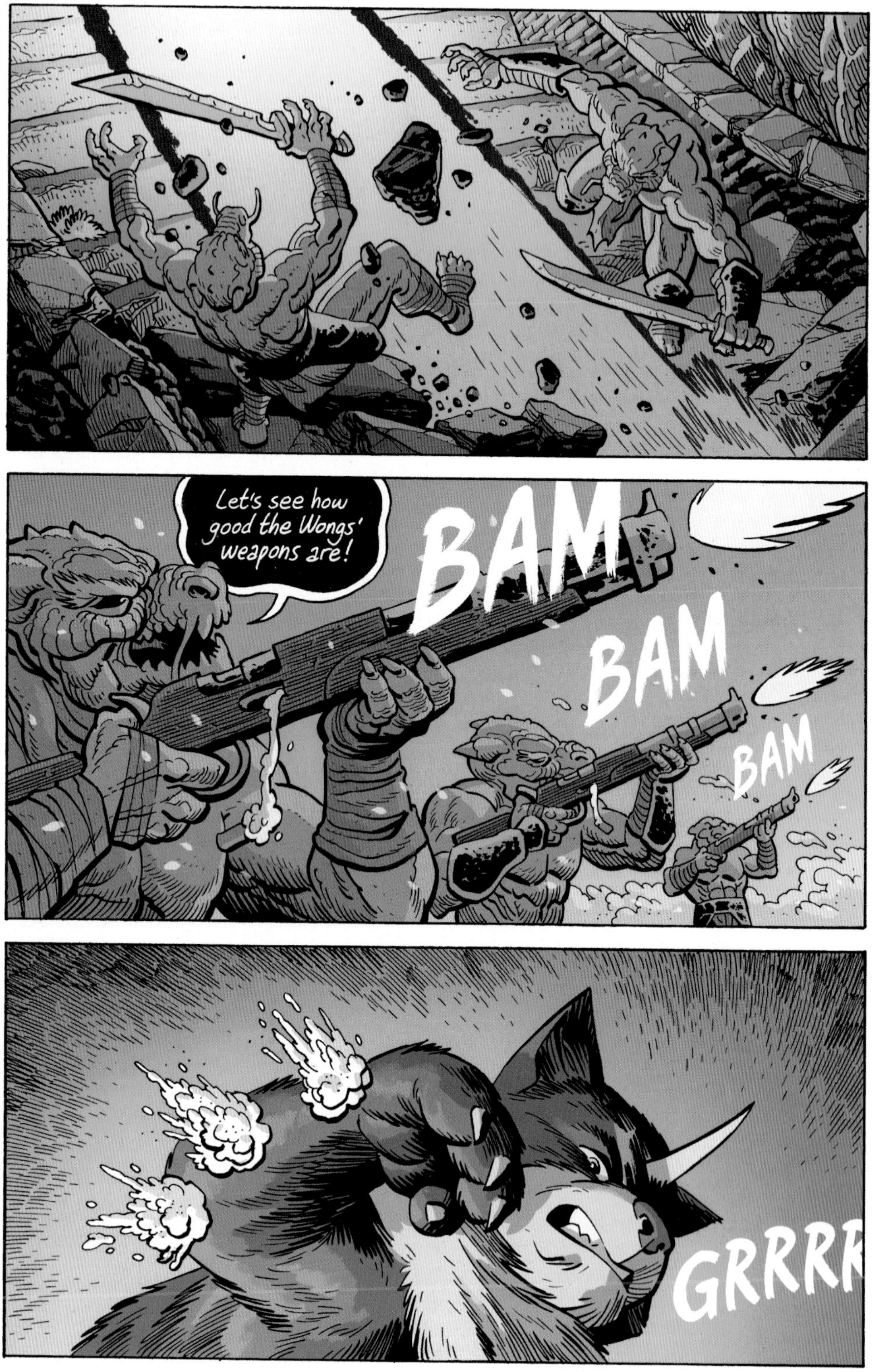
Let's see how good the Wongs' weapons are!
BAM
BAM
BAM
GRRRR

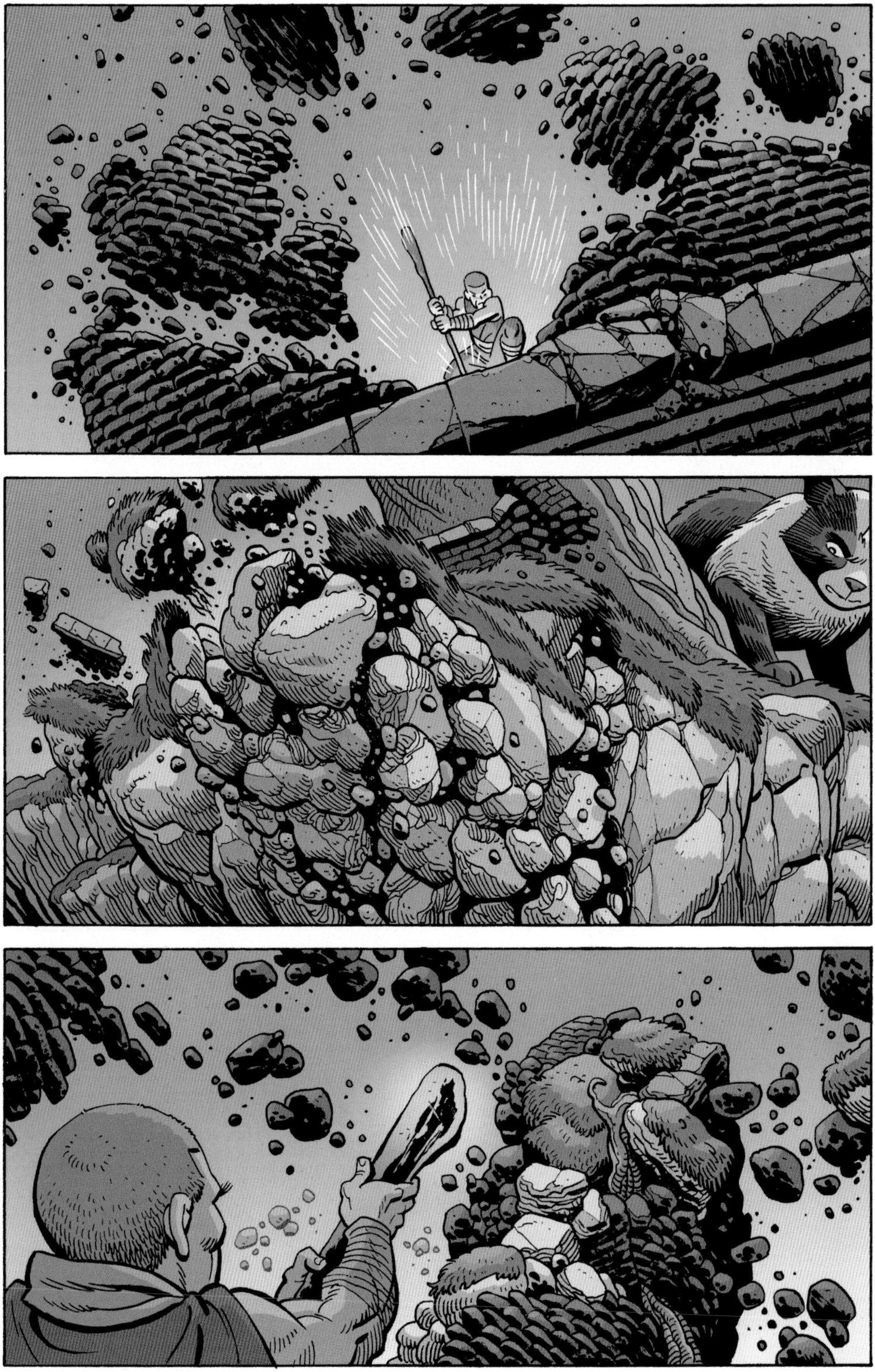

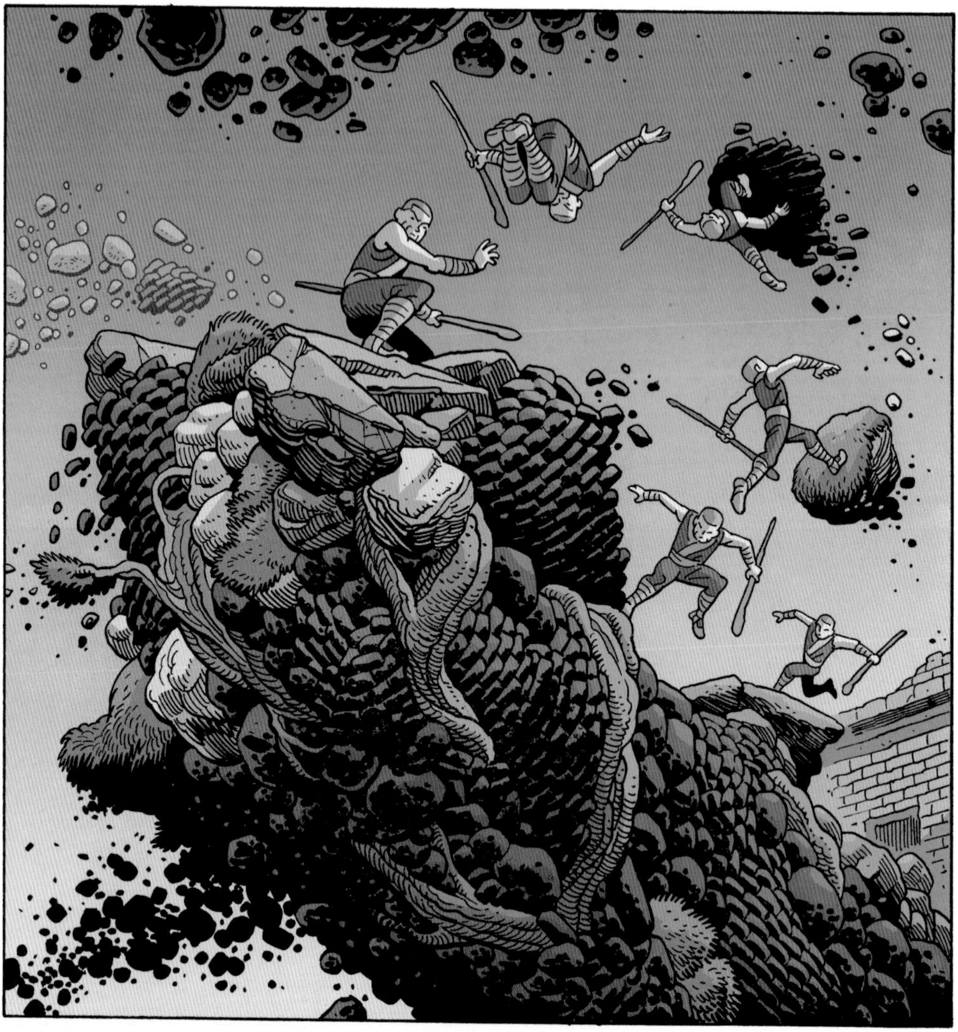

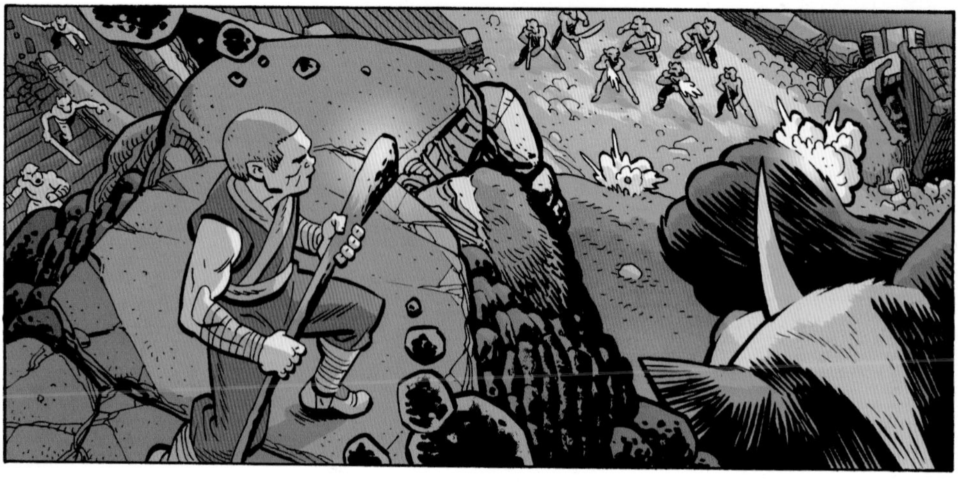

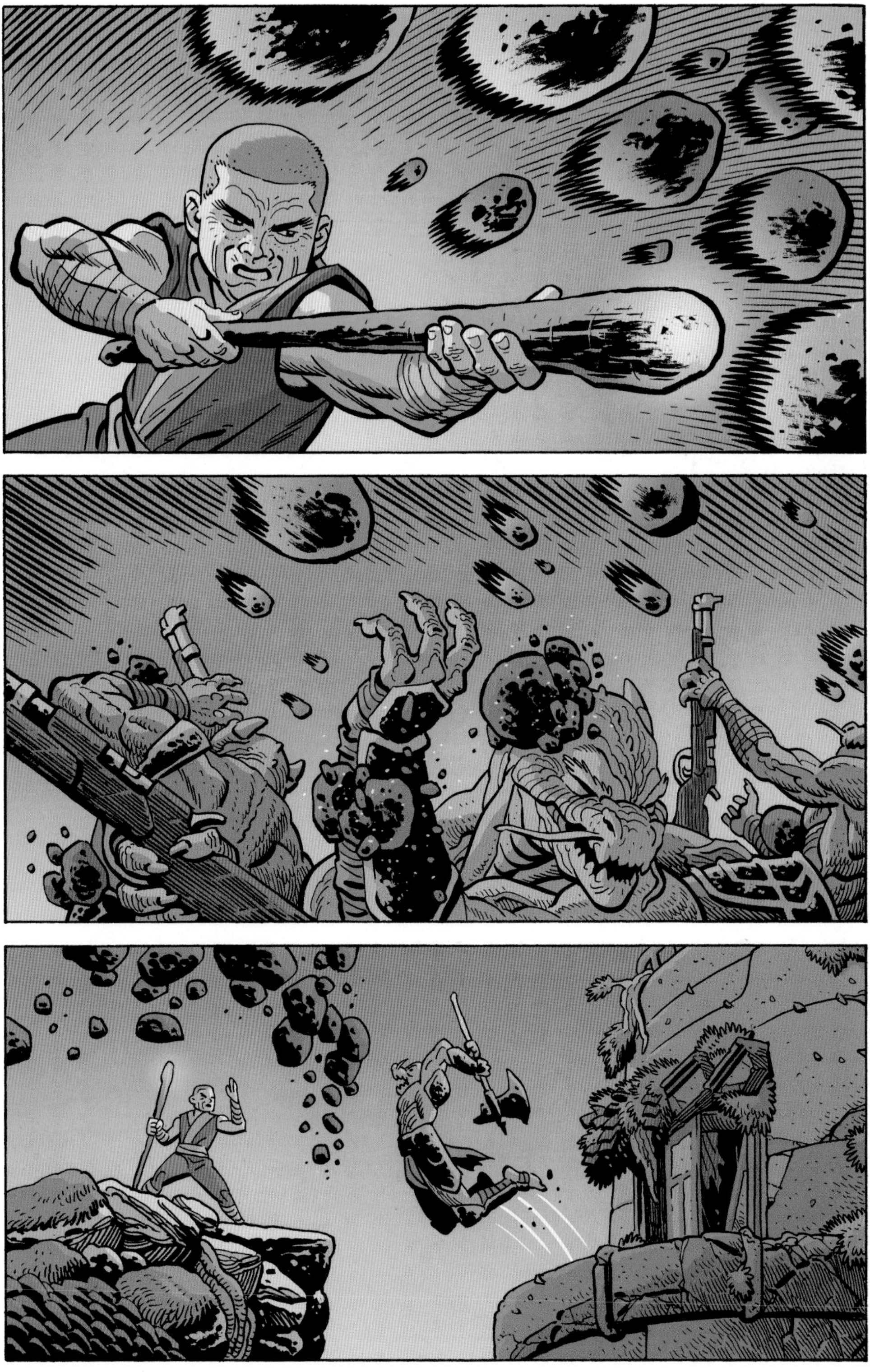

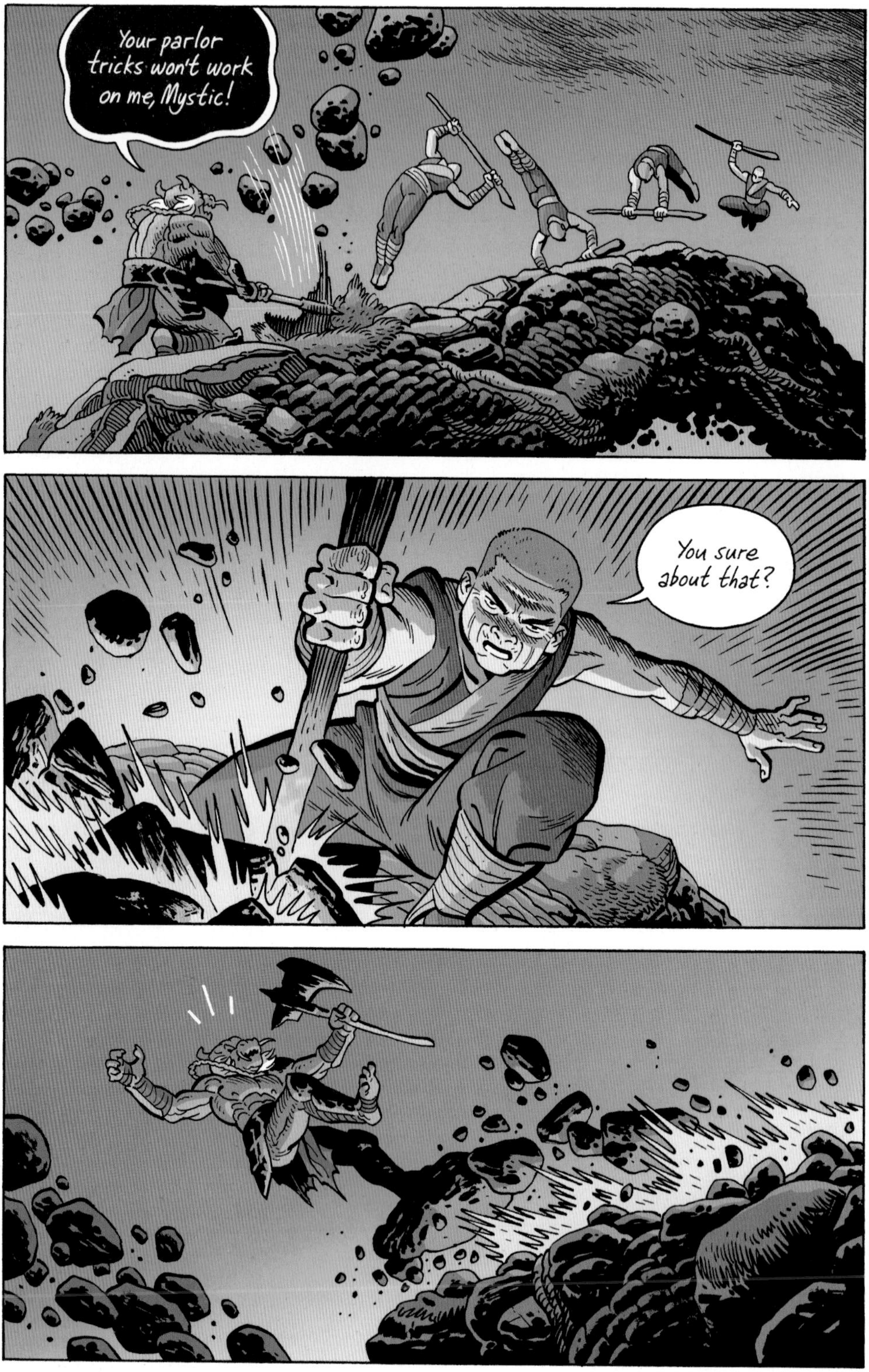
Your parlor tricks won't work on me, Mystic!
You sure about that?

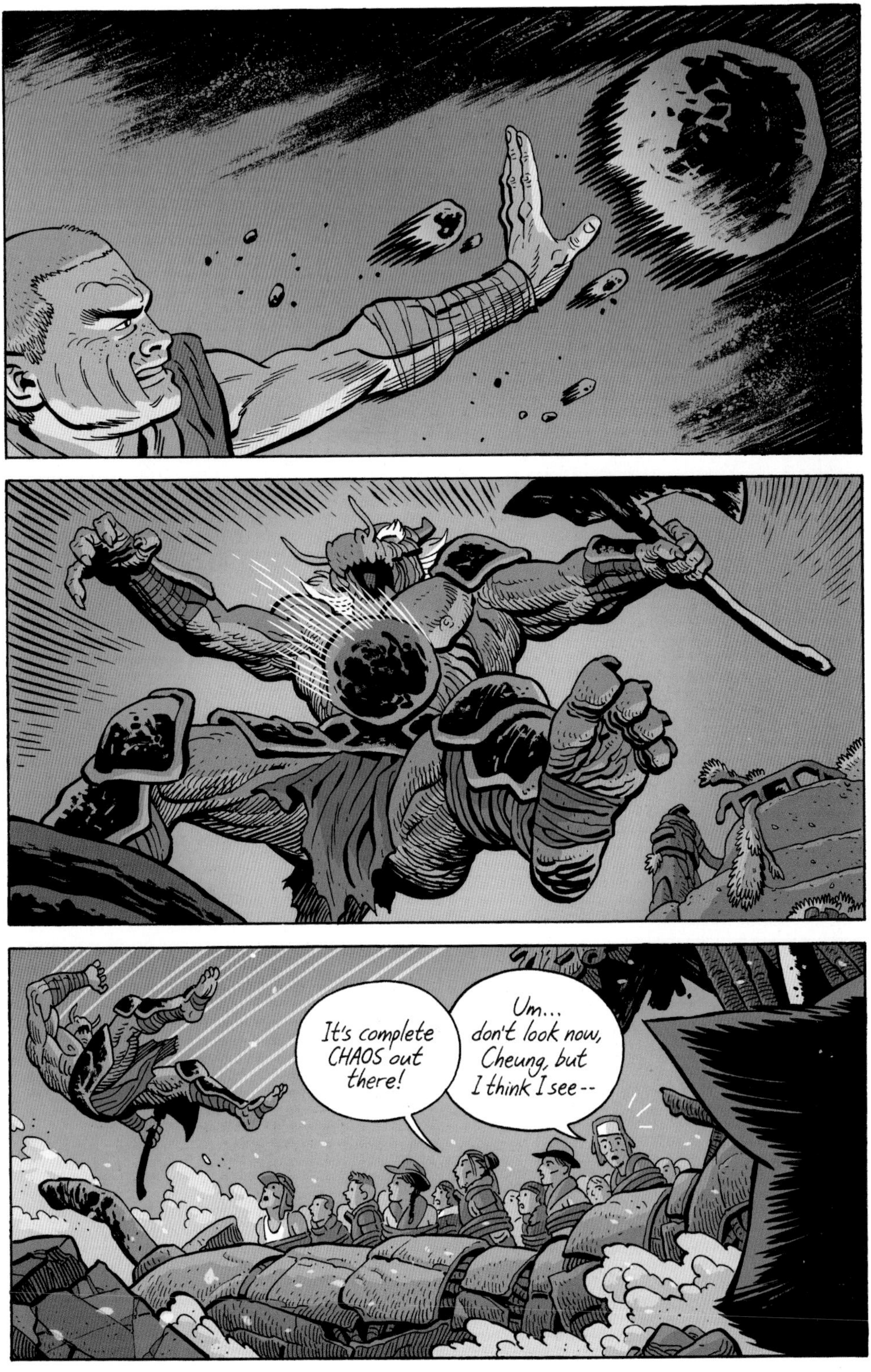
It's complete CHAOS out there!
Um... don't look now, Cheung, but I think I see--

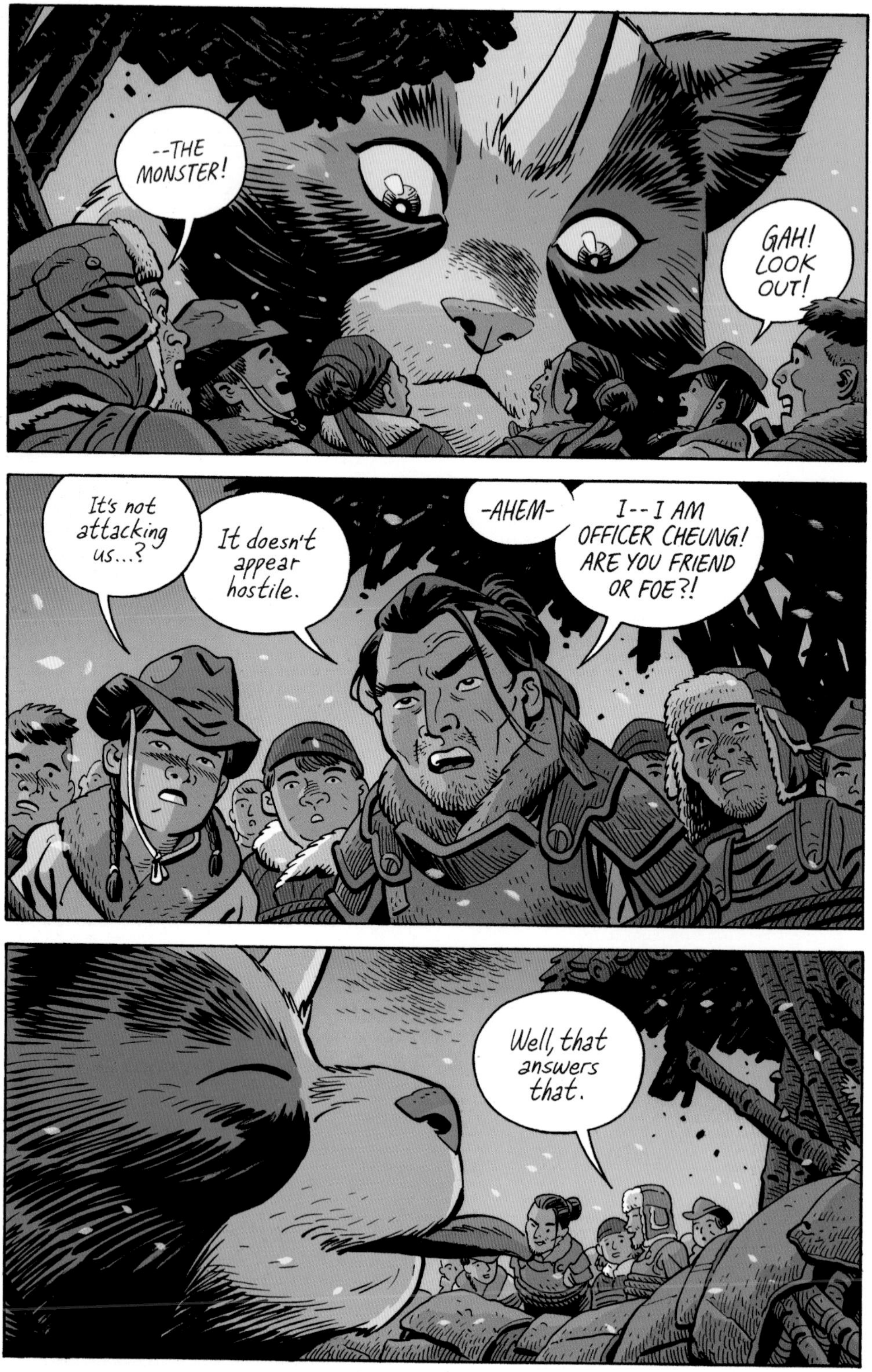
--THE MONSTER!
GAH! LOOK OUT!
It's not attacking us...?
It doesn't appear hostile.
-AHEM-
I--I AM OFFICER CHEUNG! ARE YOU FRIEND OR FOE?!
Well, that answers that.

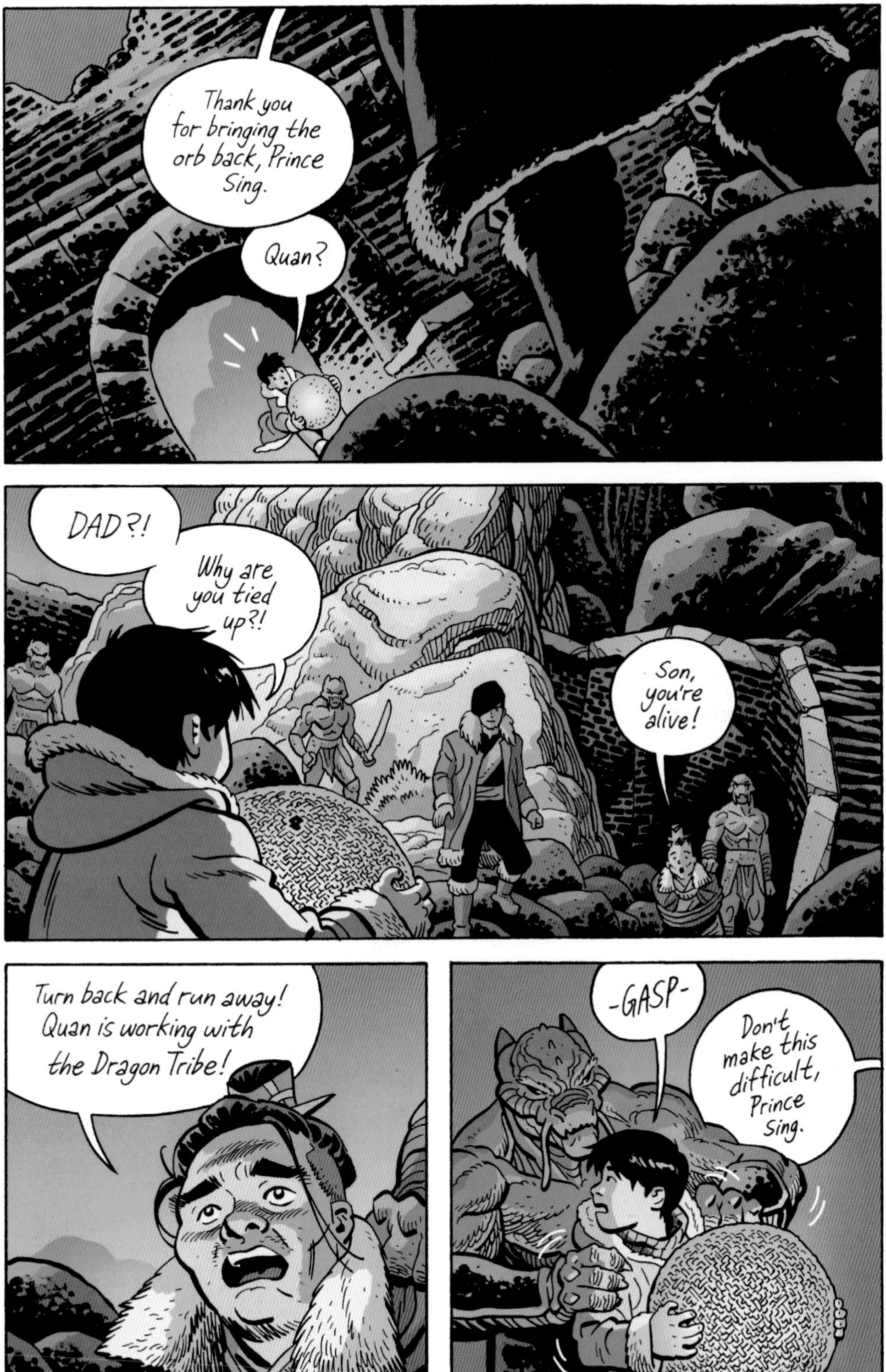
Thank you for bringing the orb back, Prince Sing.
Quan?
DAD?!
Why are you tied up?!
Son, you're alive!
Turn back and run away! Quan is working with the Dragon Tribe!
-GASP-
Don't make this difficult, Prince Sing.

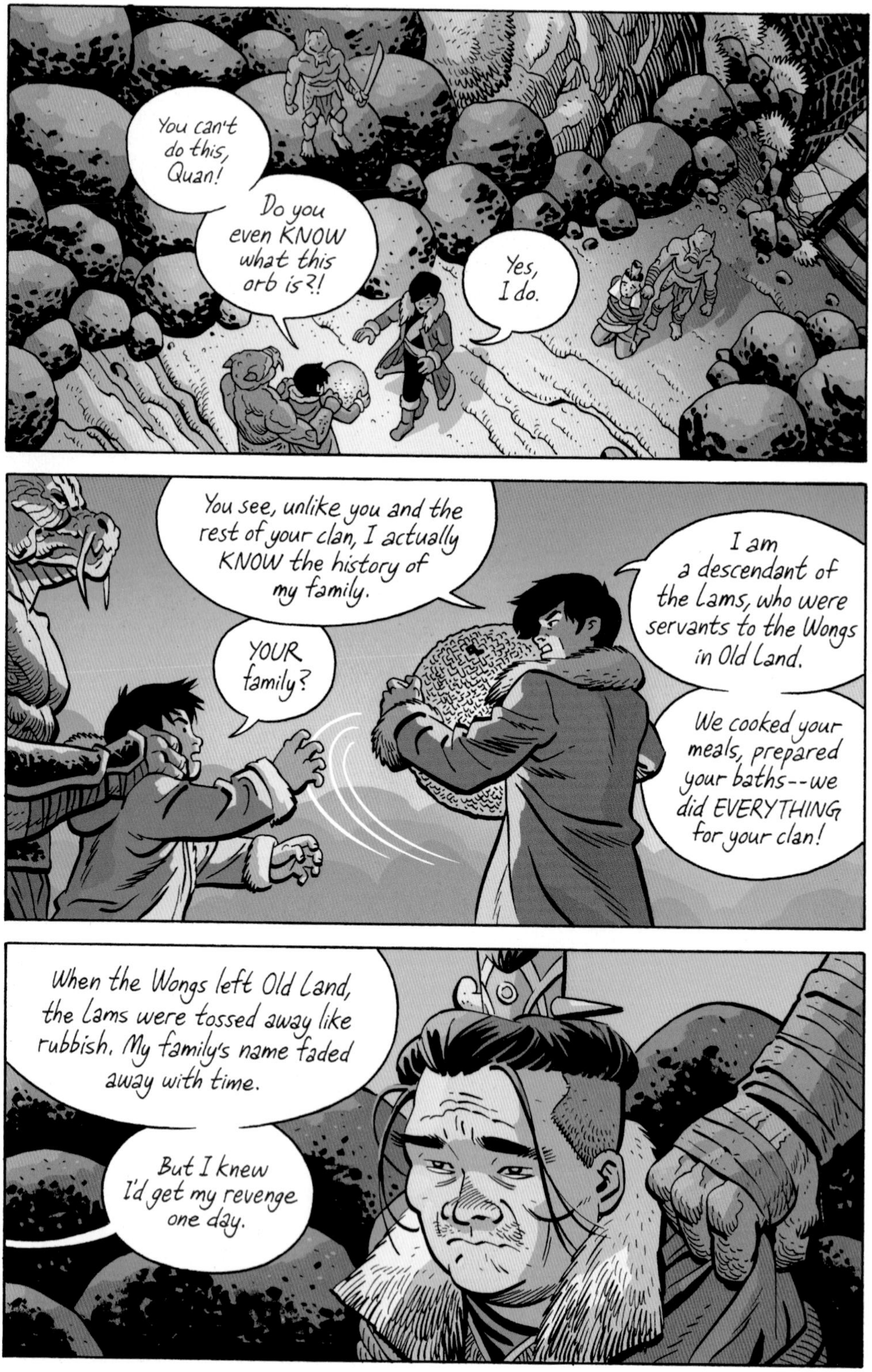
You can't do this, Quan!
Do you even KNOW what this orb is?!
Yes, I do.
You see, unlike you and the rest of your clan, I actually KNOW the history of my family.
YOUR family?
I am a descendant of the Lams, who were servants to the Wongs in Old Land.
We cooked your meals, prepared your baths--we did EVERYTHING for your clan!
When the Wongs left Old Land, the Lams were tossed away like rubbish. My family's name faded away with time.
But I knew I'd get my revenge one day.

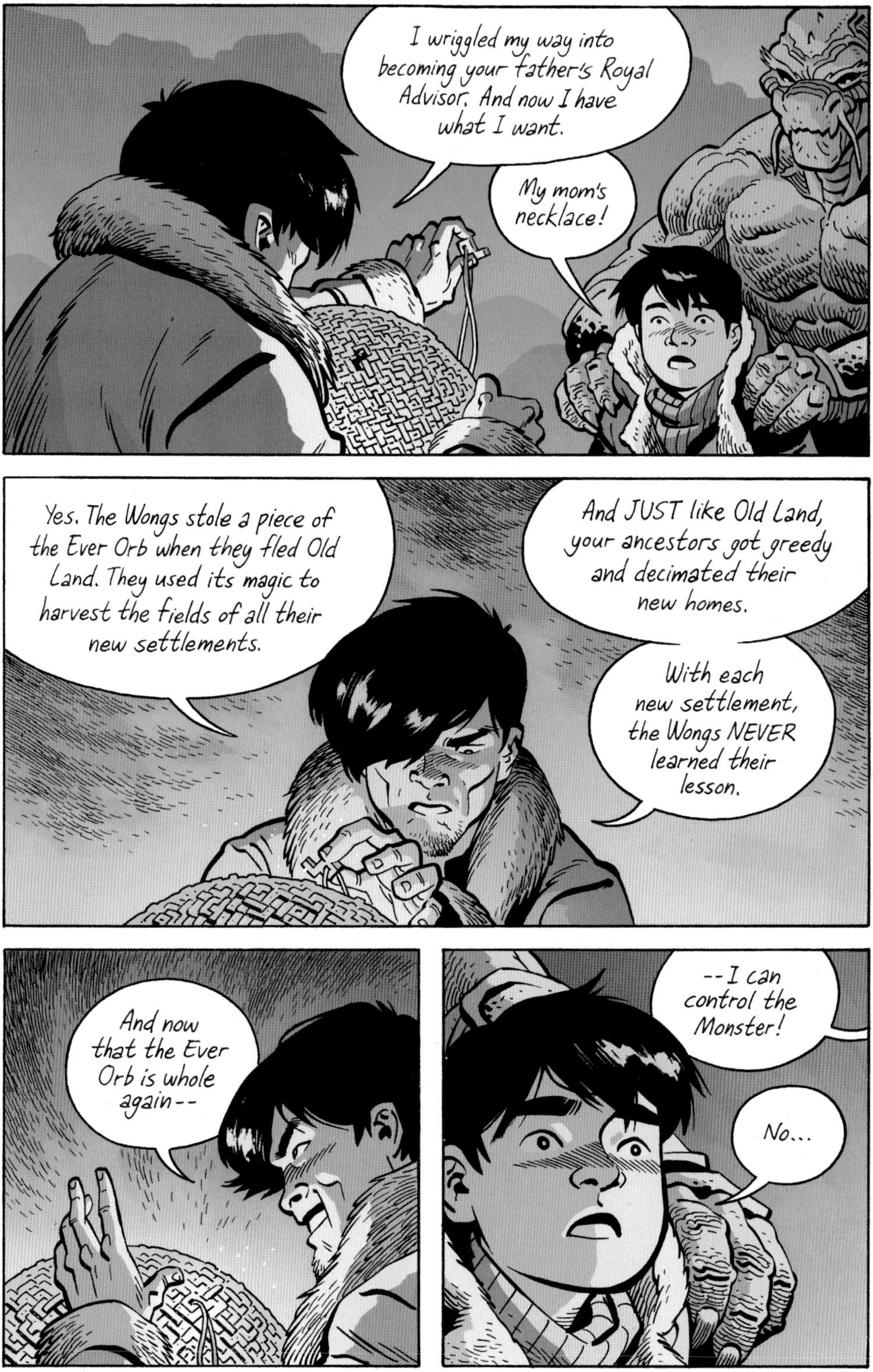
I wriggled my way into becoming your father's Royal Advisor. And now I have what I want.
My mom's necklace!
Yes. The Wongs stole a piece of the Ever Orb when they fled Old Land. They used its magic to harvest the fields of all their new settlements.
And JUST like Old Land, your ancestors got greedy and decimated their new homes.
With each new settlement, the Wongs NEVER learned their lesson.
And now that the Ever Orb is whole again--
--I can control the Monster!
No...

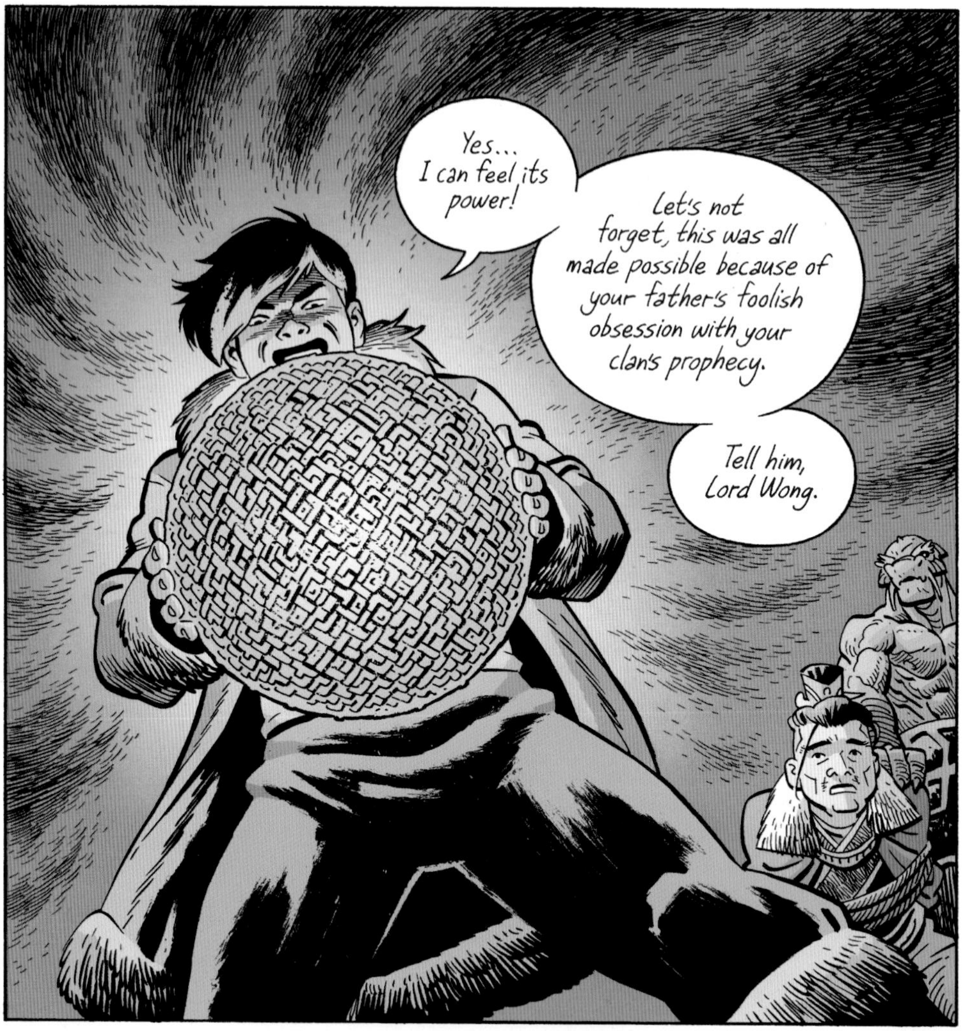
Yes... I can feel its power!
Let's not forget, this was all made possible because of your father's foolish obsession with your clan's prophecy.
Tell him, Lord Wong.

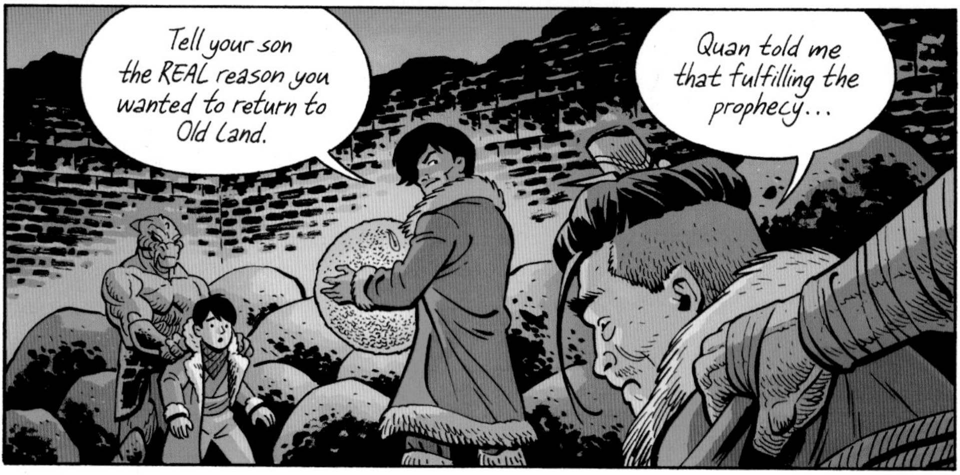
Tell your son the REAL reason you wanted to return to Old Land.
Quan told me that fulfilling the prophecy...

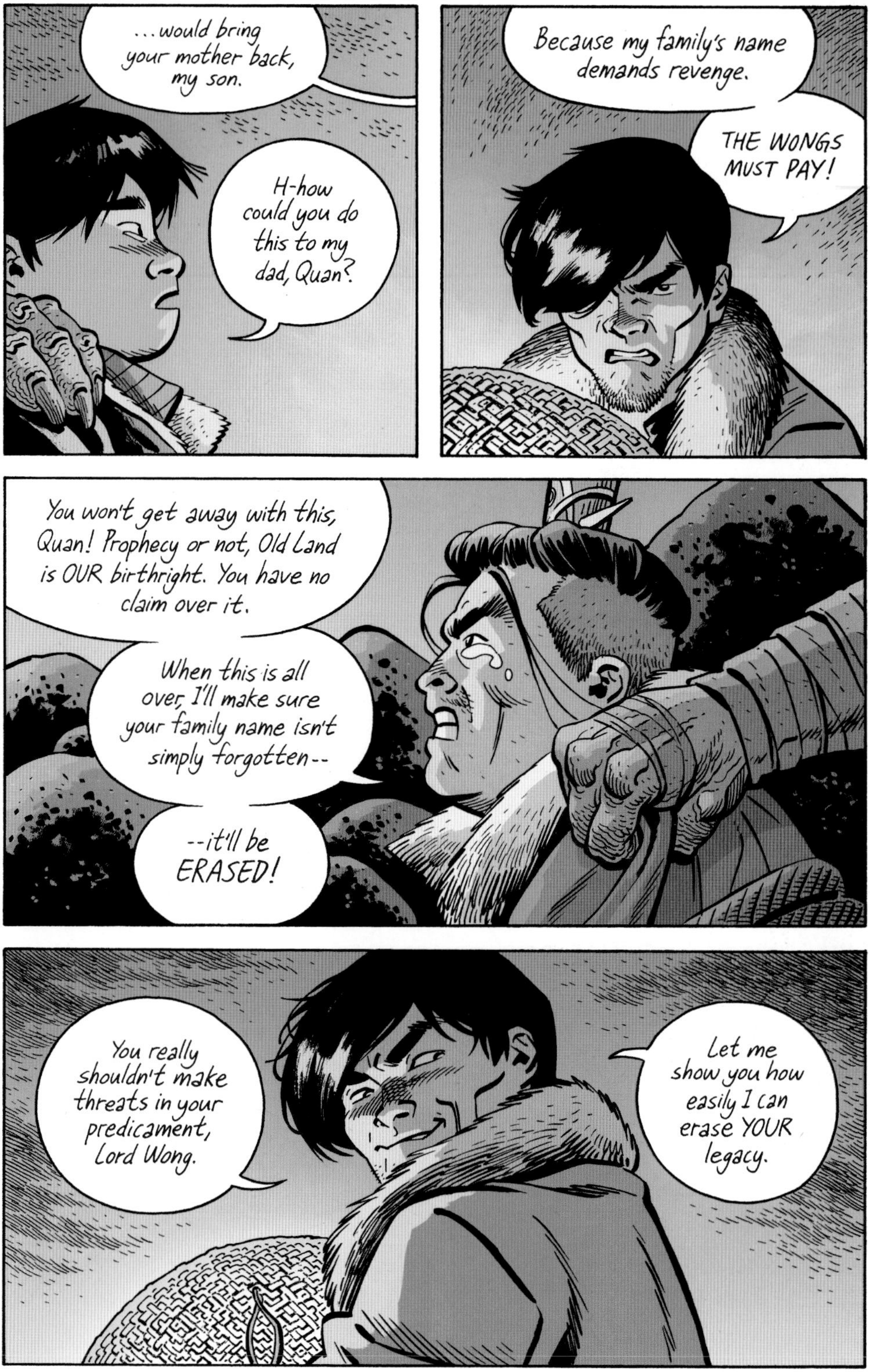
...would bring your mother back, my son.
H-how could you do this to my dad, Quan?
Because my family's name demands revenge.
THE WONGS MUST PAY!
You won't get away with this, Quan! Prophecy or not, Old Land is OUR birthright. You have no claim over it.
When this is all over, I'll make sure your family name isn't simply forgotten--
--it'll be ERASED!
You really shouldn't make threats in your predicament, Lord Wong.
Let me show you how easily I can erase YOUR legacy.

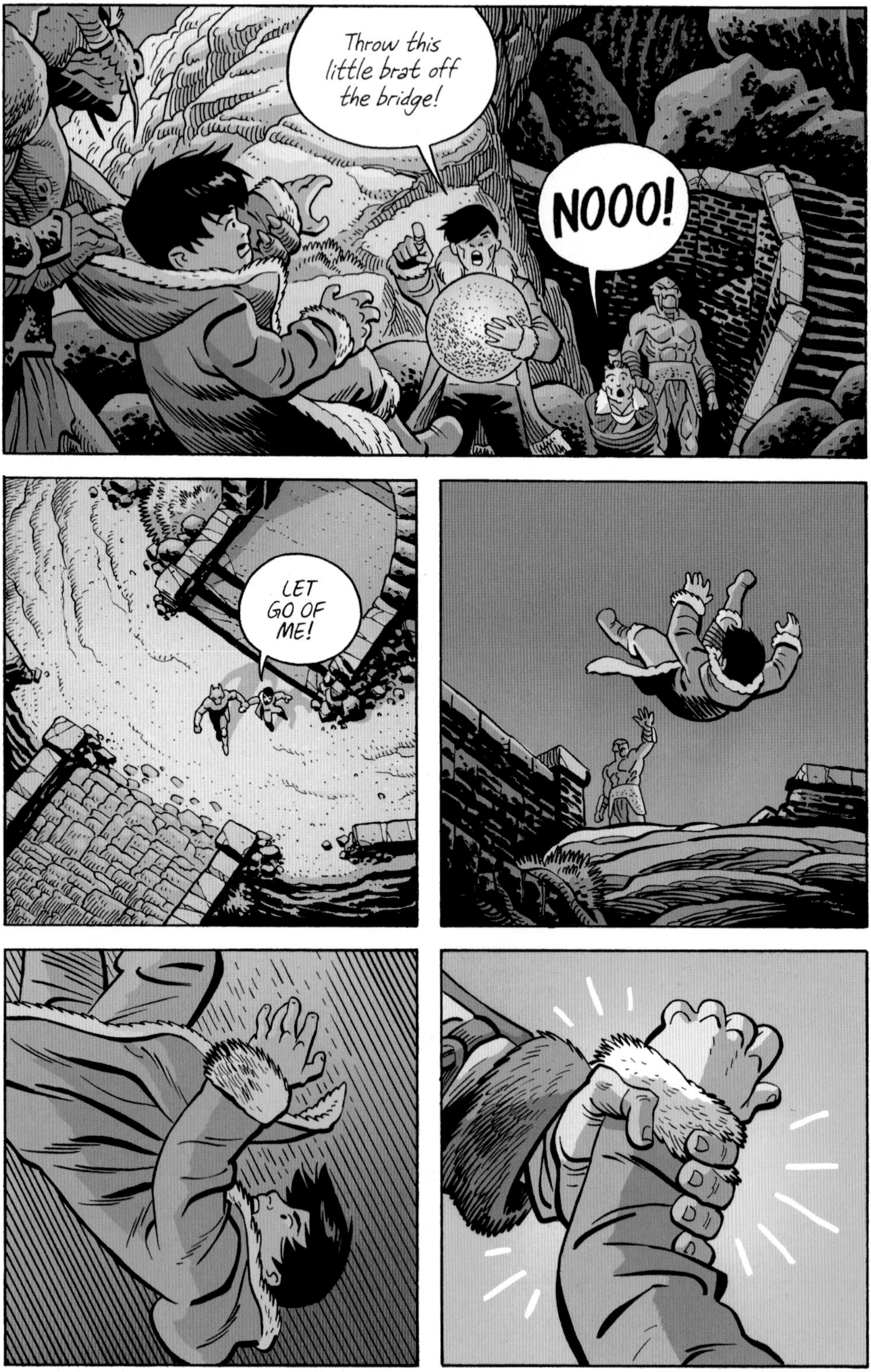

Throw this little brat off the bridge!
NOOO!
LET GO OF ME!

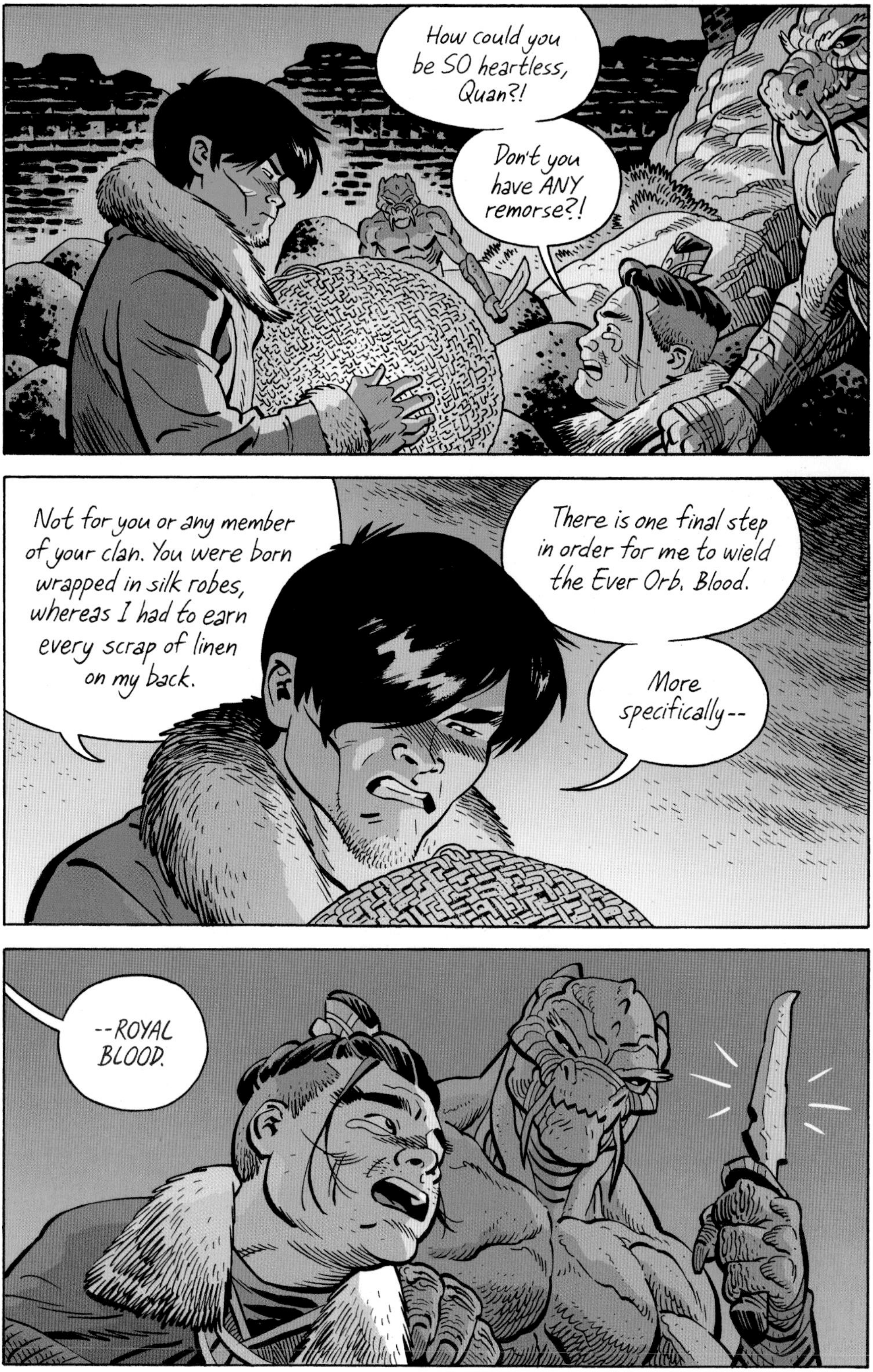
How could you be SO heartless, Quan?!
Don't you have ANY remorse?!
Not for you or any member of your clan. You were born wrapped in silk robes, whereas I had to earn every scrap of linen on my back.
There is one final step in order for me to wield the Ever Orb. Blood.
More specifically--
--ROYAL BLOOD.

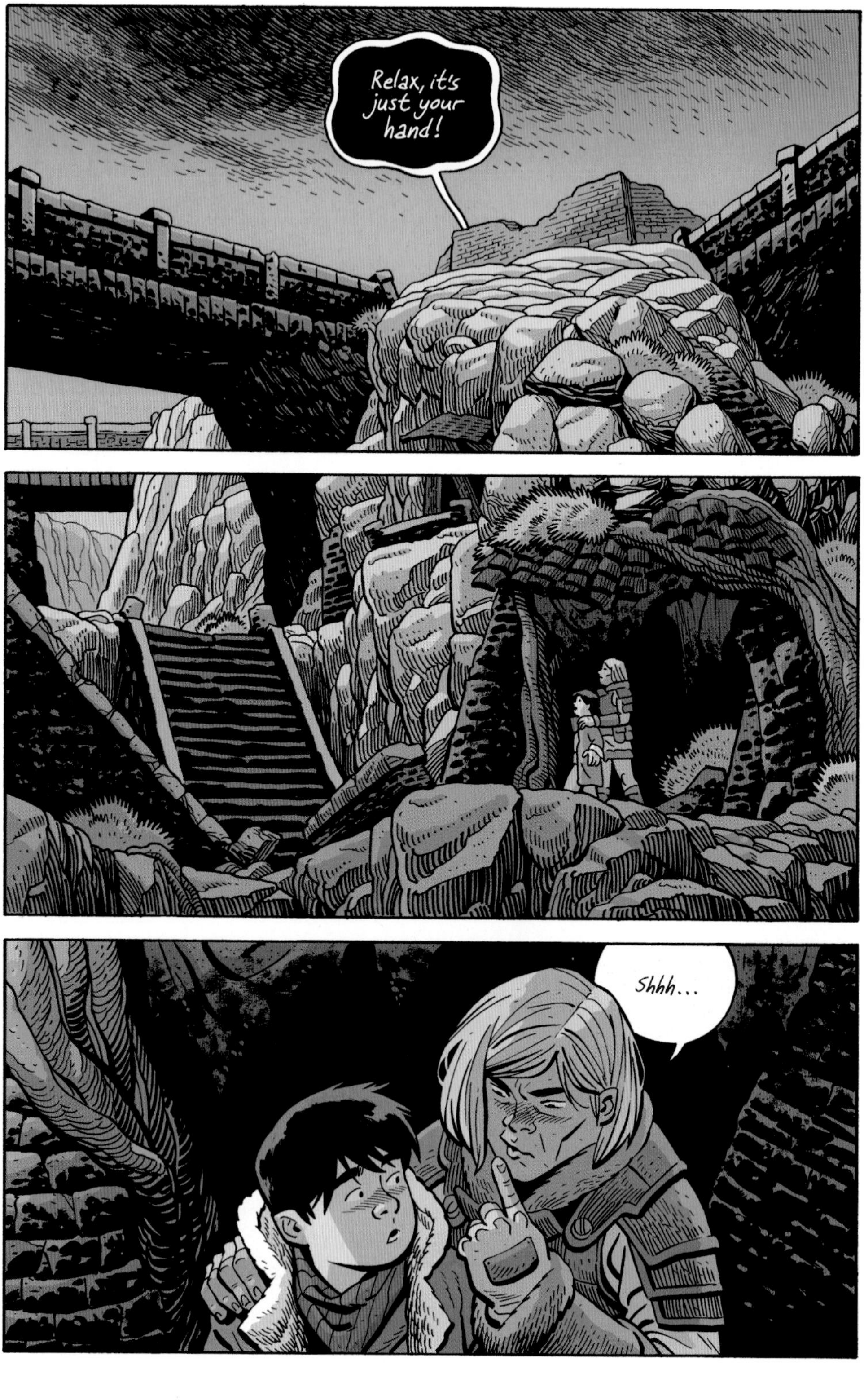
Relax, it's just your hand!
Shhh...

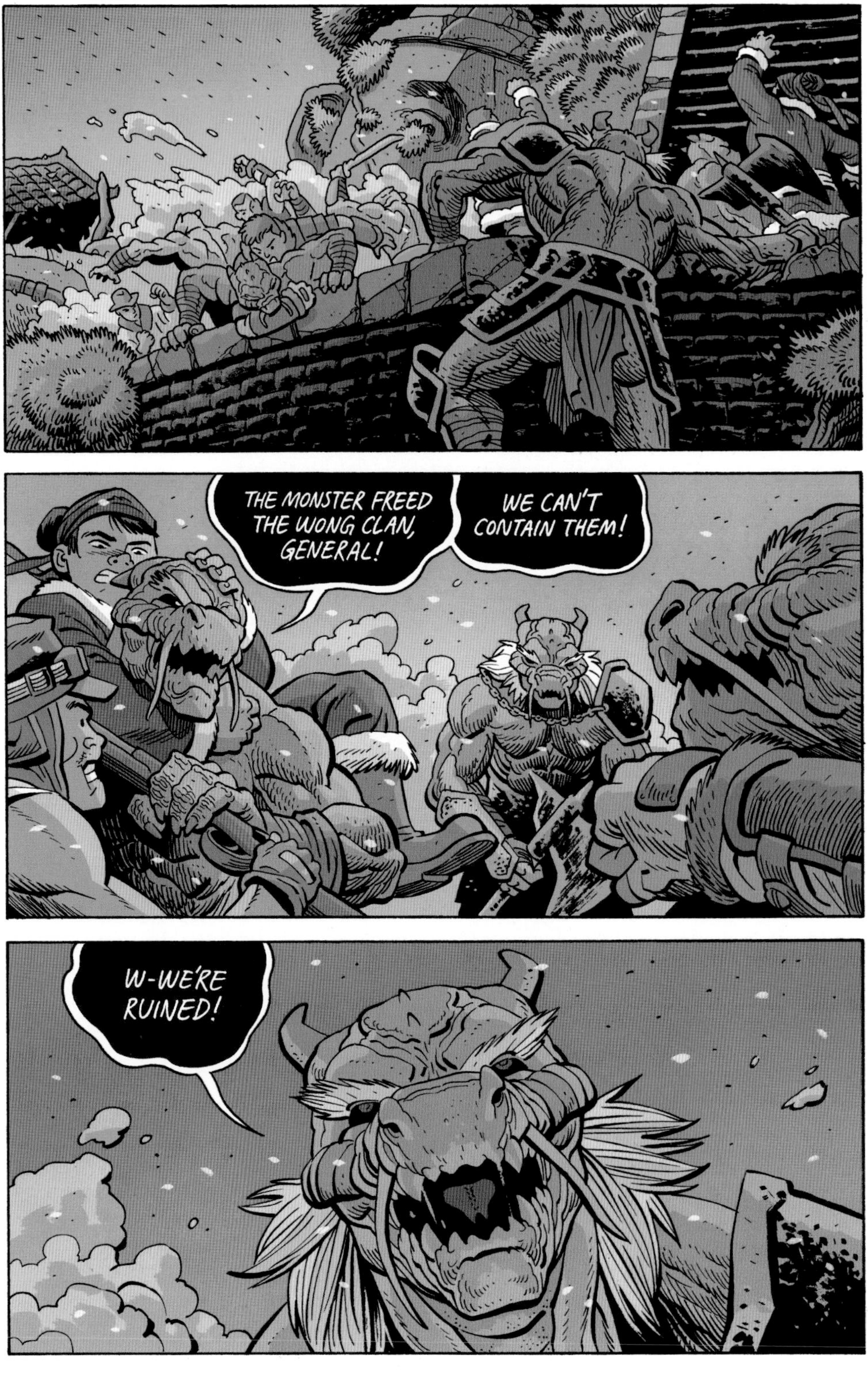
THE MONSTER FREED THE WONG CLAN, GENERAL!
WE CAN'T CONTAIN THEM!
W-WE'RE RUINED!

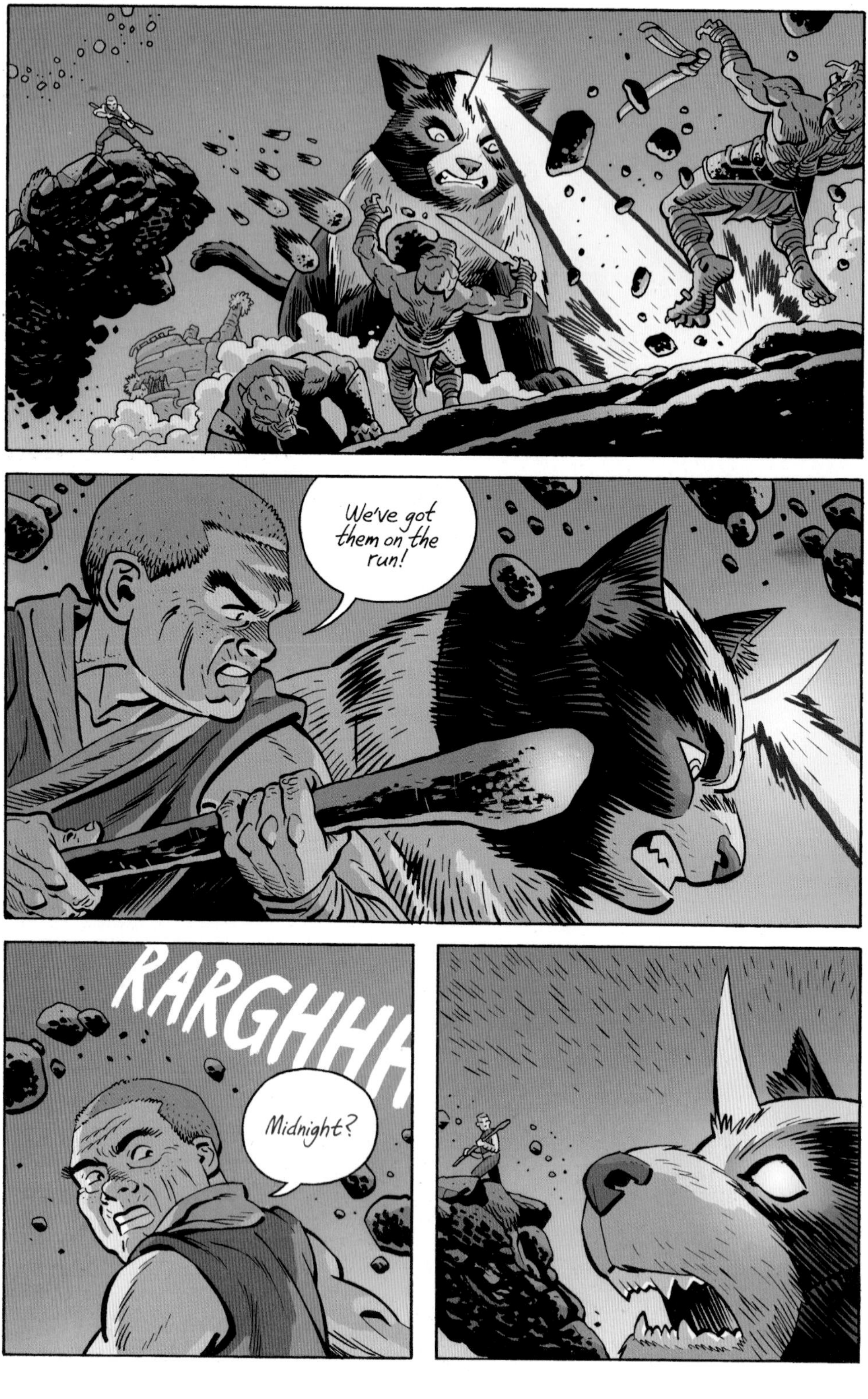
We've got them on the run!
RARGHHH
Midnight?

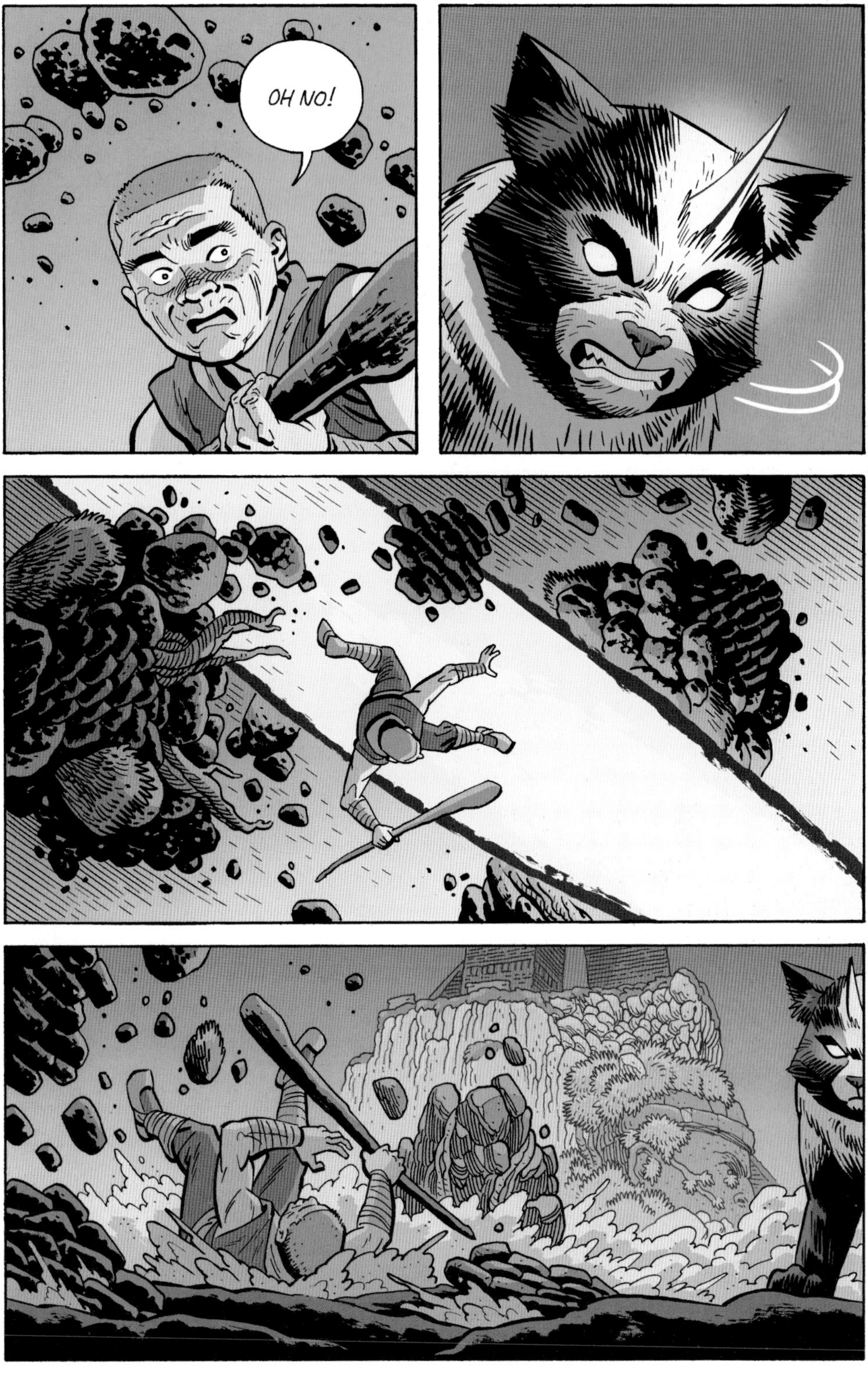
OH NO!

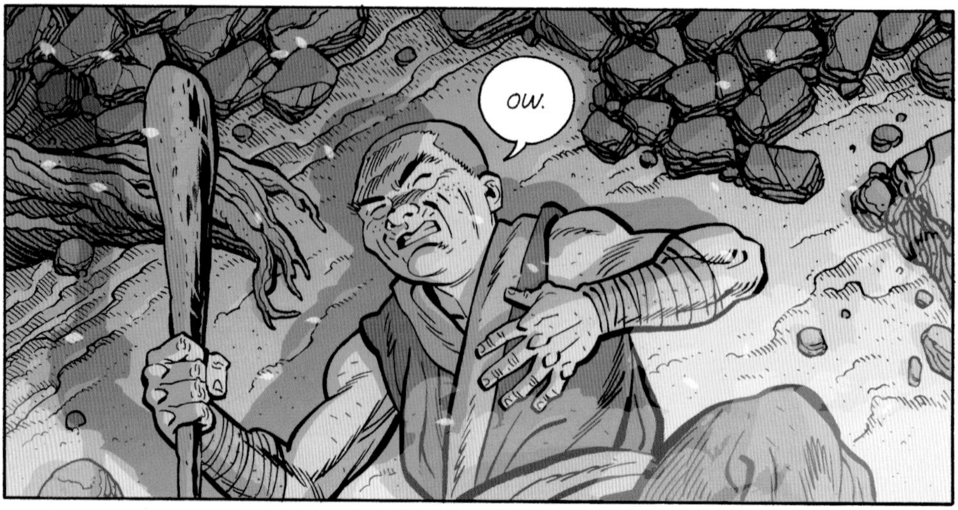
OW.

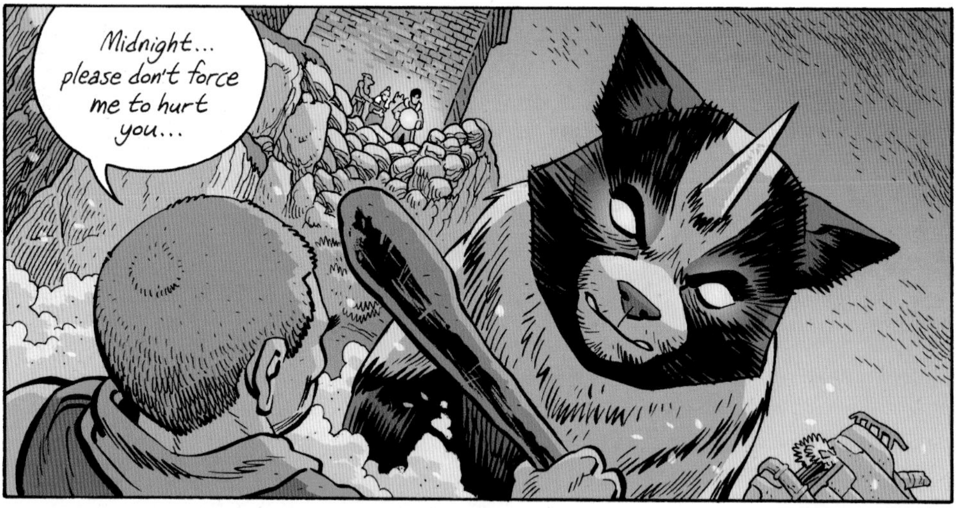
Midnight... please don't force me to hurt you...

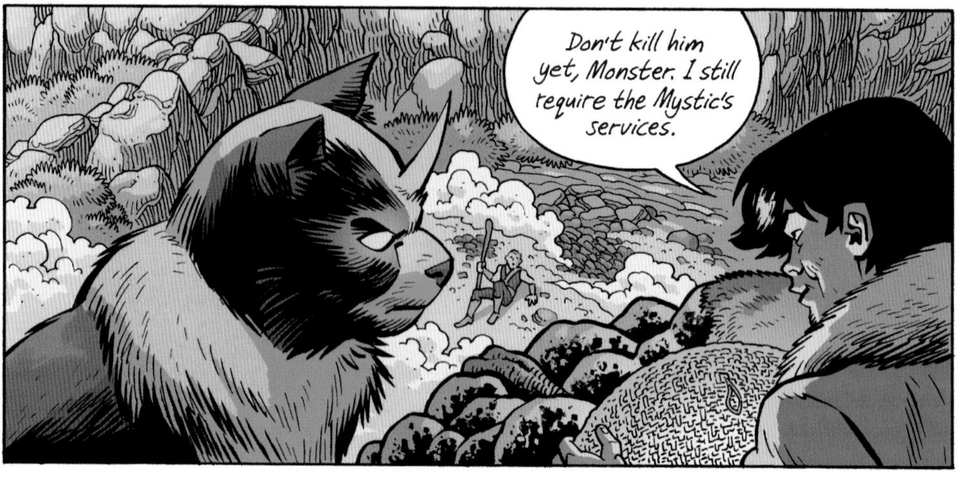
Don't kill him yet, Monster. I still require the Mystic's services.

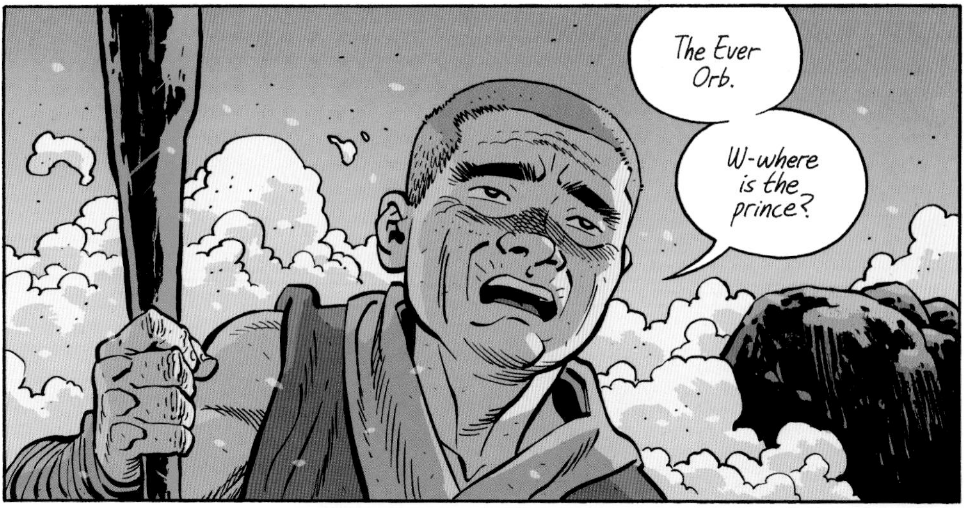
The Ever Orb.
W-where is the prince?

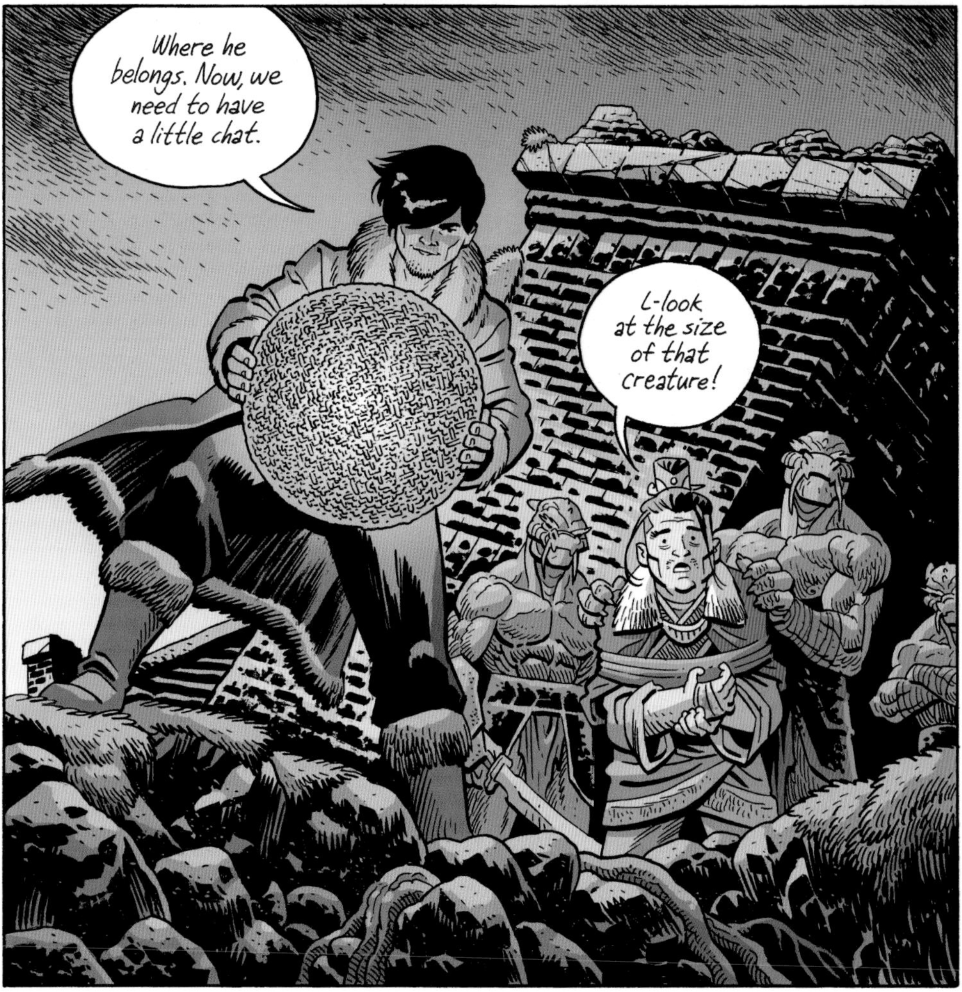
Where he belongs. Now, we need to have a little chat.
L-look at the size of that creature!

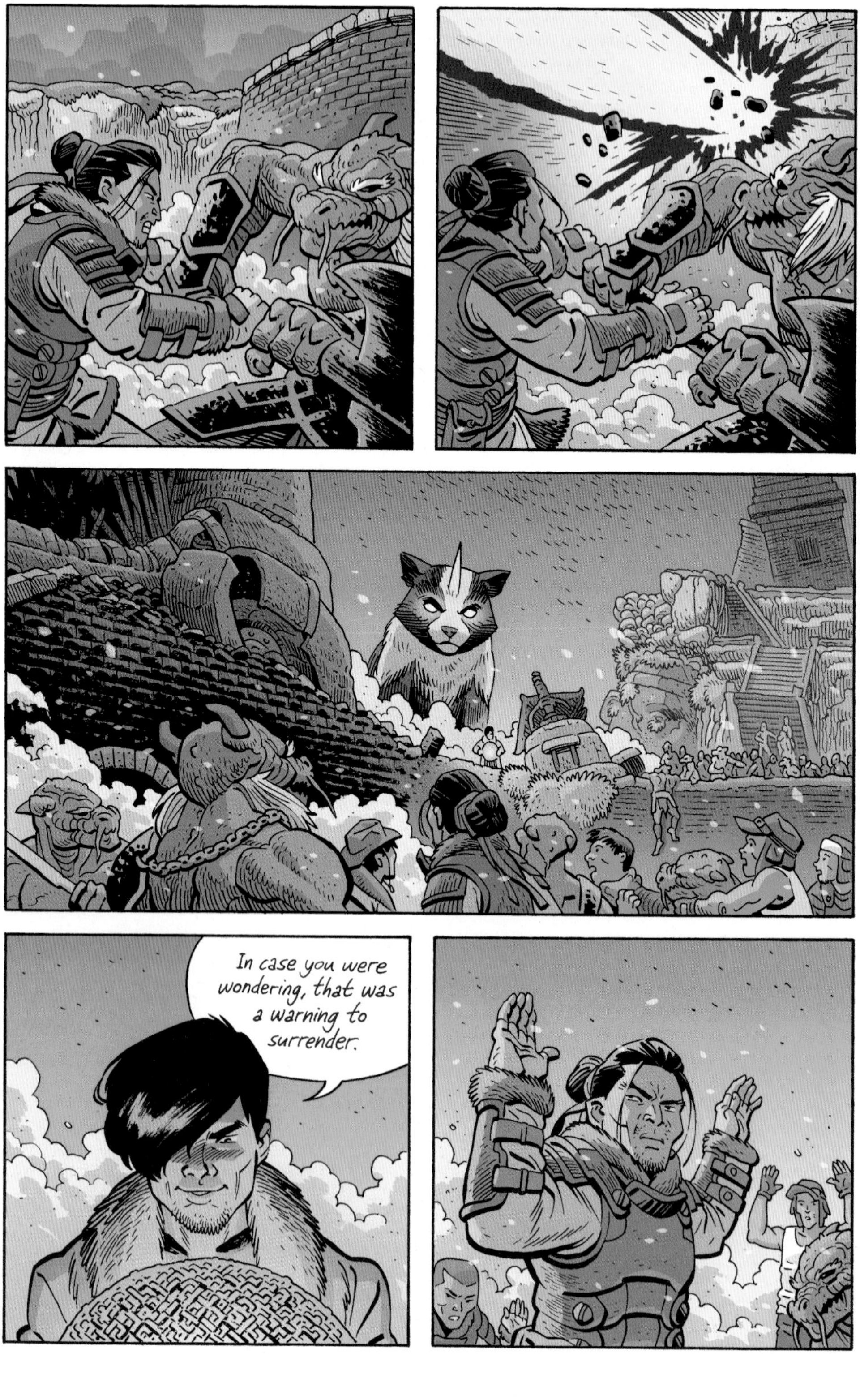
In case you were wondering, that was a warning to surrender.

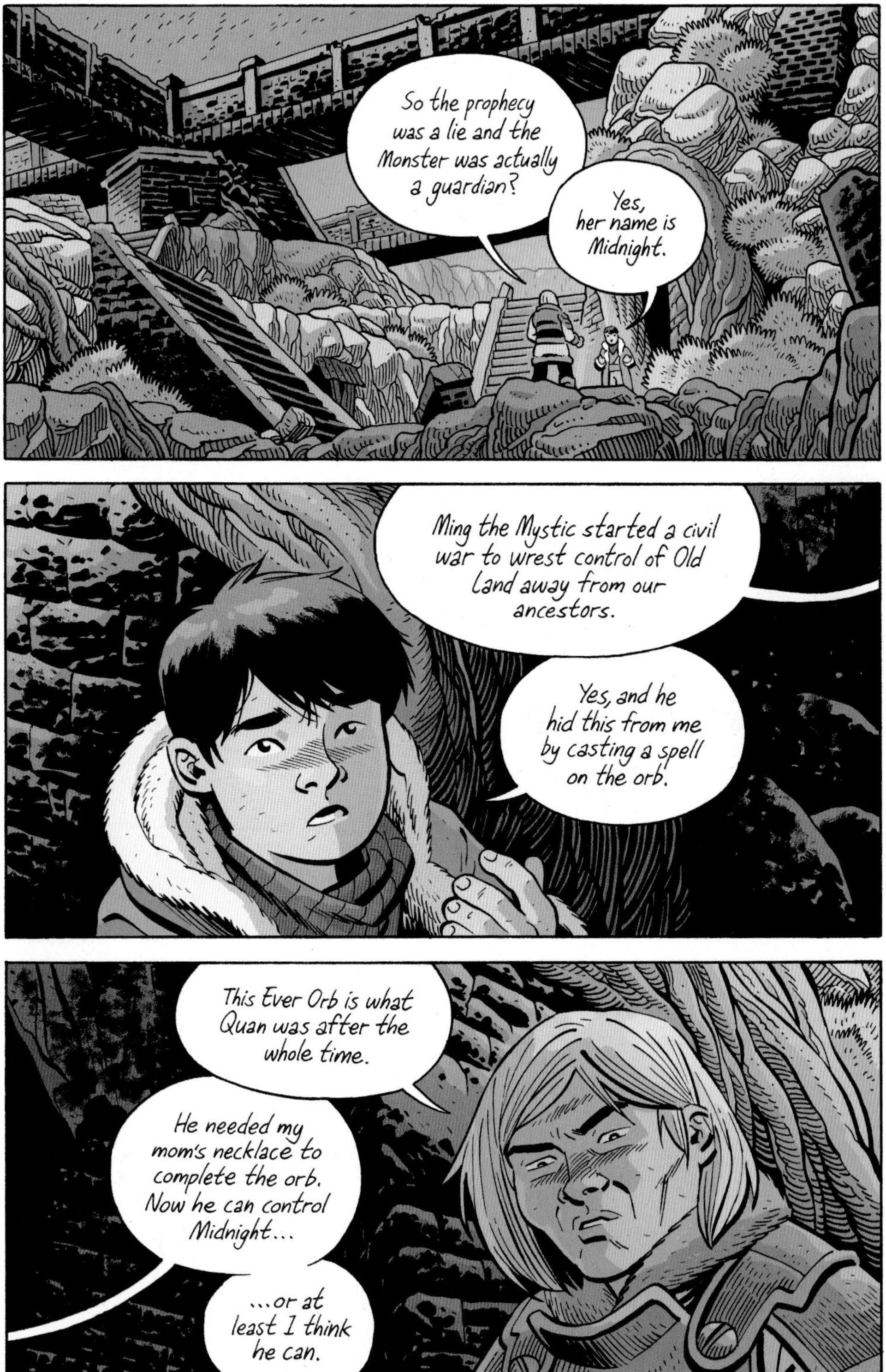
So the prophecy was a lie and the Monster was actually a guardian?
Yes, her name is Midnight.
Ming the Mystic started a civil war to wrest control of Old Land away from our ancestors.
Yes, and he hid this from me by casting a spell on the orb.
This Ever Orb is what Quan was after the whole time.
He needed my mom's necklace to complete the orb. Now he can control Midnight...
...or at least I think he can.

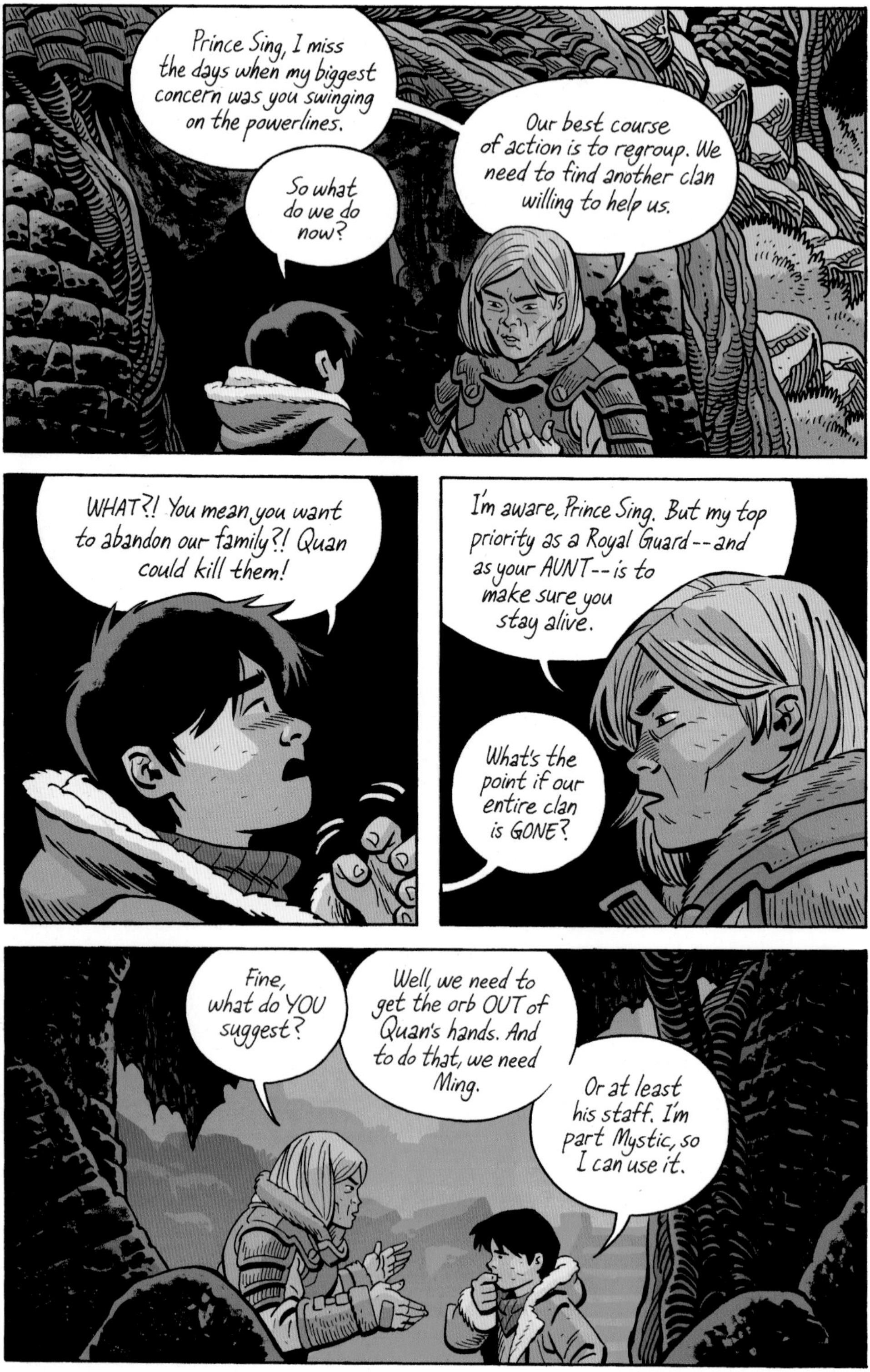
Prince Sing, I miss the days when my biggest concern was you swinging on the powerlines.
So what do we do now?
Our best course of action is to regroup. We need to find another clan willing to help us.
WHAT?! You mean you want to abandon our family?! Quan could kill them!
I'm aware, Prince Sing. But my top priority as a Royal Guard--and as your AUNT--is to make sure you stay alive.
What's the point if our entire clan is GONE?
Fine, what do YOU suggest?
Well, we need to get the orb OUT of Quan's hands. And to do that, we need Ming.
Or at least his staff. I'm part Mystic, so I can use it.

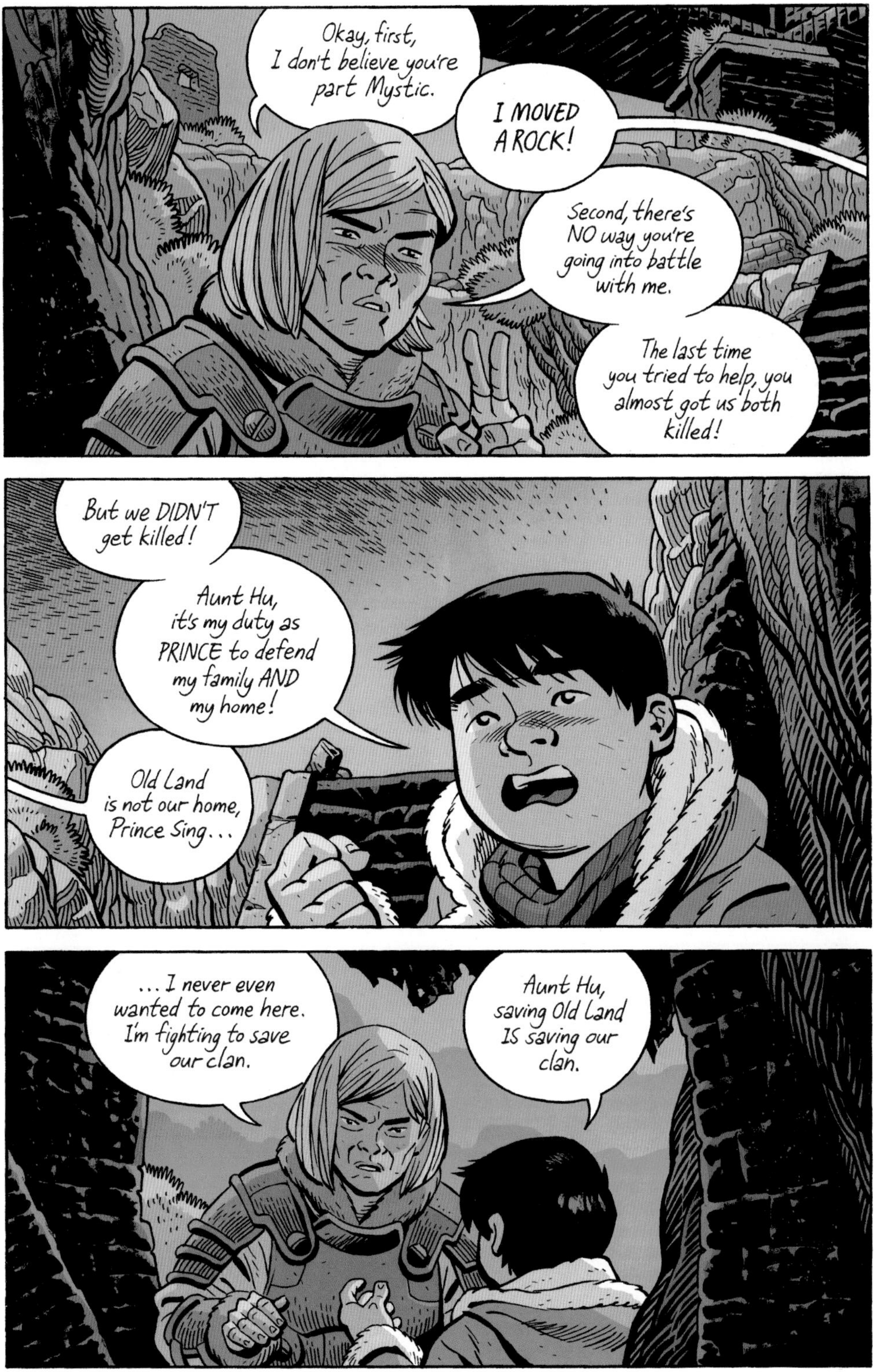
Okay, first, I don't believe you're part Mystic.
I MOVED A ROCK!
Second, there's NO way you're going into battle with me.
The last time you tried to help, you almost got us both killed!
But we DIDN'T get killed!
Aunt Hu, it's my duty as PRINCE to defend my family AND my home!
Old Land is not our home, Prince Sing...
...I never even wanted to come here. I'm fighting to save our clan.
Aunt Hu, saving Old Land IS saving our clan.

My mother once told me that we have a right to our legacy. Old Land is our legacy.

It's where we come from, and we have to protect it the same way we'd protect our family!

Prince Sing...

Come on, Aunt Hu, you KNOW I'm making a good point.

-SIGH-

You follow every single one of my commands, you got it?

GOT IT!

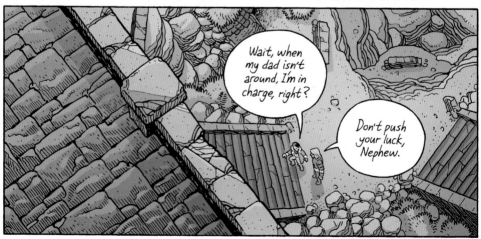

Wait, when my dad isn't around, I'm in charge, right?

Don't push your luck, Nephew.

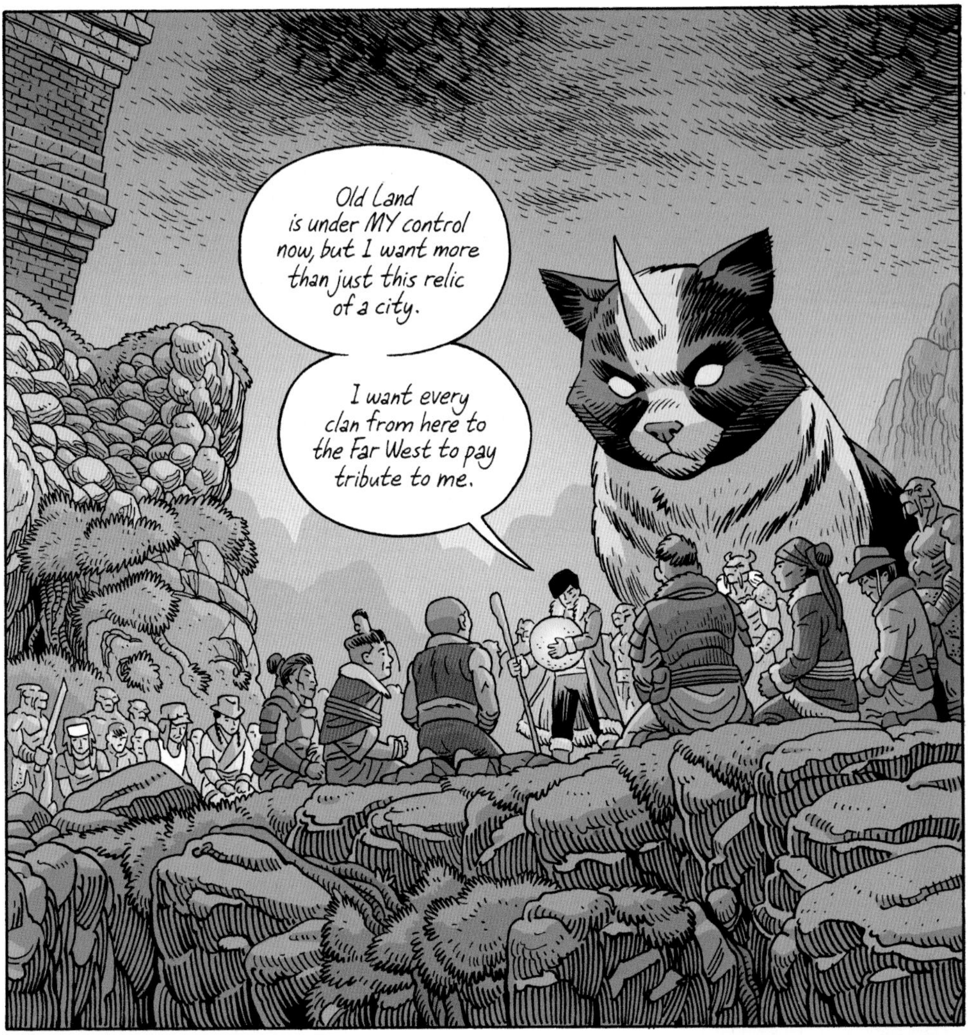
Old Land is under MY control now, but I want more than just this relic of a city.
I want every clan from here to the Far West to pay tribute to me.

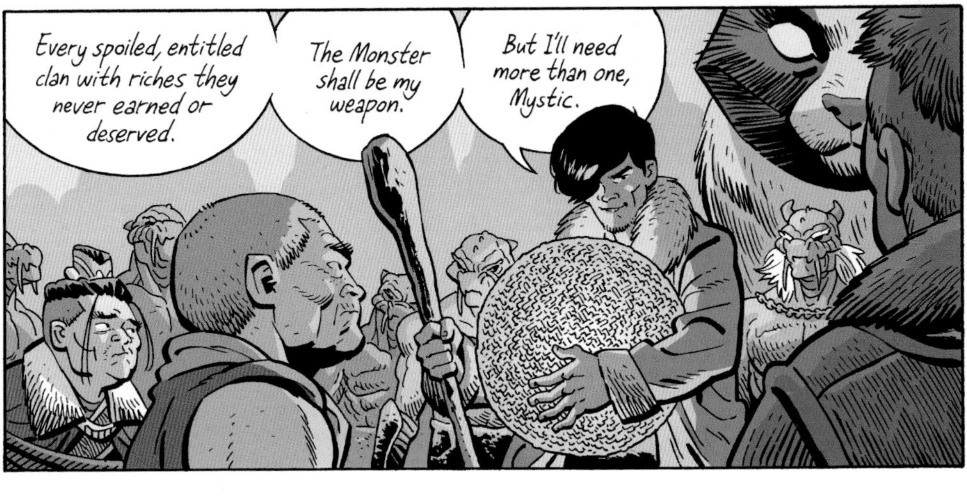
Every spoiled, entitled clan with riches they never earned or deserved.
The Monster shall be my weapon.
But I'll need more than one, Mystic.

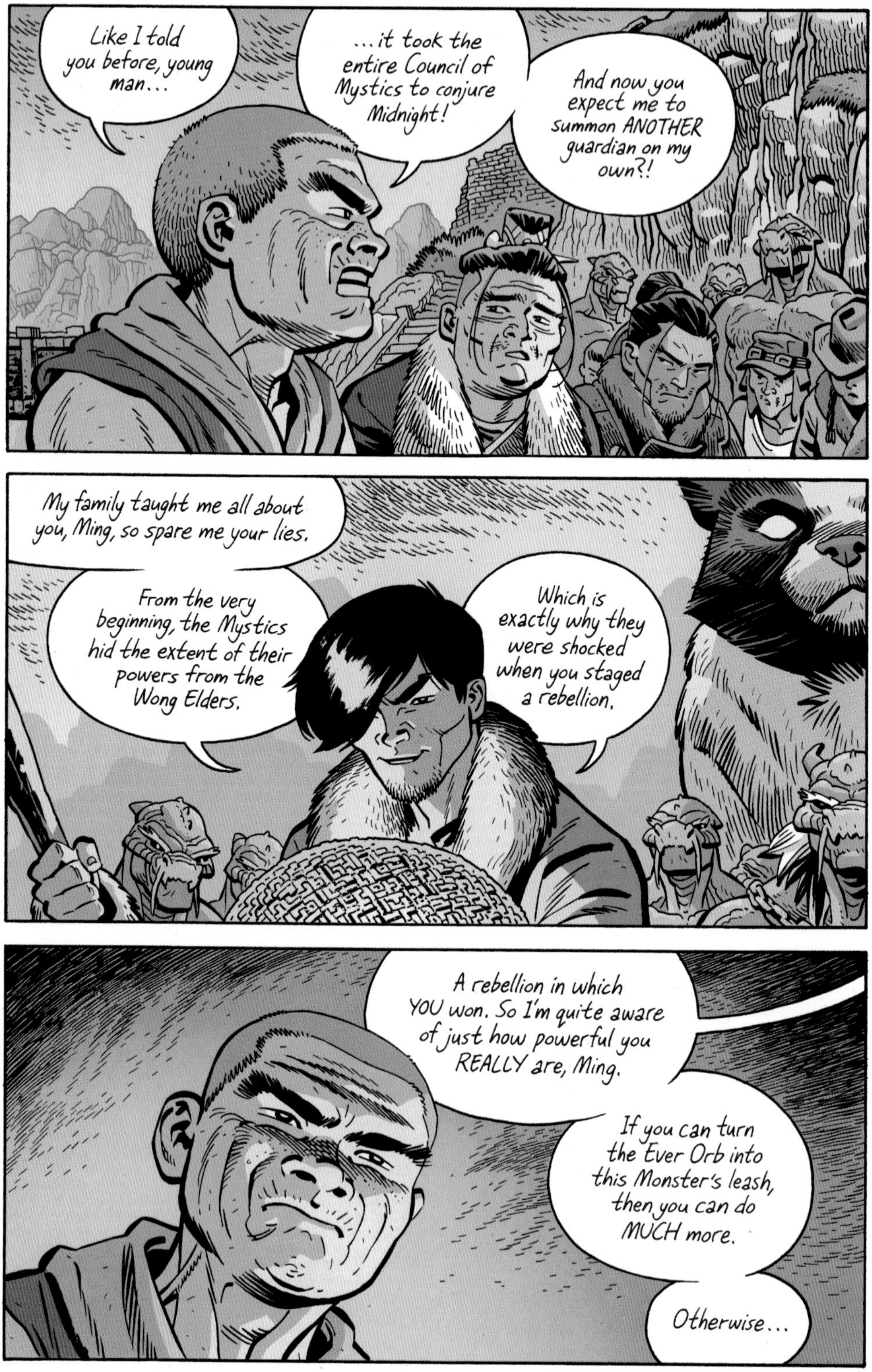
Like I told you before, young man...
...it took the entire Council of Mystics to conjure Midnight!
And now you expect me to summon ANOTHER guardian on my own?!
My family taught me all about you, Ming, so spare me your lies.
From the very beginning, the Mystics hid the extent of their powers from the Wong Elders.
Which is exactly why they were shocked when you staged a rebellion.
A rebellion in which YOU won. So I'm quite aware of just how powerful you REALLY are, Ming.
If you can turn the Ever Orb into this Monster's leash, then you can do MUCH more.
Otherwise...

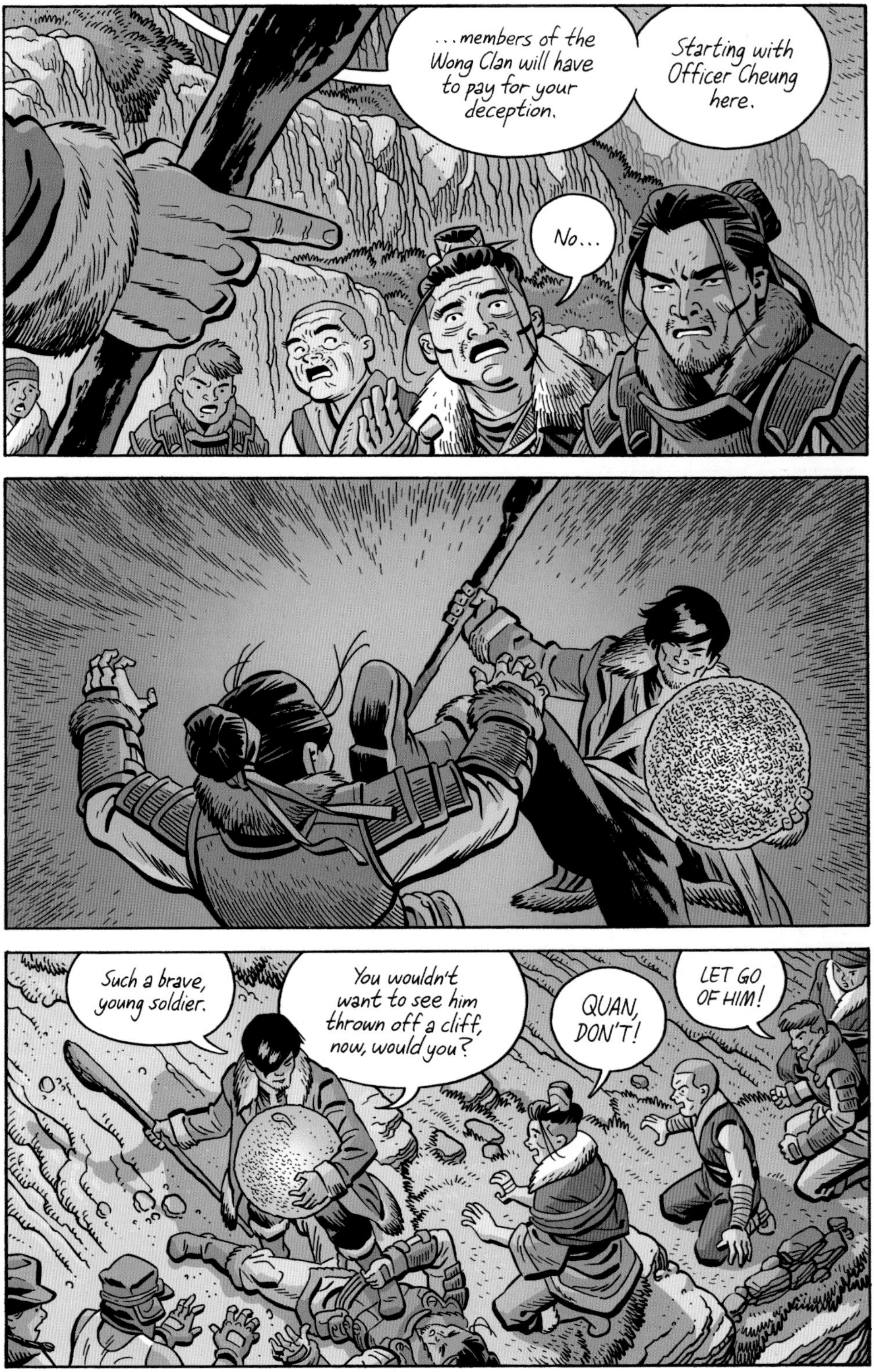

...members of the Wong Clan will have to pay for your deception.
Starting with Officer Cheung here.
No...
Such a brave, young soldier.
You wouldn't want to see him thrown off a cliff, now, would you?
QUAN, DON'T!
LET GO OF HIM!

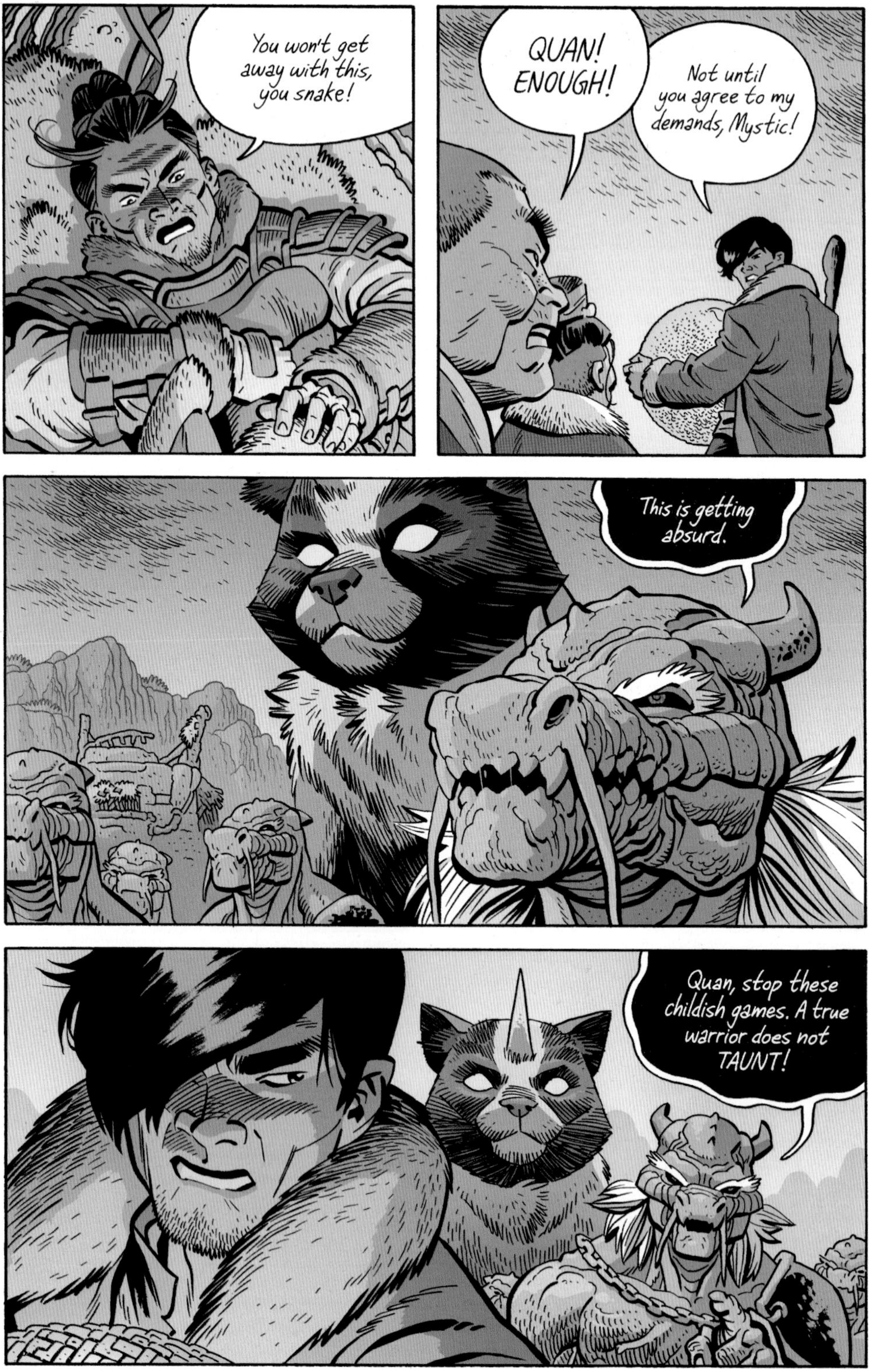
You won't get away with this, you snake!
QUAN! ENOUGH!
Not until you agree to my demands, Mystic!
This is getting absurd.
Quan, stop these childish games. A true warrior does not TAUNT!

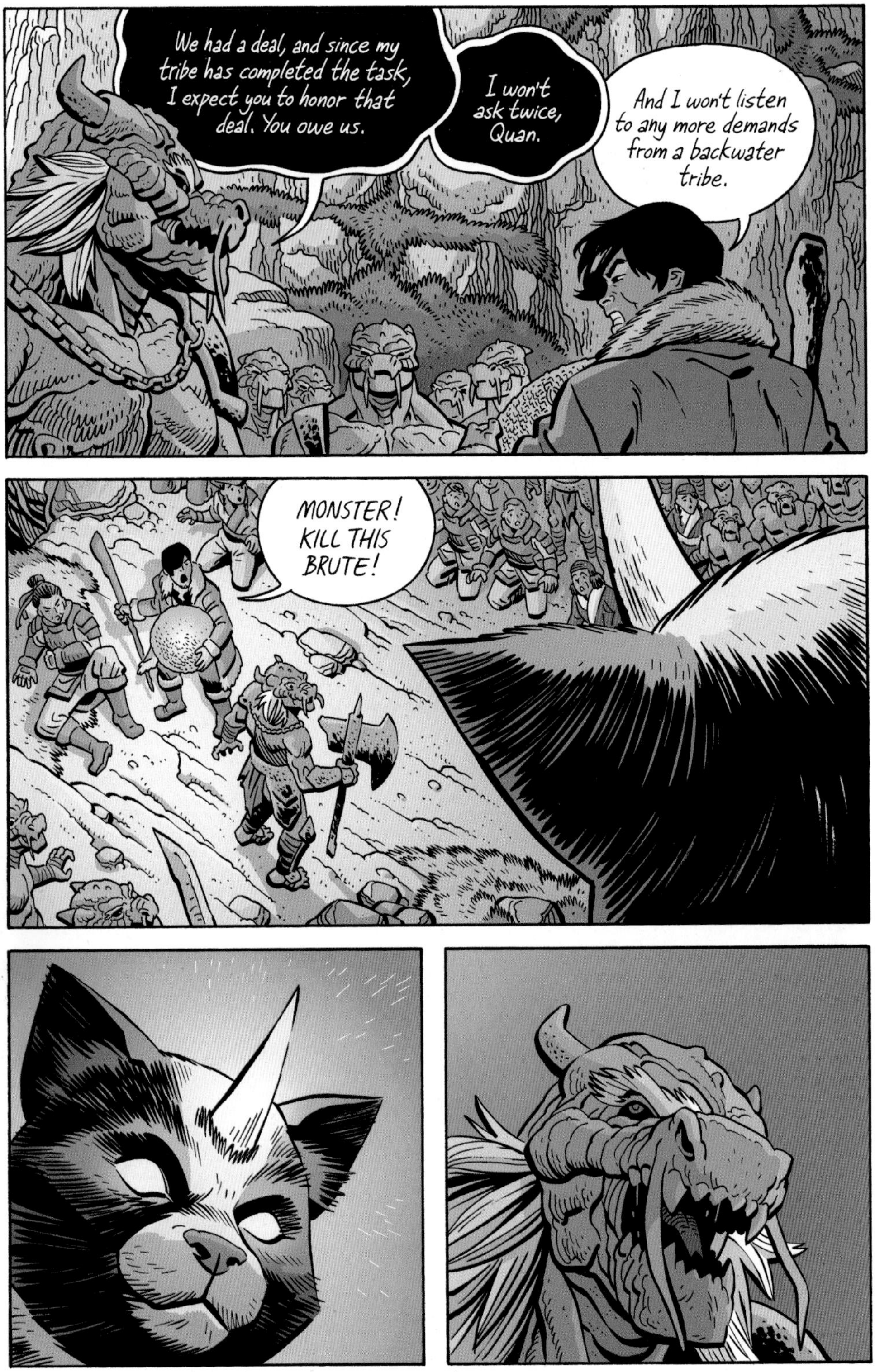
We had a deal, and since my tribe has completed the task, I expect you to honor that deal. You owe us.
I won't ask twice, Quan.
And I won't listen to any more demands from a backwater tribe.
MONSTER! KILL THIS BRUTE!

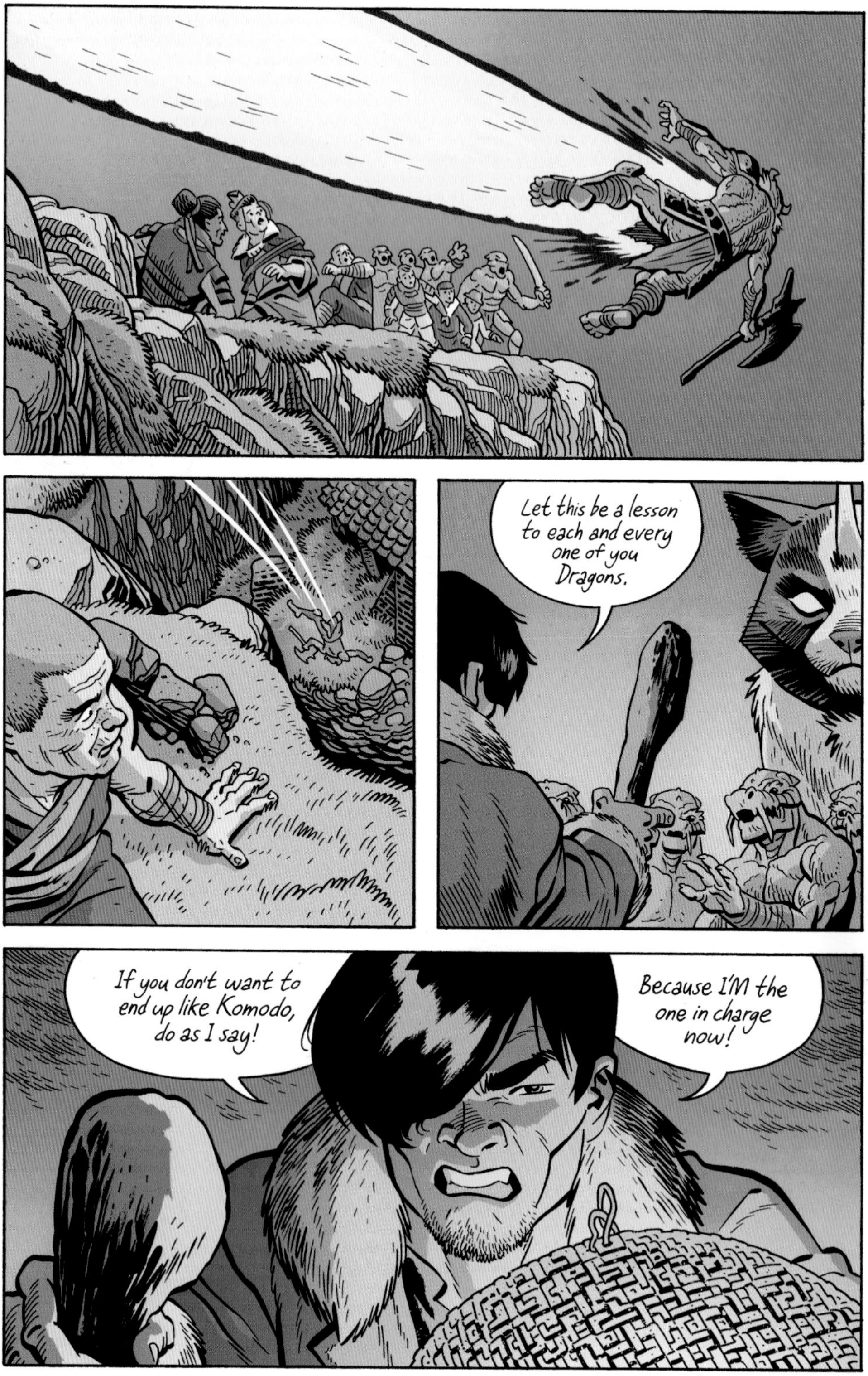
Let this be a lesson to each and every one of you Dragons.
If you don't want to end up like Komodo, do as I say!
Because I'M the one in charge now!

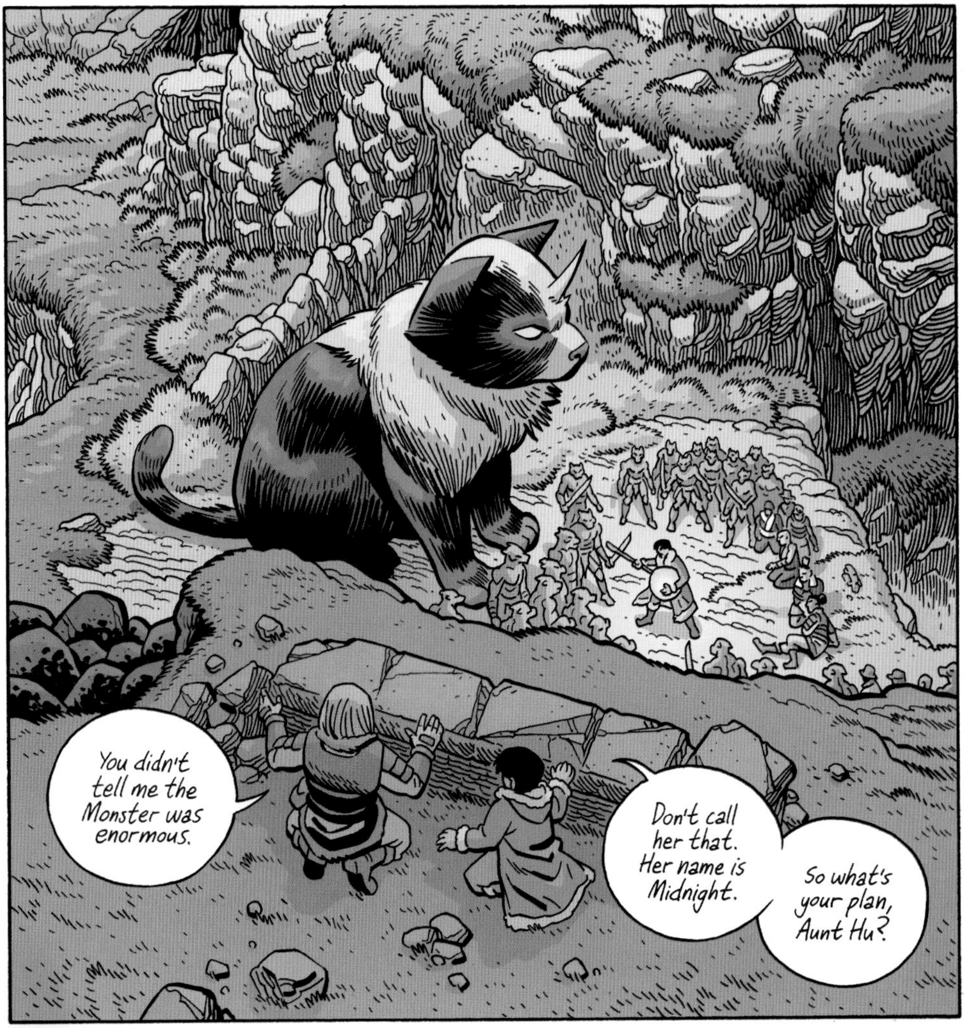
You didn't tell me the Monster was enormous.
Don't call her that. Her name is Midnight.
So what's your plan, Aunt Hu?

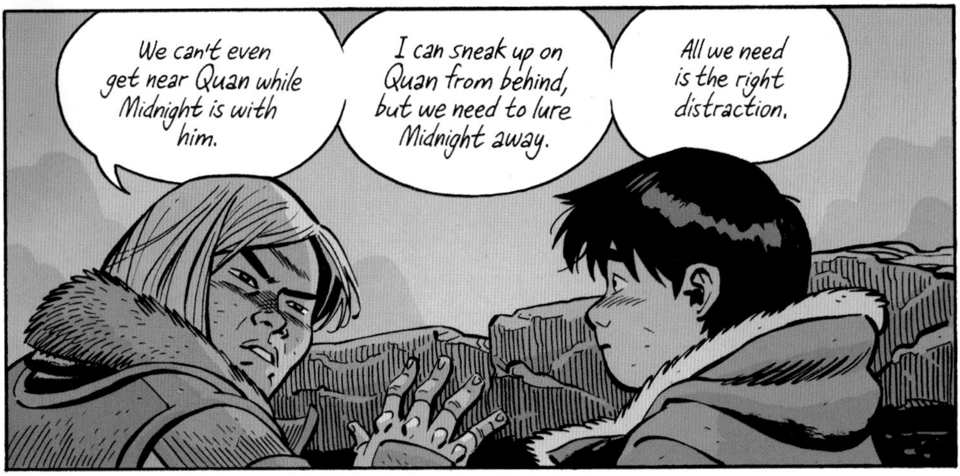
We can't even get near Quan while Midnight is with him.
I can sneak up on Quan from behind, but we need to lure Midnight away.
All we need is the right distraction.

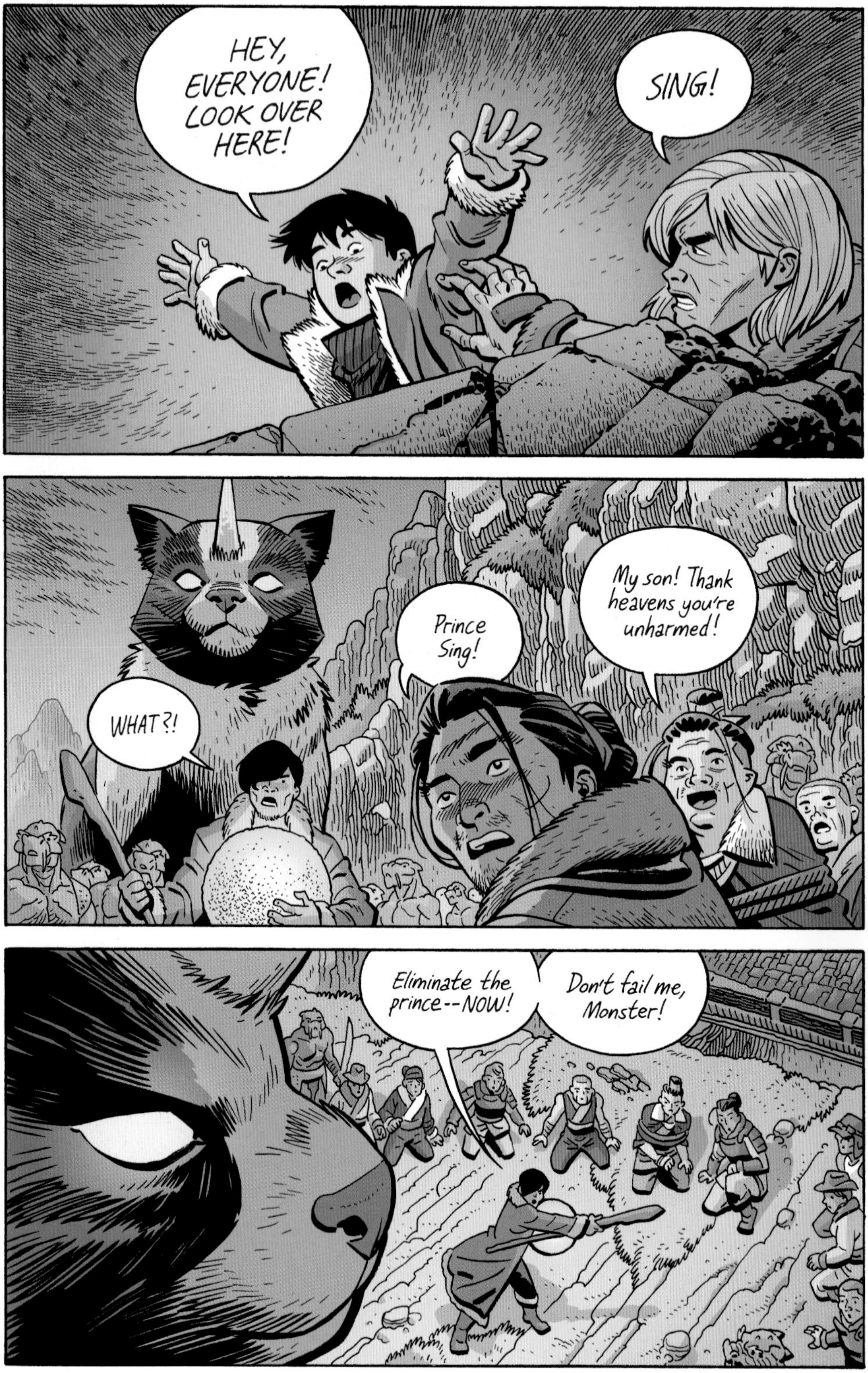
HEY, EVERYONE! LOOK OVER HERE!
SING!
WHAT?!
Prince Sing!
My son! Thank heavens you're unharmed!
Eliminate the prince--NOW!
Don't fail me, Monster!

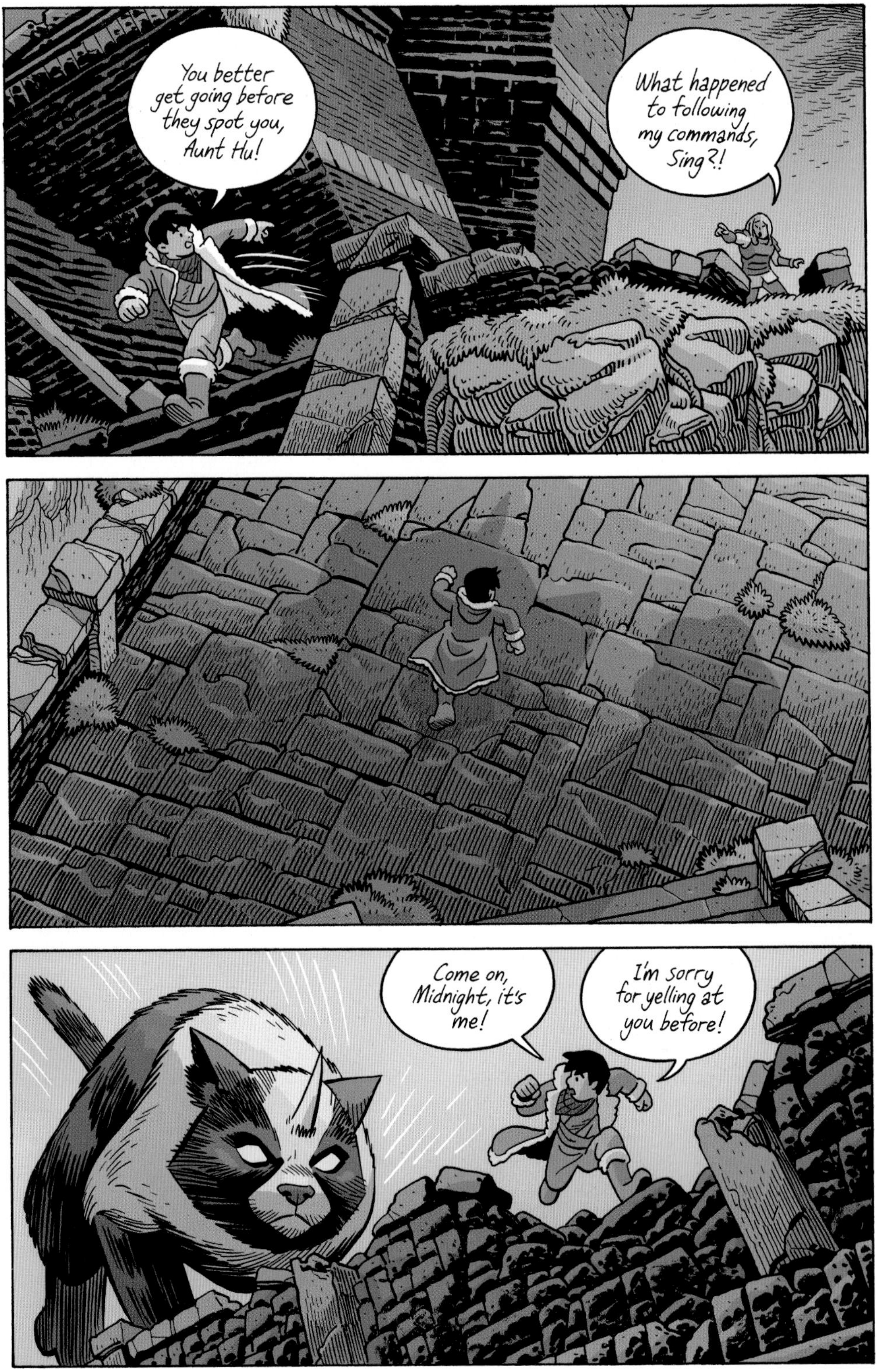
You better get going before they spot you, Aunt Hu!
What happened to following my commands, Sing?!
Come on, Midnight, it's me!
I'm sorry for yelling at you before!

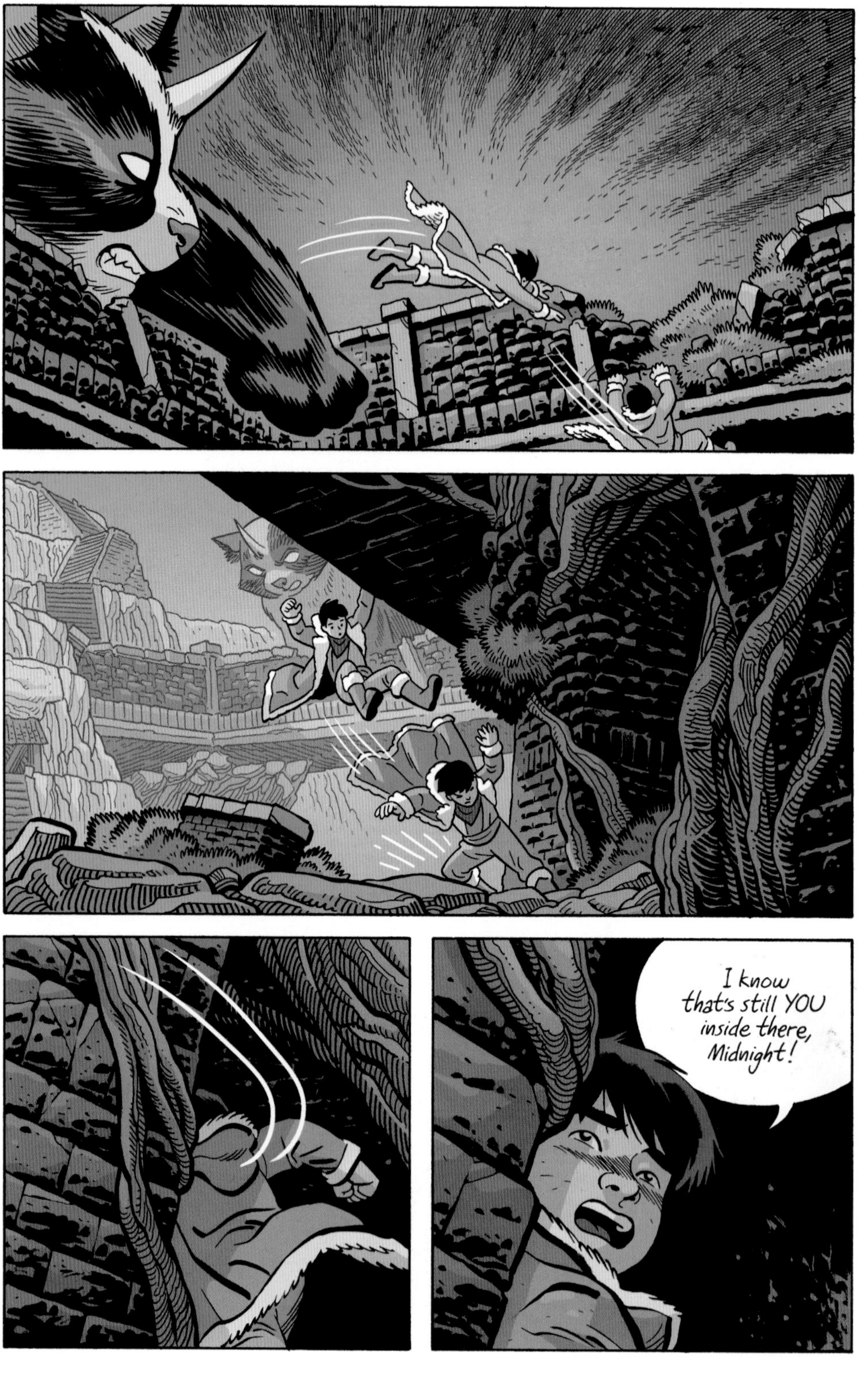
I know that's still YOU inside there, Midnight!

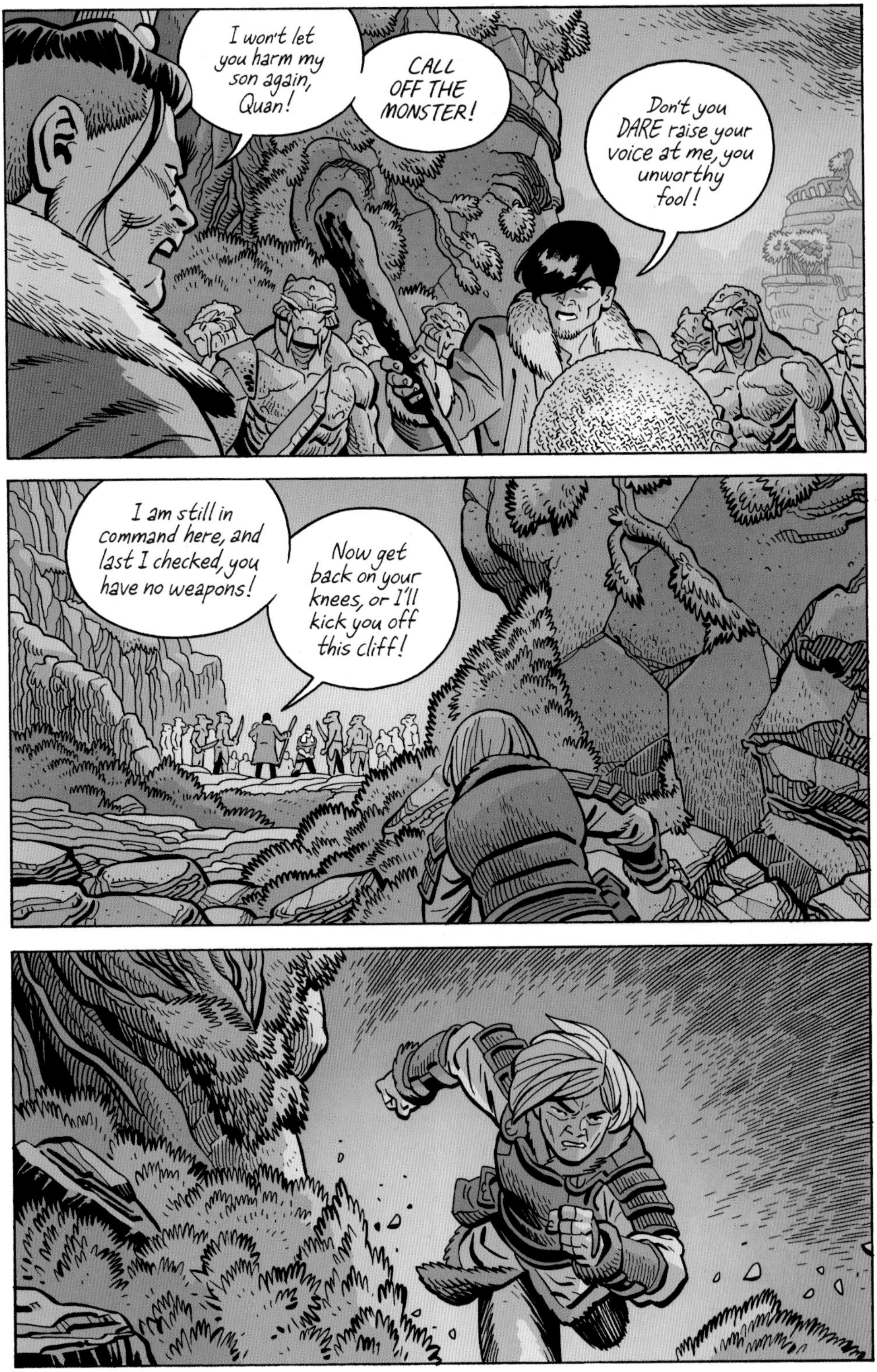
I won't let you harm my son again, Quan!
CALL OFF THE MONSTER!
Don't you DARE raise your voice at me, you unworthy fool!
I am still in command here, and last I checked, you have no weapons!
Now get back on your knees, or I'll kick you off this cliff!

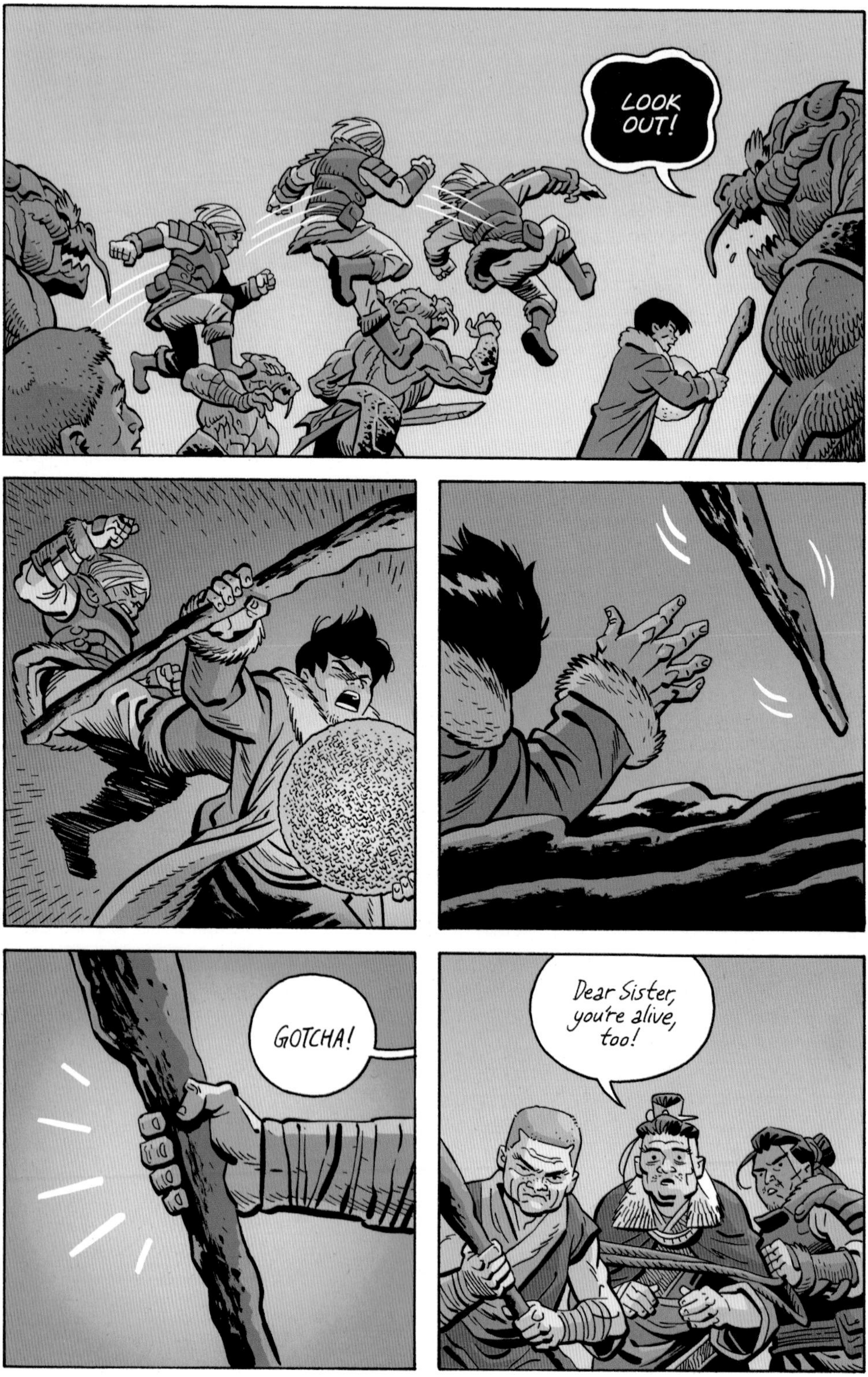
LOOK OUT!
GOTCHA!
Dear Sister, you're alive, too!

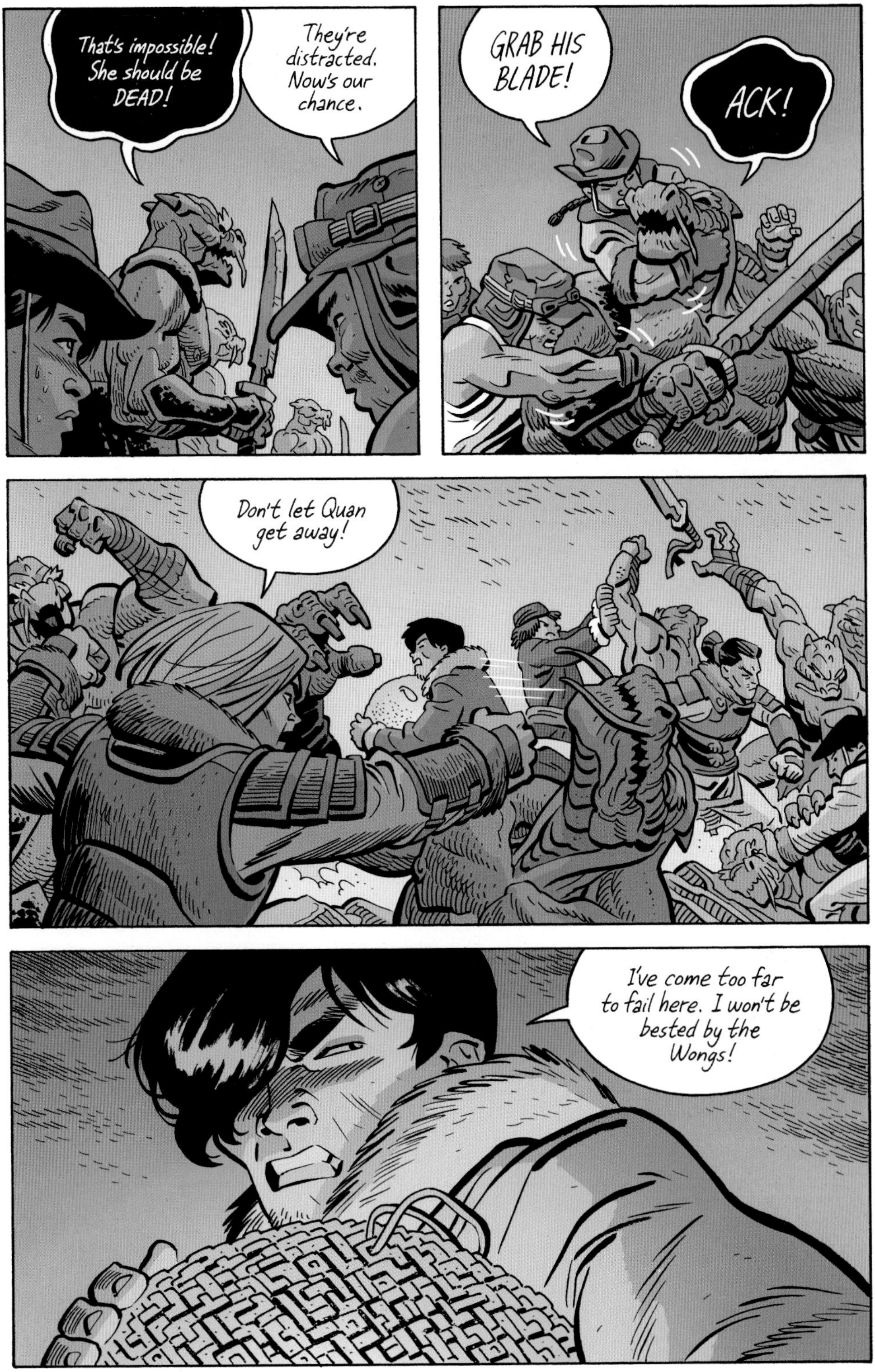

That's impossible! She should be DEAD!
They're distracted. Now's our chance.
GRAB HIS BLADE!
ACK!
Don't let Quan get away!
I've come too far to fail here. I won't be bested by the Wongs!

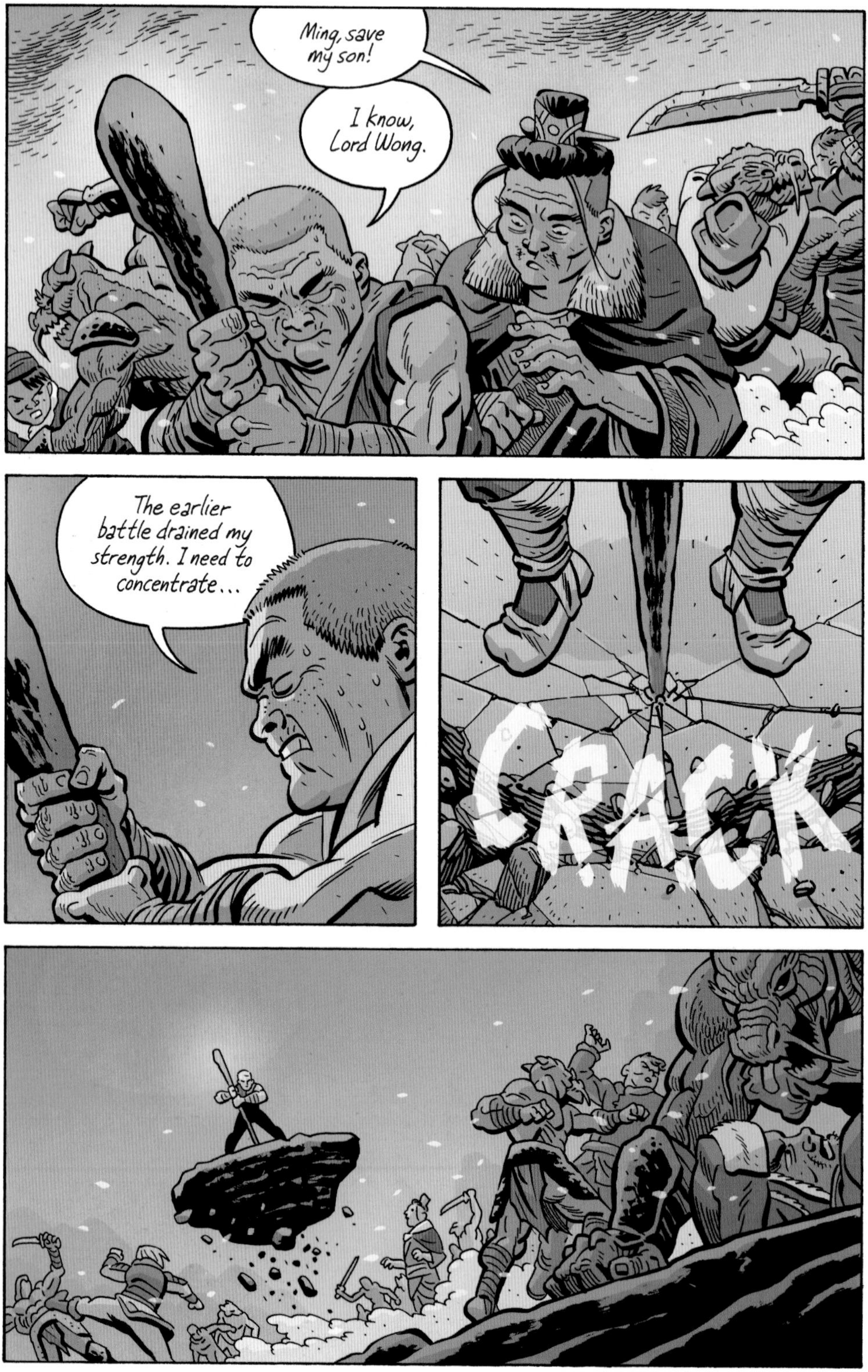
Ming, save my son!
I know, Lord Wong.
The earlier battle drained my strength. I need to concentrate...
CRACK

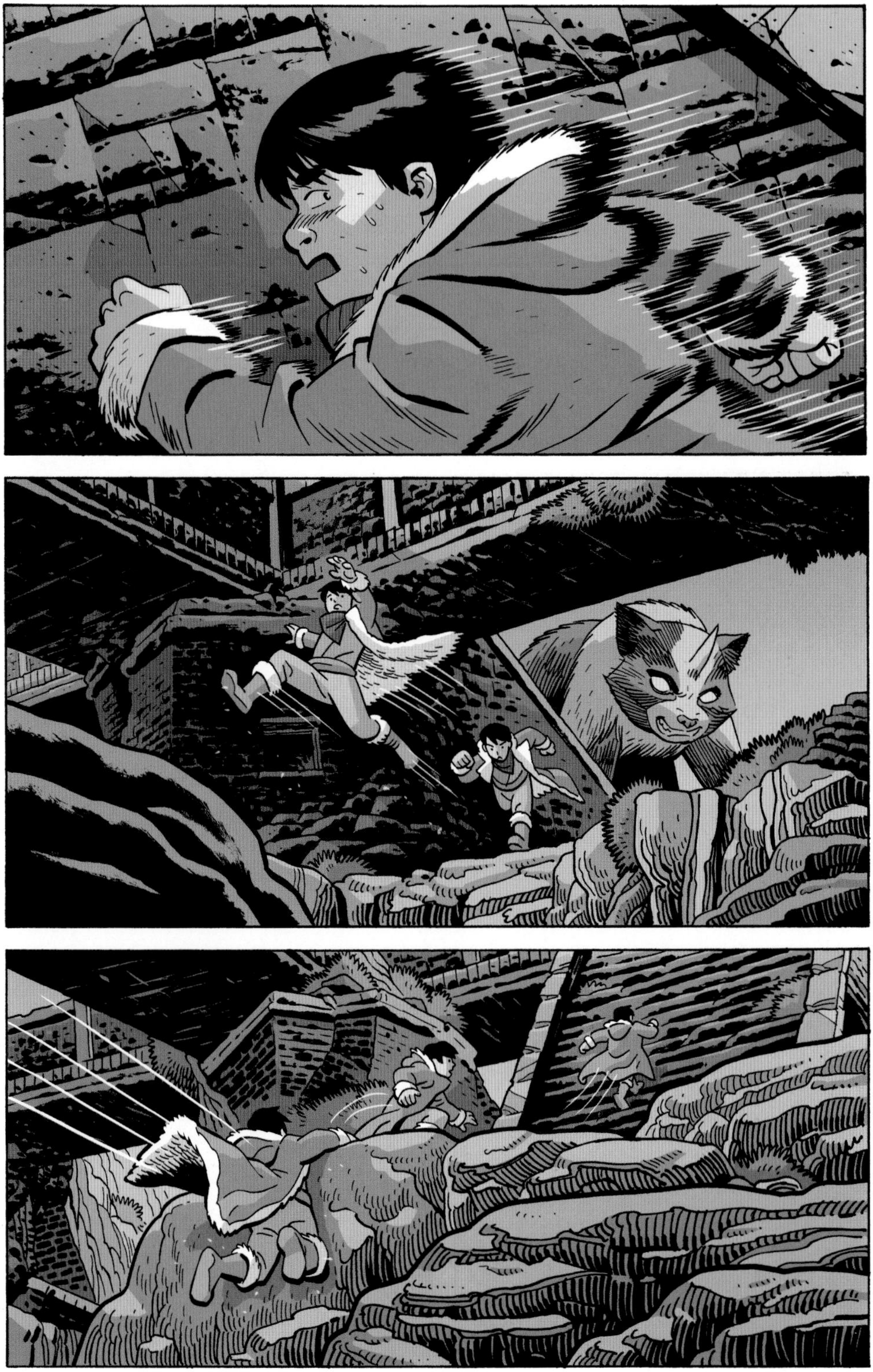

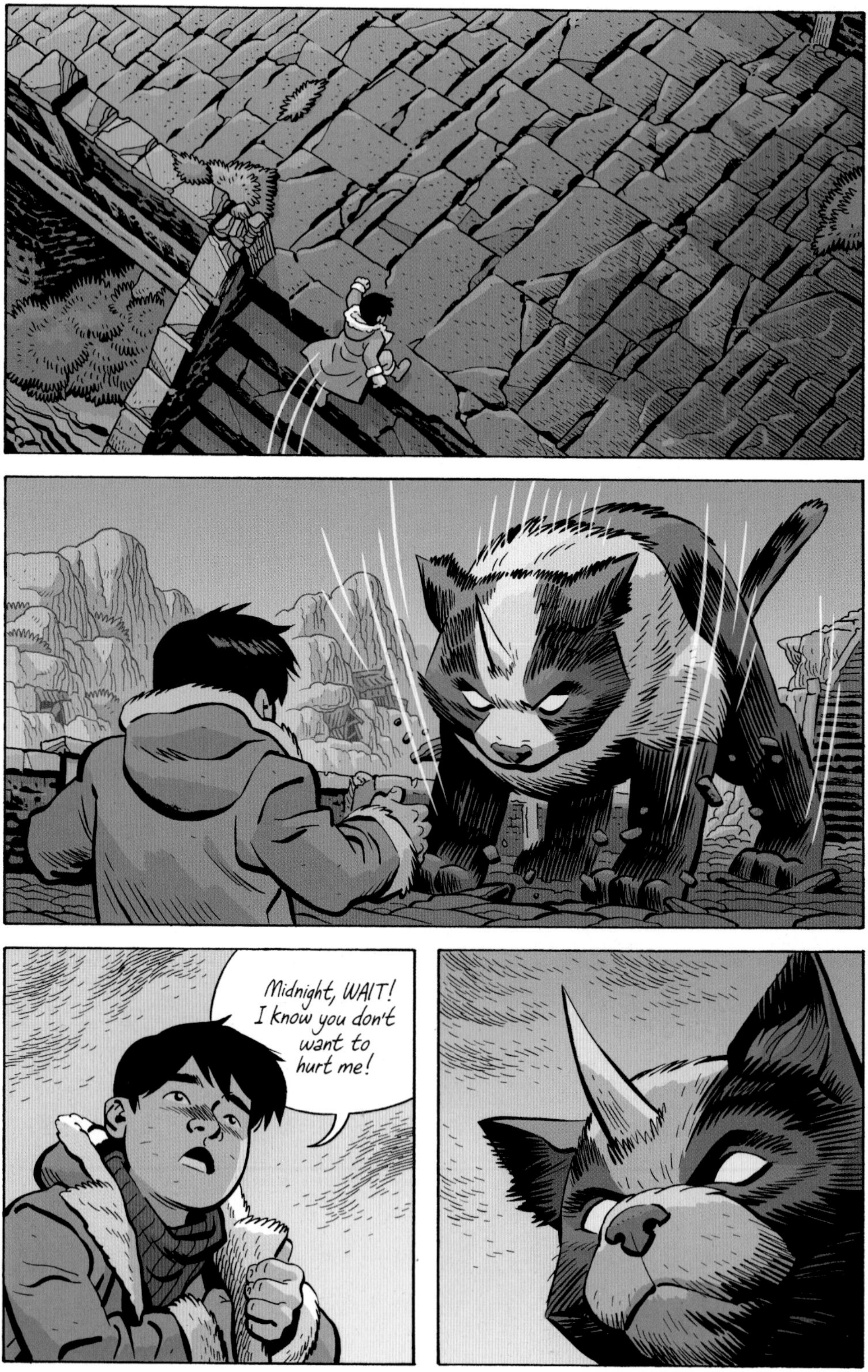
Midnight, WAIT! I know you don't want to hurt me!

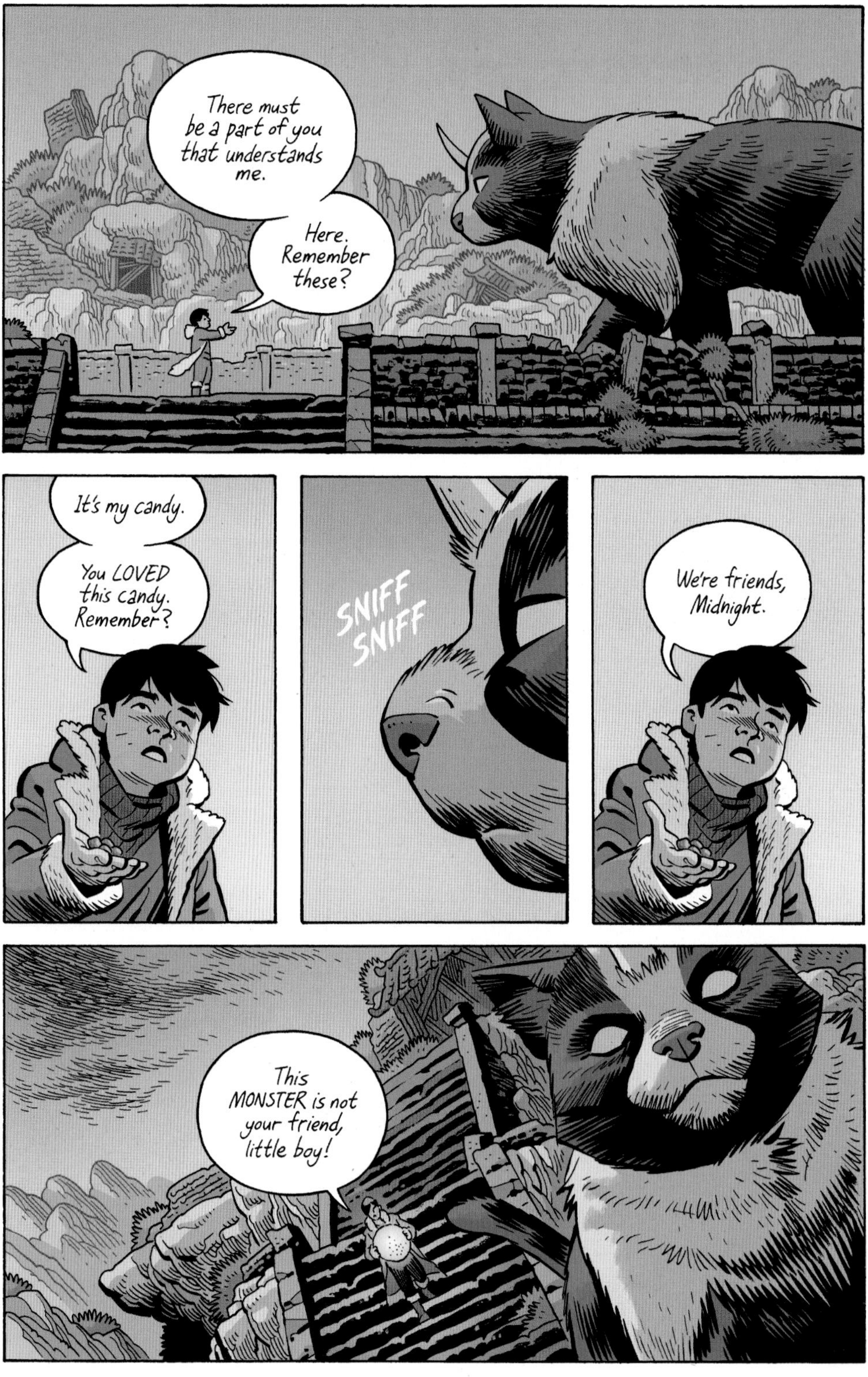
There must be a part of you that understands me.
Here. Remember these?
It's my candy.
You LOVED this candy. Remember?
SNIFF SNIFF
We're friends, Midnight.
This MONSTER is not your friend, little boy!

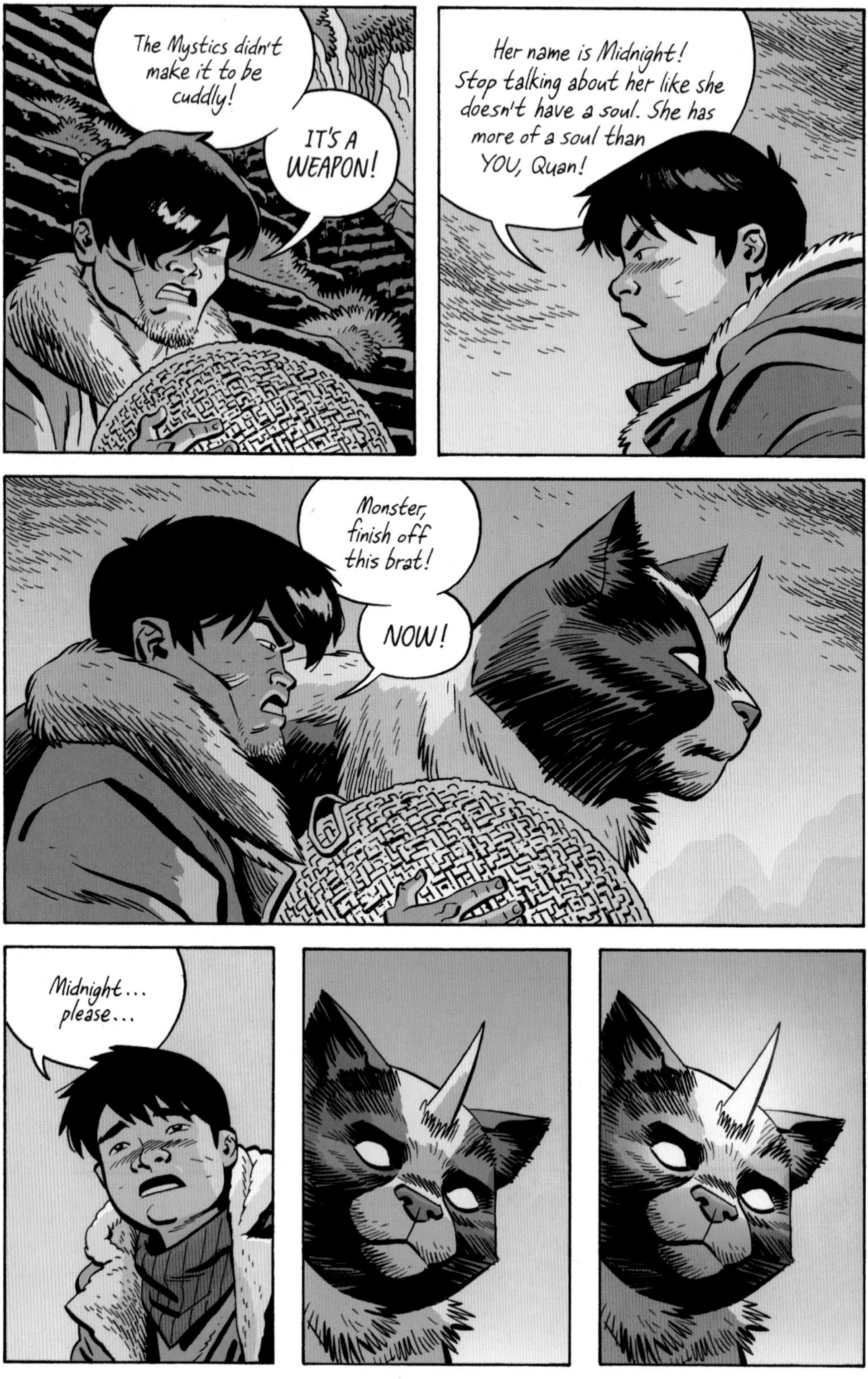
The Mystics didn't make it to be cuddly!
IT'S A WEAPON!
Her name is Midnight! Stop talking about her like she doesn't have a soul. She has more of a soul than YOU, Quan!
Monster, finish off this brat!
NOW!
Midnight... please...

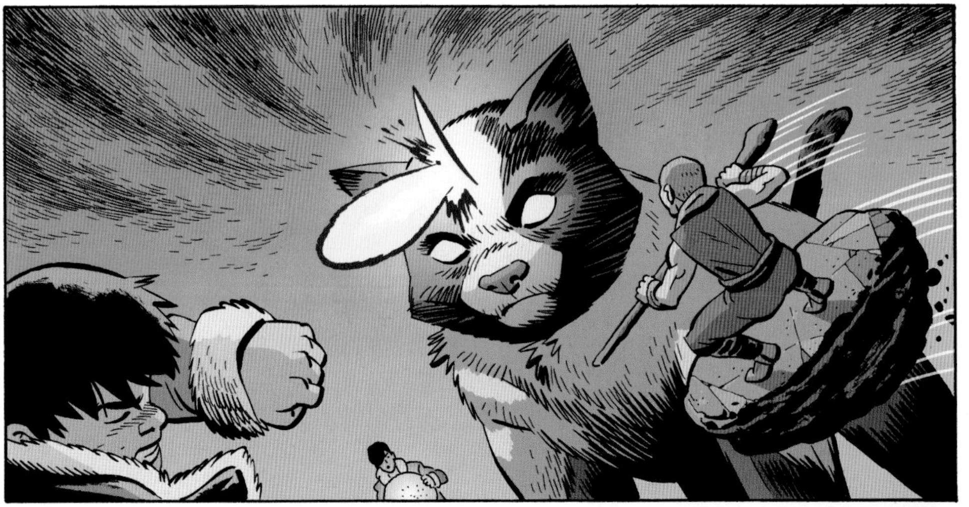

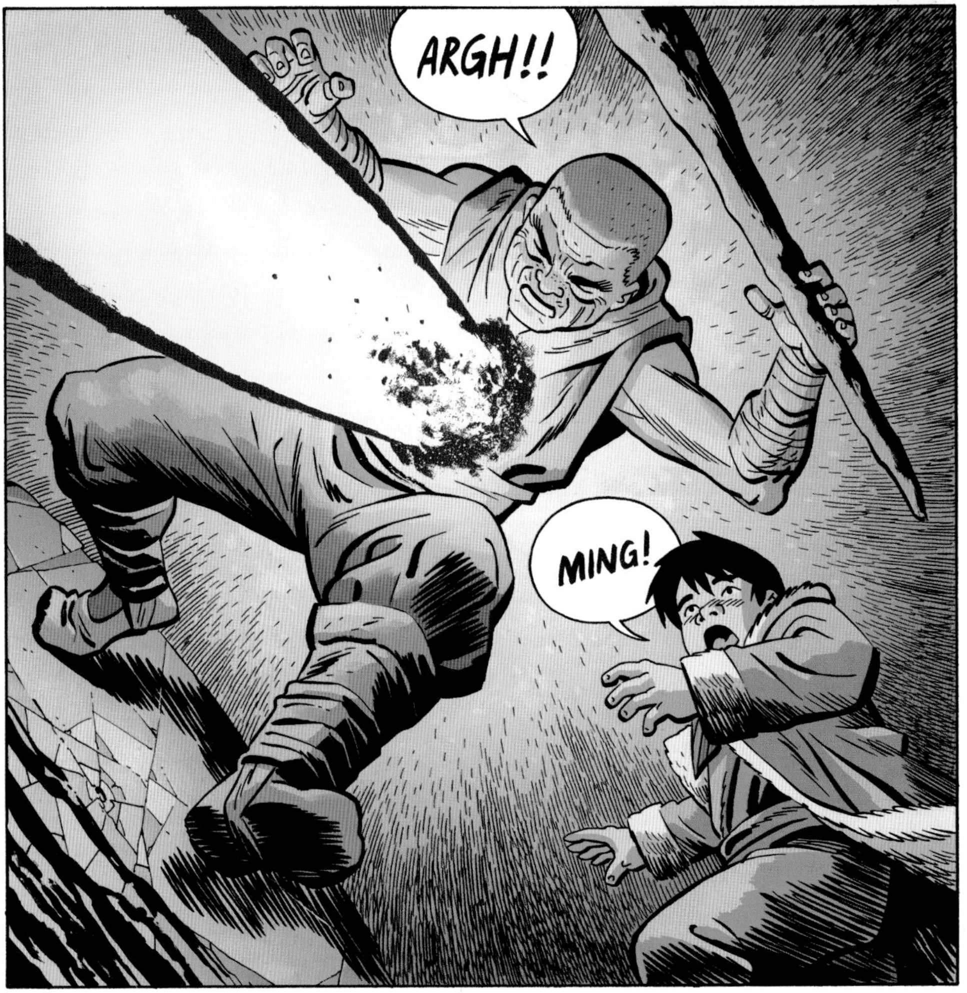
ARGH!!
MING!

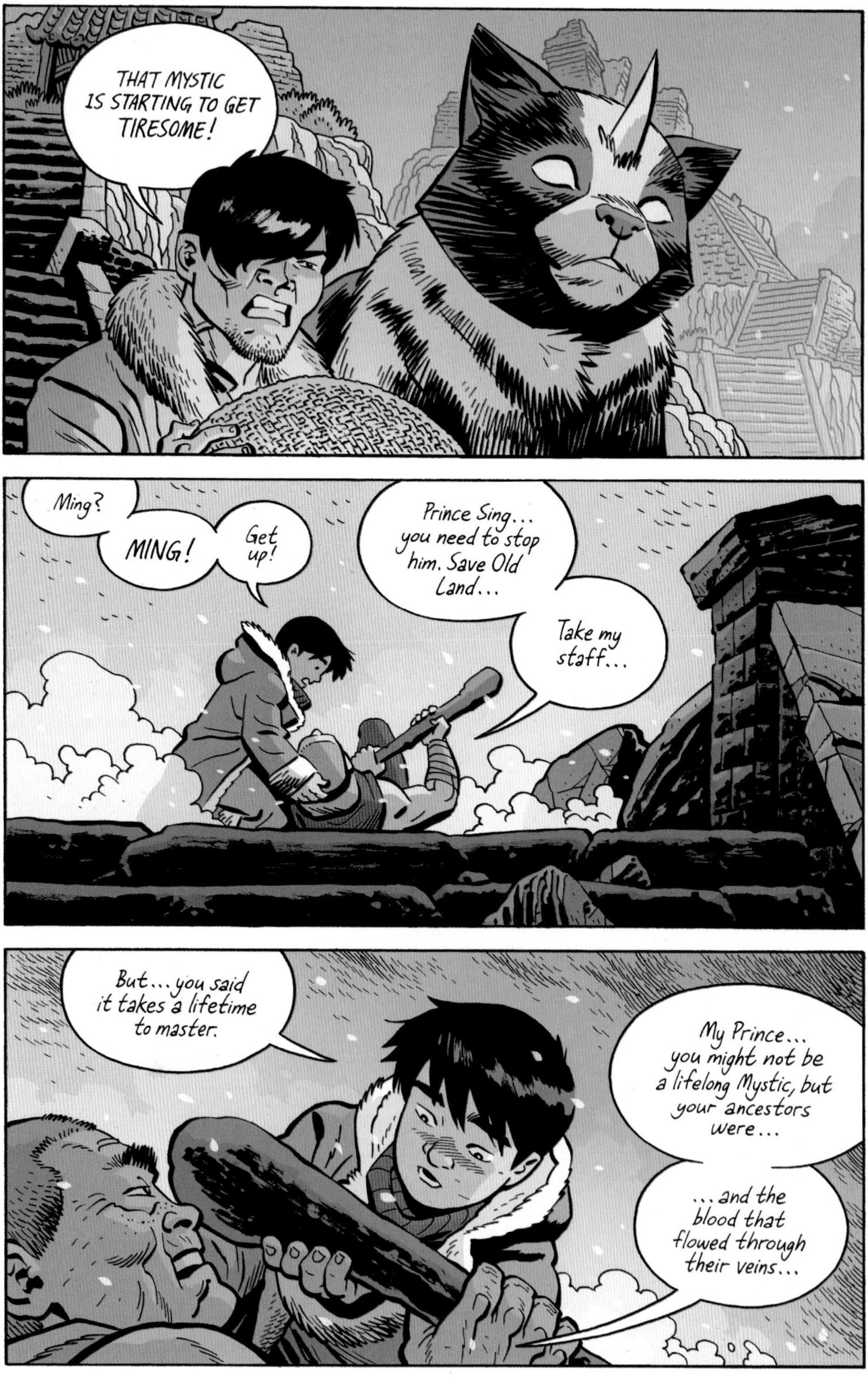
THAT MYSTIC IS STARTING TO GET TIRESOME!
Ming?
MING!
Get up!
Prince Sing... you need to stop him. Save Old Land...
Take my staff...
But... you said it takes a lifetime to master.
My Prince... you might not be a lifelong Mystic, but your ancestors were...
...and the blood that flowed through their veins...

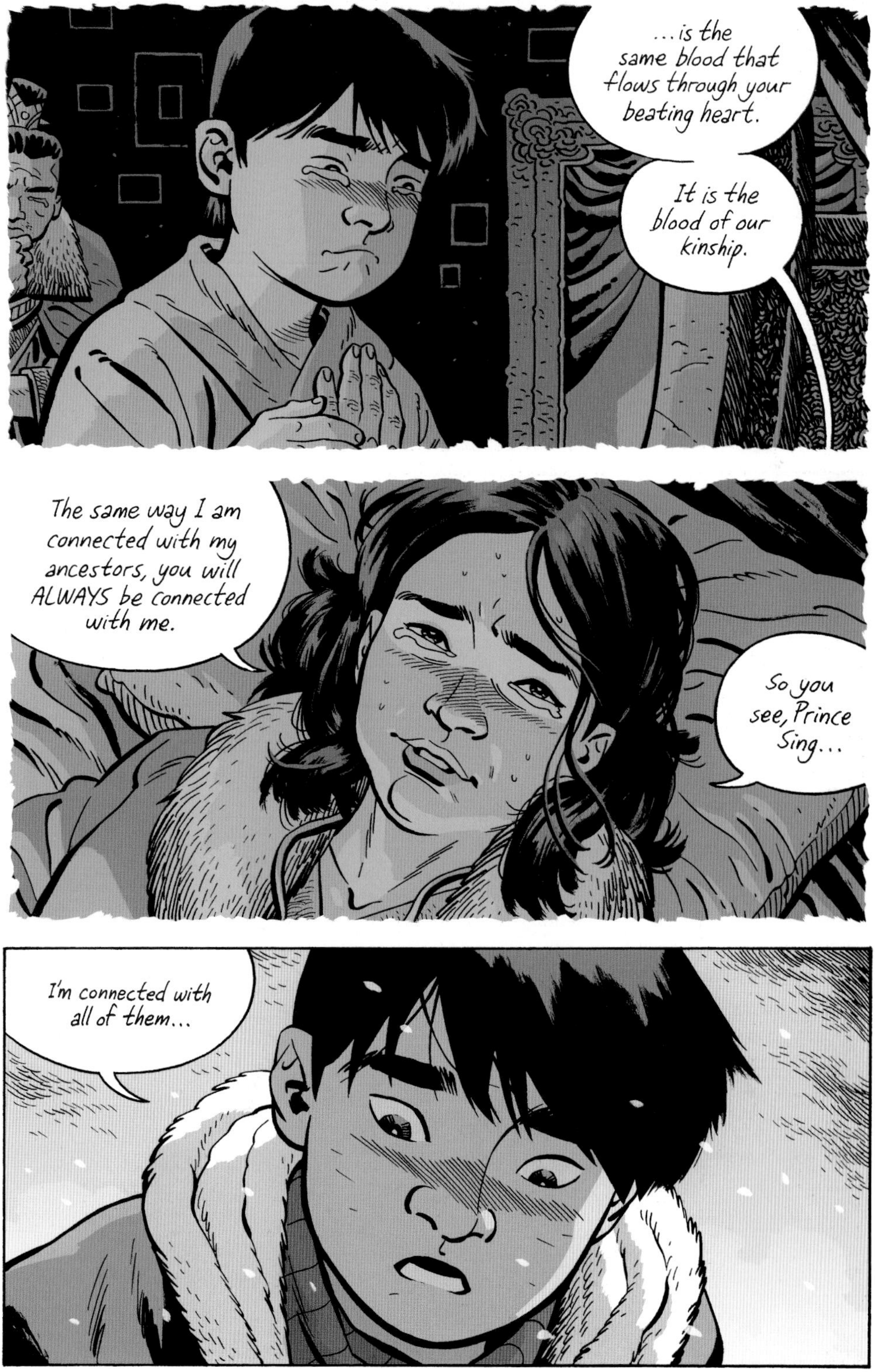
...is the same blood that flows through your beating heart.
It is the blood of our kinship.
The same way I am connected with my ancestors, you will ALWAYS be connected with me.
So you see, Prince Sing...
I'm connected with all of them...

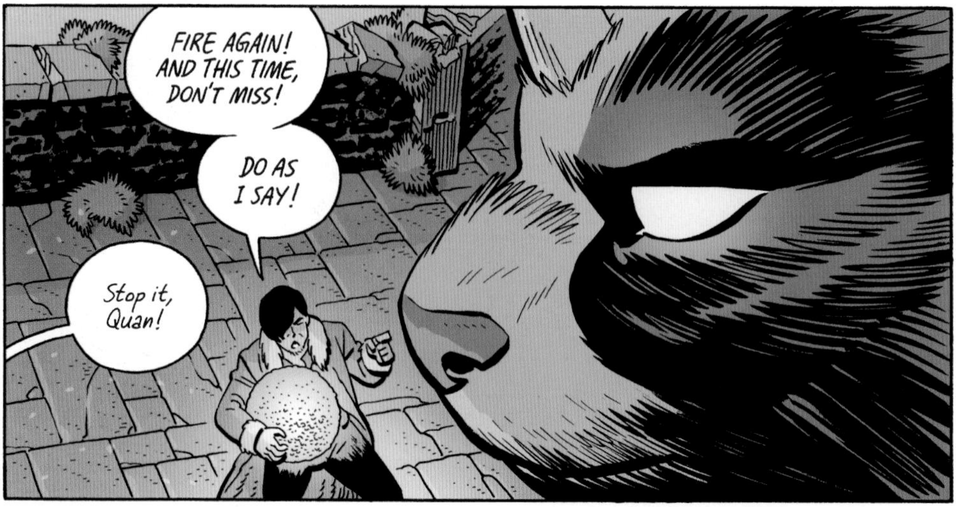
FIRE AGAIN! AND THIS TIME, DON'T MISS!
DO AS I SAY!
Stop it, Quan!

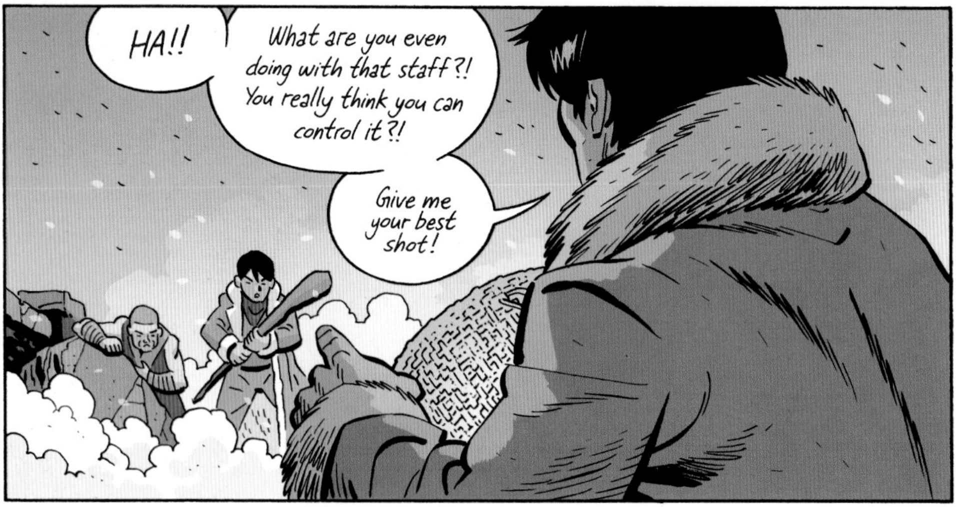
HA!!
What are you even doing with that staff?! You really think you can control it?!
Give me your best shot!

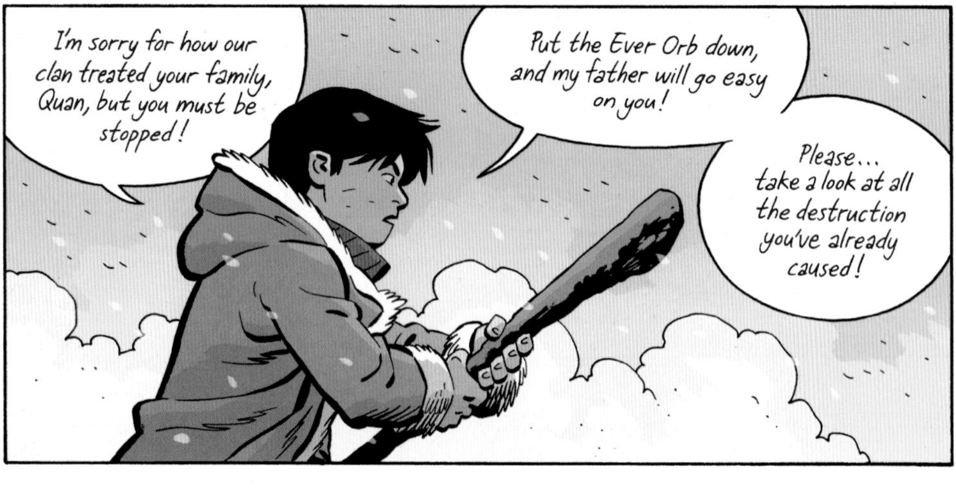
I'm sorry for how our clan treated your family, Quan, but you must be stopped!
Put the Ever Orb down, and my father will go easy on you!
Please... take a look at all the destruction you've already caused!

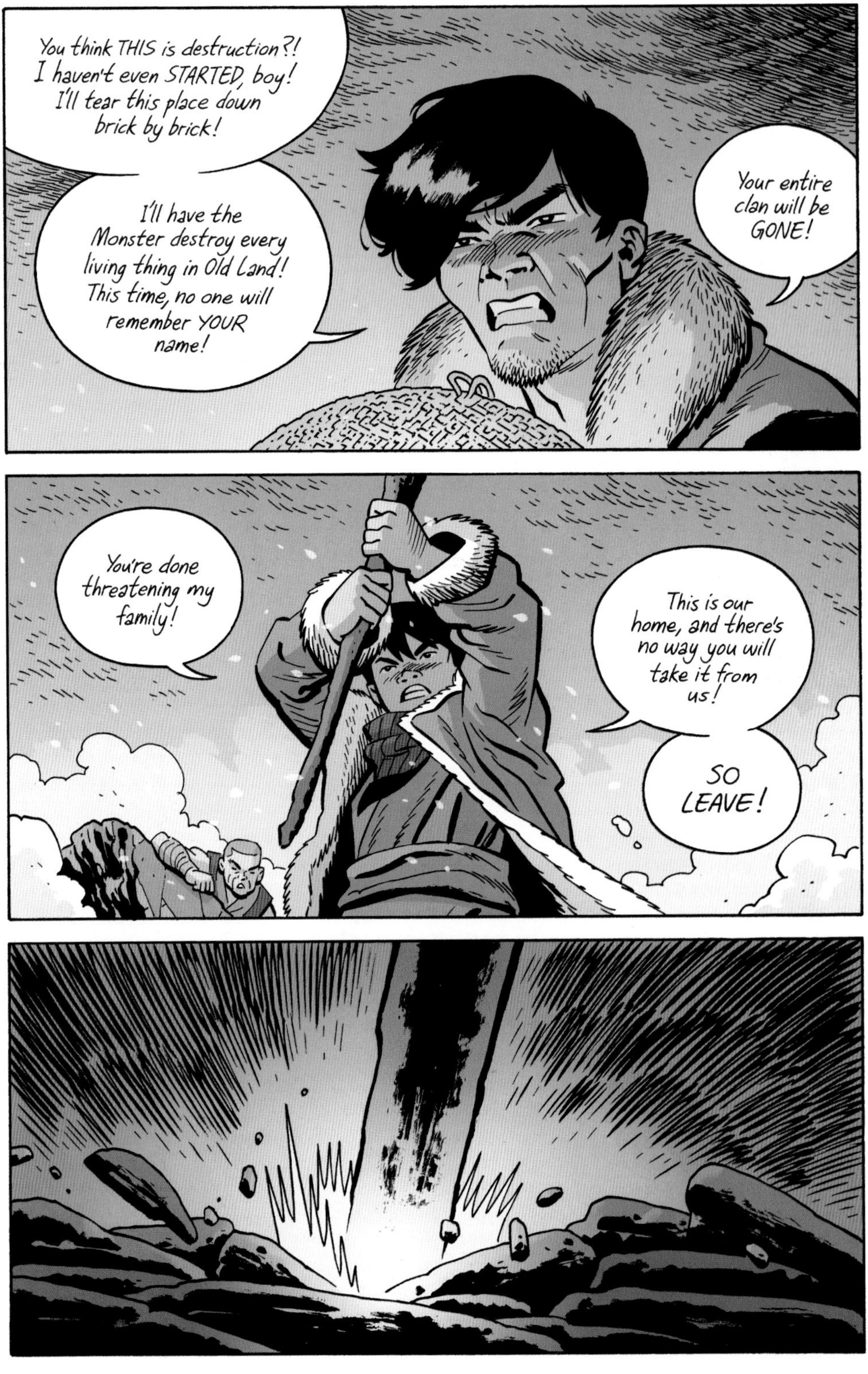
You think THIS is destruction?! I haven't even STARTED, boy! I'll tear this place down brick by brick!
I'll have the Monster destroy every living thing in Old Land! This time, no one will remember YOUR name!
Your entire clan will be GONE!
You're done threatening my family!
This is our home, and there's no way you will take it from us!
SO LEAVE!

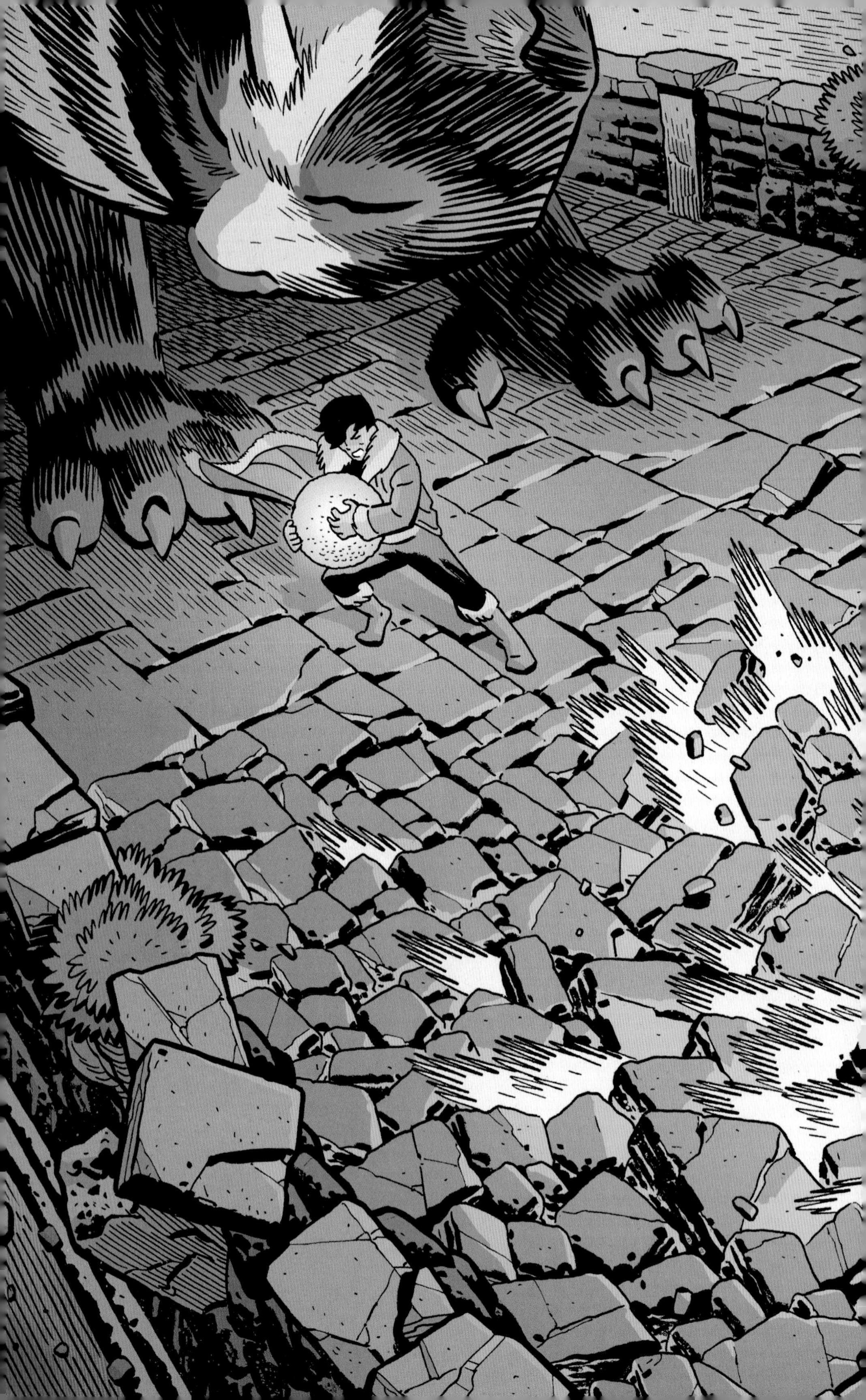

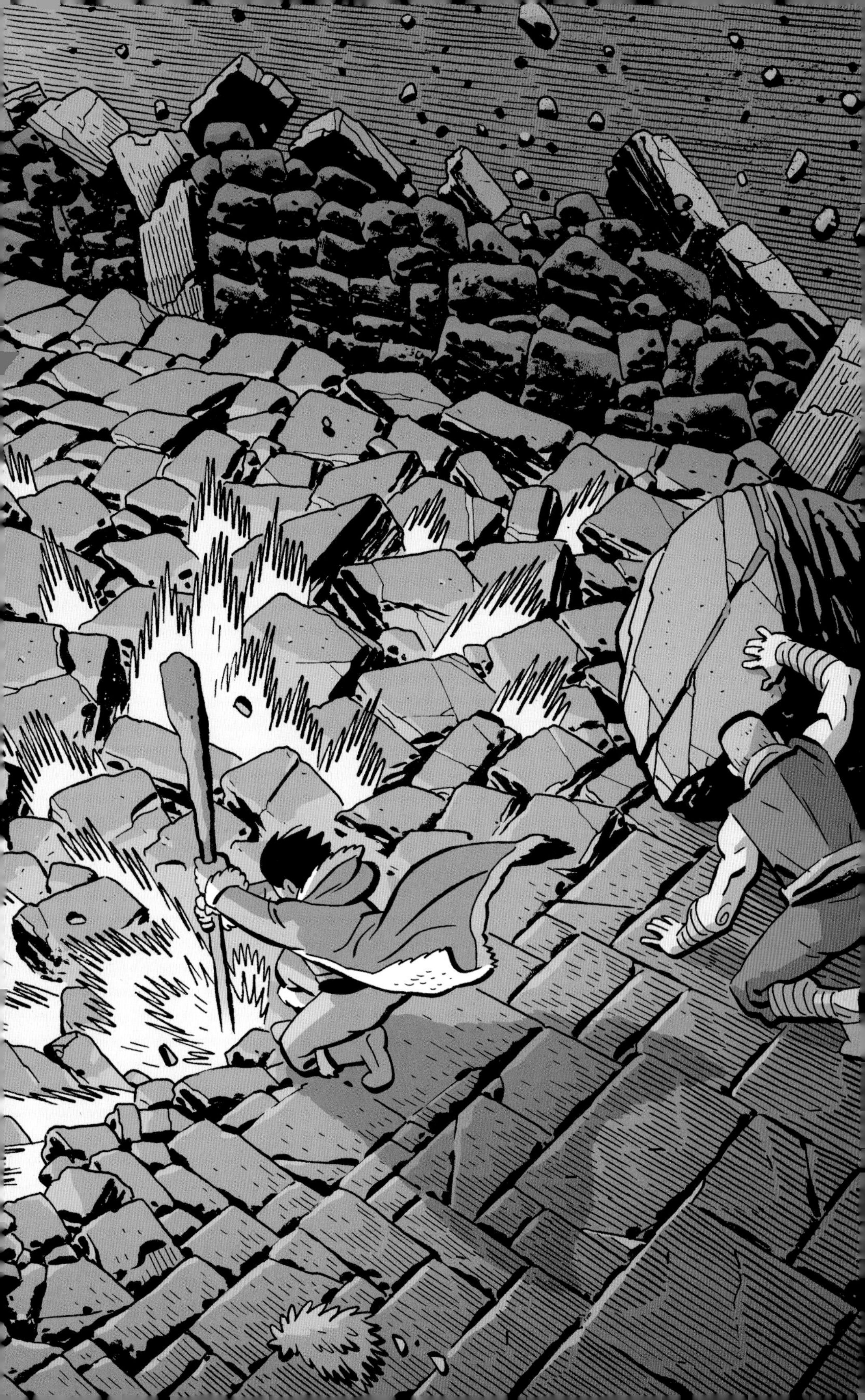

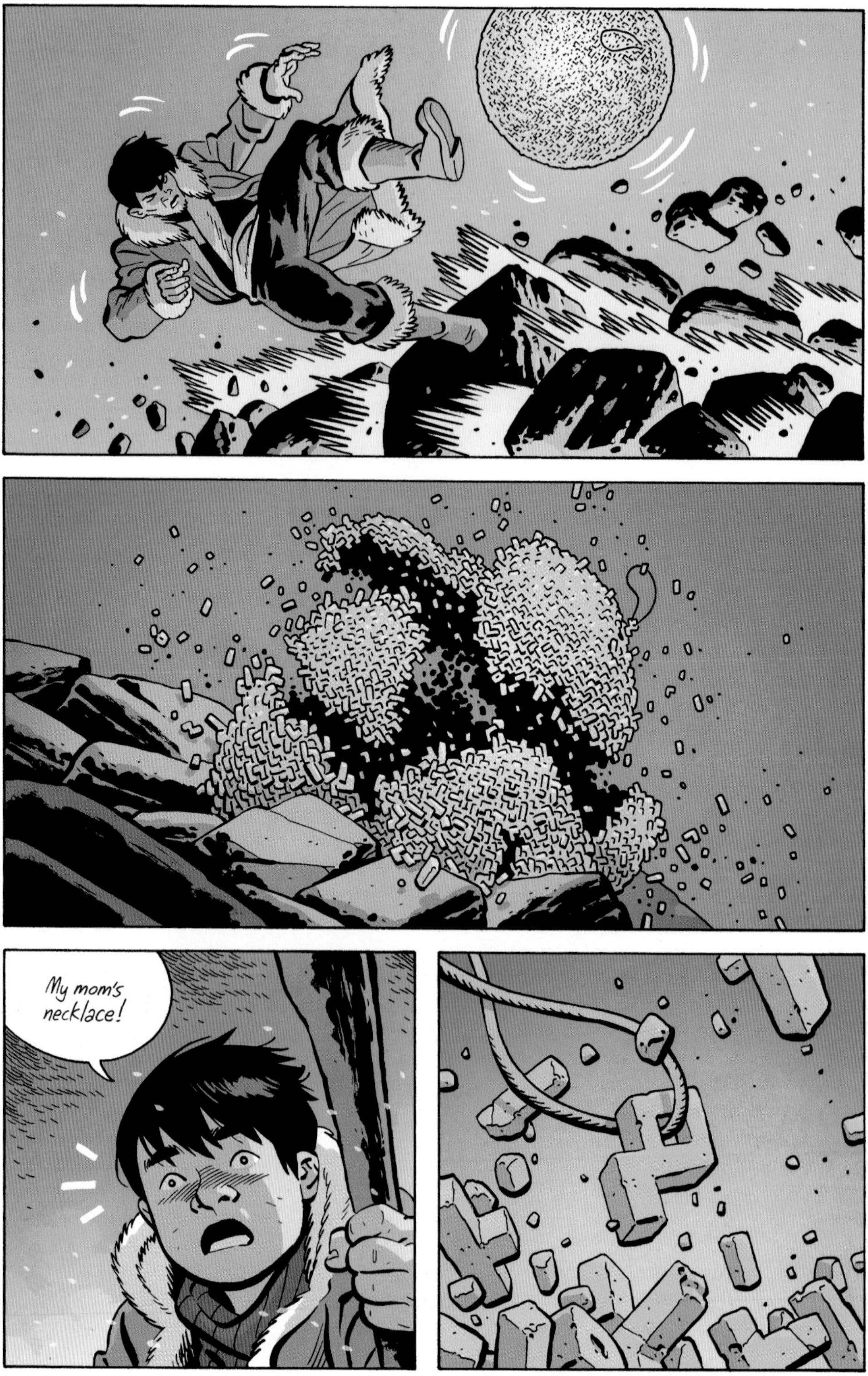
My mom's necklace!

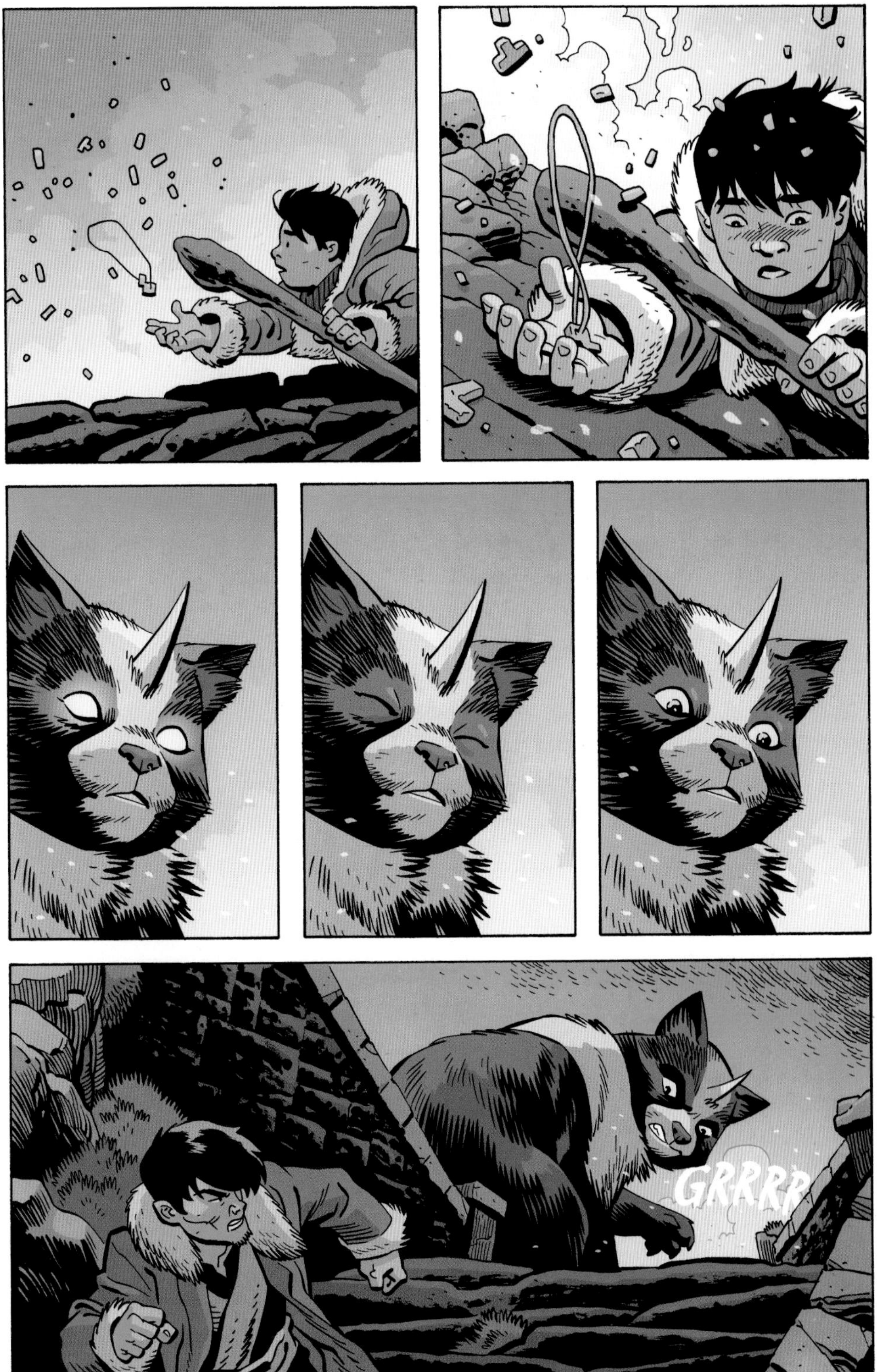
GRRRR

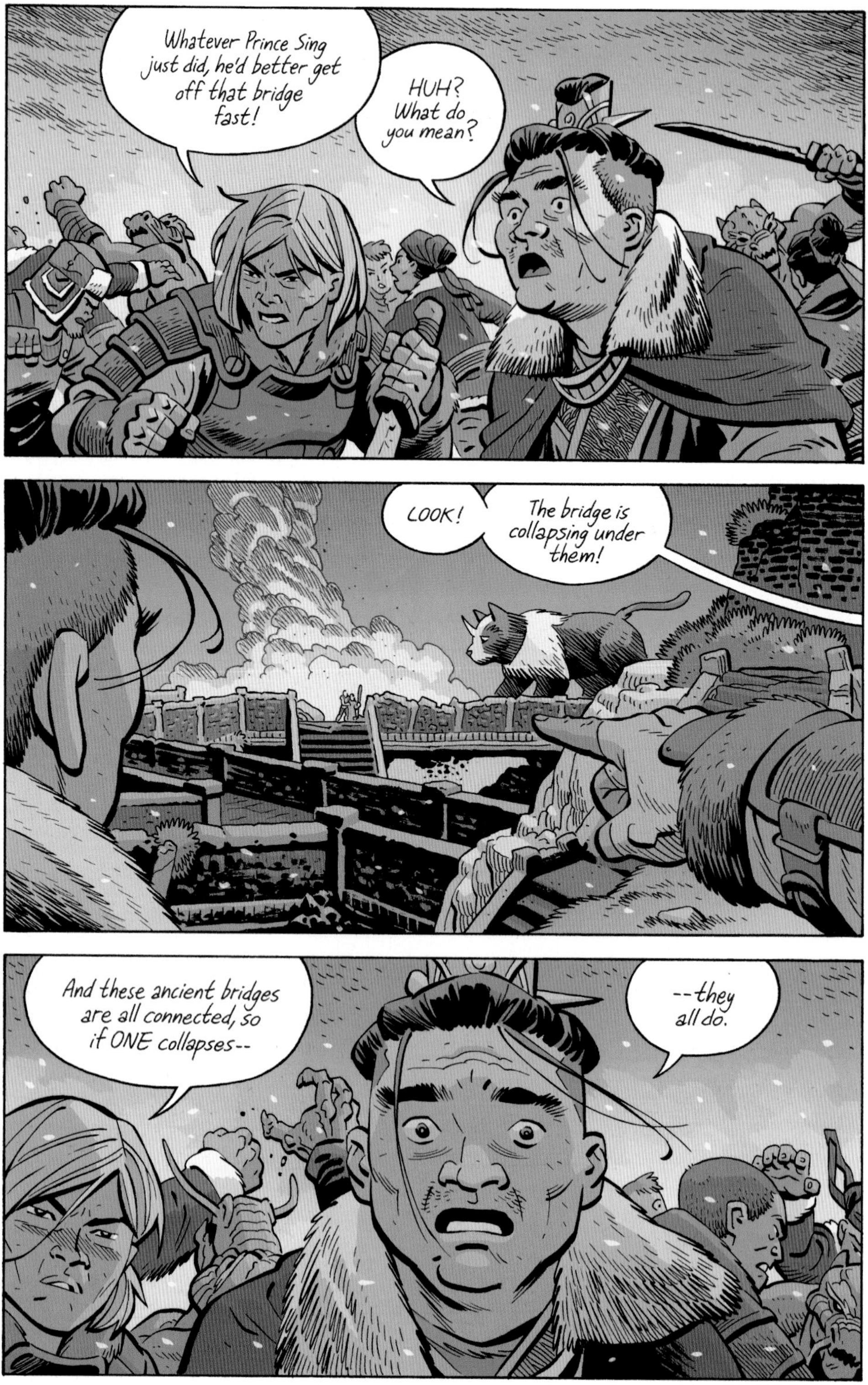
Whatever Prince Sing just did, he'd better get off that bridge fast!
HUH? What do you mean?
LOOK!
The bridge is collapsing under them!
And these ancient bridges are all connected, so if ONE collapses--
--they all do.

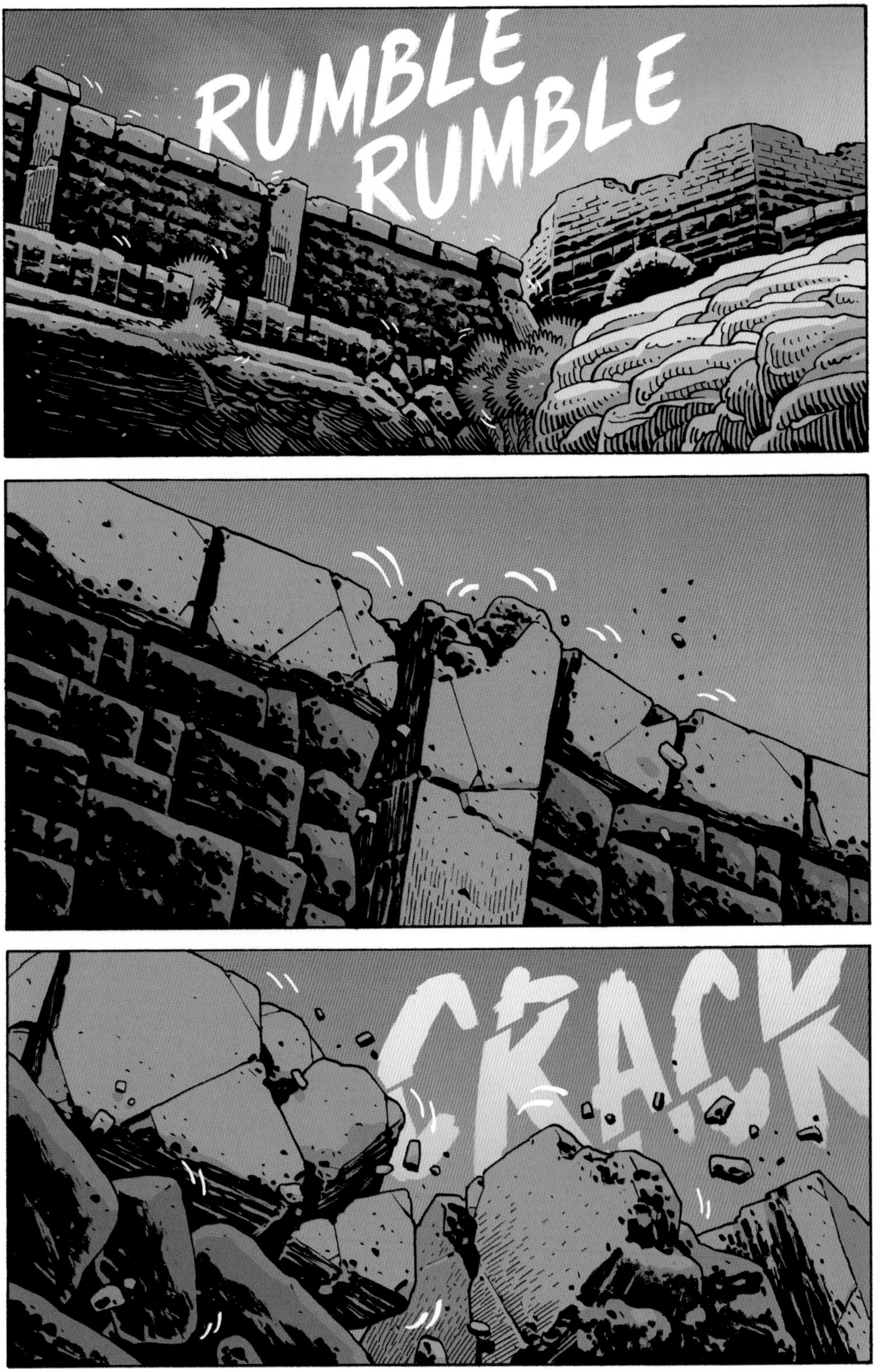
RUMBLE
RUMBLE
CRACK

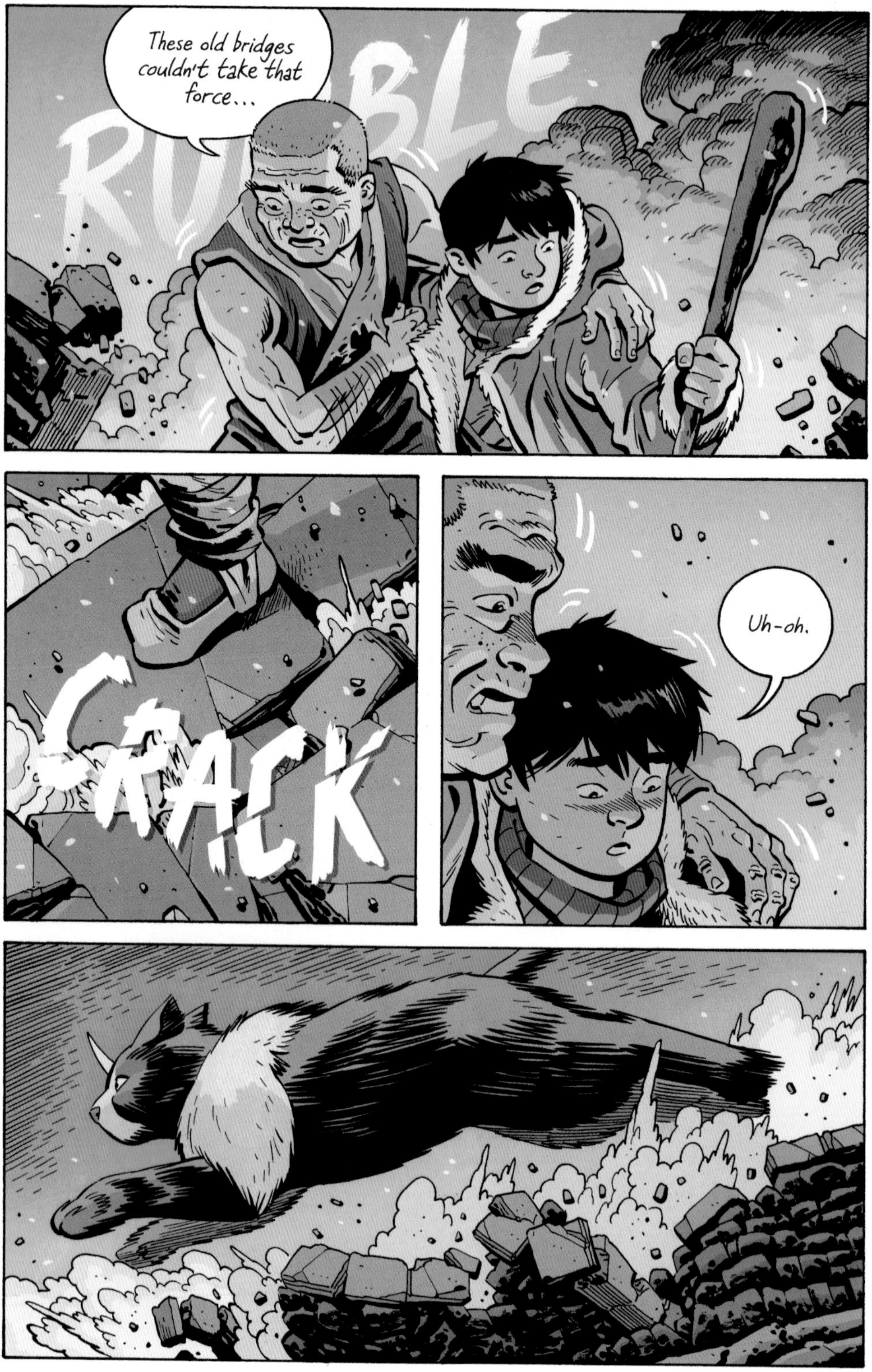
These old bridges couldn't take that force...
CRACK
Uh-oh.

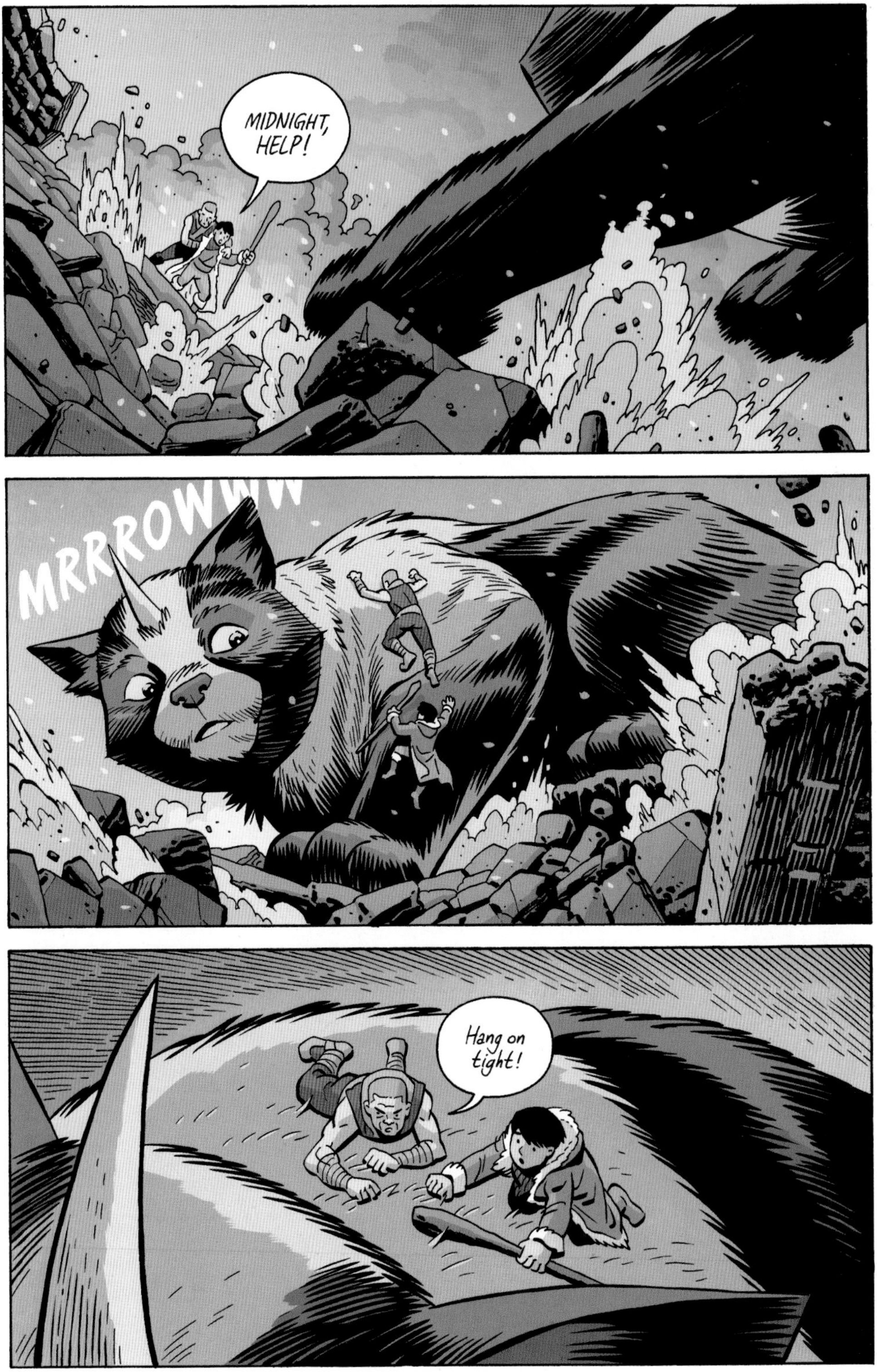
MIDNIGHT, HELP!
MRRROWWW
Hang on tight!

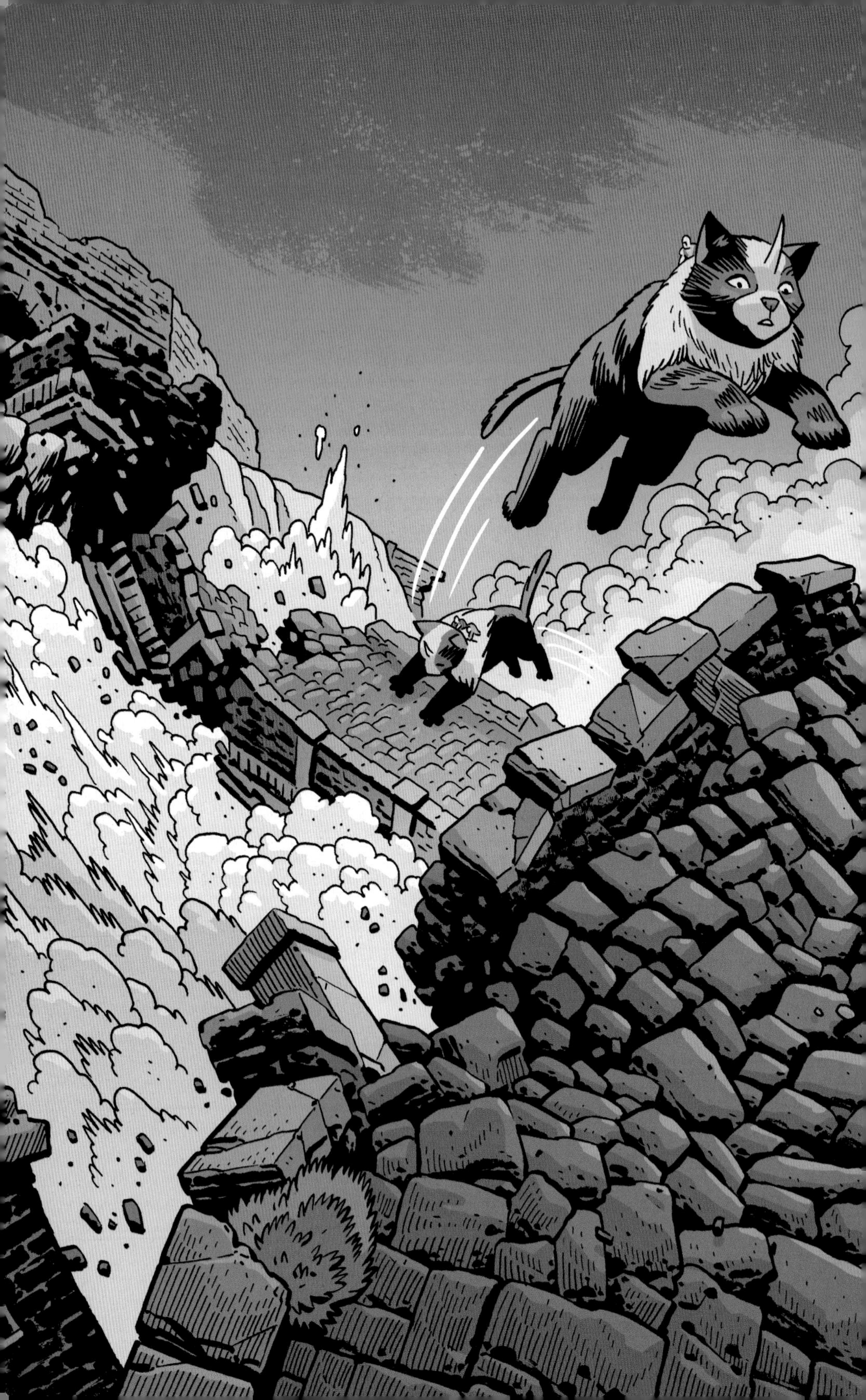

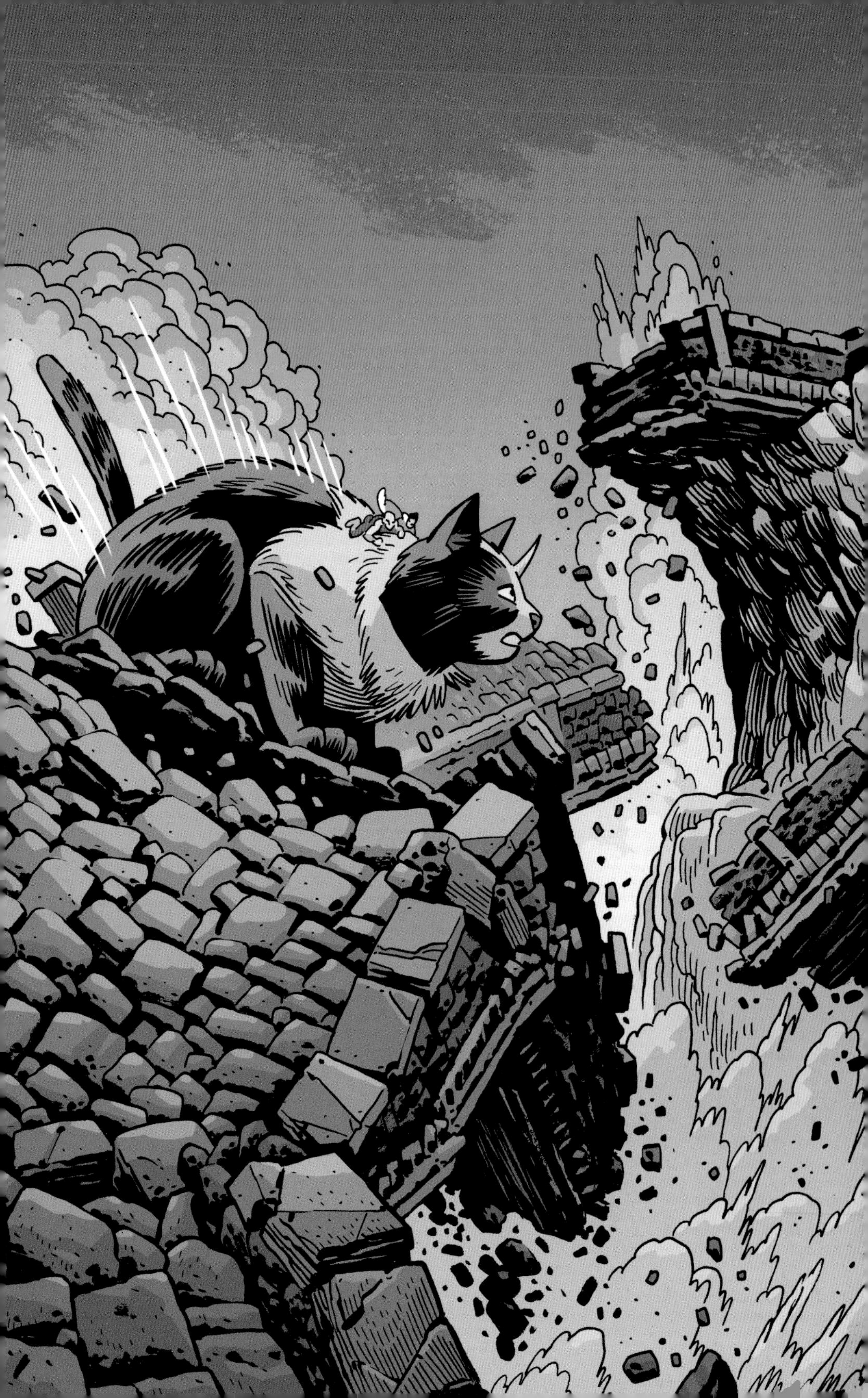

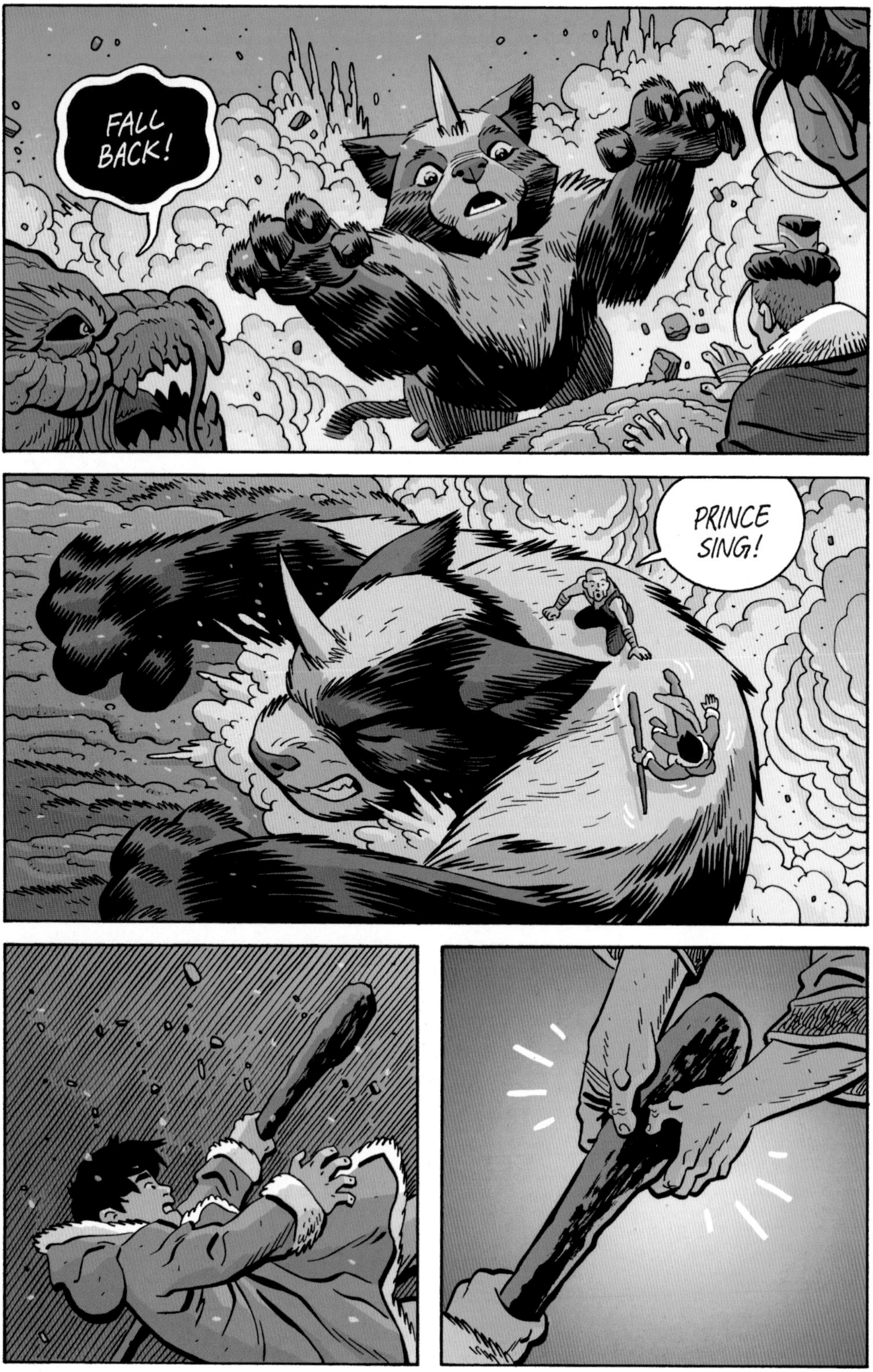
FALL BACK!
PRINCE SING!

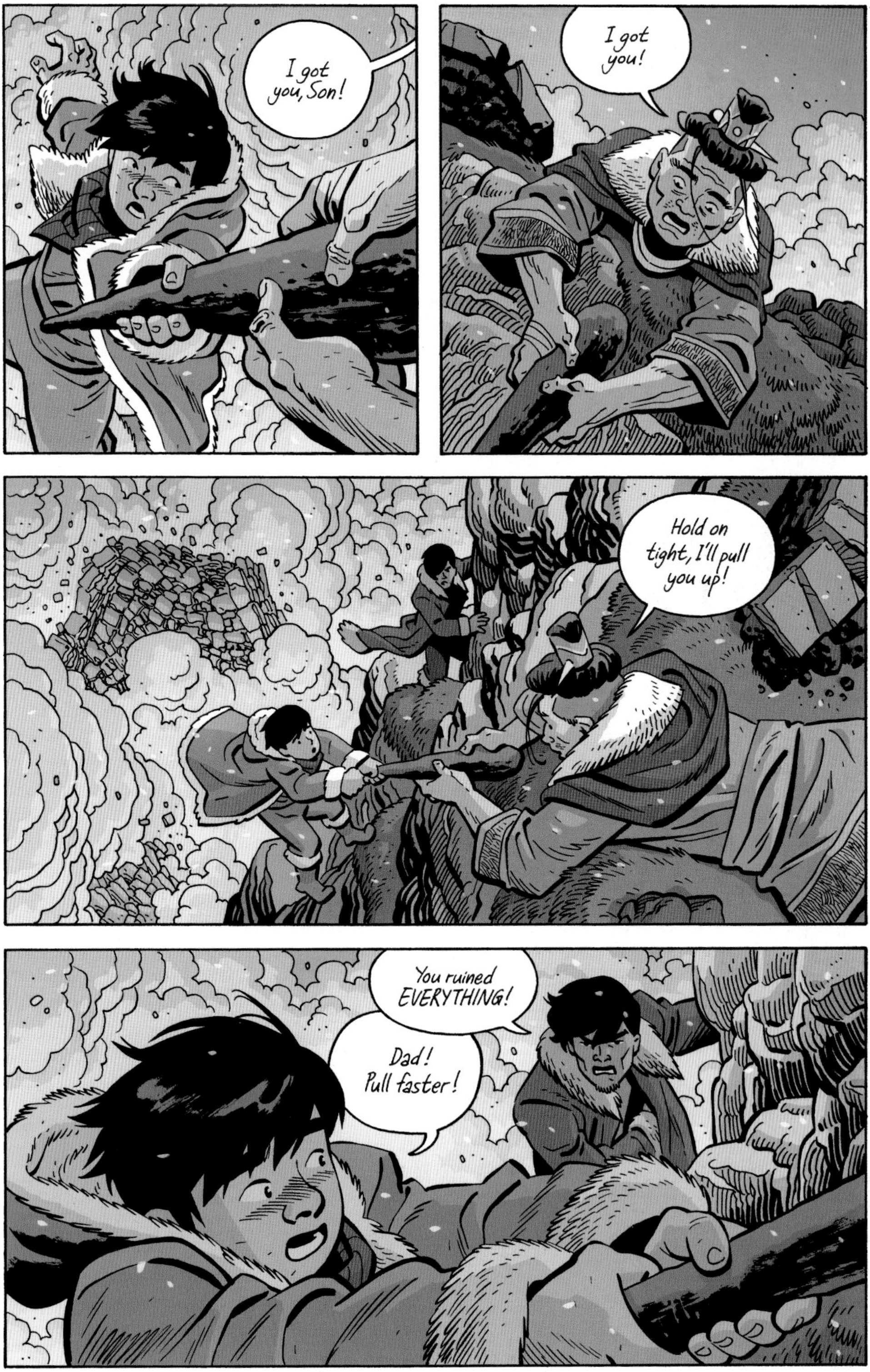
I got you, Son!
I got you!
Hold on tight, I'll pull you up!
You ruined EVERYTHING!
Dad! Pull faster!

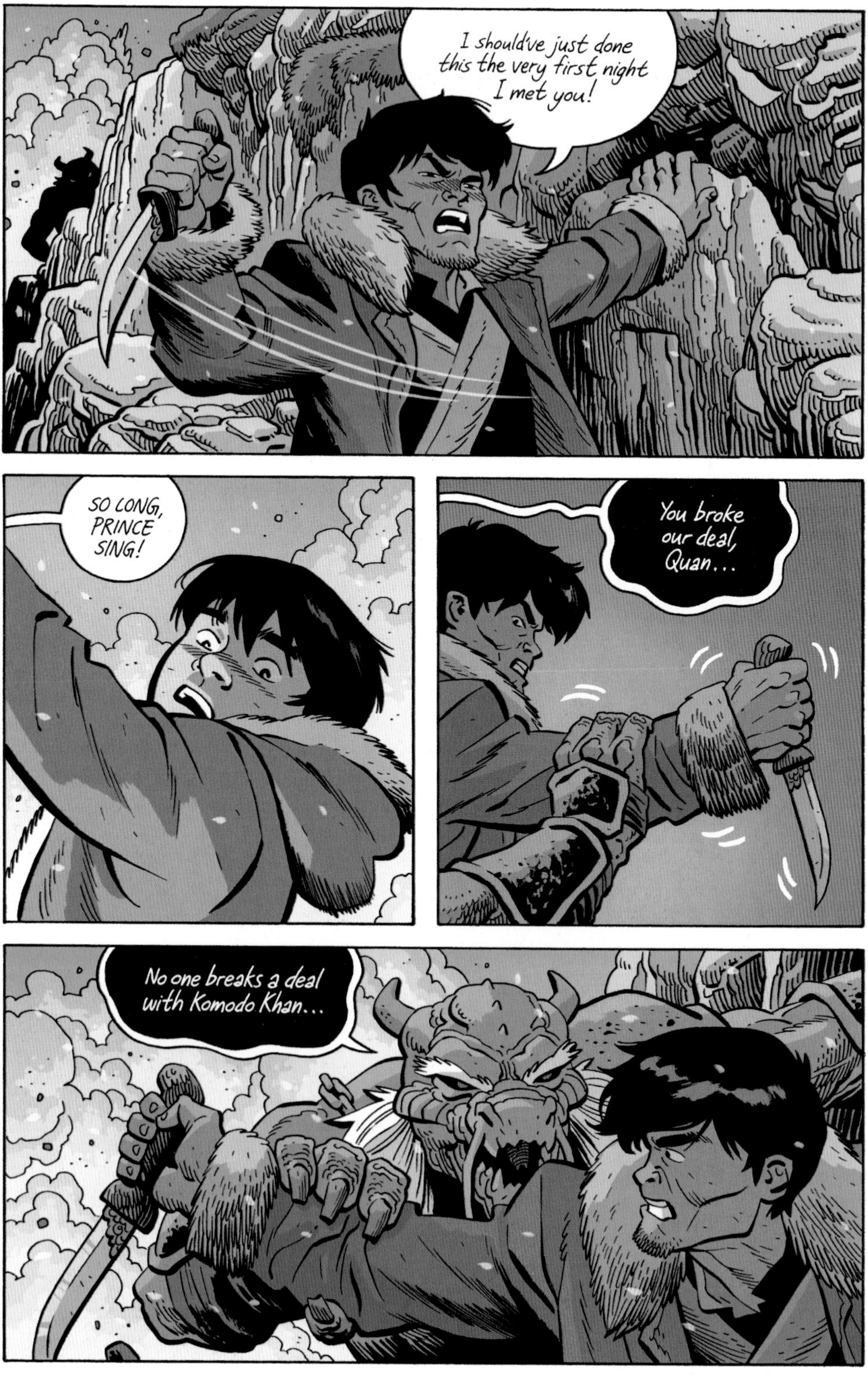
I should've just done this the very first night I met you!
SO LONG, PRINCE SING!
You broke our deal, Quan...
No one breaks a deal with Komodo Khan...

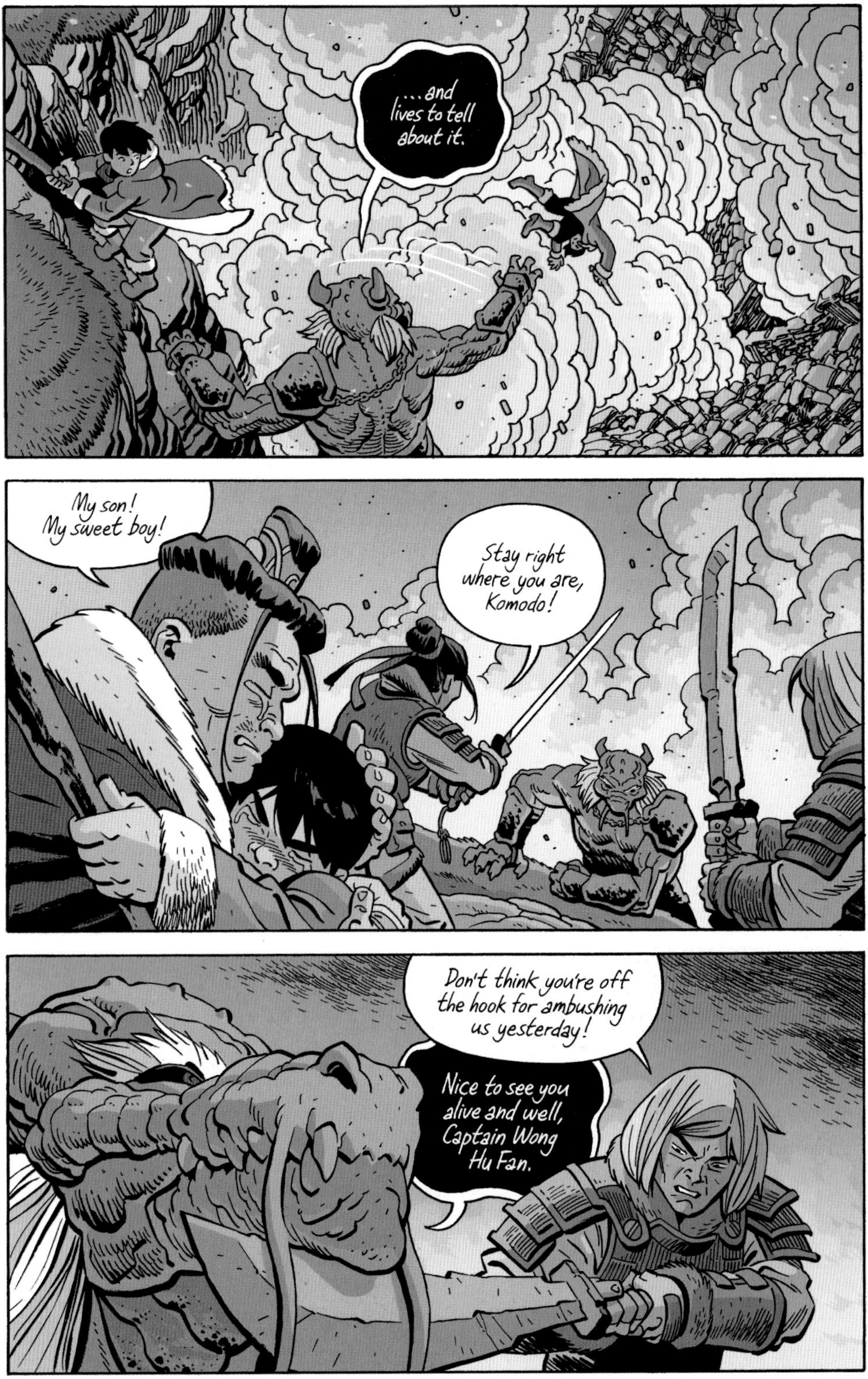
...and lives to tell about it.
My son! My sweet boy!
Stay right where you are, Komodo!
Don't think you're off the hook for ambushing us yesterday!
Nice to see you alive and well, Captain Wong Hu Fan.

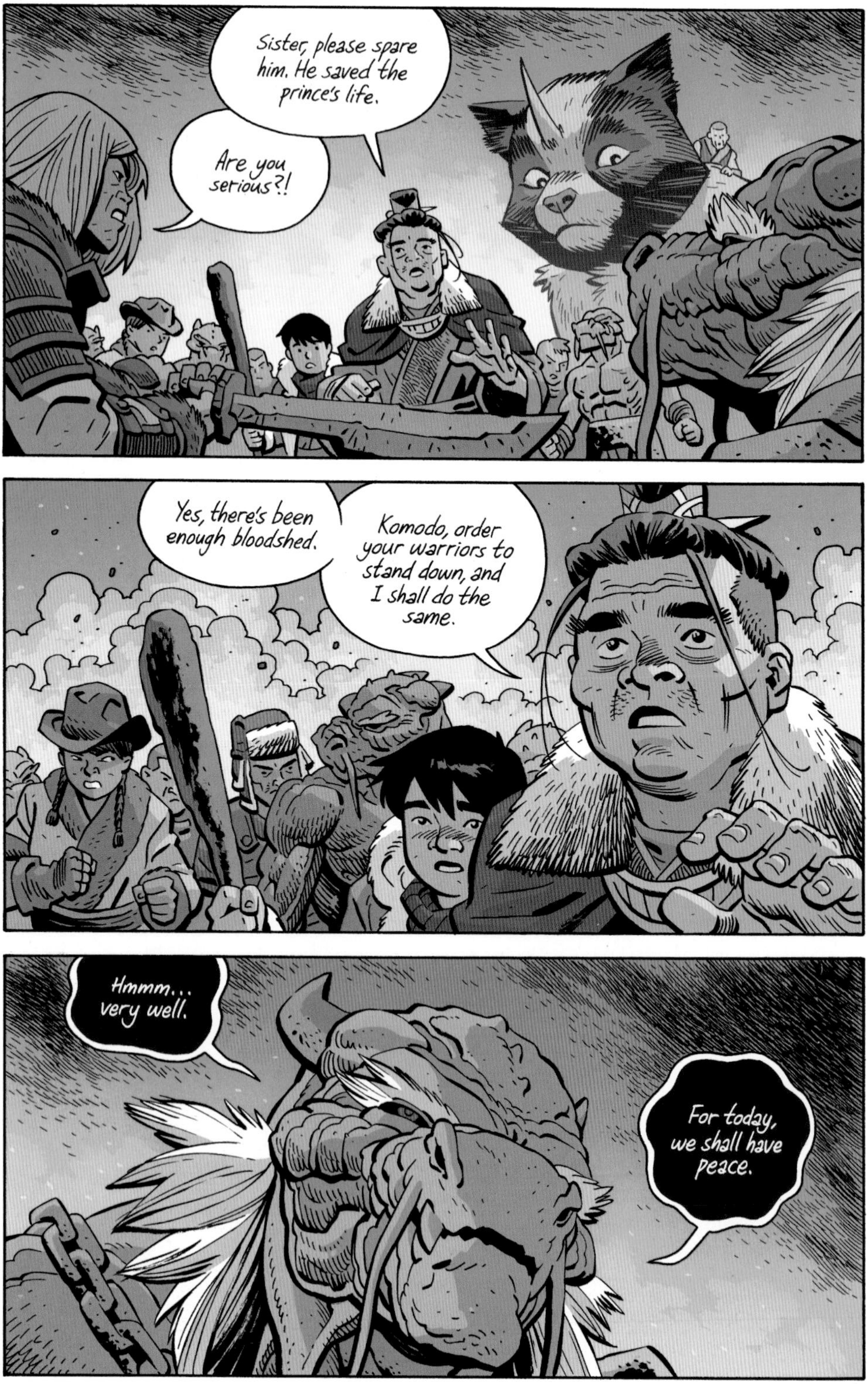
Sister, please spare him. He saved the prince's life.
Are you serious?!
Yes, there's been enough bloodshed.
Komodo, order your warriors to stand down, and I shall do the same.
Hmmm... very well.
For today, we shall have peace.

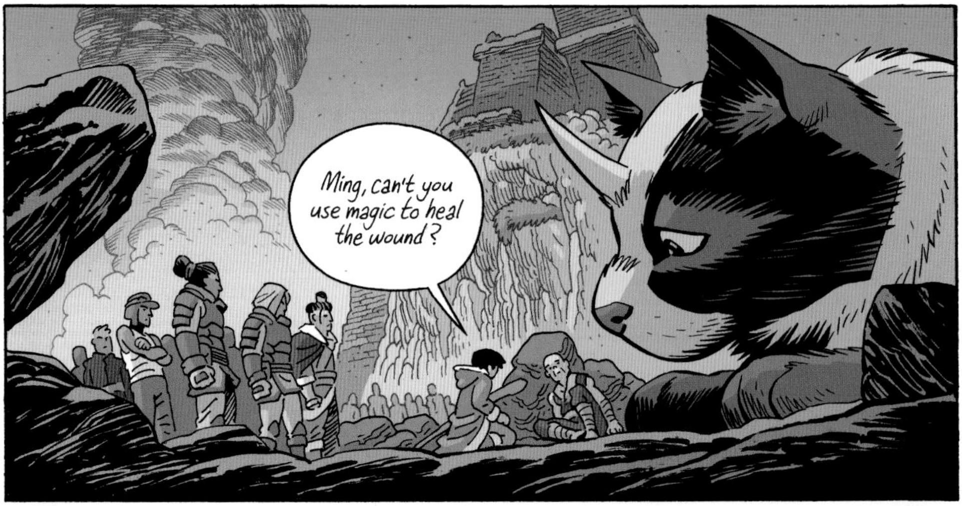
Ming, can't you use magic to heal the wound?

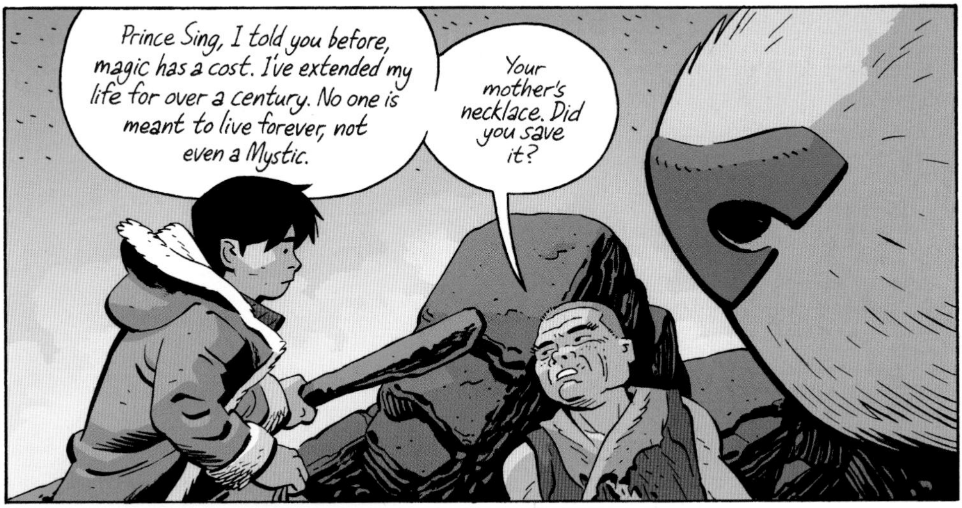
Prince Sing, I told you before, magic has a cost. I've extended my life for over a century. No one is meant to live forever, not even a Mystic.
Your mother's necklace. Did you save it?

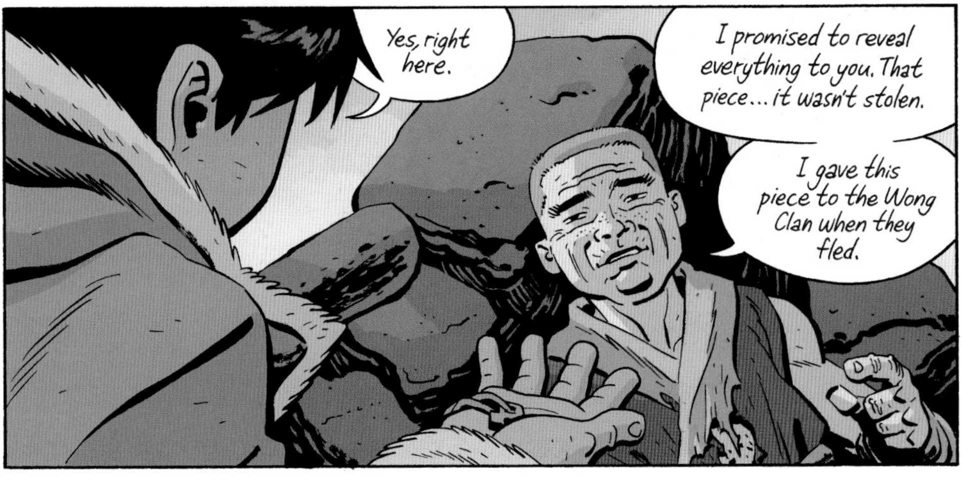
Yes, right here.
I promised to reveal everything to you. That piece... it wasn't stolen.
I gave this piece to the Wong Clan when they fled.

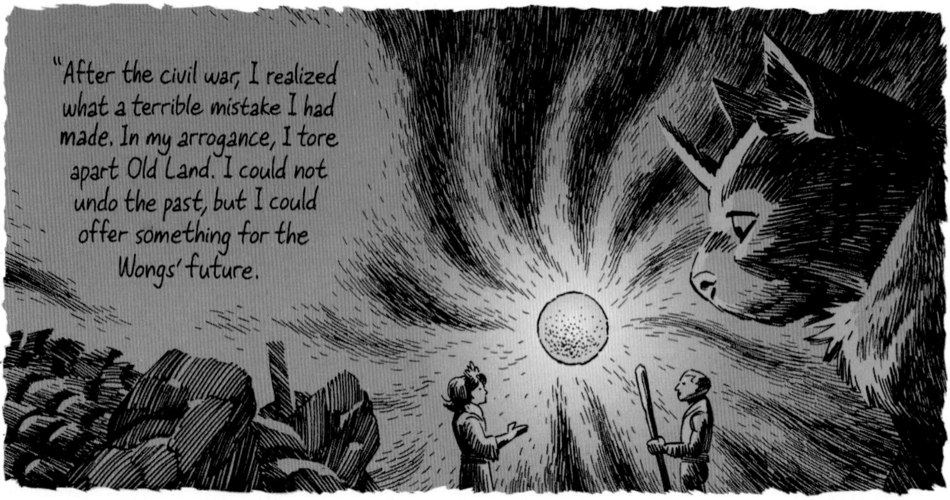
"After the civil war, I realized what a terrible mistake I had made. In my arrogance, I tore apart Old Land. I could not undo the past, but I could offer something for the Wongs' future.

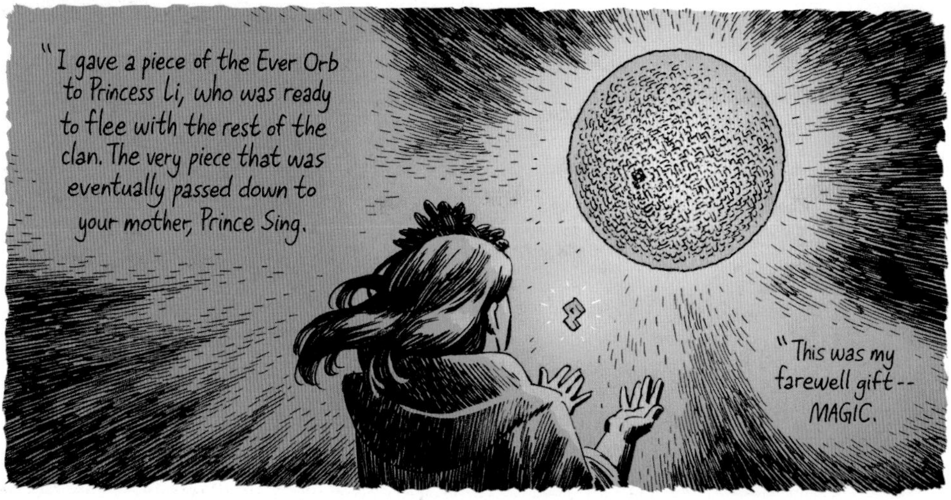
"I gave a piece of the Ever Orb to Princess Li, who was ready to flee with the rest of the clan. The very piece that was eventually passed down to your mother, Prince Sing.
"This was my farewell gift-- MAGIC.

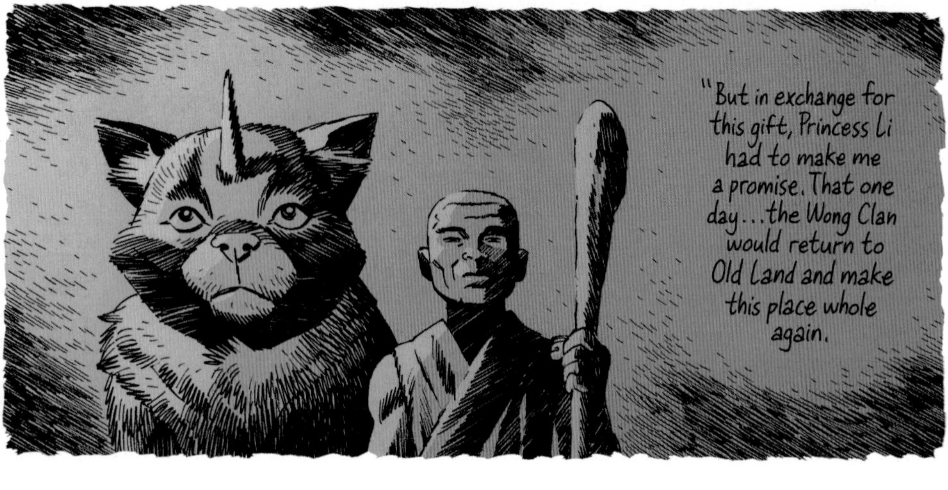
"But in exchange for this gift, Princess Li had to make me a promise. That one day...the Wong Clan would return to Old Land and make this place whole again.

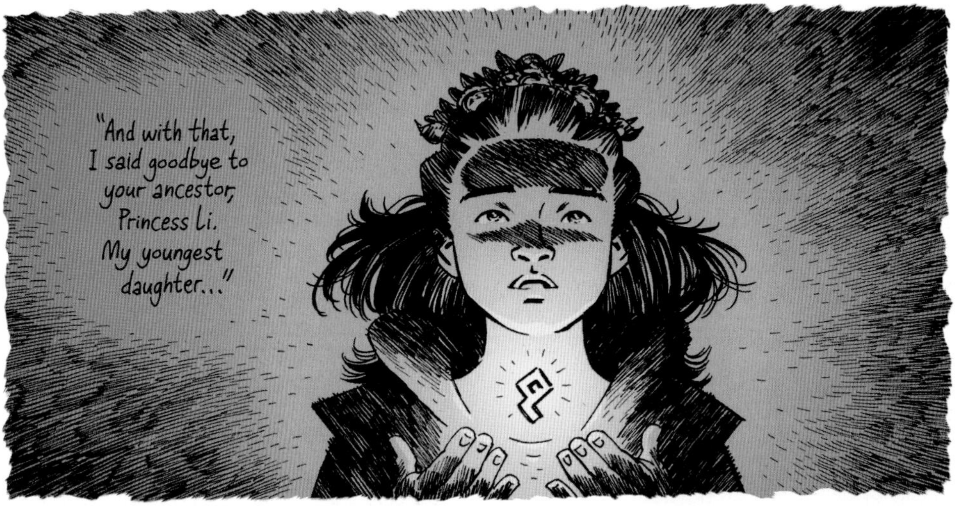
"And with that, I said goodbye to your ancestor, Princess Li. My youngest daughter..."

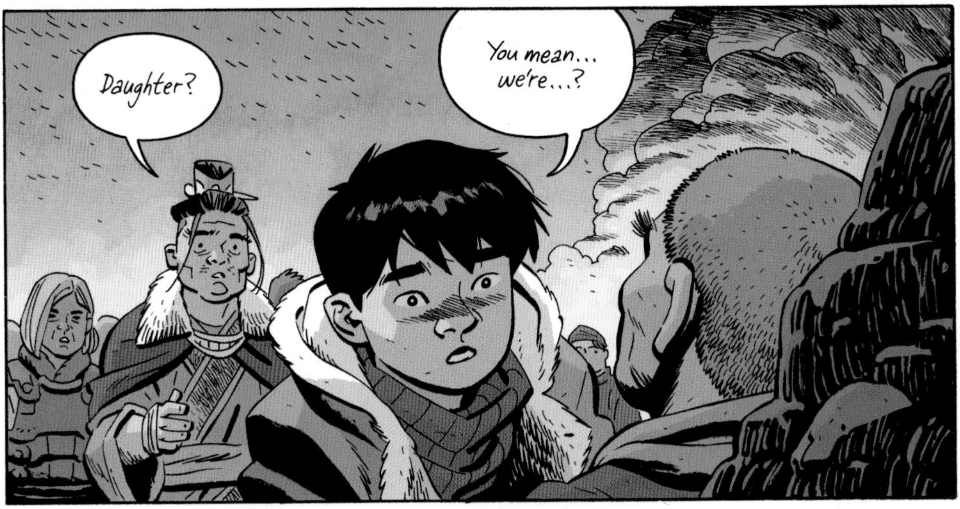
Daughter?
You mean... we're...?

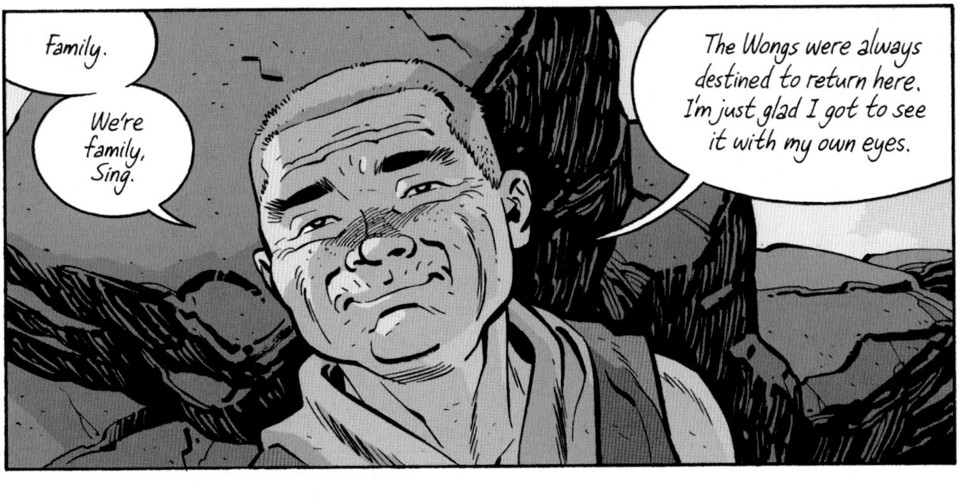
Family.
We're family, Sing.
The Wongs were always destined to return here. I'm just glad I got to see it with my own eyes.

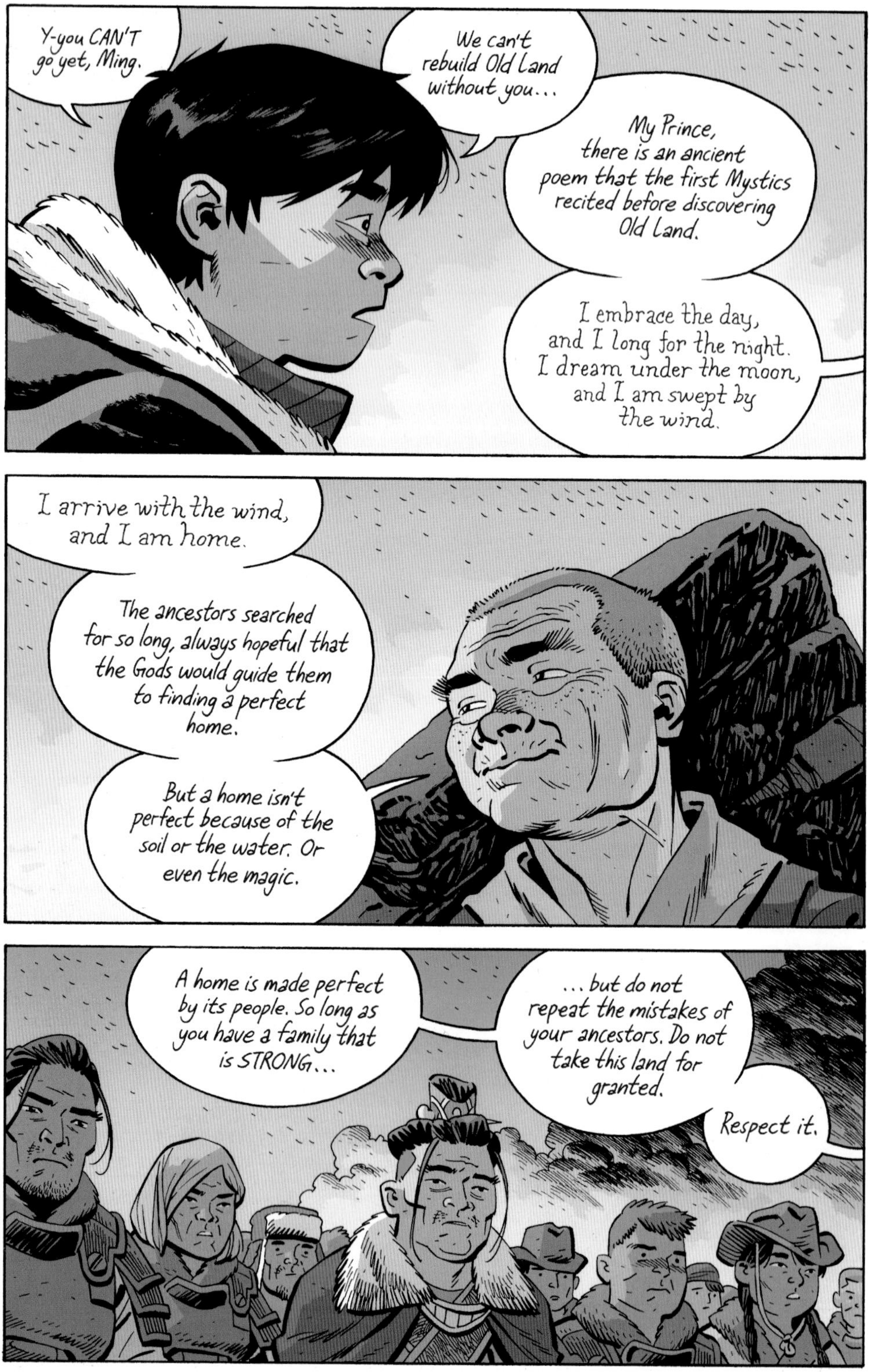
Y-you CAN'T go yet, Ming.
We can't rebuild Old Land without you...
My Prince, there is an ancient poem that the first Mystics recited before discovering Old Land.
I embrace the day, and I long for the night. I dream under the moon, and I am swept by the wind.
I arrive with the wind, and I am home.
The ancestors searched for so long, always hopeful that the Gods would guide them to finding a perfect home.
But a home isn't perfect because of the soil or the water. Or even the magic.
A home is made perfect by its people. So long as you have a family that is STRONG...
...but do not repeat the mistakes of your ancestors. Do not take this land for granted.
Respect it.

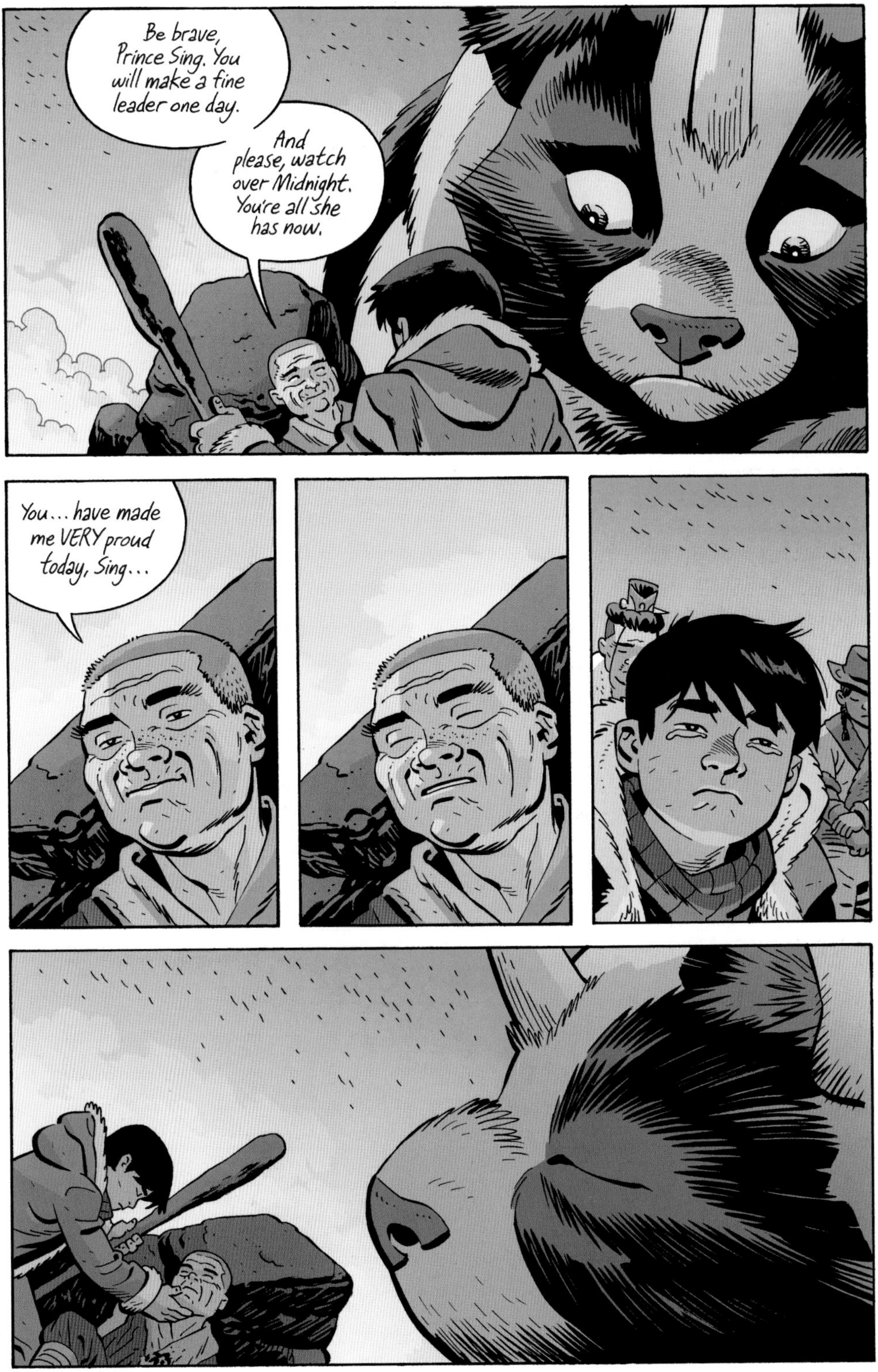
Be brave, Prince Sing. You will make a fine leader one day.
And please, watch over Midnight. You're all she has now.
You... have made me VERY proud today, Sing...

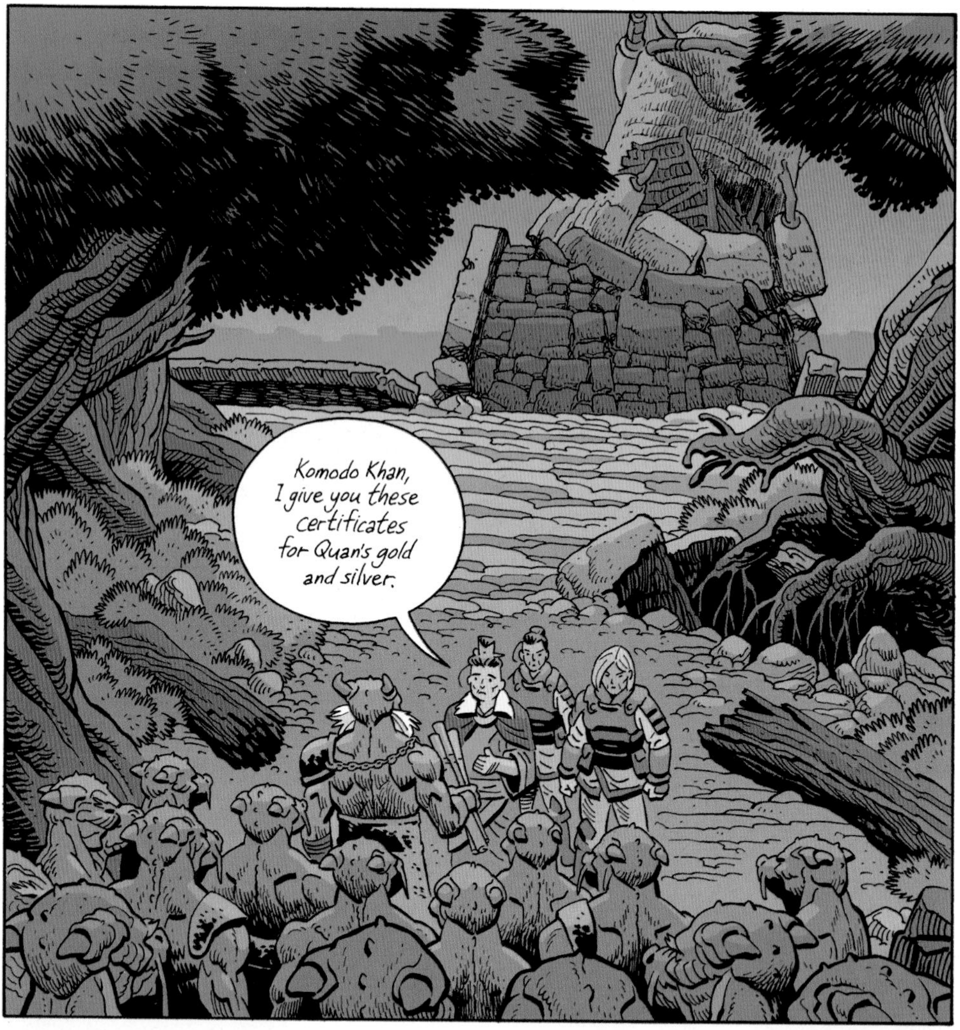
Komodo Khan, I give you these certificates for Quan's gold and silver.

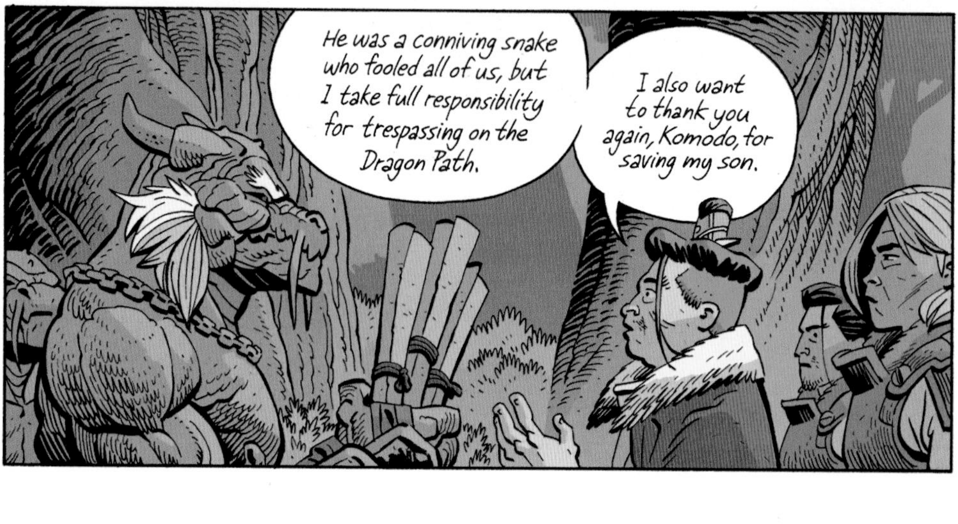
He was a conniving snake who fooled all of us, but I take full responsibility for trespassing on the Dragon Path.
I also want to thank you again, Komodo, for saving my son.

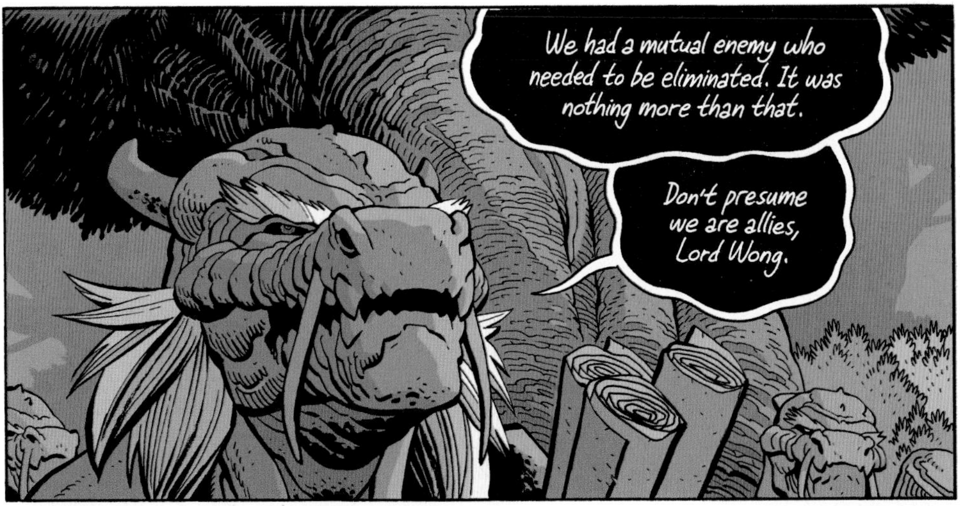
We had a mutual enemy who needed to be eliminated. It was nothing more than that.
Don't presume we are allies, Lord Wong.

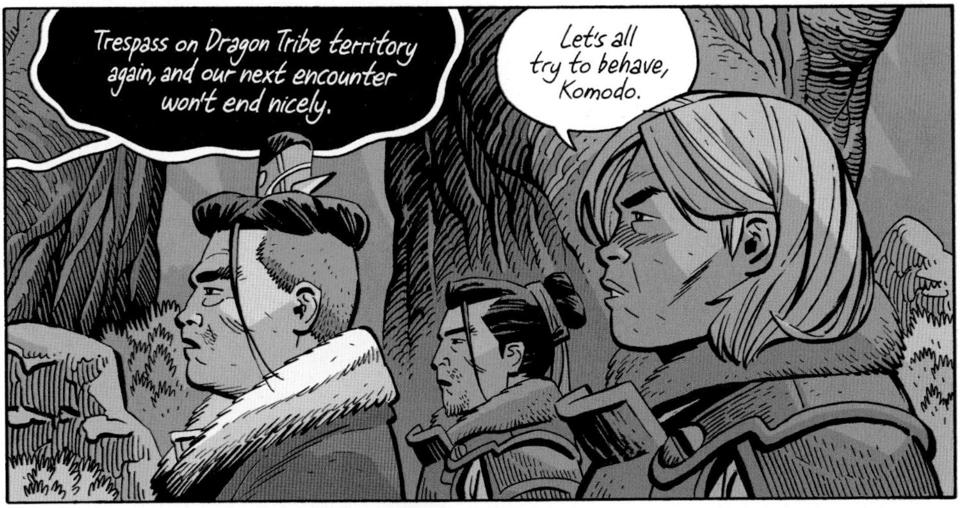
Trespass on Dragon Tribe territory again, and our next encounter won't end nicely.
Let's all try to behave, Komodo.

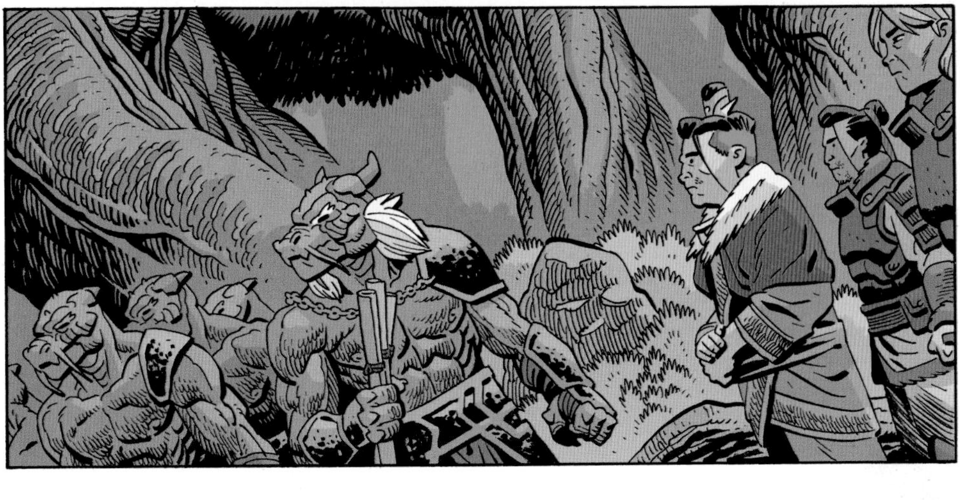

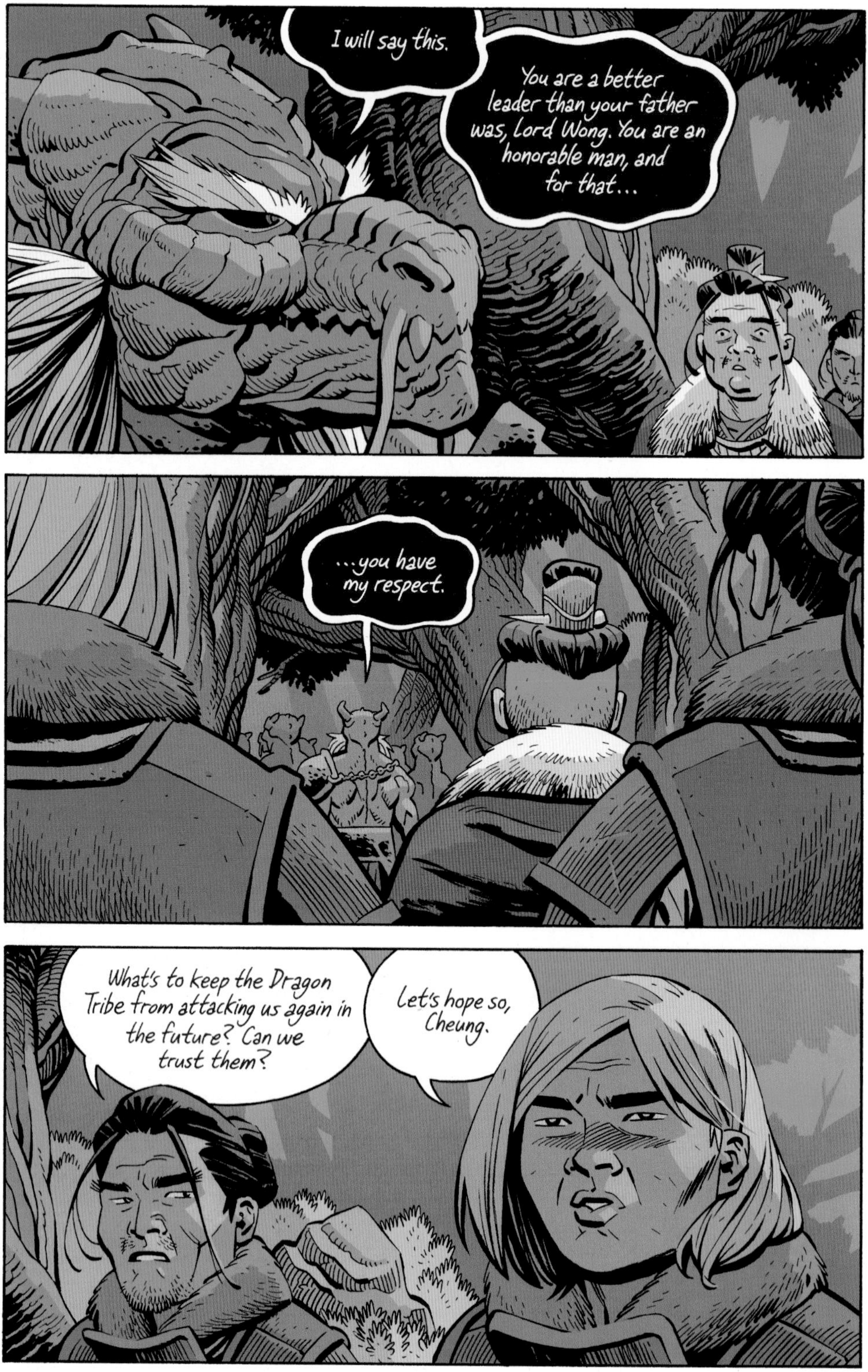
I will say this.
You are a better leader than your father was, Lord Wong. You are an honorable man, and for that...
...you have my respect.
What's to keep the Dragon Tribe from attacking us again in the future? Can we trust them?
Let's hope so, Cheung.

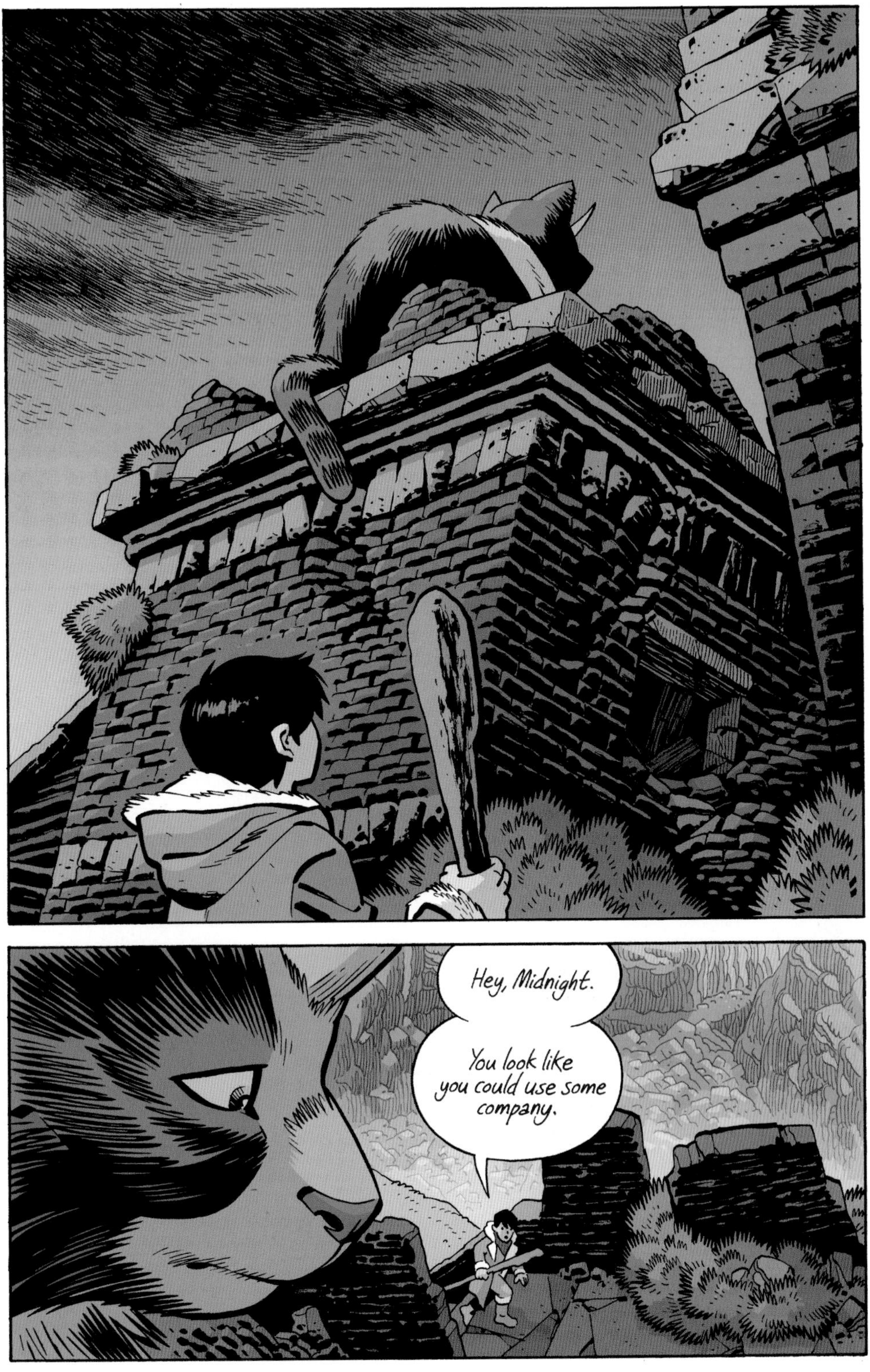
Hey, Midnight.
You look like you could use some company.

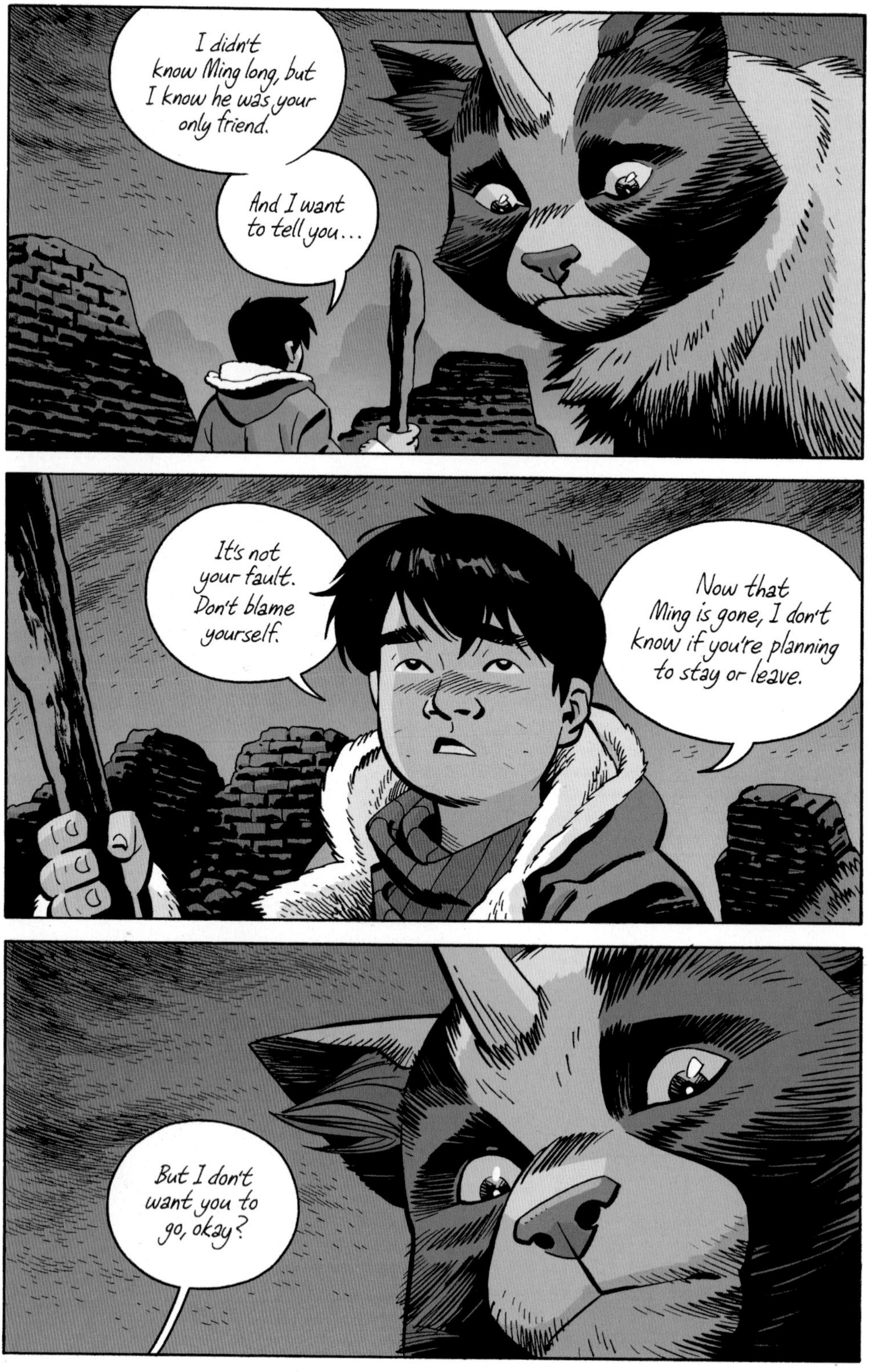
I didn't know Ming long, but I know he was your only friend.
And I want to tell you...
It's not your fault. Don't blame yourself.
Now that Ming is gone, I don't know if you're planning to stay or leave.
But I don't want you to go, okay?

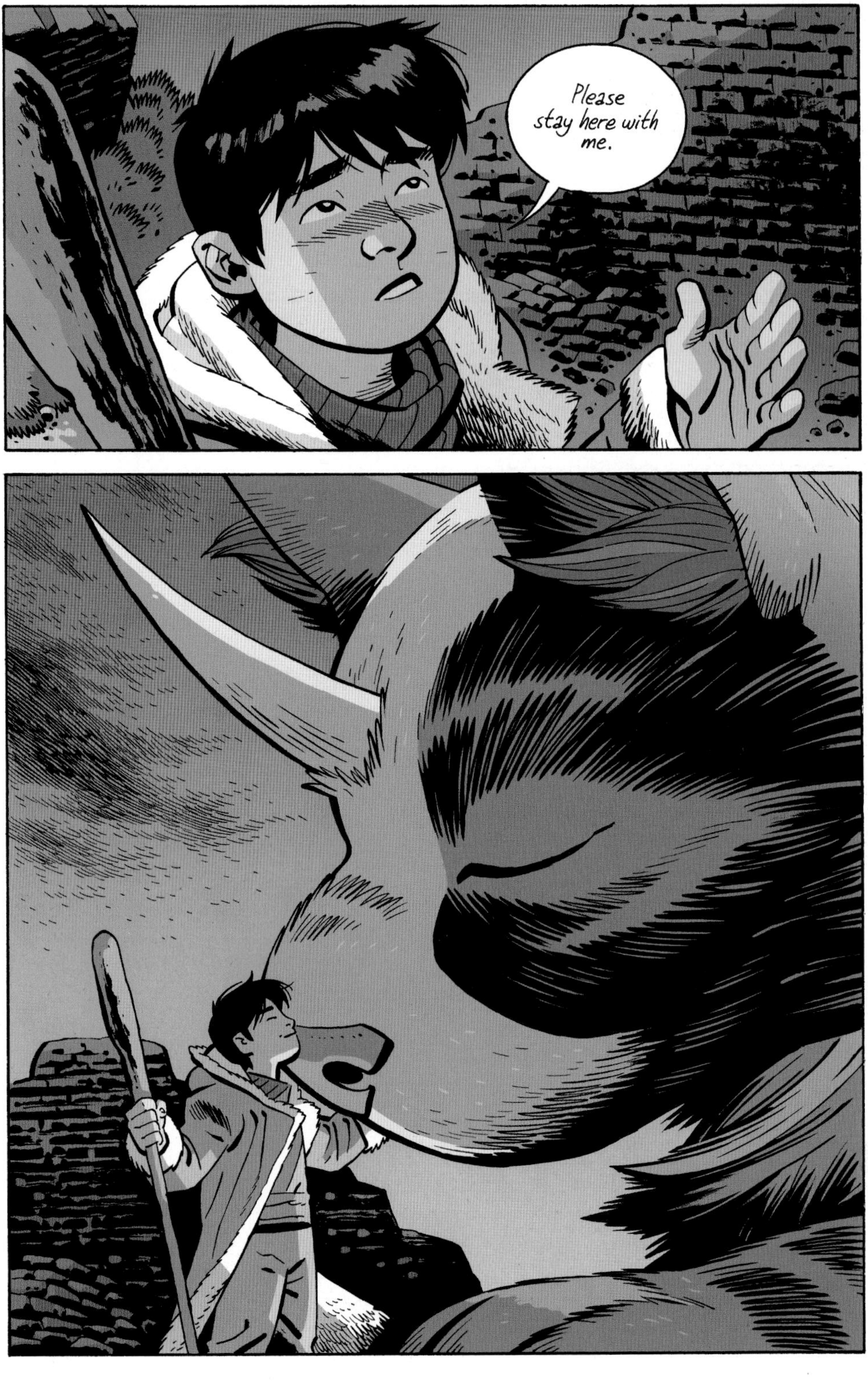
Please stay here with me.

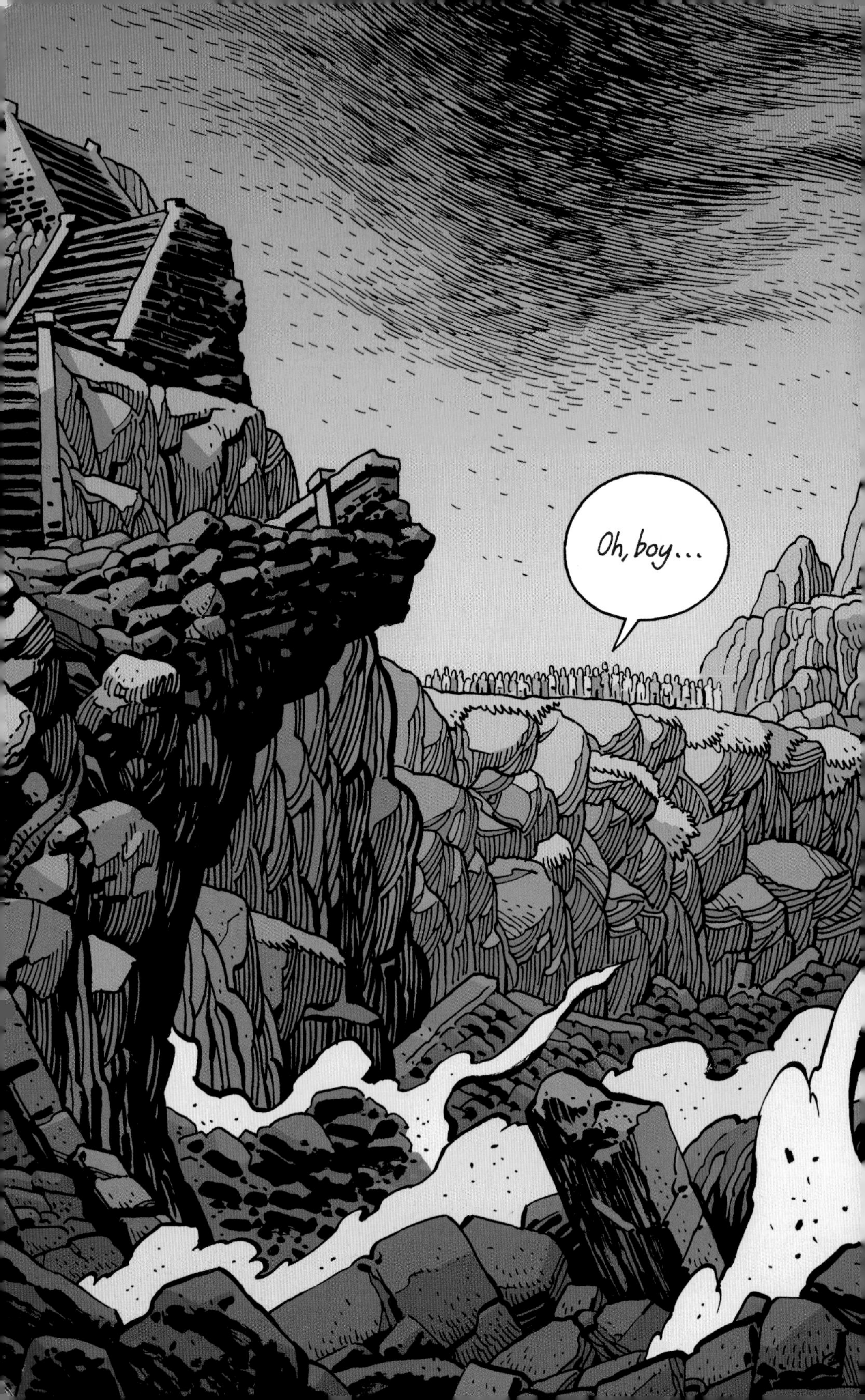
Oh, boy...

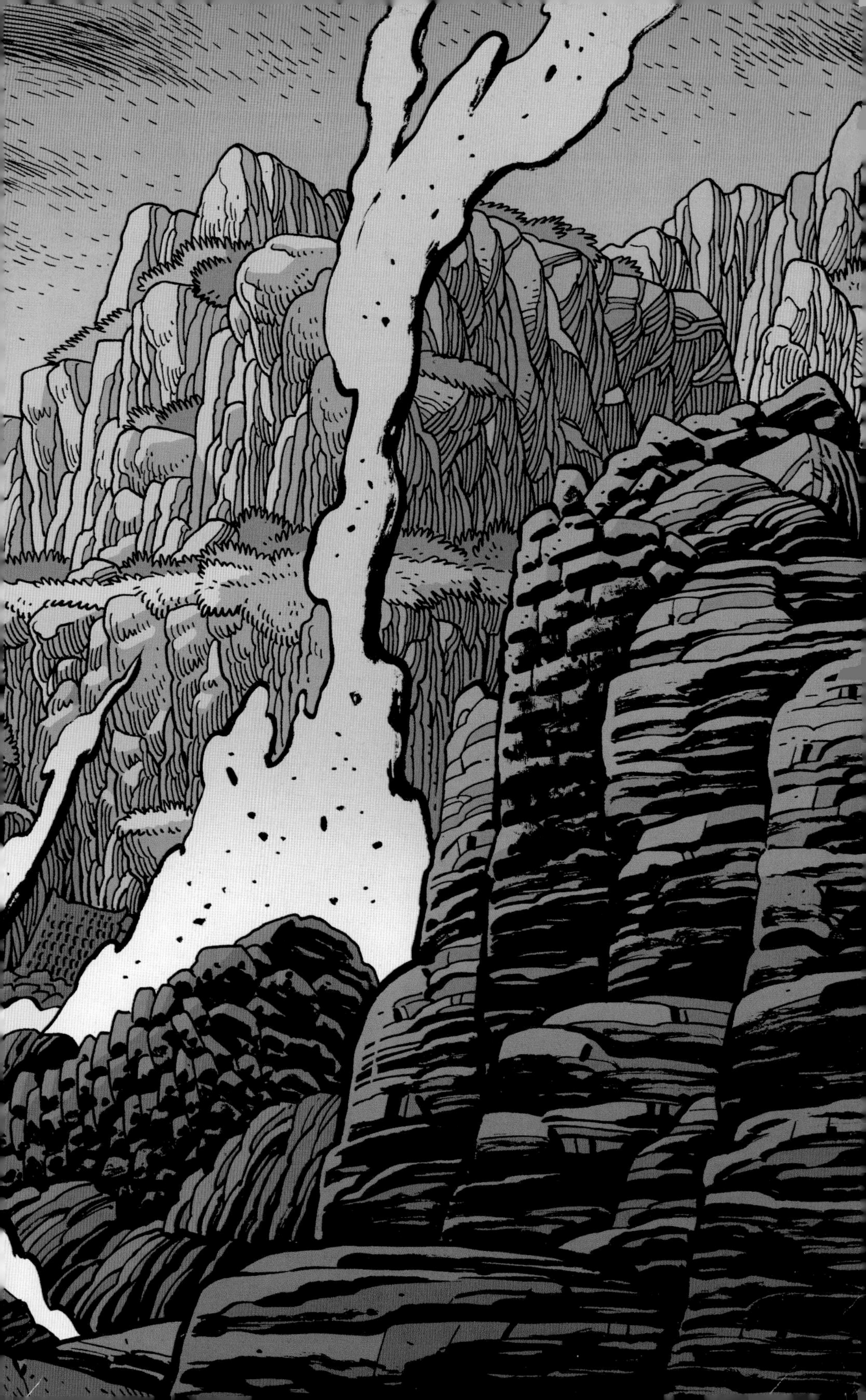

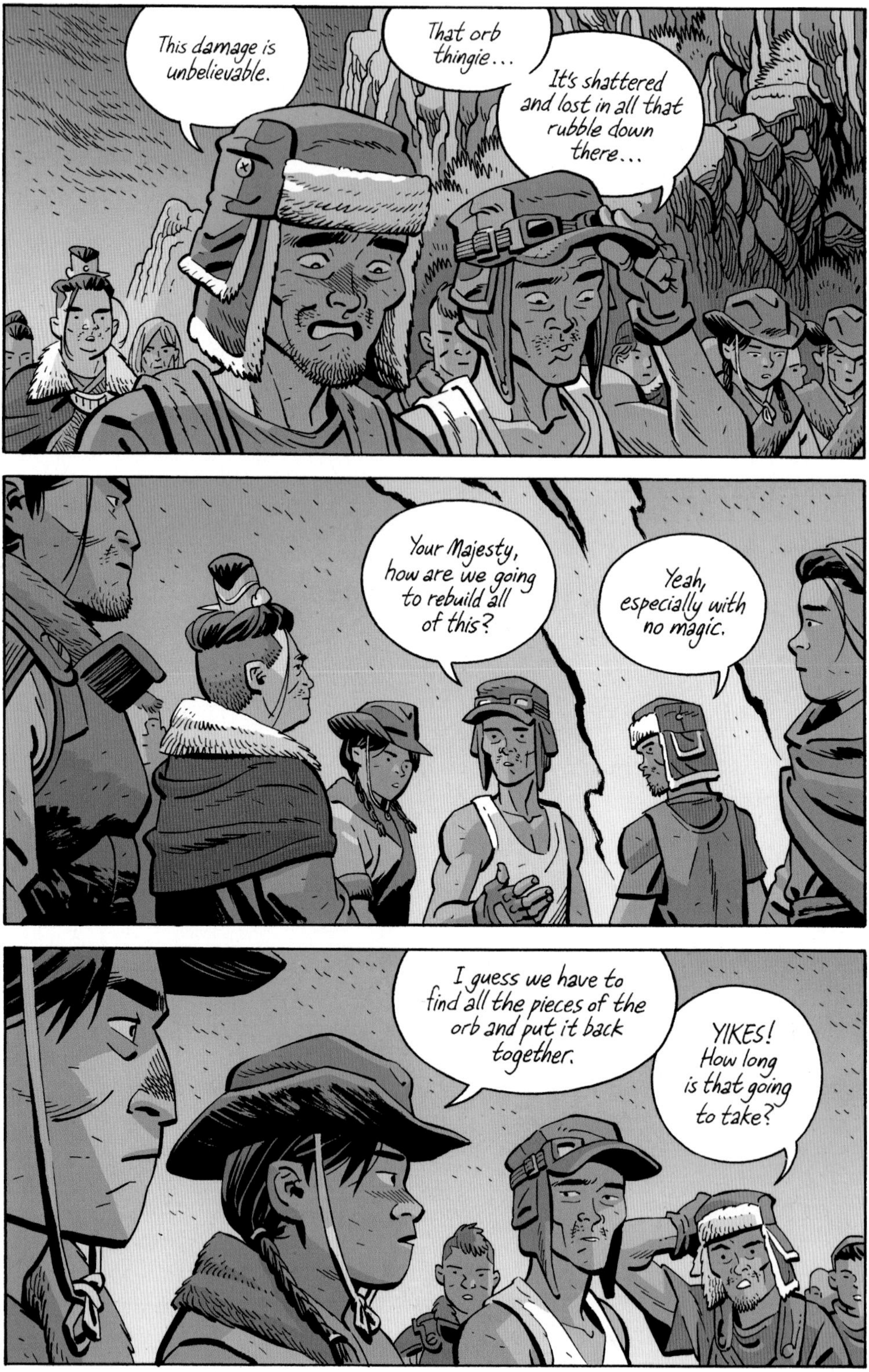
This damage is unbelievable.
That orb thingie...
It's shattered and lost in all that rubble down there...
Your Majesty, how are we going to rebuild all of this?
Yeah, especially with no magic.
I guess we have to find all the pieces of the orb and put it back together.
YIKES! How long is that going to take?

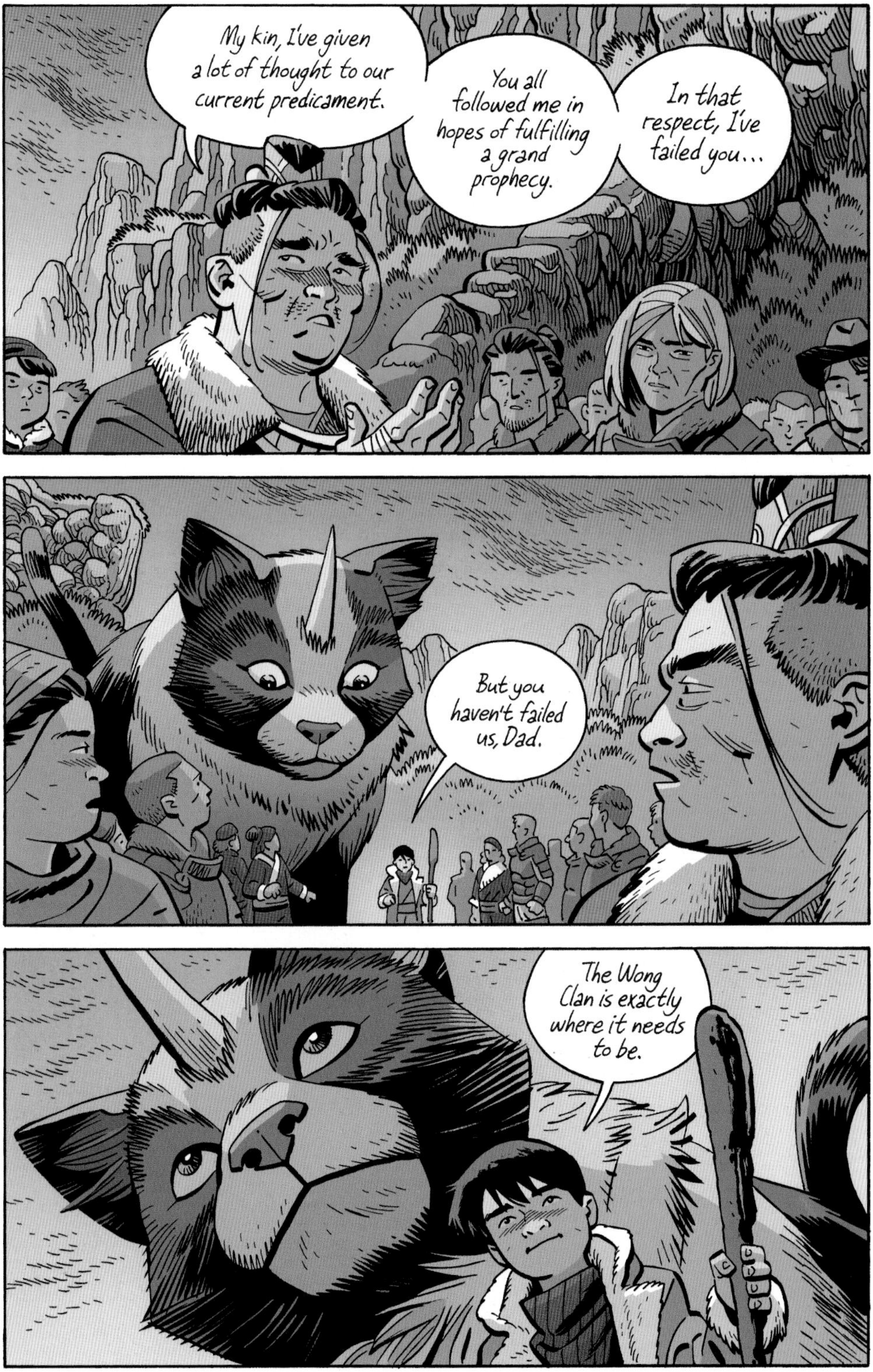
My kin, I've given a lot of thought to our current predicament.
You all followed me in hopes of fulfilling a grand prophecy.
In that respect, I've failed you...
But you haven't failed us, Dad.
The Wong Clan is exactly where it needs to be.

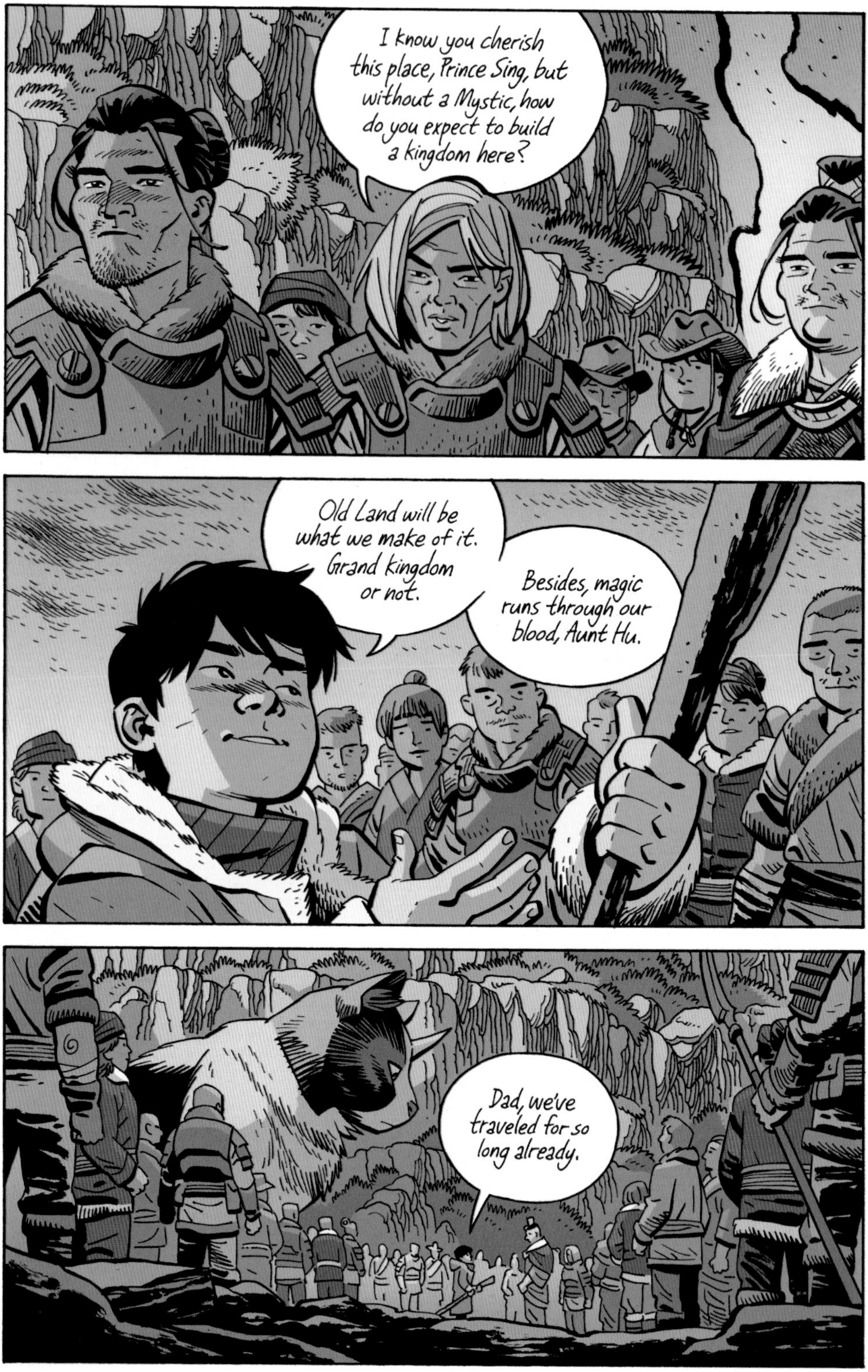
I know you cherish this place, Prince Sing, but without a Mystic, how do you expect to build a kingdom here?
Old Land will be what we make of it. Grand kingdom or not.
Besides, magic runs through our blood, Aunt Hu.
Dad, we've traveled for so long already.

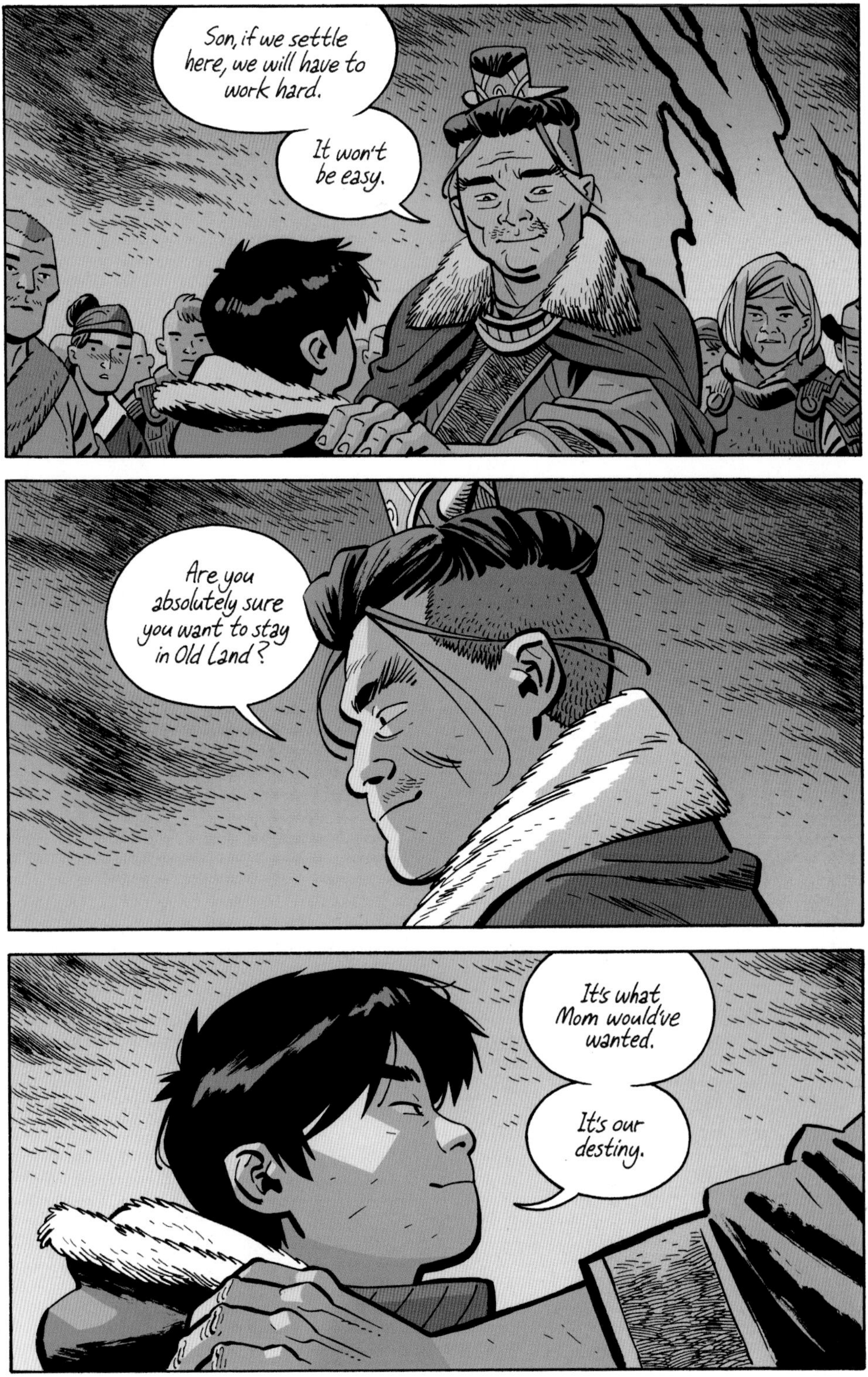
Son, if we settle here, we will have to work hard.
It won't be easy.
Are you absolutely sure you want to stay in Old Land?
It's what Mom would've wanted.
It's our destiny.

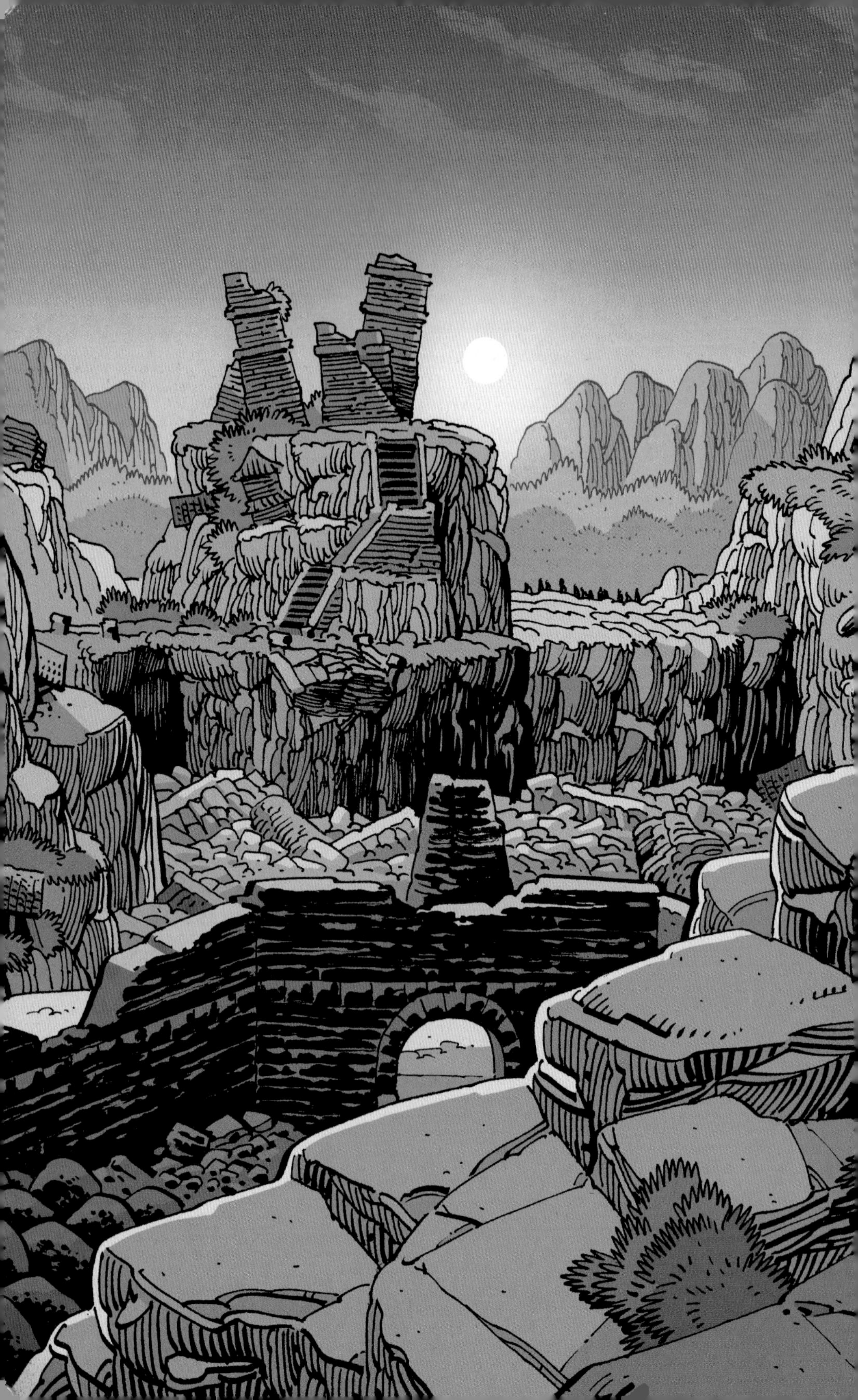

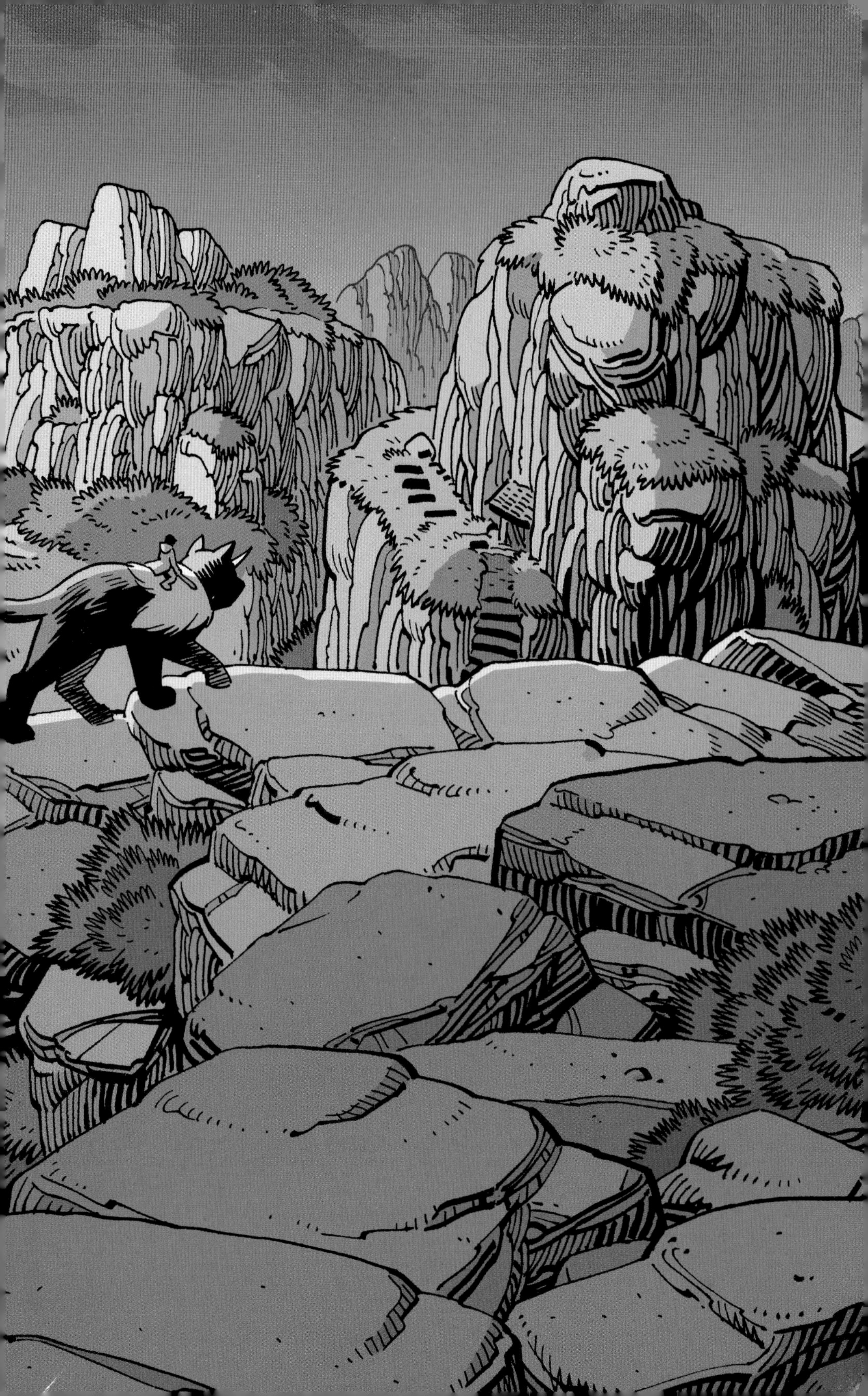

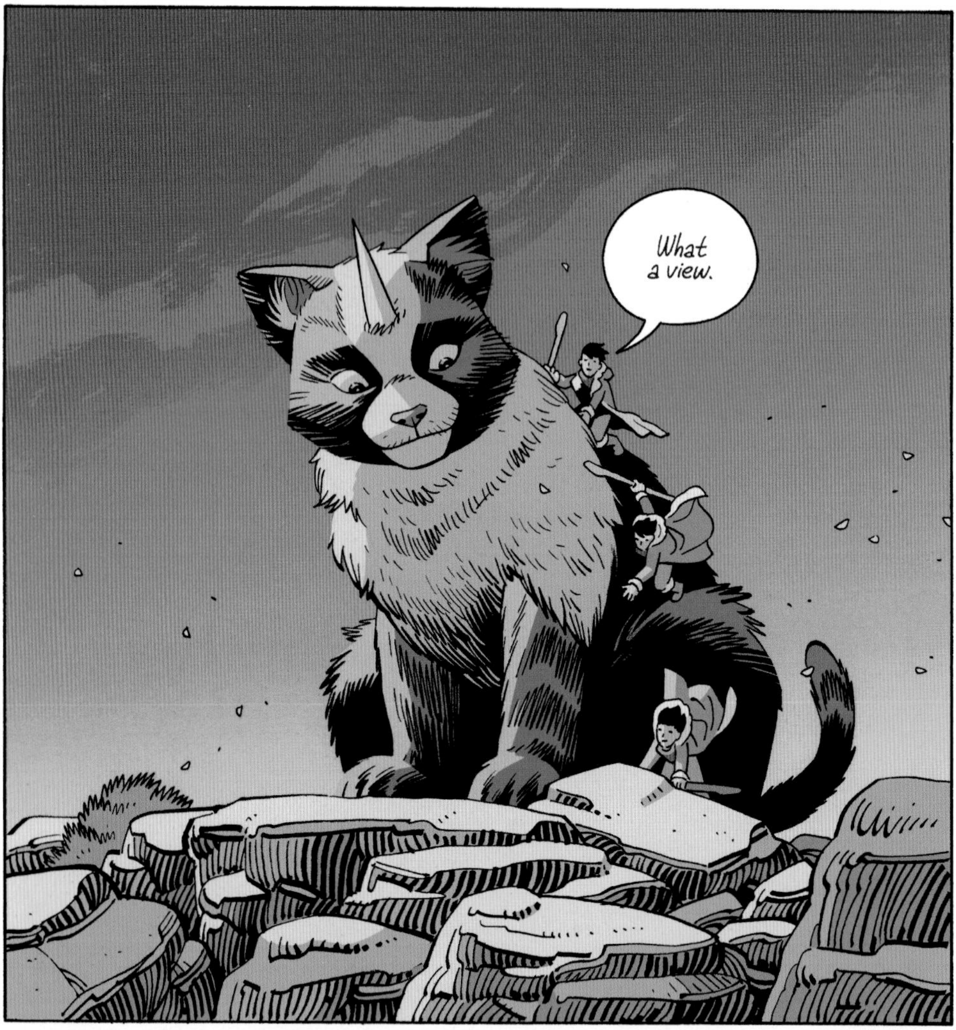
What a view.

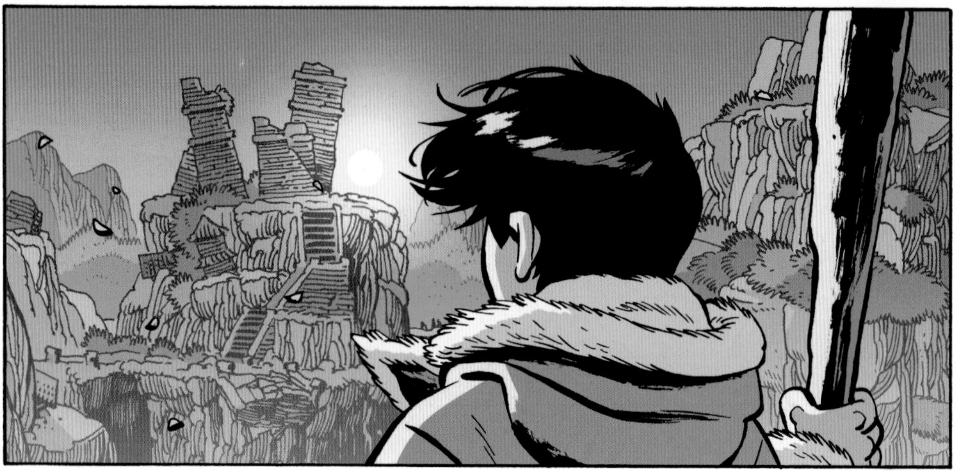

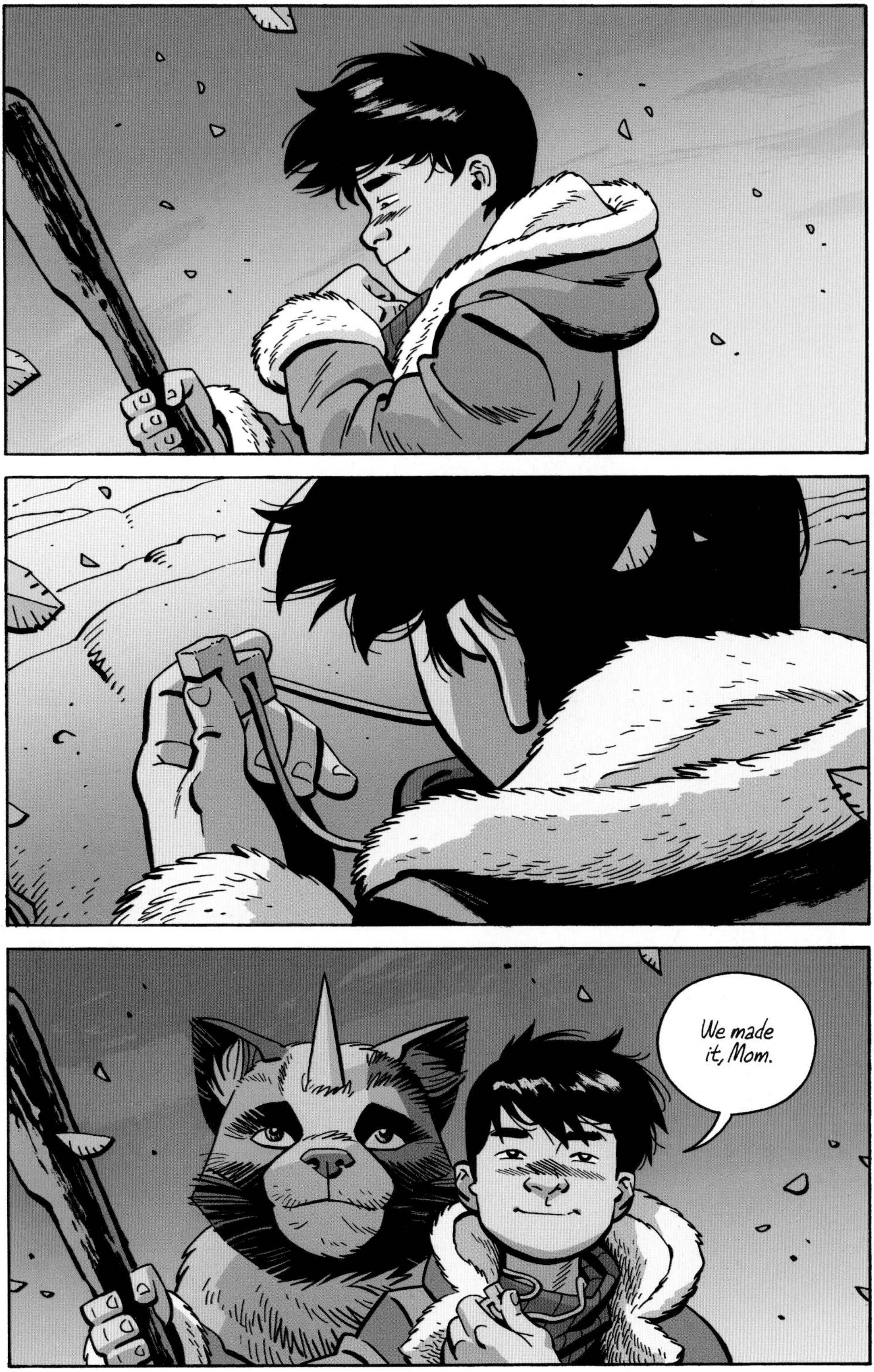
We made it, Mom.

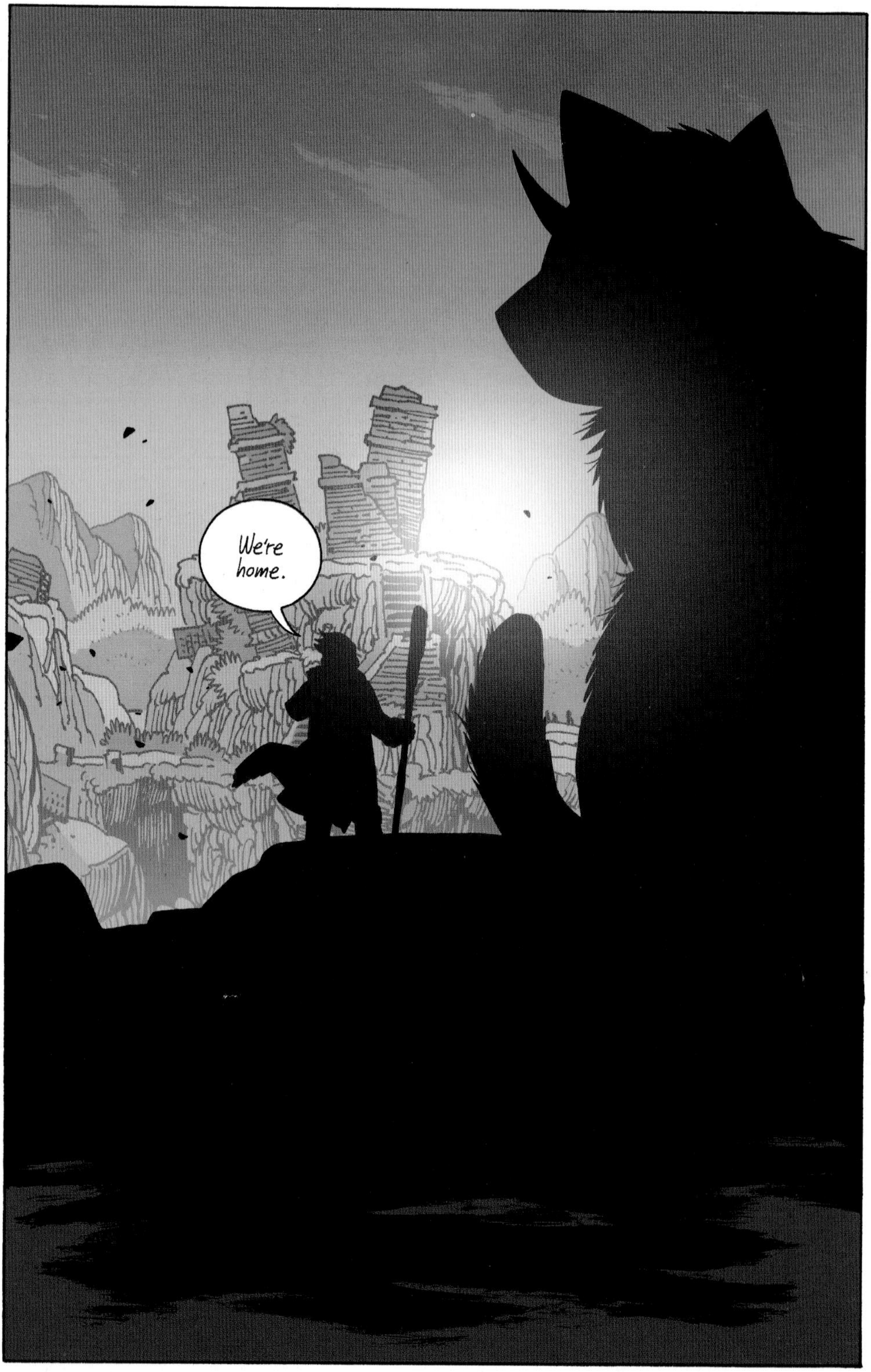
We're home.

SKETCHBOOK

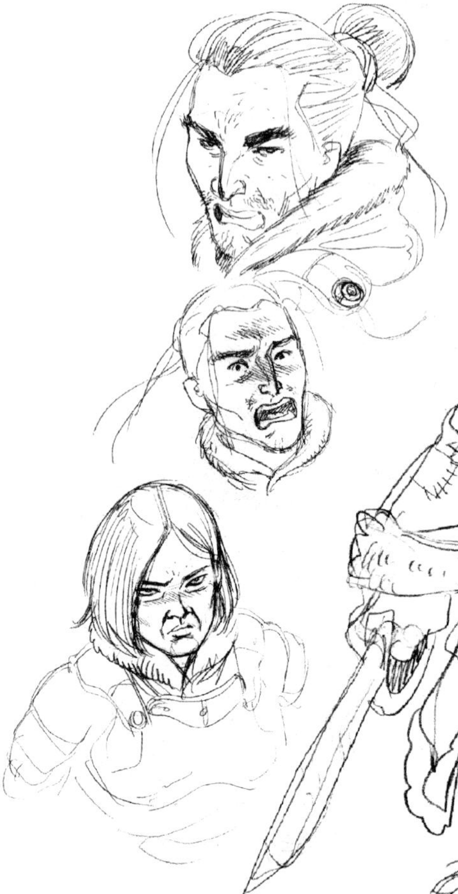

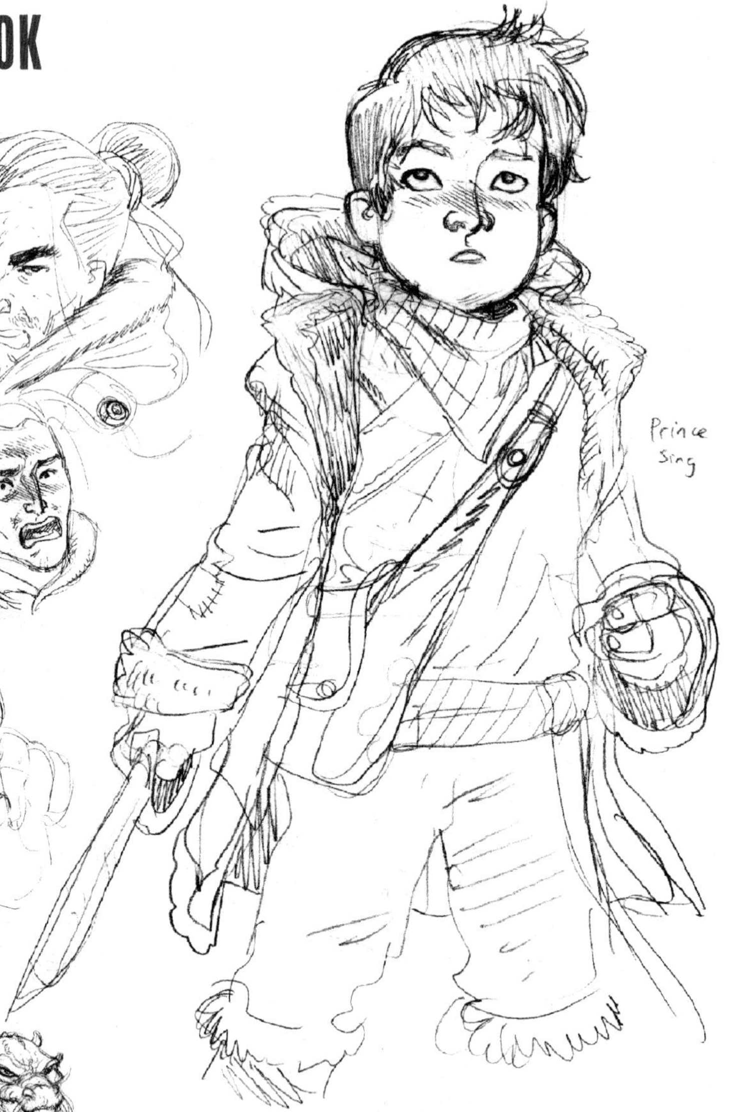
Prince Sing

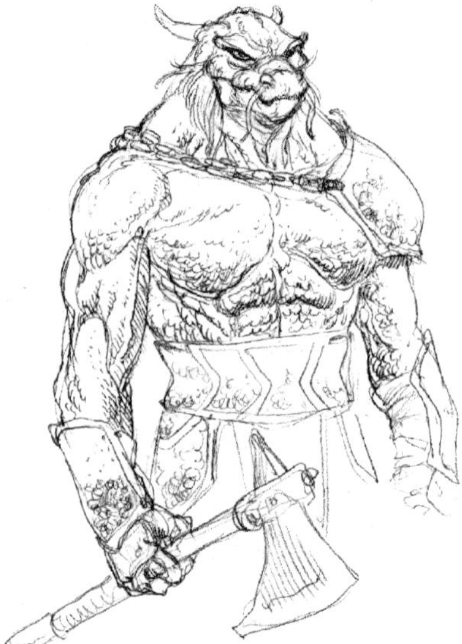

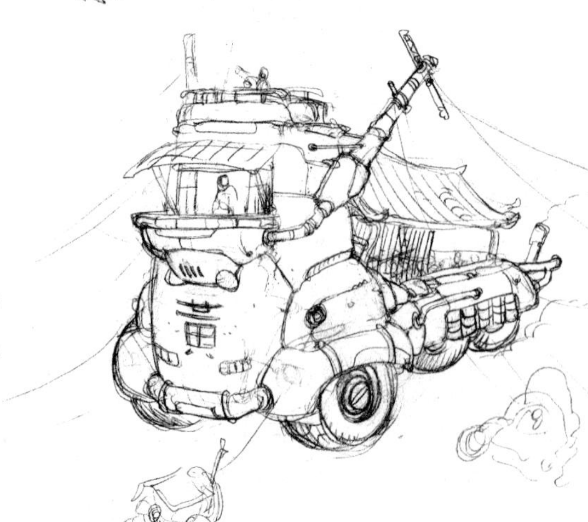

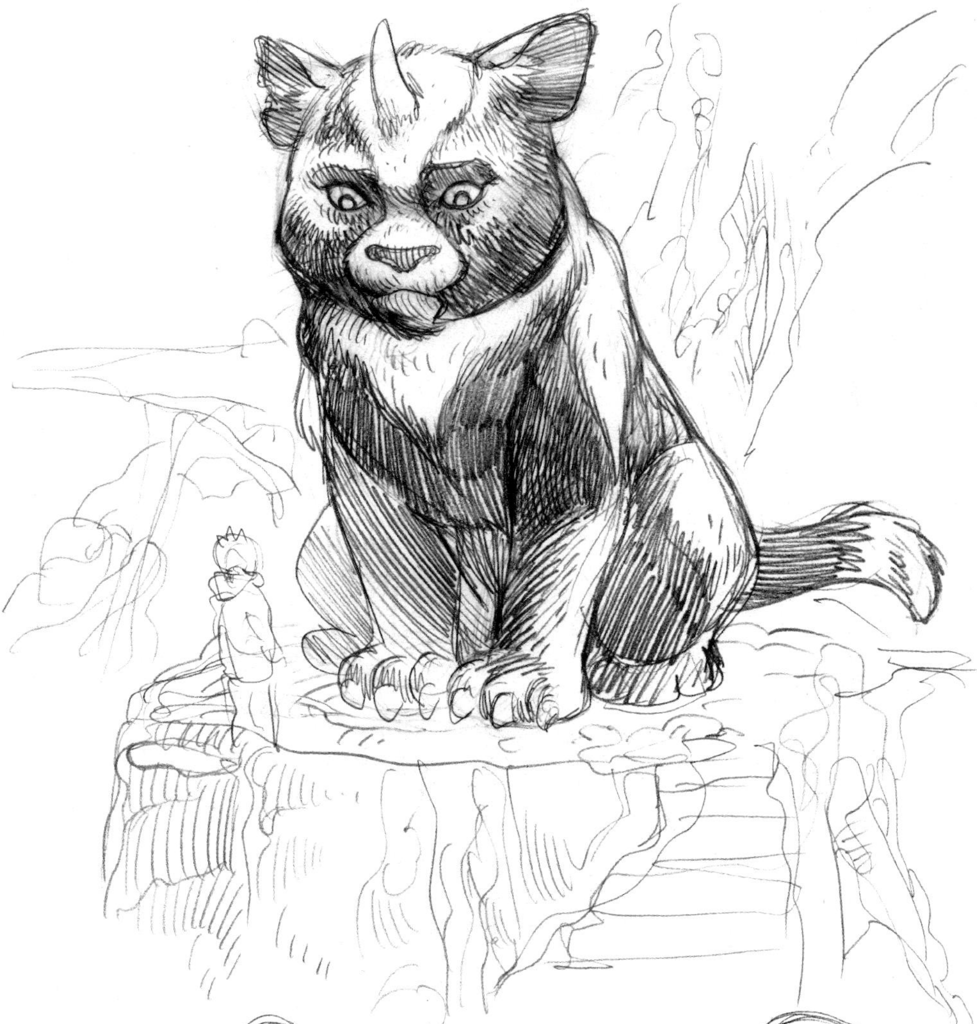

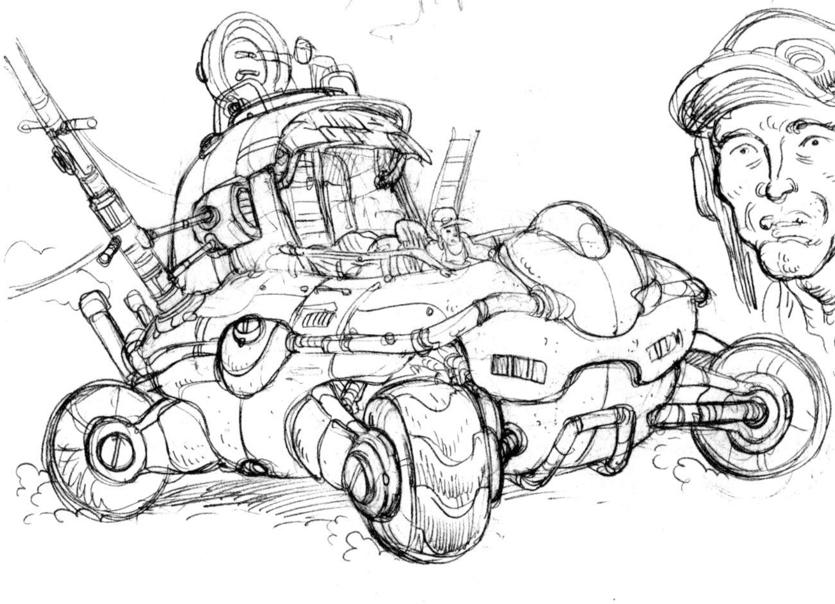

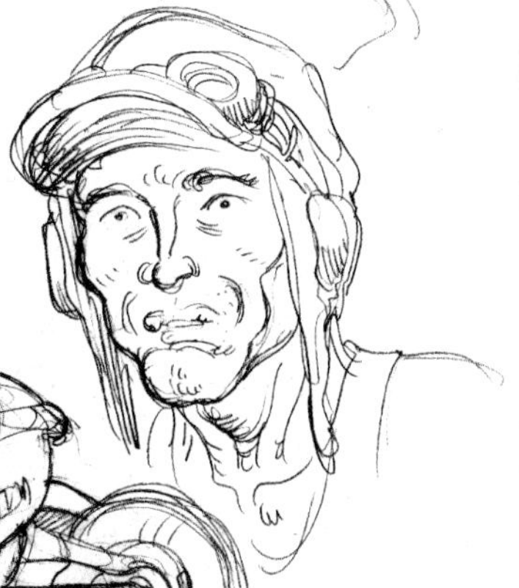

ETHAN YOUNG was born and raised in NYC to Chinese immigrant parents. Young is best known for *NANJING: The Burning City*, winner of the 2016 Reuben Award for Best Graphic Novel, which was also nominated for both the Eisner and Harvey awards. His other works include *The Battles of Bridget Lee*, *Space Bear*, and *Life Between Panels*. In addition to his comic book work, Young is also a prolific freelance illustrator and worked as character designer on the FXX animated TV show *Major Lazer*.